Selected Tales fo

Palgrave Macmillan Classics of Children's Literature

This series brings back into print some of the most important works in children's literature first published before 1939. Each volume, edited by a leading scholar, includes a substantial introduction, a note on the text, suggestions for further reading, and comprehensive annotation. While these full critical editions are an invaluable resource for students and scholars, the series is also designed to appeal to the general reader. *Classics of Children's Literature* presents wonderful stories that deserve a place in any adult's or child's library.

Series Editors:
M. O. Grenby, University of Newcastle, UK
Lynne Vallone, Rutgers University, USA

Maria Edgeworth, *Selected Tales for Children and Young People*
Edited by Susan Manly

E. Nesbit, *The Story of the Treasure Seekers* and *The Wouldbegoods*
Edited by Claudia Nelson

Little Goody Two-Shoes and Other Stories: Originally Published by John Newbery
Edited by M. O. Grenby

Hesba Stretton, *Jessica's First Prayer* and Brenda, *Froggy's Little Brother*
Edited by Elizabeth Thiel

Selected Tales for Children and Young People

Maria Edgeworth

Edited with an Introduction by

Susan Manly

Reader in English, University of St Andrews, Scotland

First published 2013 by
PALGRAVE MACMILLAN

Palgrave Macmillan in the UK is an imprint of Macmillan Publishers Limited, registered in England, company number 785998, of Houndmills, Basingstoke, Hampshire RG21 6XS.

Palgrave Macmillan in the US is a division of St Martin's Press LLC, 175 Fifth Avenue, New York, NY 10010.

Palgrave Macmillan is the global academic imprint of the above companies and has companies and representatives throughout the world.

Palgrave® and Macmillan® are registered trademarks in the United States, the United Kingdom, Europe and other countries.

ISBN: 978–0–230–36142–3 paperback

This book is printed on paper suitable for recycling and made from fully managed and sustained forest sources. Logging, pulping and manufacturing processes are expected to conform to the environmental regulations of the country of origin.

A catalogue record for this book is available from the British Library.

A catalog record for this book is available from the Library of Congress.

Contents

Acknowledgements

I thank Matthew Grenby and Lynne Vallone for instigating the Palgrave Classics of Children's Literature series and for their valuable editorial advice. Many thanks to Marilyn Butler, who first prompted my interest in Edgeworth and generously shared her expertise and enthusiasm with me; and thanks to David Butler for making archival material available to me. I am grateful for the funding provided by the Carnegie Trust for the Universities of Scotland, which enabled me to read original correspondence in the Edgeworth Papers archive held at the National Library of Ireland in Dublin; and for the assistance given by Special Collections staff at the University of St Andrews, the National Library of Ireland and the Bodleian Library, Oxford. I thank my colleagues at St Andrews, particularly Susan Sellers, Lorna Hutson, Gill Plain, Nicholas Roe, and Jane Stabler, for their encouragement. Thanks above all to Angus Stewart, for technical help as well as moral support.

Introduction

Life and Work

Maria Edgeworth (1768–1849) is widely regarded as a pioneer of children's literature. Edgeworth was an innovative writer of numerous tales and novellas for children and young people, whose work was enjoyed by generations of juvenile readers from the late eighteenth until the early twentieth century. She was also the author of *Practical Education* (1798), an important manual on early education that broke away from the speculative approach of Jean-Jacques Rousseau and the class-specificity of John Locke (both of whom focused their efforts on the education of boys) to create an experimental, scientific pedagogy, based on observations and anecdotes drawn from the experience of bringing up real girls and boys (eight of her half-siblings from her father's third marriage).[1]

Edgeworth's prolific writing for and about children was grounded in a sympathy for young people strengthened by her own turmoil in early childhood: she lost her mother when she was five years old, and her father (a virtual stranger to her) remarried within a few months. Her response to this emotional trauma was to behave so badly that she was sent away to school at seven, and did not return to live amongst the family until she was fourteen, having experienced her stepmother's loss in addition to her first bereavement. From this point in 1782 until her death in 1849, Edgeworth spent most of her time at the family home in Edgeworthstown in Ireland, not far from Longford, where she became her father's estate manager as well as taking a leading role in the education of the younger children (in total there were

---

[1] John Locke, *Some Thoughts Concerning Education* (1693), focuses on the education of young gentlemen, although it contains much generally applicable advice that Edgeworth incorporates in her own educational theory; Jean-Jacques Rousseau's *Emile, or Education* (1762) focuses mainly on the fictional boy of the title.

twenty-one Edgeworth children by his four wives). Besides *Practical Education* and her tales for younger readers, Edgeworth wrote many novels and essays about Ireland, and was acknowledged by Sir Walter Scott as a pioneer of the national tale. These include perhaps her best-known work, *Castle Rackrent* (1800), as well as *An Essay on Irish Bulls* (1802), *Ennui* (1809), *The Absentee* (1812), and *Ormond* (1817). She wrote a number of witty, complex fictions about women as authors and independent beings, often subtly reflecting on women's exclusion from public life, and on the politics of marriage and sexual liberation, including *Letters for Literary Ladies* (1795/1798), *Belinda* (1801), *Leonora* (1806), and *Helen* (1834). In addition, she wrote *Whim for Whim* (1798), a comic play focusing on political subversion in London and based on real events involving the French Queen and the parliamentary opposition; *Professional Education* (1809), about the preparation of young men for careers in the professions; *Patronage* (1814), a long, ambitious tale about two contrasting families; and *Harrington* (1817), which deals with anti-semitism in 1770s London.

This is not an exhaustive catalogue: Edgeworth was a productive and wide-ranging thinker and writer. In her heyday (1800–14), she was the most commercially successful and prestigious novelist in Britain and Ireland: the £2,100 she earned from *Patronage* trebles the £700 Scott earned from *Waverley* (1814), which John Gibson Lockhart thought unprecedented, and was seven times what Jane Austen earned from *Emma* (1816). Edgeworth herself calculated that in all she made more than £11,000 from her writing. Her reputation has suffered since, in part because of her choice of form, the philosophic or moral tale, which became unfashionable as readers began to expect a more uniform naturalism. With the publication of the 12-volume Pickering & Chatto *Novels and Selected Works of Maria Edgeworth* (1999/2003), however, and distinguished editions of individual works, as well as fresh insights in critical studies, Edgeworth's achievements as a writer and novelist of ideas are once again being recognized.[2]

---

[2] Marilyn Butler's *Maria Edgeworth: A Literary Biography* (Oxford: Clarendon Press, 1972) remains the fullest treatment of Edgeworth's life to date, and is the main source for this biographical sketch.

The tales in this edition are drawn from four collections published over eight years. Four of the tales are from the first edition of *The Parent's Assistant* (1796) ('The Little Dog Trusty', 'Lazy Lawrence', 'The Bracelets', and 'The Purple Jar'); one from the much expanded third edition of 1800 ('Waste Not, Want Not'); one, 'Rosamond's Day of Misfortunes', from *Early Lessons* (1801); one story, 'The Good Aunt', from *Moral Tales* (1801) and one, 'The Grateful Negro', from *Popular Tales* (1804).[3] While 'The Little Dog Trusty', a simple and very short tale, was meant for children aged between three and eight, most of the stories in *The Parent's Assistant* were intended for readers aged between eight and twelve, while *Moral Tales* was aimed at readers of around thirteen upwards. *Popular Tales* was presented as a work primarily for those not usually considered 'polite', and therefore relatively unengaged by tales centring on people of wealth and fashion, but it was widely read by adolescents and young adults.

Education, Enlightenment, and the 'Moral Tale'

The author of five major works for and about children between 1796 and 1804, Edgeworth is known for her realism, her technical virtuosity, her psychological acuteness in depicting the thoughts and feelings of children, her secularism, and her commitment to the increased diffusion of knowledge. Edgeworth began writing in the wake of Immanuel Kant's essay of 1784, 'What is

---

[3] There has been some discussion about the publication date of the first edition of *The Parent's Assistant*, since it is advertised in the first edition of Edgeworth's *Letters for Literary Ladies* (1795), but the likeliest date is 1796; the second edition appeared later the same year. See Butler, *Maria Edgeworth*, 159. *Practical Education* was nominally jointly authored by Maria Edgeworth and her father. Letter evidence, however, suggests that it was very largely her project, and mainly written by her: see Edgeworth Papers, National Library of Ireland MS 10,166/7/161, for instance, in which Richard Lovell Edgeworth refers to it as 'Maria's great work', and hopes that it will 'meet with as favourable a reception as her other works' (letter dated 17 July 1797). Her father contributed the chapters on grammar and mechanics, and material for the chapters on geography, geology and arithmetic, and her brother, Lovell, offered material for the chapter on chemistry; but she is responsible for the rest.

Enlightenment?': his precept for this age of enlightenment was 'Have courage to use your *own* reason', and he envisaged the result as *'man's emergence from his self-incurred immaturity'*.[4] Echoing these ideas, James Keir, one of Maria Edgeworth's father's close friends and fellow Lunar thinker,[5] celebrated the year 1789—the first year of the French Revolution—as distinguished for

> the sudden and extensive impulse which the human mind has received, and which has extended its active influence to every object of human pursuits, political, commercial, and philo- sophical. The diffusion of a general knowledge, and of a taste for science, over all classes of men [...] seems to be the charac- teristic feature of the present age.[6]

Chiming with Richard Price's assertion, also in 1789, that the Revolution was the latest sign of a 'diffusion of knowledge which has undermined superstition and error', Keir linked the democra- tization of knowledge to social transformation: 'In this age, the flame that passes over all kindles the sparks of genius wherever they happen to lurk.' Knowledge was no longer to be 'confined to public schools, or to particular classes of men'; nor was it to be confined to adults.[7] Keir responded enthusiastically the same year to *Sandford and Merton*, a children's book by another Edgeworth family friend, Thomas Day, describing it as 'more likely to be of

---

[4] Immanuel Kant, *An Answer to the Question: "What is Enlightenment?"*, trans. by H.B. Nisbet (1970; London: Penguin Books, 2009), 1.

[5] Richard Lovell Edgeworth was a member of the Lunar Society of Birmingham in the late 1760s and 1770s, although the group retained a lasting influence on him as a thinker and inventor. Other prominent members of the Lunar circle included Erasmus Darwin, Josiah Wedgwood, James Watt, Joseph Priestley and James Keir, all of them committed to sci- ence, invention, and free enquiry. For an excellent account of the Society and its influence, see Jenny Uglow, *The Lunar Men: The Friends who Made the Future, 1730–1810* (London: Faber & Faber, 2002).

[6] Keir, *The First Part of a Dictionary of Chemistry* (Birmingham & London: Printed by Pearson & Rollason for Elliot & Kay, 1789), iii.

[7] Keir, *Dictionary of Chemistry*, pp. iv, iii, cited by Mitzi Myers, 'Aufklärung für Kinder? Maria Edgeworth and the Genders of Knowledge Genres', *Women's Writing* 2.2 (1995), 113–40: 113–14; Price, *Discourse on the Love of our Country* (London: T. Cadell, 1789), 41–2.

solid service than any that has been published. It is of little use to write for grown-up people; their acquired habits will generally prevail: but young, unformed minds may be influenced into action'.[8] Maria Edgeworth's work, too, is grounded in the conviction that reading can play a part in encouraging children to be innovative, independent thinkers, and that they can thus be part of the expanding public sphere invoked by Kant, Keir and Price.

Contemporaries recognized the extent to which Edgeworthian education allied itself with enlightenment and enquiry, and some expressed disquiet at the secular moral principles that this suggested.[9] For Sarah Trimmer the secularism of *The Parent's Assistant*, Maria Edgeworth's first book for children, undermined its usefulness. To the suggestion in its Preface that gaining a distinct knowledge of children's minds through observation might be considered a 'treasure of natural history',[10] Trimmer retorts: 'Enough may be known of the infant mind to enable parents to educate their children both for Time and Eternity, without their being able to ascertain such facts as these.' Many of the stories, Trimmer felt, neglected opportunities to offer religious education to their readers: 'Lazy Lawrence', for example, depicted Jem's honesty and industry without reference to 'Christian motives', while Lawrence's idleness was not pointed out as an instance of 'sinfulness'. 'Old Poz', meanwhile, in which a cantankerous but good-hearted old magistrate is gently mocked by his daughter, is interpreted by Trimmer as actively subversive, a satire on established state authority: 'Children [...] should be taught, as their catechism directs, to "honour and obey those who are in authority under the king".'[11]

---

[8] Keir, letter to Day, 29 September 1789, cited by Myers, 'Aufklärung für Kinder?', 114. Myers makes a strong argument for reading Edgeworth as a writer bringing the values and ideas of enlightenment to children.

[9] See for instance, the review in the *British Critic* XV (1800), 210; and Sarah Trimmer, *Guardian of Education*, 5 vols (London: J. Hatchard, 1802–6), I, 2; II, 171.

[10] Richard Lovell Edgeworth, Preface to *The Parent's Assistant* (London: J. Johnson, 1796), v: Edgeworth is quoting from Thomas Reid, *Inquiry into the Human Mind*, which proposes this close scientific attention to the growth of a child's mind.

[11] Review of *Parent's Assistant* in *Guardian of Education* II (1803), 353–60, 415–18: 355, 356, 415.

Maria Edgeworth's interest in writing for children and encouraging children as thinkers was firmly rooted in family projects and interests of long standing, beginning with Richard Lovell Edgeworth's enthusiasm for Rousseau's scheme of natural education in the late 1760s and early 1770s, which led him (disastrously) to attempt to create a real-life 'Emile' in his eldest son. More productive was the 'child register' begun in 1776 by Honora Sneyd Edgeworth, Richard Lovell Edgeworth's second wife and Maria Edgeworth's first stepmother, in which she collected children's conversations as a means of establishing how they thought. In the 1790s, as she was preparing *Practical Education* and helping to bring up a large family of step-brothers and -sisters, Maria Edgeworth revived these child registers. They were an important part of the experimental approach to children's learning which was to form the foundation of her educational writing, and which informs the realistic child characters of *The Parent's Assistant* and later collections of tales for the young.

Edgeworth began telling stories while still at school in Derby (a particularly vivid one told of 'an adventurer who had a mask made of the dried skin taken from a dead man's face, which he put on when he wished to be disguised'), but her earliest published work dates from 1787.[12] Her first tales for children include the autobiographically based 'The Bracelets', written in 1787, and a saga called 'The Freeman Family', inspired by a series of stories about a large family of adventurous children, made up by Richard Lovell Edgeworth and told to his children in 1788–9. This was never published, although parts of it were used for her later novel for adults, *Patronage*. Between finishing the first draft of 'The Freeman Family' and beginning a second, Edgeworth began work on what were to become her first set of *Parent's Assistant* tales, all written between 1790 and 1795, adding eight new tales, written between 1796 and 1800, for the third edition of 1800. Like the unfinished Freeman saga, Edgeworth's tales began their textual life in oral form, as stories written on a slate, read aloud, and adjusted according to the Edgeworth children's comments, as well as editorial advice from other family members, principally

---

[12] Butler, *Maria Edgeworth*, 55; Frances Edgeworth, *A Memoir of Maria Edgeworth*, 3 vols (London: printed by Joseph Masters & Son, 1867), I, 10.

her father.[13] She often solicited ideas and suggestions from family and friends as a basis for her tales: a letter of 1797 to her cousin Sophy Ruxton, for instance, asks for 'any stories or anecdotes from the age of 5 to 15' for the third edition of *The Parent's Assistant*.[14] In 1780, her father and first stepmother had jointly written a privately printed collection of stories about two children, Harry and Lucy, making their first discoveries about the world outside their home, and Edgeworth later incorporated and added to these in her *Early Lessons* (1801), writing sequels in 1814 and 1825.[15] In the years when Edgeworth was writing the first *Parent's Assistant*, there were at least two children in the family aged between ten and thirteen, so the idea of writing for older children and adolescents naturally suggested itself: we can see *Moral Tales* (1801) as growing organically out of her first collection.[16] At the same time, her father's fourth marriage in 1798 meant that new infant half-siblings could benefit from the science-rich educational programme in the lightly fictionalized tales of *Early Lessons* (1801), which follow Harry, Lucy, Frank and Rosamond in their first discoveries about the world.

At least six of the *Parent's Assistant* tales (including two in the current selection) are set in or around Bristol, where the Edgeworth family spent two years. Maria Edgeworth's father and third stepmother, Elizabeth, and her half-brother Lovell left Ireland for England in early summer 1791 in search of treatment for her half-brother Lovell's incipient tuberculosis—the disease that had already killed his sister Honora in 1790. They left her at home in charge of her younger half-siblings, ranging in age from two to ten. On 14 October 1791 their father sent for them and for the

---

[13] Butler, *Maria Edgeworth*, 156, 157.

[14] Edgeworth Papers, National Library of Ireland, MS 10,166/7/165.

[15] The stories written by Richard and Honora were never published, and only one volume (the second) of this collection of stories, which they called *Practical Education*, was printed. There is no overlap between this earlier collection and the work of educational philosophy of the same title published in 1798.

[16] 'Mademoiselle Panache' is an interesting example of a tale that bridged the two collections, beginning in *The Parent's Assistant* with its characters as small girls, and carrying them through to adulthood in the second part, when it was transferred into *Moral Tales*.

next two years the family lived in Prince's Buildings in Clifton, a fashionable part of Bristol. Regular outings included walks on the Downs, where the children ran about hunting fossils and clambering on rocks, and visits to an excellent library in town.[17] The months when she remained behind in Edgeworthstown and the years in Clifton were clearly important times for Edgeworth as a writer: the children relied on her for tales to keep them entertained and interested, especially in Clifton, where they lived in relatively cramped conditions, and had few toys or books of their own. Many tales were written or incubated during this period.

Edgeworth's writing for children has serious purposes, but it is never unimaginative, and is often infused with humour. Although her chosen form for children was the 'moral tale', this was not the moral tale as generally understood by children's literature critics, Humphrey Carpenter and Mari Prichard for instance, who describe it as strongly didactic in tendency, hostile to fancy, preoccupied with children's self-correction, and dominated in narrative terms by adult preceptors who 'are almost always present, guiding and admonishing the children, and drawing every possible lesson from what has occurred'.[18] Mitzi Myers rejects this description and points out how inapplicable it is to Edgeworth's tales for children: 'Given the family background, the odd thing about the Edgeworth canon is the comparative dearth of lively, wise father figures and the abundance of powerful maternal figures, some wise and many anything but. Equally surprising perhaps are the numerous orphans, emigrés, and displaced persons.'[19]

Meanwhile, Alan Richardson questions the common assumption that moral tales are essentially an attempt to stamp out fairytales, the genre often thought of as most imaginative, noting the persistence of fairy-tale motif and plot in Edgeworth's first

---

[17] Butler, *Maria Edgeworth*, 105.

[18] Carpenter and Prichard, *The Oxford Companion to Children's Literature* (1984; Oxford & New York: Oxford University Press, 1995), 358–60: 359.

[19] Myers, 'Little Girls Lost: Rewriting Romantic Childhood, Righting Gender and Genre', in *Teaching Children's Literature: Issues, Pedagogy, Resources*, ed. by Glenn Edward Sadler (New York: Modern Language Association, 1992), 131–42: 133.

Rosamond story, 'The Purple Jar', with its magically attractive object of desire.[20]

Edgeworth in fact wrote 'moral tales' for both children and adults, modelled on the French genre of the moral or philosophic tale, as used by Voltaire (François-Marie d'Arouet), Stéphanie-Félicité de Genlis and Arnaud Berquin, the latter prominent and important writers for children in the 1780s, when Edgeworth was beginning her career as an author.[21] Jean-François Marmontel, whose *Contes Moraux* were published in 1763, was particularly influential in forming Edgeworth's sense of the philosophical potential of the genre. Marmontel thought of the tale as primarily a witty often comic form that prompts reflective thought. As Mitzi Myers observes, Edgeworth

> self-consciously used the term 'tale' for her fictions not because she is prudish about the novel (the usual explanation), but because she thus signals to contemporary readers the intellectual, argumentative, analytical genre she domesticates, feminizes, and frequently subverts. [...] for a woman writer who wants to be taken seriously and explore serious issues, who values her youthful protagonists and is interested in more about them than who they'll marry, the moral tale offers progressive possibilities.[22]

Edgeworth's 'moral tale' was thus vitally connected to her commitment to enlightenment.

The Parent's Assistant and *Early Lessons*

'The Little Dog Trusty' and 'The Orange-Man', simple tales for very young children, were written in 1790 or 1791. Together with 'The Purple Jar', these stories were published in the first and second

---

[20] Richardson, *Literature, Education, and Romanticism* (Cambridge: Cambridge University Press, 1994), 116.

[21] Edgeworth's 'Advertisement' to *Belinda* (1801) insists that it is a 'moral tale', not a novel; and *Harrington* (1817) was similarly conceived: see Butler, *Maria Edgeworth*, 221–2.

[22] Myers, 'Little Girls Lost', 136.

editions of *The Parent's Assistant* (1796), but were transferred to *Early Lessons* in 1801. Both 'The Little Dog Trusty' and 'The Orange-Man' address child readers directly ('Little boys, I advise you, never be afraid to tell the truth; never say, *"stay a minute,"* and *"stay a little longer,"* but run directly and tell of what you have done that is wrong'); and both end unhappily for one of the two child protagonists. 'The Little Dog Trusty' is focused, as its title suggests, on the issues of trustworthiness and obedience to parental authority, the parity between the submissive, innocent dog and the boy hero, Frank, indicated as the tale closes by the renaming of the dog (which is henceforward also to be called 'Frank').

The disciplinary impulse can be strong in Edgeworth's earliest stories although others, like 'The Bracelets' (written in 1787), present error as something that can help to develop children's moral sense. Edgeworth's own early experiences at the hands of her much admired but strict first step-mother, Honora, and her father, might have prompted the emphasis in these first stories on stern instruction and stringent punishment. Honora's preoccupation with obedience is evident in a manuscript notebook entry that shows her reflecting on the beating of her four-year-old son for refusing to recite vowel sounds, as well as in a letter expressing her conviction that

almost everything that education can give, is to be given before the age of 5 or 6—therefore I think great attention & strictness should be shewn before that age; particularly, if there is anything refractory or rebellious in the disposition, that is the time to repress it, & to substitute good habits, obedience, attention, & respect towards superiors.[23]

'The Little Dog Trusty' is true to this authoritarian model of moral education: its hero, Frank, escapes punishment by admitting his culpability in overturning a basin of milk while romping with his brother, but his brother is punished by being 'whipped, till he cried so loud with the pain, that the whole neighbourhood could hear him'. In addition, Robert is made an object of

---

[23] M.S. Eng.misc. c.895, fol.76, Bodleian Library, Oxford; letter to Mrs Margaret Ruxton, n.d. [?1776], cited in Butler, *Maria Edgeworth*, 47.

disapprobation in order to enforce the lesson for the benefit of neighbouring families (his father renames the dog with the express intention that Robert's dishonesty will be publicized among all the local children when they ask about the dog's name-change).

The story of Trusty, Frank and Robert is drawn from an incident in the Edgeworth household, related in the chapter on truth in *Practical Education*, in which 'H——' (Maria Edgeworth's half-brother Henry) broke a looking-glass while his parents were out: 'As soon as he heard the sound of the returning carriage, he ran and posted himself at the hall door. His father, the moment he got out of the carriage, beheld his erect figure, and pale, but intrepid countenance.' Instead of punishing Henry, or expressing anger on hearing his frank confession, Richard Lovell Edgeworth praised him: 'he would rather all the looking-glasses in his house should be broken, than that one of his children should attempt to make an excuse'. Maria Edgeworth urges parents in such cases to explain to children the 'great disgrace' of falsehood as opposed to the 'slight inconvenience' involved in speaking the truth.[24] In contrast, if physical punishment is used to stigmatize lying, children remain in subjection to authority, obedient from fear rather than honourable from the ambition to build and maintain integrity.

In the two Rosamond tales selected for inclusion in this edition, we see Edgeworth moving away from the punitive treatment of error. Edgeworth's endearingly fallible child heroine, Rosamond, is introduced in 'The Purple Jar' (1796), where she is seven; but she returns in further stories in *Early Lessons* (1801), in the *Continuation of Early Lessons* (1814), and finally in *Rosamond: A Sequel* (1821), by which time she is thirteen. The longevity of the character, appearing in tales spanning some 25 years, suggests her popularity and indicates the appeal that this voluble, inquisitive and irrepressible fictional child had for her creator.

As 'The Purple Jar' opens, we are plunged with Rosamond into a busy London shopping street, a world that she has not yet learnt to interpret: 'she saw a great variety of things, of which she did

---

[24] *Practical Education* (1798), ed. by Susan Manly, vol. 11 in *The Novels and Selected Works of Maria Edgeworth*, 12 vols (London: Pickering & Chatto, 2003), General editors Marilyn Butler, Mitzi Myers & W. J. Mc Cormack, 118.

not know the use, or even the names' (p.6). Despite knowing very little about the objects on sale in milliners' and jewellers' shops, Rosamond avidly admires their displays—'festoons of artificial flowers' and 'pretty baubles'—and urges her mother to buy 'all these pretty things', without pausing to consider what they are for and why they should be desired. When her amused mother asks, 'What, all! Do you wish for them all, Rosamond?' the reply is unselfconsciously and comically prompt: 'Yes, mamma, all' (p.6). Seeing through Rosamond's eyes, we cannot help but empathize with this hedonistic capacity for unthinking consumption. Yet we are also given the mother's gentle interrogation of her daughter's terms, in which she mildly questions Rosamond's superficial judgments of value and tries to prompt her to examine the objects of desire 'more attentively', and to consider redefining worth as usefulness rather than beauty (p.8). When Rosamond is invited to choose between the beautiful purple jar that she admires in a chemist's window and a new pair of shoes to replace her outworn ones, taking into consideration which will conduce most to her happiness, she is ingenious in thinking up plausible reasons for the object of her choice (the jar) and wants her mother to confirm whether she is right. But her mother urges her: 'Nay, my dear, I want you to think for yourself' (p.9). Rather than thinking for her daughter and requiring unreflective obedience, Rosamond's mother encourages the child to consider her reasons: in short, to philosophize.

Edgeworth herself saw Rosamond as 'une petite Raisonneuse', a thinker in the making.[25] Rosamond at seven is not yet equipped to make a rational choice, since happiness for her signifies transient sensory pleasure. Reasoning begins here, however, through the child's senses, in true Rousseauvian fashion, since not only is the 'beautiful colour' of the vase, as Rosamond discovers, an illusion created by a vile-smelling liquor, but the choice in its favour means days of pain, limping about in her disintegrating shoes, unable to 'run, dance [or] jump'. Rosamond ends the tale

---

[25] Maria Edgeworth to Ann Taylor, 14 March 1809, Osborne Collection, Toronto Public Library; cited by Mitzi Myers, 'Portrait of the Female Artist as a Young Robin: Maria Edgeworth's Telltale Tailpiece', in *The Lion and the Unicorn* 20 (1996), 230–63: 242.

regretting her misjudgment, but her irrepressible optimism and active desire for self-improvement predominate: 'I am sure— no, not quite sure—but, I hope, I shall be wiser another time' (p.11). Already, Rosamond is learning to consider her terms and observe her own thinking processes. She has in fact been making an experiment, learning from experience, and as Edgeworth emphasized in the second part of *Early Lessons*, trial and error are a necessary part of gaining knowledge and strengthening the reasoning powers:

Harry.   But we can try, papa.
Papa.   Yes, my dear, that is the only certain method of knowing.[26]

The glossary included in *Early Lessons* confirms that by 1801 Edgeworth is not greatly interested in enforcing obedience; she is preoccupied instead with 'embodied' learning in which moral ideas are formed through individual experiences and experiments in thinking in real-life situations. When she defines 'conduct', Edgeworth accordingly lays emphasis on this individualized process: 'People, by thinking whether they are going to do right or wrong, can judge and determine how they ought to act: their judgment conducts or leads them. Judging wisely, and acting accordingly, is good conduct; the contrary is bad conduct.' Rosamond's and her mother's conversations are part of this process of forming judgments, as the definition given to 'conversation' also suggests: 'Answering what people ask; listening to what others say; hearing from others what they know, and telling them what we know.'[27]

Humphrey Carpenter and Mari Prichard consider 'The Purple Jar' to be 'the moral tale at its most banal', and F. J. Harvey Darton wonders at its being so 'unfailingly readable', since he considers its rational mother so repellent. Darton finds Rosamond herself endearing, with 'that illuminating little hesitation about her future goodness' as the tale ends ensuring that she is 'not the

---

[26] *Harry and Lucy* Part II, in *Early Lessons*, ed. by Elizabeth Eger, vol. 12, *Novels and Selected Works of Maria Edgeworth*, 107.

[27] *Harry and Lucy* Part I, in *Early Lessons: Novels and Selected Works of Maria Edgeworth*, 84.

horrid little prig her mother wished her to be'.[28] Mitzi Myers, on the other hand, reads 'The Purple Jar' as having 'liberating potential' and suggests that Edgeworth takes up a 'progressive reformer's stance toward her period's consumerism and fashionable display', depicting the little heroine as capable of a 'rational socialization' that runs counter to contemporary stereotyping of girls and women as intellectually inferior by nature. Rosamond is guided away from being a stereotypical girl, 'seduced by beauty, glamour, and fashion', gaining power over herself.[29]

The second of the Rosamond tales included here bears out this reading. 'Rosamond's Day of Misfortunes', with its inset story, 'The Robin', amplifies the political resonances present in 'The Purple Jar'. Without losing sight of the comic potential in Rosamond's errors and self-dramatizing tendencies, Edgeworth allows her child reader to think seriously about the benefits and responsibilities of freedom and independence, and to reflect on the just use of superior power. The structure of the tale ingeniously suggests Rosamond's internalization of the lessons she learns from her mother through her re-enactment of her own progress from passivity to self-reliance, with the robin who needs her help allowing her to see herself as others see her. In this tale as in many others, Edgeworth communicates her conviction that it is attention and perseverance, which depend on the determination of the individual, that yield progress. Rosamond's mother neither indulges her nor condemns her for her self-pity and bad temper, instead gently asking her to look at and into herself to analyse her feelings by drawing her towards a mirror so that she can see herself more objectively: 'Look at this cross face [...] is that an agreeable little girl, do you think?' (p.14). Rosamond achieves a measure of self-command when, prompted by this new view of herself, she decides to 'do what was disagreeable to her', but she still feels 'dismal' (p.15) until her mother, instead of reprimanding her, encourages her to examine her thoughts and

---

[28] Carpenter and Prichard, *Oxford Companion to Children's Literature*, 358; Darton, *Children's Books in England*, rev. by Brian Alderson (3rd edition: Cambridge: Cambridge University Press, 1982), 140, 174.

[29] Myers, 'Socializing Rosamond: Educational Ideology and Fictional Form', *Children's Literature Association Quarterly* 14.2 (1989), 52–8: 52, 55.

feelings in order to ascertain why she is sure that she is going to have a bad day.

All of this connects to the story of the robin that follows. Running about to warm herself in the garden, Rosamond finds a robin, immobile on a snow-drift, eyes half-closed, starving and frozen. Like Rosamond when she awoke, the robin is cold and potentially subject to the will of those with more power; but just as her mother works to show Rosamond how free she really is—not the passive victim of misfortune, but a child who can overcome the fear of unpleasant sensations and give herself reason for self-approbation and self-esteem—Rosamond comes to the realization that the robin is not hers, but its own creature with a right to its liberty. Through this object-lesson in independence, Rosamond is being initiated into a sense of herself as self-reliant, able to draw on her own moral agency.

Like the Rosamond tales, 'The Bracelets', written in 1787, when Edgeworth was nineteen, is interesting for its depiction of the development of individual selfhood and female rationality. The action of the story takes place between 1 May and 1 June, and this two-part structure is mirrored in the competitions that take place on the first of each month as well as in the contrast that Edgeworth establishes between Cecilia and her best friend, Leonora.

The two-part structure of the tale is in fact somewhat complicated by the competing models of femininity presented through the characters: the more carefully one looks at this tale, the more ambivalent it appears on the subject of conformity to conventional gender stereotypes. Leonora is held up as a kind of model of good temper, but she is in other respects a less sympathetic character than Cecilia (something that Edgeworth signals in the narrative viewpoint, which grants her readers far more sustained access to Cecilia's thoughts and feelings). While Leonora is more considerate and more forgiving of others' foibles, she is in part man-made, for the description of her upbringing by her mother, in which she has been 'habituated to [...] restraint [...] and early accustomed to yield' (p.37), closely resembles Rousseau's sketch of his ideal girl in *Emile*: 'Girls should [...] early be accustomed to restraint [...] This habitual restraint produces a docility which woman requires all her life long, for she will always be in subjection

to a man'.[30] With her habit of submission, it is easier for Leonora
to be even-tempered and inoffensive; but as Edgeworth points out,
it also means that she lacks the powers of 'exertion to overcome
[...] disagreeable feelings of sensibility' (p.38). Cecilia's identity
is to some extent constructed along masculine lines: motherless,
she emulates her father and brother, and it is this early education,
'insensibly infused' via paternal influence, the narrator tells us,
that has formed her 'eager desire to improve', her 'enterprising,
independent spirit', and her 'abilities to excel'. As a result, her virtues have become 'such as were more estimable in a man, than
desirable in a female'. Cecilia is 'active, ambitious, enterprising'
and 'eager in the pursuit [...] of her wishes', highly motivated by
the desire to 'do what was right', and 'anxious to please' her companions; Leonora is 'unaspiring', 'proud', 'too indolent to govern',
and only 'anxious to avoid what was wrong' (pp.36, 33).

Encouraged by her father's approbation for public displays of
magnanimity and candour, Cecilia desires her companions' admiration, which she is tempted to win through what she self-
doubtingly calls a 'parade of [...] generosity' (p.43). Her exhibition
of largesse puts her in danger of losing her best friend, since she
sells a small silver box given to her by Leonora as a keepsake in
order to buy a showy gift for a third girl, Louisa. Cecilia's biggest
mistake is to undervalue the small gifts that symbolize and per-
petuate bonds of private affection; with her male-influenced upbringing, she regards all 'small objects', as well as 'small errors', as
'trifles' (p.36). This gains particular significance when we consider
that for Edmund Burke, theorist of the sublime and beautiful, femininity is consistently associated with smallness and with beauty,
whereas the sublime is linked with greatness and masculinity.[31]
The omniscient narrator in the tale notes Cecilia's divergence
from conventional ideas of proper femininity with some disap-
proval, but her efforts to unite 'masculine' ambition and 'fem-
inine' regard for others' feelings are drawn sympathetically.

---

[30] Rousseau, *Emile*, trans. by Barbara Foxley (London & Toronto: J. M.
Dent, 1911), 332–3.

[31] Burke, *A Philosophical Enquiry into the Origin of Our Ideas of the Sublime
and Beautiful* (London: R. & J. Dodsley, 1757): see especially part III, sec-
tions XIII ('Beautiful objects small') and XVI ('Delicacy'), 96–7; 101–2.

Critics of 'The Bracelets' differ in their assessments of its gender politics. Elizabeth Kowaleski-Wallace views it as a vehicle for 'the message that Edgeworth's maternal persona most often conveys to its female readers [...] the necessity for the cultivation of a separate series of female attributes and virtues'. The 'purpose' of 'The Bracelets' is 'to teach young girls the necessary social skills that enable them to accommodate themselves to a life with and among other women', rather than for the public life, among men, that boys have in view.[32] In contrast, Mitzi Myers's reading of the tale recognizes its ambivalences: she notes that 'The Bracelets' is about both 'the pleasures and pains of interdependence', since it depicts 'a subjectivity constructed in community, with life's happiness depending on the "pleasures of sympathy" and "the suffrages of others"'. In addition, she comments on the ways in which this tale, originally written as a surprise gift for Edgeworth's father, 'both idealizes and critiques the educational practices of the parent whom it addresses'.[33]

'Lazy Lawrence', published in the first edition of *The Parent's Assistant*, similarly invests in the non-conformity and indomitability of its hero, Jem, a resilient, active and inventive boy who through his own energy and persistence earns enough money for his widowed mother to pay her rent and keep their beloved horse, Lightfoot. Although we might expect the tale to be a cautionary history focusing on the lazy Lawrence of the title, Edgeworth seems more interested in depicting Jem's tireless efforts and busy creativity than Lawrence's moral errors. Jem epitomizes the Edgeworthian child hero of stories like 'The Orphans' and 'Simple Susan'; as Marilyn Butler observes, he is typified by 'courage and determination to act on his own, often

---

[32] Kowaleski-Wallace, *Their Fathers' Daughters* (New York & Oxford: Oxford University Press, 1991), 118–19.

[33] Myers, 'De-Romanticizing the Subject: Maria Edgeworth's "The Bracelets", Mythologies of Origin, and the Daughter's Coming to Writing', in *Romantic Women Writers: Voices and Countervoices*, ed. by Paula R. Feldman and Theresa M. Kelley (Hanover NH & London: University Press of New England, 1995), 88–110: 108, 101, 108. The phrases about sympathy and the suffrages of others are drawn from Edgeworth's chapter on vanity, pride and ambition in *Practical Education* (174), which has clear relevance to 'The Bracelets'.

in defiance of the adults and children about him'.[34] Jem is given gardening work by a lady to whom he has sold some fossils, and subsequently invents a way of weaving doormats out of heather, which the lady sells to her friends. Her benevolent patronage is clearly crucial to Jem's fortunes, but she forfeits the reader's sympathy, which has been strongly engaged by Jem's optimistic outlook and incessant activity, when she reacts with cold suspicion to his discovery that the money he has earned is gone, and that the horse might have to be sold after all. As readers, we know that Jem is a truthful boy and sympathize with his refusal to respond to the lady's hostile questions. Perhaps significantly, a lucky penny plays an important role in solving this impasse: Jem needs luck as well as resourcefulness and perseverance to achieve the aims that he has set himself.

'Waste Not, Want Not', published in 1800, echoes the emphasis placed in 'Lazy Lawrence' upon the inventive capacities of children, although here the problem-solving child is relatively well off. Again, as in so many of the stories, Edgeworth begins with a contrasting pair of characters, here, two boys named Ben and Hal. More directly political than 'Lazy Lawrence', this tale interrogates the conspicuous excess of aristocratic presumption and vanity, and posits, through its use of the motif of threads, the importance of reciprocal social bonds. Along the way it also questions what the conservative thinker Edmund Burke had considered the natural loyalty to the 'little platoon', those local, quasi-familial attachments which Burke thought integral to the maintenance of 'public affections'.[35] In his preface to *The Parent's Assistant*, Richard Lovell Edgeworth queries the ways in which vanity and partiality work 'in opposition to the abstract love of justice, and the general desire to increase the wisdom and happiness of mankind'.[36] Maria Edgeworth's story accordingly probes unreflective conformity and loyalty to the 'little platoon' as an element in the perpetuation of inequality and injustice.

---

[34] Butler, *Maria Edgeworth*, 161–2.

[35] Burke, *Reflections on the Revolution in France* (3rd edition, London: J. Dodsley, 1790), 68.

[36] Edgeworth, *The Parent's Assistant*, vi.

One of the tale's central characters, Hal (a princely name recalling Shakespeare's playboy of *Henry IV Part I*) has uncritically 'imbibed' (p.74) the idea that gentlemen should be conspicuously profligate. The other—pointedly called 'Ben', after one of the authors of American independence, Benjamin Franklin—is a more thoughtful child. Hal freely spends his money on luxuries and sweets and a flashy uniform for an archery competition devised by Lady Diana Sweepstakes, and patronizes Ben 'with the look of superiority, which he had been taught to think *the rich* might assume towards those, who were convicted either of poverty or economy' (p.82). The difference between the two boys is quickly established when their uncle asks each to unpack a parcel done up with whipcord—Hal impatiently cuts his to pieces, Ben examines the knot and undoes the cord so as to be able to reuse it—and the cord is later proved to be as useful as Ben has intuited, enabling him to win an archery competition when his bow-string breaks. But Hal's violent rupture of these ties that bind, and the value placed on them by Ben, have deeper metaphorical and political resonance. Ben thinks for himself, but acts for others. Hal's extravagance and his obedience to what William Godwin called the 'love of distinction' means that he, by contrast, cannot truly feel his connection to society at large, or at least not to those he has been brought up to consider his inferiors.[37] Meeting a ragged, half-blind boy in the Cathedral, the two boys accompany him to his mother's house, where they find her sitting up in her 'wretched bed', 'winding worsted', with her four 'meagre, ill-clothed, pale children' beside her, sorting rags to make paper (p.86). Again, the imagery of threads and of connected fabrics is prominent, but Hal, who has spent his money on 'good things' for himself, satisfies himself with an outpouring of sentiment about the poverty he is seeing, for the first time, from the inside of one of the 'terrible, tumble-down places' he has frequently glimpsed from 'mamma's carriage' (p.86). He immediately forgets the scene of misery once they leave, 'and the gay shops in Wine-street, and the idea of his green and white uniform wholly occupied his imagination' (p.86).

---

[37] Godwin, *An Enquiry Concerning Political Justice*, 2 vols (Dublin: Luke White, 1793), II, 357.

Hal has no conception of what might tie him to that 'spectacle of misery' (p.86), becoming completely enveloped in the ostentatious display of social and economic superiority to which he feels entitled. He is, as his uncle jokes, 'Mr Uniform' (p.93), conforming unreflectively to the 'little platoon' of rich boys (led by the sons of Lady Diana Sweepstakes). Ben chooses to share the money left over from the purchase of a coat with the ragged boy, buying him a warm coat as well: both rich and poor boy need protection from the cold, as he recognizes. Eventually, Edgeworth ensures that Ben emerges as the hero of this story, winning the archery competition without donning the uniform of the other wealthy boys, and able to aim steadily without shaking because he has acknowledged this shared need.

'Lazy Lawrence' and 'Waste Not, Want Not' take their place alongside other tales in the third edition of *The Parent's Assistant*, such as 'Simple Susan', 'The Basket-Woman' and 'The Orphans', which focus attention on the resourcefulness and quiet heroism of working-class children. Andrew O'Malley argues that Edgeworth's working-class child heroes 'exhibit the kind of industrious application and internalization of middle-class ideology (writ small) that such reform efforts as [Hannah More's] Cheap Repository Tract Society were trying to promote in the poor', and that her representations implicitly recommend the virtuous subordination of the deserving poor as a source of individual contentment and social improvement.[38] Edgeworth's depictions of social injustice are more subtle than this interpretation suggests, however: Lawrence and the ragged boy of 'Waste Not, Want Not' have much to teach more socially privileged characters and readers about self-reliance and integrity. There is also a fairy-tale element to the successful endeavours of Lawrence, Susan (in 'Simple Susan'), and the children of 'The Orphans': they defeat real-life ogres—oppressive land-agents, homelessness, public calumny—through their own efforts, modelling a heroism equal to that of Jack the Giant-killer, but recognizably modern rather than fantastical.

---

[38] O'Malley, *The Making of the Modern Child: Children's Literature and Childhood in the Late Eighteenth Century* (New York & London: Routledge, 2003), 46.

Moral Tales and *Popular Tales*

Edgeworth's earliest stories for younger readers—those in *The Parent's Assistant* and *Early Lessons*—show their child heroes beginning to think for themselves, to achieve rational self-command and to solve problems, whether moral or mechanical. Her tales for older readers—adolescents and young or less literary adults—are often more complex in terms of subject matter and treatment. Contemplating political questions of justice and social progress, Edgeworth avoids clear or open didacticism in favour of allusion and intertextuality as a means of creating food for thought: she plants references to other books and to historical events and political debates that can be followed up by alert readers to expand their own powers of mind as well as the possibilities of interpretation. Edgeworth thus fosters the critical abilities that she and other reformist writers of the period thought integral to a modern, progressive society.

Richard Lovell Edgeworth's preface to *Moral Tales* signals the connection that the Edgeworths made between reading and flexible, inventive thinking. He argues that those who take pleasure in reading literature by authors such as Arnaud Berquin, Thomas Day or Anna Barbauld—the authors Maria Edgeworth emulated—are those who later pursue 'a demonstration of Euclid, or a logical deduction, with as much eagerness, and with more rational curiosity'. Tales are thus part of a programme of mental exercise calculated to 'enure the mind to athletic vigour'. This was not to be restricted to those of the middle and upper classes: the preface to *Popular Tales* refers to Edmund Burke's estimate that there were 80,000 readers in Britain, and declares that *Popular Tales* is intended for this new reading public, in particular those not usually considered 'polite'. Advances in the 'art of printing' had opened up new channels of entertainment and information to those previously excluded from enlightened education, and this access to intelligence was desired 'by the wise and good of all ranks', and by both sexes.[39]

---

[39] Preface, *Moral Tales*, ed. by Clíona Ó Gallchoir, vol. 10 in *Novels and Selected Works of Maria Edgeworth*, 169; Preface, *Popular Tales*, in *Tales and Novels by Maria Edgeworth*, 18 vols (London: Baldwin & Cradock, 1832), IV, iii–iv.

Popular Tales was thus optimistically conceived as a democratic, progressive work. In his influential article about *Popular Tales* in the *Edinburgh Review*, Francis Jeffrey sees Edgeworth's populism as of a different order from the dangerous variety peddled by Thomas Paine, author of *Rights of Man* (1791–2), or William Wordsworth in *Lyrical Ballads* (1798). While they had sought to spread 'disaffection and infidelity' among 'common people', and to disseminate 'pernicious absurdities', Jeffrey judges Edgeworth's tales to be designed to impress upon the minds of their readers 'the inestimable value and substantial dignity of industry, perseverance, prudence, good humour', and other 'vulgar and homely virtues' that conduce to happiness but are largely unadmired.[40] A more recent commentator, Alan Richardson, concurs in Jeffrey's evaluation of the politics of *Popular Tales*: he sees Edgeworth as the inventor of 'a fictional discourse which implicitly counters the popular radicalism of Paine, without vulgarizing a polite literary form in the manner of Wordsworth' and views her work as rendering attractive in fictional shape qualities 'that would enable a lower-class reader eager for self-improvement to make the most of his or her limited opportunities without expecting to rise too fast or too high'. Any hard worker can succeed in *Popular Tales*, argues Richardson, but to do so he 'must cut himself off from other workers [...] never forgetting his humble beginnings and the "gratitude" owed to a benevolent patron.'[41] Richardson's assessment carries obvious weight when applied to 'The Grateful Negro', although even here the politics of the tale are less clear-cut than Richardson claims.

'The Good Aunt'

Written in 1797, 'The Good Aunt' is interesting from many points of view, as a story about the aspiration for social status versus the ambition to be useful, about the difficulties of moral decisions for individuals enmeshed within systems of oppression, and the importance of being oneself and striving for self-improvement rather than bowing to others' opinions or allowing oneself to be discouraged by unjust representations. This is a story that, in

---

[40] *Edinburgh Review* 8 (July 1804), 330.
[41] Richardson, *Literature, Education, and Romanticism*, 225.

Myers's words, redefines heroism as 'benign and powerful maternal governance', 'a female mode of cultural reform directed toward improvement of both self and community'.[42] Although the focus of the tale is on the thoughts and actions of three boys at public schools (that is to say, privately run boys' schools for the social elite), the quiet, nurturing presence of the titular 'good aunt' is crucial. Her determined financial independence, her interest in reason, in ideas and in philosophical conversation, and her steady but hands-off encouragement of her nephew, Charles Howard, create models for his own behaviour. Under Mrs Howard's guidance, Charles eventually excels in the male world of school—an embryonic public sphere of politicking, power-play, and knowledge-acquisition. In addition, however, he learns from her example the role of being a nurturing parent to the younger boy, Oliver. Oliver, who is newly arrived from Jamaica, is described in terms that suggestively position him as analogous to an enslaved child; as the tale unfolds Charles plays an important part in his emancipation into his full potential.

This sketch tracing the diverse themes, plotting and ideas in 'The Good Aunt' supports Myers's point that critics simplify Edgeworth when they portray her as 'an amanuensis wielding her father's pen or a puppet ventriloquizing his ideas'.[43] In fact, Richard Lovell Edgeworth's claim that the stories in *Moral Tales* 'were written to illustrate the opinions delivered in *Practical Education*' is only partly true when we look closely at individual examples from his daughter's tales. 'The Good Aunt' is much more than a mere fictionalized scheme of education, although

---

[42] Myers, 'Impeccable Governesses, Rational Dames and Moral Mothers', *Children's Literature* 14 (1986), 31–56: 54, 55. Myers argues that women writers' moral tales in the Georgian period often 'smuggle in their own symptomatic fantasies, dramatizing female authority figures, covertly thematizing female power' by creating heroines who are 'rational educators' (34, 35); they thus present motherhood as a means of attaining what Mary Wollstonecraft called 'civic existence', and suggest that 'nurture [is] power' (54).

[43] Myers, 'Romancing the Moral Tale: Maria Edgeworth and the Problematics of Pedagogy', in *Romanticism and Children's Literature in Nineteenth-Century England*, ed. by James Holt McGavran, Jr (Athens, GA: University of Georgia Press, 1991), 96–128: 100.

the rights and wrongs of private and public education are certainly among its preoccupations, subjects explored in chapter
XIX of *Practical Education*. Edgeworth's father presents 'The Good
Aunt' in the preface to *Moral Tales* as a fable about 'judicious early
education'. While he concedes that large public schools can form
a character and develop a boy's potential, he argues that the 'solid
advantages' of school education must be 'secured by previous domestic instruction'.[44] Richard Lovell Edgeworth's presentation of
the story's preoccupations thus registers the significance of the
domestic sphere and of parental or quasi-parental influence in the
realization of the child's full potential; but he does not remark
upon the absence of good biological parent-figures in the tale,
or the prominence of the *female* mentor (the 'mentoria', to use
Myers's term[45]) in this scene of early instruction.

One of Edgeworth's sources (alluded to in a footnote) is Edward
Gibbon's memoir, in which Gibbon explores his intellectual roots
in his childhood experiences, and in particular the fulfilment of
the 'maternal office' by his mother's sister, Mrs Catherine Porten.
This surrogate parenting was acknowledged by Gibbon as being
of tremendous significance in making him a reader and thinker.
He apostrophizes his aunt as 'the true mother of my mind', and
notes that 'to her kind lessons I ascribe my early and invincible
love of reading, which I would not exchange for the treasures of
India. [...] Mrs. Porten [...] was more prone to encourage than to
check a curiosity above the strength of a boy'. When his grandfather's finances ran adrift, his aunt was left destitute, but 'scorned
a life of obligation and dependence', choosing to support herself
by keeping a boarding-house for boys at Westminster School.[46]

Clearly, Edgeworth draws creatively on this source for her own
purposes: her fictional aunt's circumstances and character re-
semble Mrs Porten's, but she is more fully realized as the mother
of Charles's mind, and as a thinker in her own right. Mrs Howard
prioritizes Charles's pleasure in reading at an impressionable age,

---

[44] *Novels and Selected Works of Maria Edgeworth,* ed. Ó Gallchoir, X, 170.

[45] Myers, 'Impeccable Governesses', 38.

[46] *Miscellaneous Works of Edward Gibbon, Esq., with Memoirs of His Life
and Writings*, 2 vols (London: A. Strahan, T. Cadell & W. Davies, 1796): I,
19, 24–6.

introducing him to books on subjects 'which she thought would excite his curiosity to know *more*' and encouraging him to 'talk to her freely about what he read' (p.101). In *The Enquirer* (1797), cited approvingly in *Practical Education*, William Godwin insists upon the importance of the child's first teacher as the creative influence whose responsibility it is to 'awaken his mind', and to inspire him with the desire to learn: this injunction is taken seriously by Mrs Howard. Godwin stresses that 'the first lesson of a judicious education is, Learn to think, to discriminate, to remember and to enquire'. But he begins his essay on private and public education by reflecting on the isolation and lack of self-esteem experienced by the boy who is not so fortunate. Without the nurturing of his efforts which is, Godwin thinks, 'the first thing that gives spring and expansion to the infant learner', a boy is left with nothing to 'inspire [him] with self-value'.[47]

In Edgeworth's tale, however, Charles is able to give Oliver this 'spring and expansion' and 'self-value' because he has previously received the gift of confident self-improvement from his aunt. She consistently stands for the idea (central to the philosophy of *Practical Education*) that 'genius' is not solely an innate capacity; rather, talent and achievement are the product of sustained, determined effort and self-defined ambition. Early in the story, Charles, anxious to help his aunt and to be 'of use' as she faces financial ruin, asks her: 'What would *you* wish me to be, ma'am?—because that's what I will be—if I can.' Her response—'I wish you to be what you are' (p.109)—is initially disappointing to the eager boy, but it is this sense of her esteem for him as a developing individual, and crucially, as a trusted friend with whom she openly shares her thoughts, that helps Charles believe in his own powers. Charles is inspired to make the effort to win an essay-prize by the anticipated pleasure of giving joy to his aunt, his tutor and Oliver (dreaming of the medal, he sees each of their smiling faces in turn imprinted on the prize medallion). Similarly, Oliver is 'inspired' by Charles, who passes on his aunt's philosophy: '[Oliver's] own opinion of himself rose with the opinion which he saw his instructor had of his abilities. He was convinced that

---

[47] Godwin, *The Enquirer* (London: G. G. and J. Robinson, 1797), 3, 6, 57–8; cited in *Practical Education*, 133.

he was not doomed to be a dunce for life; his ambition was rekindled; his industry was encouraged by hope, and rewarded by success.' (p.120)

In the course of the tale, Charles finds more assurance and a greater sense of self-worth through the friendship that he offers to Oliver, becoming his 'good genius' (p.120). In addition to these themes of benign guidance, self-making, and independent thinking, however, an uneasy undercurrent consisting of reflection on the meanings and effects of slavery, on violent and punitive assertions of social superiority and the ownership of others, runs beneath the surface of the tale. Oliver, described as a 'Creole' (a term that does not necessarily indicate African lineage, but may do so) is beset by feelings of inferiority: feelings that partly arise from his lack of prior schooling, which gives rise to thrice-weekly floggings by masters who label him as unteachable and backward, and partly arise from being claimed by Augustus (the third boy in the tale) as a 'negro-slave', to be used and abused at will in his role as Augustus's 'fag' (p.117).[48] As the plot unfolds, it becomes clear that it is Oliver and the Jamaican ex-slave, Cuba, who hold the keys to the restoration of the good aunt's fortunes, a fairy-tale reward that is indirectly the result of the aunt's refusal to inherit a slave plantation in Jamaica, and her emancipation of some of the slaves on the estate.

'The Grateful Negro'

Edgeworth's interest in debates about slavery and abolition, visible in 'The Good Aunt' in 1801, is very evident in 'The Grateful Negro', published three years later. The controversy about the morality of slavery and the slave trade had by this time been active for at least 28 years, and abolitionism had gained widespread popular support by 1789, when William Wilberforce introduced twelve resolutions against the slave trade in the House of Commons. In 1790, a select committee of the House of Commons had undertaken extensive interviewing of witnesses involved in the slave trade.

---

[48] Edgeworth defines 'fags' as boys 'forced to wait upon and obey their...luxurious masters'. Oliver is described as having a 'dark complexion' that masks his blushes of shame at his errors (pp.114–15).

The campaign was given added salience in 1791 when there was a mass slave uprising in Saint-Domingue, and when Wilberforce again tried, and failed, to advance the issue in Parliament. The following year, in 1792, the House of Commons voted to phase out the British slave trade by 1796, but the motion was blocked in the House of Lords. Outside Parliament, anti-saccharitism (a boycott on slave-produced sugar) had gained large-scale public backing by March 1792, when James Gillray published a carica-ture of the King and Queen taking unsweetened tea in support of 'the poor Blackamoors'.[49] But Wilberforce's continued efforts in Parliament went on failing. The year 1804 saw the last of several unsuccessful abolition attempts again blocked by the Lords; it was not until 1807 that the Abolition of the Slave Trade Act finally passed into law. Edgeworth was well aware of the debates of the 1790s over the conditions suffered by the millions of Africans seized by slave traders and sold into slavery in the West Indies. Several of the Edgeworth family's friends, including Thomas Day and Erasmus Darwin, published works that made their opposition to slavery and the slave trade clear. Edgeworth herself was familiar with the facts as reported to Parliament, as a letter to her cousin, Sophy Ruxton, shows, and had read a pamphlet summarizing these reports that aroused strong indignation in her.[50] This might well have been *A Short Sketch of the Evidence, for the Abolition of the Slave Trade, Delivered Before a Committee of the House of Commons* (Glasgow, 1792), which condenses into nineteen pages the eye-witness accounts of the tortures, mutilations, and other atrocities visited upon slaves, both on board the slave-ships and on West Indian plantations, based on the enormous body of evidence presented to Parliament.

'The Grateful Negro' takes significant plot and character details from Bryan Edwards's pro-slavery *History of the West Indies* (1793), but it is also informed by abolitionist sources like the *Short Sketch*, Anna Barbauld's 'Epistle to William Wilberforce' (1791) and August von Kotzebue's play of 1795, *The Negro Slaves* (translated into English in 1796). Edgeworth's tale centres on two Jamaican

---

[49] Gillray, 'Anti-Saccharrites', BMC 8074.
[50] Edgeworth to Sophy Ruxton, 5 March 1792 (MS 10, 166/7/88, National Library of Ireland).

planters: Jefferies, who is 'thoughtless' and avaricious, indifferent
to the sufferings of his slaves, or capable only of 'momentary compassion' (p.175); and Edwards, who has 'humane views', is alert to
the 'voice of distress', and is keen to 'make our negroes as happy
as possible', though 'convinced, by the arguments of those who
have the best means of obtaining information, that the sudden
emancipation of the negroes would rather increase than diminish
their miseries' (pp.176, 177, 179, 176). Similarly, there are two central slave characters: Jefferies' slave, Hector, a man of 'superior
fortitude and courage', and leader of a conspiracy to 'extirpate'
the whites in revenge for their tyranny and cruelty; and Caesar,
once another of Jefferies' slaves, but now the property of Edwards
(p.181). He is described as 'frank, fearless, martial, and heroic',
but also 'grateful' (p.180). Caesar regards Edwards as 'my benefactor—my friend!', since by buying them both, Edwards has enabled
him to stay with his wife-to-be, Clara; and after a 'violent and
painful' internal conflict, in which Caesar wrestles with his feelings of loyalty to his fellow-slaves, he finally decides to honour
his sense of 'gratitude' to his 'friend' (pp.182, 183). He warns him
of the approaching uprising and elects to give up his hopes of
liberty; he does, however, secure his fellows' future by making
Edwards promise that they will not be punished.

  In the course of the unfolding of the plot, Edgeworth makes
it clear that the uprising is the necessary consequence of oppression: 'The cruelties practised by Durant, the overseer of Jefferies'
plantation, had exasperated the slaves under his dominion', and
their conspiracy is driven by 'all the courage of despair' (p.181).
In narrative terms, she justifies and explains the slave rebellion
by showing Jefferies and other planters carousing and feasting,
deaf to the cries of distress nearby as Jefferies' overseer has 'recourse to that brutality which he considered as the only means of
governing black men', flogging four slaves 'unmercifully' (p.188).
She reinforces this representation of corrupt luxury and vicious
abuse by describing another decisive incident, when Mrs Jefferies,
a 'languid beauty' who spends her days 'reclining on a couch'
being fanned by slaves, orders a female slave who has inadvert-
ently torn a new gown to be 'severely chastised' (pp.189, 190).
Edgeworth is surely remembering Barbauld's 'Epistle to William
Wilberforce' (1791), in which Barbauld scathingly describes a

'pale Beauty' who 'courts the breeze,/Diffus'd on sofas of voluptuous ease', with 'arm recumbent wield[ing] the household scourge', 'Contriving torture, and inflicting wounds' (ll. 57–70). As the story draws to its conclusion, Edgeworth implicitly justifies the negligent and avaricious plantation owner's financial ruin and the brutal overseer's grisly demise—burnt in his house, he 'died in tortures, inflicted by the hands of those who had suffered most by his cruelties' (p.194)—as the natural consequence of their injustice and inhumanity.

'The Grateful Negro' poses pressing questions about the legitimacy of forced labour and the treatment of people as property, and ends with a veiled warning about the consequences of unthinking and irrational negligence and exploitation in the form of the Jefferies family's ruin and their overseer's death. Edgeworth riskily names one of her characters after a prominent defender of the plantocracy, Bryan Edwards, yet criticizes his refusal to debate the possibility of abolition by giving some of his opinions to Jefferies. Characteristically, she avoids polemic, preferring to stimulate her readers' powers of thought. This avoidance of explicit judgment and the ambivalent presentation of slavery and slave-owning means that 'The Grateful Negro' has aroused considerable controversy and disagreement among its recent critics.

Suvendrini Perera sees the tale as marked by contradiction and discontinuity; similarly, Moira Ferguson remarks that 'Edgeworth's entire tale concentrates on conflict', giving a voice to the slave rebels who urge armed resistance, and showing the fictional Mr Edwards himself in two minds about emancipation, unresolved on whether it should be prepared for slowly with the introduction of small areas of freedom (such as allowing couples to stay together), or whether it should be immediately effected, and slaves turned into free wage labourers. Ferguson argues that 'the ending quietly questions whether the counterblasts of abused men and women can be termed treacherous', since '[t]he power that enslaves Hector and his allies is nothing more than brute force and atrocities, all categorically condemned'.[51]

---

[51] Perera, *Reaches of Empire* (New York: Columbia University Press, 1991), 33–4; Ferguson, *Subject to Others* (New York & London: Routledge, 1992), 231–4.

George Boulukos, on the other hand, reads Edgeworth's tale as an 'attempt to reimagine slavery as humane'. Boulukos holds that Edgeworth 'was one of many writers to take the sentimental acknowledgment of slaves' humanity only as the ground for understanding them as psychological beings, to be managed and manipulated like any other worker' and concludes that 'she was, in fact, a lukewarm, ameliorationist supporter of slavery'.[52] Boulukos's article has been very influential in representing Edgeworth as ideologically conservative, and important in drawing attention to the relationship between Edgeworth's tale and Bryan Edwards's pro-slavery *History of the West Indies* (1793); yet its case is not unassailable. Elizabeth Kim, for example, notes that Edgeworth makes significant changes to Bryan Edwards's ideas. Edwards aims to shock his readers with explicit accounts of slaves' violence, and with graphic descriptions of the punishment of insurgents, whereas Edgeworth avoids such descriptions of violent acts or underplays their effects, except where they seem to be unequivocally deserved. Hence Hector's stabbing of Caesar is not fatal, the rebels are not punished, and only Durant, Jefferies and his wife are subjected to just retribution. Kim sees the tale as a warning to unjust or negligent landowners: 'Like the absentee or negligent Anglo-Irish landlords in her Irish novels, the abusive Jamaican colonial master in this story must reform his ways or face rebellion and elimination'.[53]

Frances R. Botkin argues that Edgeworth is 'firmly in the progressive, abolitionist camp' and challenges Boulukos's claim that Edgeworth largely uncritically echoes Bryan Edwards's *History*. Botkin draws attention to the web of intertextual references in the tale and argues that 'the tensions between these texts resist and subvert the notion that Edgeworth's tale relies upon and contributes to discourses unambiguously supportive of slavery and the slave trade'. Edgeworth signals her support for abolition, according to Botkin, through the suggestion that

---

[52] Boulukos, 'Maria Edgeworth's "Grateful Negro" and the Sentimental Argument for Slavery', *Eighteenth Century Life* 23 (1999), 12–29: 13, 22.

[53] Kim, 'Maria Edgeworth's *The Grateful Negro*: A Site for Rewriting Rebellion', *Eighteenth-Century Fiction* 16.1 (2003), 103–26: 110–12.

wage labourers inevitably work harder and better than slaves, since they may personally benefit from their labour, unlike those who are forced to work without remuneration, without hope of bettering their circumstances, and under the threat of severe punishment.[54]

Finally, Alison Harvey argues that Edgeworth may not align herself with a 'radical view of slaves' emancipation efforts', but that she does offer 'a critique of the hegemonic power assumed by white English patriarchal society', and in Caesar creates an 'ambiguous case of gratitude in which gratitude itself serves as an opportunity for Edgeworth to question inequitable power relations'. Edgeworth does not depict the cause of the rebels as unjust, rather implying that their means of achieving their emancipation through armed uprising risks injustice, especially as slave rebellions often entailed massive death-tolls for slaves themselves, and could set back abolition efforts by stimulating British fears of social disorder and of colonial race war.[55]

As these conflicting readings indicate, Edgeworth's writing for adolescents and young adults has considerable complexity, and often deploys footnotes and allusions to invoke ideas and arguments that work against the apparent tendency of the narrative. As such, her tales 'awaken the mind', to use Godwin's phrase:[56] they elicit enquiry, and inform their readers about political and ethical debates of the day. The process of enlightenment, of independent use of the understanding, that Edgeworth encourages her child readers to pursue in *The Parent's Assistant*, continues to be fundamental to *Moral* and *Popular Tales*.

---

[54] Botkin, 'Questioning the "Necessary Order of Things": Maria Edgeworth's "The Grateful Negro", Plantation Slavery, and the Abolition of the Slave Trade', in *Discourses of Slavery and Abolition*, ed. by Brycchan Carey, Markman Ellis, and Sara Salih (Basingstoke: Palgrave Macmillan, 2004), 194–208: 194, 195, 196.

[55] 'West Indian Obeah and English "Obee": Race, Femininity, and Questions of Colonial Consolidation in Maria Edgeworth's *Belinda*', in *New Essays on Maria Edgeworth*, ed. by Julie Nash (Aldershot & Burlington, VT: Ashgate, 2006), 1–29: 2, 19.

[56] Godwin, *The Enquirer*, 3.

Conclusion

The tales collected in this edition are a small sample of Edgeworth's extensive oeuvre for young people, but they display her wit, her empathetic representation of children's thoughts and actions, her interest in promoting debate, and her gift for realistic characterization. *The Parent's Assistant* was warmly praised by the *Monthly Review* as the production of a 'writer of the first order', and as a collection of 'amusing and interesting tales' of 'great ingenuity, [...] happily contrived to excite curiosity and awaken feeling, without the aid of improbable fiction or extravagant adventure', to be ranked alongside the best work of Anna Barbauld and John Aikin, the authors of *Evenings at Home* (1792–6).[57] Yet Edgeworth was sometimes controversial, particularly in relation to her secularism. In contrast with Francis Jeffrey's assessment of her as a conservative, John Foster condemned her for her irreligiousness, especially improper in a woman, while John Wilson Croker attacked her in 1820 for defending her father's reputation as an educationalist, alleging that her work for children was tainted by his atheism.[58]

More recent accounts of Edgeworth's writings have been similarly divergent in their assessment of her politics, as is clear in the very different critical interpretations of 'The Grateful Negro', surveyed above. While Andrew O'Malley sees her as a propagandist for middle-class values of self-reliance and industry, Gary Kelly argues that her fiction sustains 'the impulse of revolutionary feminism' and pursues a meritocratic social order in which 'inherited rank and wealth or ascribed status' cede their political dominance to a new class who have raised themselves through education and determined effort, a possibility for 'subaltern classes' as well as for the bourgeoisie.[59] Part of the reason for these contrasting assessments is that Edgeworth, in the interests of stimulating enquiry and debate, often avoids direct moralizing, or complicates

---

[57] *Monthly Review* 21 (September 1796), 89.

[58] *Eclectic Review*, 8 (1812), 1000; *Quarterly Review*, 23 (1820), 544.

[59] O'Malley, *The Making of the Modern Child*, 46; Kelly, 'Class, Gender, Nation, and Empire: Money and Merit in the Writing of the Edgeworths', *The Wordsworth Circle* 25.2 (Spring 1994), 92, 91.

it by attending sympathetically to the oppressions that give rise to conflict, or smuggles oppositional ideas in through the use of allusion. An edition such as this helps to uncover the network of allusions and intertextuality through which Edgeworth creates her effects, particularly in the tales for adolescent and young adult readers. It also advances the work of reinstating her as an author who was important in her own time and who influenced successive generations of writers for children.

Note on the Texts

The texts for the tales from *The Parent's Assistant* (1796 and 1800), *Early Lessons* (1801) and *Popular Tales* (1804) have been taken from the first editions in which each tale appeared. The text for 'The Good Aunt', from *Moral Tales* (1801), is based on the seventh edition (London: R. Hunter and Baldwin, Cradock & Joy, 1816).

Some archaic spellings have been changed (e.g. 'chuse', 'scissars', 'shew'). Edgeworth's footnotes to the tales are marked with asterisks and other symbols; mine are marked with numbered superscripts, or annotate her notes within square brackets.

Further Reading

Manly, Susan. 'Maria Edgeworth and "The Light of Nature": Artifice, Autonomy, and Anti-Sectarianism in *Practical Education* (1798)'. In *Repossessing the Romantic Past*. Ed. by Heather Glen and Paul Hamilton. Cambridge: Cambridge University Press, 2006. 140–59.

Manly, Susan. ' "Take a *poon*, Pig": Property, Class, and Common Culture in Maria Edgeworth's "Simple Susan" '. *Children's Literature Association Quarterly* 37.3 (Fall 2012). 306–22.

Myers, Mitzi. 'Daddy's Girl as Motherless Child: Maria Edgeworth and Maternal Romance; an Essay in Reassessment'. In *Living By the Pen: Early British Women Writers*. Ed. by Dale Spender. New York & London: Teachers College Press, 1992. 137–59.

Myers, Mitzi. 'The Erotics of Pedagogy: Historical Intervention, Literary Representation, the "Gift of Education", and the Agency of Children'. *Children's Literature* 23. Ed. by Elizabeth Lennox Keyser. New Haven & London: Yale University Press, 1995.

Myers, Mitzi. 'Canonical "Orphans" and Critical *Ennui*: Rereading Edgeworth's Cross-Writing'. *Children's Literature* 25. Ed. by Francelia Butler, R. H. W. Dillard, and Elizabeth Lennox Keyser, guest ed. Mitzi Myers and U. C. Knoepflmacher. New Haven & London: Yale University Press, 1997. 116–36.

Myers, Mitzi. 'Reading Rosamond Reading: Maria Edgeworth's "Wee-Wee Stories" Interrogate the Canon'. In *Infant Tongues: The Voice of the Child in Literature*. Ed. by Elizabeth Goodenough, Mark A. Heberle and Naomi Sokoloff. Detroit: Wayne State University Press, 1999. 57–79.

Myers, Mitzi. ' "Anecdotes from the Nursery" in Maria Edgeworth's *Practical Education* (1798): Learning from Children "Abroad and At Home" '. *Princeton University Library Chronicle* 60.2 (Winter 1999). 220–50.

Ó Gallchoir, Clíona. *Maria Edgeworth: Women, Enlightenment and Nation*. Dublin: University College Dublin Press, 2005.

Robinson, Fiona. 'Peculiar Dearness: Sentimental Commerce in Maria Edgeworth's "The Bracelets" '. *Children's Literature Association Quarterly* 37.3 (Fall 2012). 323–43.

'The Little Dog Trusty; or, The Liar and the Boy of Truth'

Very, very little children must not read this story, for they cannot understand it; they will not know what is meant by a liar, and a boy of truth.

Very little children, when they are asked a question, say "yes," and "no," without knowing the meaning of the words; but you, children, who can speak quite plain, and who can tell, by words, what you wish for, and what you want, and what you have seen, and what you have done; you, who understand what is meant by the words "I have done it," or "I have not," you may read this story, for you can understand it.[1]

Frank and Robert were two little boys, about eight years old. Whenever Frank did any thing wrong, he always told his father and mother of it; and when any body asked him about any thing which he had done or said, he always told the truth; so that every body who knew him believed him: but nobody who knew his brother Robert believed a word which he said, because he used to tell lies. Whenever he did any thing wrong, he never ran to his father and mother to tell them of it; but when they asked him about it, he denied it, and said he had not done the things which he had done. The reason that Robert told lies was, because he was afraid of being punished for his faults if he confessed them. He was a coward, and could not bear the least pain; but Frank was a brave boy, and could bear to be punished for little faults; his mother never punished him so much for such little faults, as she did Robert for the lies which he told, and which she found out afterward.

One evening these two little boys were playing together in a room by themselves; their mother was ironing in a room next to them, and their father was out at work in the fields, so there was nobody in the room with Robert and Frank: but there was the little dog Trusty lying by the fire-side. Trusty was a pretty playful little dog, and the children were very fond of him.

"Come," said Robert to Frank, "there is Trusty lying beside the fire asleep, let us go and waken him, and he will play with us."— "Oh yes, do let us," said Frank. So they both ran together towards the hearth to waken the dog. Now there was a basin of milk standing upon the hearth, and the little boys did not see whereabouts it stood, for it was behind them; as they were both playing with the dog, they kicked it with their feet, and threw it down; and the basin broke, and all the milk ran out of it over the hearth, and about the floor; and when the little boys saw what they had done, they were very sorry and frightened, but they did not know what to do: they stood for some time looking at the broken basin and the milk, without speaking. Robert spoke first.

"So we shall have no milk for supper tonight," said he, and he sighed—

"No milk for supper!— why not," said Frank, "is there no more milk in the house?"

"Yes, but we shall have none of it; for do not you remember last Monday, when we threw down the milk, my mother said we were very careless, and that the next time we did so, we should have no more,—and this is the next time; so we shall have no milk for supper to-night."

"Well then," says Frank, "we must do without it, that's all; we will take more care another time; there's no great harm done; come, come, let us run and tell my mother. You know she bid us always tell her directly when we broke any thing; so come," said he, taking hold of his brother's hand. "I will come just now," said Robert, "don't be in such a hurry, Frank; can't you stay a minute." So Frank stayed. And then he said, "Come now, Robert;" but Robert answered, "Stay a little longer, for I dare not go yet—I am afraid."

Little boys, I advise you, never be afraid to tell the truth; never say, "*stay a minute,*" and "*stay a little longer,*" but run directly and tell of what you have done that is wrong. The longer you stay, the more afraid you will grow; till at last, perhaps, you will not dare to tell the truth at all.—Hear what happened to Robert.

The longer he stayed, the more unwilling he was to go to tell his mother that he had thrown the milk down; and at last he pulled his hand away from his brother, and cried, "I won't go at all; Frank, can't you go by yourself?" "Yes," said Frank, "so I will; I am not afraid to go by myself; I only waited for you out of good nature, because I thought you would like to tell the truth too."

"Yes, so I will; I mean to tell the truth when I am asked; but I need not go now, when I do not choose it:—and why need you go either?—can't you wait here?—surely my mother can see the milk when she comes in." Frank said no more, but as his brother would not come he went without him. He opened the door of the next room, where he thought his mother was ironing, but when he went in, he saw that she was gone, and he thought she was gone to fetch some more clothes to iron. The clothes he knew were hanging on the bushes in the garden; so he thought his mother was gone there, and he ran after her to tell what had happened.

Now whilst Frank was gone, Robert was left in the room by himself; and all the while he was alone he was thinking of some excuses to make to his mother: and he was sorry that Frank was gone to tell her the truth. He said to himself, "If Frank and I both were to say, that we did not throw down the basin, she would believe us, and we should have milk for supper; I am very sorry Frank would go to tell her about it," Just as he said this to himself he heard his mother coming down stairs. "Oh ho!" said he to himself, "then my mother has not been out in the garden, and so Frank has not met her, and cannot have told her; so now I may say what I please."

Then this naughty cowardly boy determined to tell his mother a lie.

She came into the room, but when she saw the broken basin, and the milk spilled, she stopped short, and cried—

"So, so!—what a piece of work is here! Who did this, Robert?"

"I don't know ma'am," said Robert, in a very low voice.

"You don't know, Robert!—tell me the truth—I shall not be angry with you, child—you will only lose the milk at supper; and as for the basin, I would rather have you break all the basins I have, than tell me one lie.—So don't tell me a lie.—I ask you, Robert, did you break the basin?"

"*No ma'am,* I did not," said Robert, and he coloured as red as fire.

"Then where's Frank? Did he do it?" "No, mother, he did not," said Robert; for he was in hopes, that when Frank came in he should persuade him to say, that he did not do it.

"How do you know," said his mother, "that Frank did not do it?"

"Because—because—because ma'am," said Robert, hesitating, as liars do for an excuse; "because I was in the room all the time, and I did not see him do it."

"Then how was the basin thrown down? If you have been in the room all the time you can tell."

Then Robert, going on from one lie to another, answered—

"I suppose the dog must have done it."—"Did you see him do it?" says his mother. "Yes," said this wicked boy. "Trusty, Trusty," said his mother, turning round; and Trusty, who was lying before the fire, drying his legs, which were wet with the milk, jumped up and came to her. Then she said, "Fie! fie! Trusty !" and she pointed to the milk. "Get me a switch out of the garden, Robert; Trusty must be beat for this." Robert ran for the switch, and in the garden he met his brother; he stopped him, and told him, in a great hurry, all that he had said to his mother; and he begged of him not to tell the truth, but to say the same as he had done.

"No, I will not tell a lie," said Frank. "What! and is Trusty to be beat!—he did not throw down the milk, and he shan't be beat for it—let me go to my mother."

They both ran toward the house—Robert got first home, and he locked the house door, that Frank might not come in. He gave the switch to his mother. Poor Trusty! he looked up, as the switch was lifted over his head, but *he* could not speak to tell the truth; just as the blow was falling upon him, Frank's voice was heard at the window.—"Stop, stop! dear mother, stop!" cried he, as loud as ever he could call, "Trusty did not do it—let me in—I and Robert did it;—but do not beat Robert."

"Let us in, let us in," cried another voice, which Robert knew to be his father's, "I am just come from work, and here's the door locked." Robert turned as pale as ashes when he heard his father's voice, for his father always whipped him when he told a lie.

His mother went to the door, and unlocked it. "What's all this?" cried his father, as he came in; so his mother told him all that had happened;—how the milk had been thrown down; how she had asked Robert whether he had done it; and he said that he had not, nor that Frank had not done it, but that Trusty the dog had done it; how she was just going to beat Trusty, when Frank came to the window and told the truth.[2] "Where is the switch with which you were going to beat Trusty?" said the father.

Then Robert, who saw by his father's looks that he was going to beat him, fell upon his knees, and cried for mercy; saying, "Forgive me this time, and I will never tell a lie again."

But his father caught hold of him by the arm, "I will whip you now," said he, "and then, I hope, you will not." So Robert was whipped, till he cried so loud with the pain, that the whole neighbourhood could hear him.

"There," said his father when he had done, "now go to supper; you are to have no milk to-night, and you have been whipped. See how liars are served!" Then turning to Frank, "Come here, and shake hands with me, Frank; you will have no milk for supper, but that does not signify; you have told the truth, and have not been whipped, and every body is pleased with you. And now I'll tell you what I will do for you, I will give you the little dog Trusty, to be your own dog. You shall feed him, and take care of him, and he shall be your dog; you have saved him a beating, and I'll answer for it, you'll be a good master to him. Trusty, Trusty, come here." Trusty came; then Frank's father took off Trusty's collar. "Tomorrow I'll go to the brazier's," added he, "and get a new collar made for your dog; from this day forward he shall always be called after you, *Frank:* and, wife! whenever any of the neighbours' children ask you why the dog *Trusty* is to be called *Frank*, tell them this story of our two boys: let them know the difference between a liar and a boy of truth."

'The Purple Jar'

Rosamond, a little girl of about seven years old, was walking with her mother in the streets of London. As she passed along, she looked in at the windows of several shops, and she saw a great variety of different sorts of things, of which she did not know the use, or even the names. She wished to stop to look at them, but there were a great number of people in the streets, and a great many carts, and carriages, and wheelbarrows, and she was afraid to let go her mother's hand.

"Oh! mother, how happy I should be," said she, as she passed a toy-shop, "if I had all these pretty things!"

"What, all! Do you wish for them all, Rosamond ?"

"Yes, mamma, all."

As she spoke they came to a milliner's shop; the windows were hung with ribbons and lace, and festoons of artificial flowers.

"Oh, mamma, what beautiful roses! Won't you buy some of them?"

"No, my dear."

"Why?"

"Because I don't want them, my dear."

They went on a little farther, and they came to another shop, which caught Rosamond's eye. It was a jeweller's shop, and there were a great many pretty baubles, ranged in drawers behind glass.

"Mamma, you'll buy some of these?"

"Which of them, Rosamond?"

"Which,—I don't know which;—but any of them, for they are all pretty."

"Yes, they are all pretty; but what use would they be of to me?"

"Use! Oh I'm sure you could find some use or other, if you would only buy them first."

"But I would rather find out the use, first."

"Well, then, mamma, there are buckles: you know buckles are useful things, very useful things."

"I have a pair of buckles, I don't want another pair," said her mother, and walked on. Rosamond was very sorry that her mother wanted nothing. Presently, however, they came to a shop, which appeared to her far more beautiful than the rest. It was a chemist's shop, but she did not know that.

"Oh, mother! oh!" cried she, pulling her mother's hand; "Look, look, blue, green, red, yellow, and purple! Oh, mamma, what beautiful things! Won't you buy some of these?"

Still her mother answered as before; "What use would they be of to me, Rosamond?"

"You might put flowers in them, mamma, and they would look so pretty on the chimney-piece;—I wish I had one of them."

"You have a flower-pot," said her mother, "and that is not a flower-pot."

"But I could use it for a flower-pot, mamma, you know."

"Perhaps if you were to see it nearer, if you were to examine it, you might be disappointed."

"No, indeed, I'm sure I should not; I should like it exceedingly."

Rosamond kept her head turned to look at the purple vase, till she could see it no longer.

"Then, mother," said she, after a pause, "perhaps you have no money."

"Yes, I have."

"Dear, if I had money, I would buy roses, and boxes, and buckles, and purple flower-pots, and every thing." Rosamond was obliged to pause in the midst of her speech.

"Oh, mamma, would you stop a minute for me; I have got a stone in my shoe, it hurts me very much."

"How comes there to be a stone in your shoe?"

"Because of this great hole, mamma—it comes in there; my shoes are quite worn out; I wish you'd be so very good as to give me another pair."

"Nay, Rosamond, but I have not money, enough to buy shoes, and flower-pots, and buckles, and boxes, and every thing."

Rosamond thought that was a great pity. But now her foot, which had been hurt by the stone, began to give her so much pain that she was obliged to hop every other step, and she could think of nothing else. They came to a shoemaker's shop soon afterwards.

"There! there! mamma, there are shoes; there are little shoes that would just fit me; and you know shoes would be really of use to me."

"Yes, so they would, Rosamond.—Come in."—She followed her mother into the shop.

Mr. Sole, the shoemaker, had a great many customers, and his shop was full; so they were obliged to wait.

"Well, Rosamond," said her mother, "you don't think this shop so pretty as the rest?"

"No, not nearly; it's black and dark, and there are nothing but shoes all round; and, besides, there's a very disagreeable smell."

"That smell is the smell of new leather."

"Is it?—Oh!" said Rosamond, looking round, "there is a pair of little shoes; they'll just fit me, I'm sure."

"Perhaps they might; but you cannot be sure till you have tried them on, any more than you can be quite sure that you should like the purple vase *exceedingly,* till you have examined it more attentively."

"Why, I don't know about the shoes certainly, till I've tried; but, mamma, I am quite sure I should like the flower-pot."

"Well, which would you rather have, that jar, or a pair of shoes? I will buy either for you."

"Dear mamma, thank you—but if you could buy both?"

"No, not both."

"Then the jar, if you please."

"But I should tell you, that I shall not give you another pair of shoes this month."

"This month!—that's a very long time indeed!—You can't think how these hurt me; I believe I'd better have the new shoes—but yet, that purple flower-pot!—Oh, indeed, mamma, these shoes are not so very, very bad; I think I might wear them a little longer; and the month will be soon over; I can make them last till the end of the month; can't I?—Don't you think so, mamma?"

"Nay, my dear, I want you to think for yourself: you will have time enough to consider about it, whilst I speak to Mr. Sole about my clogs."

Mr. Sole was by this time at leisure; and whilst her mother was speaking to him, Rosamond stood in profound meditation, with one shoe on, and the other in her hand.

"Well, my dear, have you decided?"

"Mamma!—yes,—I believe.—If you please—I should like the flower-pot; that is, if you won't think me very silly, mamma."

"Why, as to that, I can't promise you, Rosamond; but, when you are to judge for yourself, you should choose what will make you the happiest; and then it would not signify who thought you silly."

"Then, mamma, if that's all, I'm sure the flower-pot would make me the happiest," said she, putting on her old shoe again; "so I choose the flower-pot."

"Very well, you shall have it; clasp your shoe and come home."

Rosamond clasped her shoe, and ran after her mother; it was not long before the shoe came down at the heel, and many times was she obliged to stop, to take the stones out of her shoe, and often was she obliged to hop with pain; but still the thoughts of the purple flower-pot prevailed, and she persisted in her choice.

When they came to the shop with the large window, Rosamond felt her joy redouble upon hearing her mother desire the servant, who was with them, to buy the purple jar, and bring it home. He had other commissions, so he did not return with them. Rosamond, as soon as she got in, ran to gather all her own flowers, which she had in a corner of her mother's garden.

"I'm afraid they'll be dead before the flower-pot comes, Rosamond," said her mother to her when she was coming in with the flowers in her lap.

"No, indeed, mamma, it will come home very soon, I dare say;—and shan't I be very happy putting them into the purple flower-pot?"

"I hope so, my dear."

The servant was much longer returning home than Rosamond had expected; but at length he came, and brought with him the long-wished for jar. The moment it was set down upon the table, Rosamond ran up, with an exclamation of joy. "I may have it now, mamma?"—"Yes, my dear, it is yours." Rosamond poured the flowers from her lap, upon the carpet, and seized the purple flower-pot.

"Oh, dear mother!" cried she, as soon as she had taken off the top, "but there's something dark in it—it smells very disagreeably—what is it? I didn't want this black stuff."

"Nor I neither, my dear."

"But what shall I do with it, mamma?"

"That I cannot tell."

"But it will be of no use to me, mamma."

"That I can't help."

"But I must pour it out, and fill the flower-pot with water."

"That's as you please, my dear."

"Will you lend me a bowl to pour it into, mamma?"

"That was more than I promised you, my dear, but I will lend you a bowl."

The bowl was produced, and Rosamond proceeded to empty the purple vase. But what was her surprise and disappointment, when it was entirely empty, to find that it was no longer a *purple* vase. It was a plain white glass jar, which had appeared to have that beautiful colour, merely from the liquor with which it had been filled.

Little Rosamond burst into tears.

"Why should you cry, my dear?" said her mother; "it will be of as much use to you now, as ever, for a flower-pot."

"But it won't look so pretty on the chimney-piece:—I am sure, if I had known that it was not really purple, I should not have wished to have it so much."

"But didn't I tell you that you had not examined it; and that perhaps you would be disappointed?"

"And so I am disappointed, indeed; I wish I had believed you before hand. Now I had much rather have the shoes; for I shall not be able to walk all this month: even walking home that little way hurt me exceedingly. Mamma, I'll give you the flower-pot back again, and that purple stuff and all, if you'll only give me the shoes."

"No, Rosamond, you must abide by your own choice; and now the best thing you can possibly do is, to bear your disappointment with good humour."

"I will bear it as well as I can," said Rosamond, wiping her eyes; and she began slowly and sorrowfully to fill the vase with flowers.

But Rosamond's disappointment did not end here; many were the difficulties and distresses into which her imprudent choice brought her, before the end of the month. Every day her shoes grew worse and worse, till at last she could neither run, dance, jump or walk in them. Whenever Rosamond was called to see any thing, she was pulling her shoes up at the heels, and was sure to be too late. Whenever her mother was going out to walk, she could not take Rosamond with her, for Rosamond had no soles to her shoes; and, at length, on the very last day of the month, it happened, that her father proposed to take her with her brother to a glass-house, which she had long wished to see. She was very happy; but, when she was quite ready, had her hat and gloves on, and was making haste down stairs to her brother and her father, who were waiting at the hall-door for her, the shoe dropped off; she put it on again in a great hurry, but, as she was going across the hall, her father turned round. "Who is that who is walking slip-shod? no one must walk slip-shod with me; why, Rosamond," said he, looking at her shoes with disgust, "I thought that you were always neat; go, I cannot take you with me."

Rosamond coloured and retired.——

"Oh, mamma," said she, as she took off her hat; "how I wish that I had chosen the shoes—they would have been of so much more use to me than that jar: however, I am sure—no, not quite sure—but, I hope, I shall be wiser another time."

'Rosamond's Day of Misfortunes'

"Many a cloudy morning turns out a fine day."[3]

"Are you getting up so soon?" said Rosamond to her sister; "it seems to be a cold morning; it is very disagreeable to get up from one's warm bed, in cold weather; I will not get up yet."

So Rosamond, who was covered up warmly, lay quite still, looking at Laura, who was dressing herself as quickly as she could.

"It is a cold morning indeed," said Laura; "therefore I'll make haste, that I may go down and warm myself, afterwards, at the fire in mamma's dressing-room."

When Laura was about half dressed, she called again to Rosamond, and told her that it was late, and that she was afraid she would not be ready for breakfast.

But Rosamond answered, "I shall be ready, I shall be ready; for you know, when I make a great deal of haste, I can dress very quickly indeed. Yesterday morning, I did not begin to dress till you were combing the last curl of your hair, and I was ready *almost* as soon as you were. Nay, Laura, why do you shake your head? I say *almost*—I don't say quite."

"I don't know what you call *almost*," said Laura, laughing; "I had been drawing some time before you came down stairs."

"But I looked at your drawing," said Rosamond, "the minute I came into the room, and I saw only three legs and a back of a chair; you know that was not much; it was hardly worth while to get up early to do so little."

"Doing a little and a little every morning makes something in time," said Laura.

"Very true," replied Rosamond; "you drew the whole of mamma's dressing-room, dressing-table and glass, and every thing, little by little, in—what do you call it?—perspective—before breakfast! I begin to wish, that I could get up as you do; but then I can't draw in perspective."

"But, my dear Rosamond, whilst you are talking about perspective, you don't consider how late it is growing," said Laura; "why don't you get up now?"

"Oh, because it is too late to get up early now," argued Rosamond.

Satisfied with this reflection, Rosamond closed her eyes, and turned to go to sleep again. "When you come to the last curl, Laura, call me once more," said she, "and then I'll get up."

But in vain Laura called her again, warning her that she was "come to the last curl."

Rosamond was more sleepy than ever, and more afraid of the cold; at last, however, she was roused by the breakfast bell: she started up, exclaiming, "Oh, Laura, what shall I do? I shall not be ready—my father will be displeased with me—And I've lost my lace—and I can't find my pocket-handkerchief—and all my things are gone.—This will be a day of misfortunes, I'm sure—and the clasp is come out of my shoe," added she; and as she uttered these words, in a doleful tone, she sat down upon the side of the bed and began to cry.

"Nay, don't cry," said Laura, "or else it *will* be a day of misfortunes; look, here's your pocket-handkerchief."

"But my lace!" said Rosamond, wiping her eyes with her handkerchief, "how can I be ready for breakfast without my lace; and my father will be very, very————"

"Very what?" said Laura, good humouredly; "here's the lace; sit up a minute, and I'll draw it out for you." Rosamond laughed, when she found that she was sitting upon her own lace, and she thanked her sister, who was now sewing the clasp into her shoe. "Well, I don't think it will be a day of misfortunes," said Rosamond, "you see I'm almost dressed, hey, Laura? and I shall be ready in pretty good time, and I shall be just as well as if I had got up an hour ago, hey, Laura?" But at this moment, Rosamond, in her violent haste, pulled the string of her cap into a knot, which she could not untie. Laura was going out of the room, but she called her back, in a voice of distress, and begged she would be so very good as to do one thing more for her; and, as Rosamond spoke, she held up her chin and showed the hard knot. Laura, whose patience was not to be conquered even by a hard knot, began very kindly to help her sister; but Rosamond, between her dislike of the cold, and her fear that she should not be ready for breakfast, and that her father would be displeased with her, became more and more fretful; she repeated, "This *will* be a day of misfortunes, after all—it tires me, Laura, to hold up my chin so long." Laura knelt down to relieve her chin; but no sooner was this complaint removed, than Rosamond began to shiver extremely, and exclaimed, "It is so cold, I cannot bear it any longer, Laura—This will be a day of misfortunes—I would rather untie the knot myself—Oh, that's my father's voice; he is dressed! he is dressed, and I am not half dressed!"

Rosamond's eyes were full of tears, and she was a melancholy spectacle, when her mother, at this instant, opened the room door. "What! not ready yet, Rosamond!—and in tears. Look at this cross face," said her mother, leading her to a looking-glass: "is that an agreeable little girl, do you think?"

"But I'm very cold, mamma; and I can't untie this knot; Laura, I think you have made it worse," said Rosamond, reproachfully.

At these words her mother desired Laura to go down stairs to breakfast. "Rosamond," added she, "you will not gain any thing by ill-humour: when you have done crying, and when you have dressed yourself, you may follow us down to breakfast."

As soon as her mother had shut the door and left her, Rosamond began to cry again; but, after some time, she considered, that her tears would neither make her warm, nor untie the knot of her cap; she therefore dried her eyes, and once more tried to conquer the grand difficulty. A little patience was all that was necessary; she untied the knot and finished dressing herself, but she felt ashamed to go into the room to her father and mother, and brothers and sister. She looked in the glass to see whether her eyes continued red. Yes, they were very red, and her purple cheeks were glazed with tears. She walked backwards and forwards between the door and the looking-glass several times, and the longer she delayed the more unwilling she felt to do what was disagreeable to her. At length, however, as she stood with the door half open, she heard the cheerful sound of the voices in the breakfast-room, and she said to herself, "Why should not I be as happy as every body else is?" She went down stairs, and resolved, very wisely, to tell her father what had happened, and to be good-humoured and happy.

"Well, Rosamond," said her mother, when she came into the room, and when she told her father what had happened, "you look rather more agreeable now than you did when I saw you a little while ago. We are glad to see that you can command yourself. Come now, and eat some breakfast."

Laura set a chair for her sister at the table near the fire, and Rosamond would have said, "Thank you," but that she was afraid to speak lest she should cry again. She began to eat her breakfast as fast as possible, without lifting up her eyes.

"You need not put quite such large pieces in your little mouth," said her mother; "and you need not look quite so dismal; all your misfortunes are over now, are they not?"

But at the word *misfortunes*, Rosamond's face wrinkled up into a most dismal condition, and the large tears, which had gradually collected in her eyes, rolled over her cheeks.

"What is the matter now, Rosamond?" said her mother.

"I don't know, mamma."

"But try to find out, Rosamond," said her mother; "think, and tell me what it is that makes you look so miserable; if you can find out the cause of this woe, perhaps you will be able to put an end to it. What is the cause, can you tell?"

"The cause is—I believe, mamma,—because," said Rosamond, sobbing,—"because I think to-day will be a—will be a day of—a day of—a day of misfortunes."

"And what do you mean by a day of misfortunes, Rosamond? a day on which you are asked not to put large pieces of bread into your mouth?"

"No, mamma," said Rosamond, half laughing, "but—"

"But what? a day when you cannot immediately untie a knot?"

"Not *only* that, mamma," answered Rosamond: "but a day when every thing goes wrong."

"When you do not get up in proper time, for instance?"

"Yes, mamma."

"And whose fault was that, Rosamond—yours or the day's?"

"Don't you think it was partly the day's fault, mamma, because it was so cold? It was the cold that first prevented me from getting up; and then my not getting up was the cause of my being in a great hurry afterwards, and of my losing my lace and my pocket-handkerchief, and of my pulling the strings of my cap into a knot, and of my being cross to Laura, who was so good to me, and of your being displeased with me, and of all my misfortunes."

"So the *cold,* you think, was the cause of all these misfortunes, as you call them: but do you think that nobody has felt the cold this morning except yourself? Laura and I have felt the cold; and how comes it that we have had no misfortunes?"

"O mamma!" said Rosamond; "but you and Laura do not mind such little misfortunes. It would be very odd indeed, mamma," (and she burst out a laughing at the idea), "it would be very droll, indeed, mamma, if I were to find you crying because you could not untie the strings of your cap."

"Or because I was cold," added her mother, laughing with her.

"I was very foolish, to be sure, mamma," resumed Rosamond; "but there are two things I could say for myself, that would be some excuse."

"Say them then, my dear; I shall be glad to hear them."

"The first is, mamma, that I was a great deal longer in the cold this morning than any body else; therefore, I had more reason to cry, you know. And the second thing I have to say for myself is—"

"Gently," interrupted her mother; "before you go to your second excuse, let us consider whether your first is a good one.—How came you to stay longer in the cold, this morning, than any body else did?"

"Because, mamma, you sent Laura down stairs, and told me, I must untie the knot myself."

"And why did I send Laura down stairs, and say you must untie the knot for yourself?"

"Because I was cross to Laura, I believe."

"And what made you cross to Laura?"

"I was cross because I could not untie the knot that the strings of my cap had got into."

"*Had got into, Rosamond!* Did the strings get into a knot of themselves?"

"I mean I pulled them into a knot."

"And how came you to do that?"

"Because I was in a hurry."

"And how came you to be in a hurry?"

"Oh, I see, mamma, that you will say it was my own fault that I did not get up in proper time.—But now for the second thing I have to say for myself: the strings of my cap are a great, great deal too short; and this more than the cold was the cause of all my misfortunes. You and Laura might have felt the cold, as you say, as much as I did; but neither of you had short strings to your caps—mamma," continued Rosamond, with an emphasis—"But," (pausing to reflect), she added—"I do not think that the cold or the strings were the *real* cause of my misfortunes. I don't think that I should have cried the first time, and I am almost sure that I should not have cried the second and third time, if it had not been for—something else. I am afraid, mamma, to tell you of this *something else,* because I know you will say, that was more foolish than all the rest."

"But tell it to me, notwithstanding," said her mother, smiling, "because the way to prevent yourself from being foolish again is to find out what made you so just now. If you tell me what you think, and what you feel, perhaps I may help you to manage yourself so as to make you wise, and good and happy; but unless I know what passes in your little mind, I shall not be able to help you."

"I'll tell you directly, mamma; it was my thinking that to-day would be a day of misfortunes, that made me cry the second and third time; and do you know, mamma," continued Rosamond in a faltering, mournful voice, "I don't know why—but I can hardly help feeling almost ready to cry when the same thing comes into my head again now. Do you think to-day *will* be a day of misfortunes, mamma?"

"I think, my dear," answered her mother, "that it will depend entirely upon yourself, whether it is or no. If you recollect, we have just discovered, that all your past *misfortunes*, as you call them—"

"Were my own fault, you are going to say, mamma," interrupted Rosamond; "that's the worst of it! That makes me more sorry, and not pleased with myself, nor with anything else, and ready to cry again, because I can't help it all now."

"Since you cannot help it all now," said her mother, "why should you cry about it? Turn your thoughts to something else. We cannot help what is past; but we can take care of the future."

"The future," repeated Rosamond; "aye, the time to come. To-morrow, let it be ever so cold, I'll get up in good time: and, as for to-day, I can't get up in good time to-day; but I may do something else that is right; and that may make me pleased with myself again—hey, mamma?—There's a great deal of this day to come yet; and, if I take care, perhaps it will not be a day of misfortunes, after all. What do you think I had better do first, mamma?"

"Run about and warm these purple hands of yours, I think," said her mother.

"And, after that, mamma, what shall I do next?"

"Do that first," said her mother, "and then we will talk about the next thing."

"But, mamma," said Rosamond, casting a longing, lingering look at the fire, "it is *very* disagreeable to leave this nice warm room, and to go out to run in the cold."

"Don't you remember, Rosamond, how warm you made yourself by running about in the garden yesterday? you said that you felt warm for a great while afterwards, and that you liked that kind of warmth better than the warmth of the fire."

"Yes; it is very true, mamma; one gets cold sooner after being at the fire—I mean, soon after one goes away from it: but still, it is disagreeable at first to go out in the cold; don't you think so, mamma?"

"Yes, I do; but I think also, that we should be able to do what is a little disagreeable, when we know that it will be for our good afterwards; and by putting off whatever is not quite agreeable to us to do, we sometimes bring ourselves into difficulties. Recollect what happened to a little girl this morning who did not get up because the cold was disagreeable."

"True, mamma; I will go."

"And I am going to walk," said her mother.

"In the garden, mamma, whilst I run about? I am very glad of that, because I can talk to you between times, and I don't feel the cold so much when I'm talking. The snow is swept off the gravel walk, mamma, and there's room for both of us, and I'll run and set your clogs at the hall door, ready for your feet to pop into them."

The Robin

Rosamond found it cold when she first went out, but she ran on as fast as she could, singing,

Good, happy, gay,
One, two, three, and away,

till she made herself quite warm.

"Feel my hands, mamma," said she, "not my purple hands, now—feel how warm they are. You see, mamma, I'm able to do what is a little disagreeable to me, when it is for my good afterwards, as you said, mamma."

Rosamond, who was now warm enough to be able to observe, saw, while she was speaking to her mother, a robin redbreast, which was perched at a little distance from her upon a drift of snow. He did not seem to see Rosamond, which rather surprised her. "He must be very cold, or very tame, or very stupid," whispered she; "I'll go nearer to him." At her approach he hopped back a few paces, but then stood still. "Poor robin! pretty robin! he opens his eyes, he looks at me, he is not stupid, he likes me, I dare say, and that is the reason he does not fly away. Mamma, I think he would let me take him up in my hand—may I, mamma? he does not stir."

"I am afraid he is hurt, or ill—take care that you don't hurt him, Rosamond."

"I'll take the greatest care, mamma," said Rosamond, stooping down softly, and putting her hand over the little bird—"Hush! I have him safe, mamma—his little claws stick to the snow—he is very cold, for he trembles—and he is frightened—there is something come over his eyes—he is ill—what shall I do with him, mamma? May I take him into the house and hold him to the fire, and then give him a great many crumbs to make him quite well?"

Rosamond's mother advised her not to hold the bird to the fire, but said that she might take him into the house and warm him by degrees in her warm hands.

"How lucky it is that my hands are warm, and how glad I am that I came out," cried Rosamond. "Pretty robin, he is better, mamma—he opened his eyes—I'll take him in and show him to Laura."

This poor robin had been almost starved by cold and hunger, but he was gradually recovered by Rosamond's care, and she rejoiced that she had saved the little bird's life. Her mother gave her some crumbs of bread for him; and whilst the robin redbreast was picking up the crumbs, Rosamond stood by watching him with great delight.

"What are become of all your misfortunes, Rosamond?" said her mother.

"*My* misfortunes!—what misfortunes?—Oh, I had quite forgot—I was thinking of the robin's misfortunes."

"Which were rather greater than yours, hey, Rosamond?"

"Yes, indeed, mamma," said Rosamond, laughing; "my knot was no great misfortune; I wonder I could *think* about such little things. But you see, mamma, this has not been a day of misfortunes after all. I am very happy now—I am pleased with myself,—I have saved the life of this poor little robin; and, if I had cried all day long, it would not have done so much good; it would not have done any good. There is only one thing I don't feel quite pleased with myself about yet—Laura! I'm sorry I was cross to Laura about the knot—what can I do to make amends for that, mamma?—I'll never be cross again; I'll tell her so, hey, mamma?"

"No, I advise you not to tell her so, Rosamond, lest you should not be able to keep your promise—"

"If there should come another knot to-morrow, mamma! but I think it would be a good thing to prevent that. Mamma, will you be so good as to give me two long bits of tape, and I will sew them on my cap."

Her mother said that she thought it was wise of Rosamond to prevent *misfortunes*, instead of crying about them after they had happened: she gave her the two bits of tape, and Rosamond sewed them on her cap.

As soon as she had finished this affair, she returned to her robin, who was now flying about the room, and Laura was looking at him. "Laura, is not it a pretty robin?"

"Very pretty, indeed," said Laura.

"Should not you like to have such a robin very much, Laura?" continued Rosamond.

"I like to see him, and to hear him sing, and to feed him," answered Laura.

"Well, but should you not like to have him in a cage for your own?" said Rosamond; and at the same moment she whispered to her mother, "Mamma, do you know I intend to give him to Laura?"

But how much was Rosamond surprised and disappointed when her sister answered, "No, I should not like to keep him in a cage, because I do not think he would be happy. I have heard that robin redbreasts die soon if they are kept in cages."

"Dear, that is very unlucky indeed," said Rosamond, "particularly as I was just going to offer to give you my robin. But you know you need not keep him in a cage, he may fly about in this room as he does now, and you may feed him every day; should not you like that, Laura? and should not you be much obliged to me then?"

Laura perceived that Rosamond was anxious she should answer *yes*, and she was unwilling to displease her by refusing to accept of her offer, she therefore hesitated a little.

"Why don't you say yes or no?" said Rosamond, in rather an impatient tone:—she had at this instant need of all her command over herself, to keep to her late excellent resolution, "*never to be cross again*"—Her mother's eye luckily was upon her, and, with a sudden change of countenance, Rosamond smiled and said, "No, mamma, I have not forgot—you see I am good humoured—I am only a little sorry that Laura does not seem to like to have my little robin—I thought she would be so pleased with him."

"So I am pleased with him," replied Laura, "and very much obliged to you for offering to give him to me, but I do not wish to keep him; I once took care of a poor robin, and fed him almost all winter; but at last a sad accident happened to him; don't you remember, Rosamond? he flew upon the bars of the grate in mamma's dressing-room, and he was terribly burnt! and he died."

Rosamond was touched by the recollection of this poor bird's sufferings; and, after expressing some regret at the thoughts of parting with the pretty robin, which was now upon the table, she determined to open the window, and to let the bird fly away, or stay, whichever he liked best. The robin fluttered for some time near the window, then returned to the crumbs upon the table, pecked them, hopped about, and seemed in no haste to be gone; at last, however, he flew. "O mamma, he is gone for ever!" said Rosamond; "but I did right to let him do as he pleased, did not I, mamma? it was very disagreeable to me indeed to open the window; but you know, mamma, you told me, that we must sometimes do what is disagreeable, when it is to be for our good afterwards; this is not for my good, but for the bird's good. Well, I hope it will be for his good! at any rate, I have done rightly."

Whilst Rosamond was yet speaking, the robin returned and perched upon the window-stool. Laura scattered some crumbs upon the floor within sight of the window; the bird hopped in, and flew away with one of the crumbs in his beak. "I dare say," said Rosamond, "he will often come back; every day, per-haps, Laura:—Oh, how glad I should be of that! would not you, mamma?"

"My dear little girl," said her mother, "I should be glad of it: I am very much pleased to see that you can command your tem-per, and that you can use your understanding to govern yourself." Rosamond's mother stroked her daughter's hair upon her forehead as she spoke, and then gave her two kisses.

"Ah, mamma," said Rosamond, "this is not a day of misfor-tunes, indeed."

"No, my dear," said her mother, "it is not; and I wish in all your little and great misfortunes you may manage yourself as well as you have done to-day."

Rosamond's prudent precaution, in sewing longer strings to her cap, proved successful; for a whole month she was dressed in proper time; and her father, to reward her for keeping her good resolutions, lent her a nice little machine of his for drawing per-spective; she was allowed to use it before breakfast only, and she felt the advantage of getting up in proper time.[4]

The robin redbreast returned regularly every day to the win-dow to be fed, and when the window happened to be shut, he pecked at it with his little beak till it was opened for him. He at last grew so familiar that he would eat out of Rosamond's hand.

"How much pleasure I should have lost, mamma," said Rosamond, one morning, when the bird was eating out of her hand, "if I had not done what was a little disagreeable to me on that cold day—which I thought would have been a day of misfortunes."

'The Bracelets'

In a beautiful and retired part of England lived Mrs. Villars; a lady whose accurate understanding, benevolent heart, and steady temper peculiarly fitted her for the most difficult, as well as most important, of all occupations—the education of youth. This task she had undertaken; and twenty young persons were put under her care, with the perfect confidence of their parents. No young people could be happier; they were good and gay, emulous, but not envious of each other; for Mrs. Villars was impartially just; her praise they felt to be the reward of merit, and her blame they knew to be the necessary consequence of ill-conduct: to the one, therefore, they patiently submitted, and in the other consciously rejoiced. They rose with fresh cheerfulness in the morning, eager to pursue their various occupations; they returned in the evening with renewed ardour to their amusements, and retired to rest satisfied with themselves, and pleased with each other.

Nothing so much contributed to preserve a spirit of emulation in this little society as a small honorary distinction, given annually, as the prize of successful application. The prize this year was peculiarly dear to each individual, as it was the picture of a friend whom they all dearly loved—it was the picture of Mrs. Villars in a small bracelet. It wanted neither gold, pearls, nor precious stones to give it value.

The two foremost candidates for this prize were Cecilia and Leonora: Cecilia was the most intimate friend of Leonora, but Leonora was only the favourite companion of Cecilia.[5]

24

Cecilia was of an active, ambitious, enterprising disposition; more eager in the pursuit, than happy in the enjoyment of her wishes. Leonora was of a contented, unaspiring, temperate character; not easily roused to action, but indefatigable when once excited. Leonora was proud, Cecilia was vain: her vanity made her more dependent upon the approbation of others, and therefore more anxious to please than Leonora; but that very vanity made her, at the same time, more apt to offend: in short, Leonora was the most anxious to avoid what was wrong, Cecilia the most ambitious to do what was right. Few of their companions loved, but many were led by Cecilia, for she was often successful; many loved Leonora, but none were ever governed by her, for she was too indolent to govern.

On the first day of May, about six o'clock in the evening, a great bell rung to summon this little society into a hall, where the prize was to be decided. A number of small tables were placed in a circle in the middle of the hall; seats for the young competitors were raised one above another, in a semicircle, some yards distant from the table; and the judges chairs, under canopies of lilacs and laburnums, forming another semicircle, closed the amphitheatre. Every one put their writings, their drawings, their works of various kinds, upon the tables appropriated for each. How unsteady were the last steps to these tables! How each little hand trembled as it laid down its claims. Till this moment everyone thought herself secure of success, but now each felt an equal certainty of being excelled; and the heart which a few minutes before exulted with hope, now palpitated with fear.

The works were examined, the preference adjudged; and the prize was declared to be the happy Cecilia's. Mrs. Villars came forward smiling with the bracelet in her hand: Cecilia was behind her companions, on the highest row; all the others gave way, and she was on the floor in an instant. Mrs. Villars clasped the bracelet on her arm: the clasp was heard through the whole hall, and an universal smile of congratulation followed. Mrs. Villars kissed Cecilia's little hand, and "now," said she, "go and rejoice with your companions, the remainder of the day is yours."

Oh! you whose hearts are elated with success, whose bosoms beat high with joy, in the moment of triumph command yourselves; let that triumph be moderate, that it may be lasting. Consider, that though you are good, you may be better; and though wise, you may be weak.

As soon as Mrs. Villars had given her the bracelet, all Cecilia's little companions crowded round her, and they all left the hall in an instant: she was full of spirits and vanity—she ran on: running down the flight of steps which led to the garden, in her violent haste, Cecilia threw down the little Louisa. Louisa had a china mandarin in her hand, which her mother had sent her that very morning; it was all broken to pieces by her fall.[6]

"Oh! My mandarin!" cried Louisa, bursting into tears. The crowd behind Cecilia suddenly stopped: Louisa sat on the lowest step, fixing her eyes upon the broken pieces; then turning round, she hid her face in her hands upon the step above her. In turning, Louisa threw down the remains of the mandarin; the head, which she had placed in the socket, fell from the shoulders, and rolled bounding along the gravel walk. Cecilia pointed to the head, and to the socket, and burst out a laughing: the crowd behind laughed too. At any other time they would have been more inclined to cry with Louisa; but Cecilia had just been successful, and sympathy with the victorious often makes us forget justice. Leonora, however, preserved her usual consistency. "Poor Louisa!" said she, looking first at her, and then reproachfully at Cecilia. Cecilia turned sharply round, colouring half with shame and half with vexation. "I could not help it, Leonora," said she.

"But you could have helped laughing, Cecilia."

"I didn't laugh at Louisa; and I surely may laugh, for it does nobody any harm."

"I am sure, however," replied Leonora, "I should not have laughed if I had—"

"No, to be sure you wouldn't, because Louisa is your favourite; I can buy her another mandarin the next time that the old pedlar comes to the door, if that's all.—I *can* do no more—*Can* I?" said she, turning round to her companions.

"No, to be sure," said they, "that's all fair."

Cecilia looked triumphantly at Leonora: Leonora let go her hand; she ran on, and the crowd followed. When she got to the end of the garden, she turned round to see if Leonora had followed her too; but was vexed to see her still sitting on the steps

with Louisa. "I'm sure I can do no more than buy her another!—
Can I?" said she, again, appealing to her companions.

"No, to be sure," said they, eager to begin their plays.

How many did they begin and leave off before Cecilia could be
satisfied with any: her thoughts were discomposed, and her mind
was running upon something else; no wonder then, that she did
not play with her usual address. She grew still more impatient; she
threw down the ninepins: "Come, let us play at something else—
at threading-the-needle," said she, holding out her hand.[7] They all
yielded to the hand which wore the bracelet. But Cecilia, dissatis-
fied with herself, was discontented with every body else: her tone
grew more and more peremptory.—One was too rude, another too
stiff; one, too slow; another too quick; in short, every thing went
wrong, and every body was tired of her humours.

The triumph of *success* is absolute, but short. Cecilia's companions at length recollected, that though she had embroidered a
tulip and painted a peach better than they, yet that they could
play as well, and keep their tempers better: she was thrown out.
Walking towards the house, in a peevish mood, she met Leonora;
she passed on.

"Cecilia!" cried Leonora.

"Well, what do you want with me?"

"Are we friends?"

"You know best."

"We are; if you will let me tell Louisa, that you are sorry——"

Cecilia, interrupting her, "Oh! Pray let me hear no more about
Louisa!"

"What! Not confess that you were in the wrong? Oh, Cecilia! I
had a better opinion of you."

"Your opinion is of no consequence to me now; for you don't
love me."

"No, not when you are unjust, Cecilia."

"Unjust! I am not unjust: and if I were, you are not my
governess."

"No; but am not I your friend?"

"I don't desire to have such a friend!—who would quarrel with
me for happening to throw down little Louisa—how could I tell
that she had a mandarin in her hand? And when it was broken,
could I do more than promise her another?—Was that unjust?"

"But you know, Cecilia——"

"*I know*," ironically, "I know, Leonora, that you love Louisa better than you do me; that's the injustice!"

"If I did," replied Leonora, gravely, "it would be no injustice, if she deserved it better."

"How can you compare Louisa to me!" exclaimed Cecilia, indignantly.

Leonora made no answer, for she was really hurt at her friend's conduct: she walked on to join the rest of her companions. They were dancing in a round upon the grass: Leonora declined dancing, but they prevailed upon her to sing for them; her voice was not so sprightly as usual, but it was sweeter than usual.— Who sung so sweetly as Leonora? or who danced so nimbly as Louisa?

Away she was flying, all spirits and gaiety, when Leonora's eyes, full of tears, caught her's: Louisa silently let go her companion's hands, and, quitting the dance, ran up to Leonora to enquire what was the matter with her.

"Nothing," replied she, "that need interrupt you.—Go, my dear; go and dance again."

Louisa immediately ran away to her garden, and pulling off her little straw hat, she lined it with the freshest strawberry leaves; and was upon her knees before the strawberry bed when Cecilia came by. Cecilia was not disposed to be pleased with Louisa at that instant for two reasons; because she was jealous of her, and because she had injured her. The injury, however, Louisa had already forgotten; perhaps, to tell things just as they were, she was not quite so much inclined to kiss Cecilia as she would have been before the fall of her mandarin, but this was the utmost extent of her malice, if it can be called malice.

"What are you doing there, little one?" said Cecilia, in a sharp tone. "Are you eating your early strawberries here all alone?"

"No," said Louisa, mysteriously; "I am not eating them."

"What are you doing with them? can't you answer then?—I'm not playing with you, child!"

"Oh! as to that, Cecilia, you know I need not answer you unless I choose it; not but what I would, if you would only ask me civilly—and if you would not call me *child*."

"Why should not I call you child?"

"Because—because——I don't know: but I wish you would stand out of my light, Cecilia, for you are trampling upon all my strawberries."

"I have not touched one, you covetous little creature!"

"Indeed—indeed, Cecilia, I am not covetous; I have not eaten one of them—they are all for your friend Leonora. See how unjust you are."

"Unjust! that's a cant word you have learned of my friend Leonora, as you call her; but she is not my friend now."

"Not your friend now!" exclaimed Louisa; "then I am sure you must have done something *very* naughty."

"How!" said Cecilia, catching hold of her.

"Let me go—Let me go!" cried Louisa, struggling; "I won't give you one of my strawberries, for I don't like you at all!"

"You don't, don't you?" said Cecilia, provoked; and catching the hat from Louisa, she flung the strawberries over the hedge.

"Will nobody help me!" exclaimed Louisa, snatching her hat again, and running away with all her force.

"What have I done?" said Cecilia, recollecting herself; "Louisa! Louisa!" She called very loud, but Louisa would not turn back; she was running to her companions.

They were still dancing hand in hand upon the grass, whilst Leonora, sitting in the middle, sung to them.

"Stop! stop! and hear me!" cried Louisa, breaking through them; and rushing up to Leonora, she threw her hat at her feet, and panting for breath—"It was full—almost full, of my own strawberries," said she; "the first I ever got out of my own garden.—They should all have been for you, Leonora—but now I have not one left. They are all gone!" said she, and she hid her face in Leonora's lap.

"Gone! gone where?" said every one at once, running up to her.

"Cecilia! Cecilia!" said she, sobbing.

"Cecilia," repeated Leonora, "what of Cecilia?"

"Yes, it was—it was."

"Come along with me," said Leonora, unwilling to have her friend exposed; "Come, and I will get you some more strawberries."

"Oh, I don't mind the strawberries indeed; but I wanted to have had the pleasure of giving them to you."

Leonora took her up in her arms to carry her away; but it was too late.

"What Cecilia! Cecilia, who won the prize!—it could not surely be Cecilia!" whispered every busy tongue.

At this instant the bell summoned them in. "There she is!—There she is!" cried they, pointing to an arbour, where Cecilia was standing ashamed and alone: and as they passed her, some lifted up their hands and eyes with astonishment, others whispered and huddled mysteriously together, as if to avoid her; Leonora walked on, her head a little higher than usual.

"Leonora!" said Cecilia, timorously, as she passed.

"Oh, Cecilia! Who would have thought that you had a bad heart?"

Cecilia turned her head aside, and burst into tears.

"Oh no, indeed, she has not a bad heart!" cried Louisa, running up to her, and throwing her arms round her neck: "She's very sorry!—Are not you, Cecilia?—But don't cry any more, for I forgive you with all my heart—and I love you now, though I said I did not, when I was in a passion."

"Oh, you sweet-tempered girl!—how I love you," said Cecilia, kissing her.

"Well then, if you do, come along with me, and dry your eyes, for they are so red!"

"Go, my dear, and I'll come presently."

"Then I will keep a place for you next to me; but you must make haste, or you will have to come in when we have all sat down to supper, and then you will be so stared at!—So don't stay now!"

Cecilia followed Louisa with her eyes, till she was out of sight— "And is Louisa," said she to herself, "the only one who would stop to pity me? Mrs. Villars told me that this day should be mine; she little thought how it would end!" Saying these words, Cecilia threw herself down upon the ground; her arm leaned upon a heap of turf which she had raised in the morning, and which, in the pride and gaiety of her heart, she had called her throne.

At this instant Mrs. Villars came out to enjoy the serenity of the evening, and passing by the arbour where Cecilia lay, she started; Cecilia rose hastily.

"Who is there?" said Mrs. Villars.

"It is I, madam."

"And who is I?"

"Cecilia."

"Why, what keeps you here, my dear—where are your companions? this is, perhaps, one of the happiest days of your life."

"God forbid, madam!" said Cecilia, hardly able to repress her tears.

"Why, my dear, what is the matter?"

Cecilia hesitated.

"Speak, my dear; you know that when I ask you to tell me any thing as your friend, I never punish you as your governess: therefore you need not be afraid to tell me what is the matter."

"No, madam, I am not afraid, but ashamed. You asked me, why I was not with my companions?"

"Yes."

"Why, madam, because they have all left me; and——"

"And what, my dear?"

"And I see that they all dislike me: and yet I don't know why they should, for I take as much pains to please as any of them; all my masters seem satisfied with me; and you yourself, ma'am, were pleased this very morning to give me this bracelet, and I am sure you would not have given it to any one who did not deserve it."

"Certainly not: you did deserve it for your application—for your successful application. The prize was for the most assiduous, not for the most amiable."

"Then if it had been for the most amiable it would not have been for me?"

Mrs. Villars, smiling—"Why, what do you think yourself, Cecilia? you are better able to judge than I am; I can determine whether or no you apply to what I give you to learn; whether you attend to what I desire you to do, and avoid what I desire you not to do; I know that I like you as a pupil, but I cannot know that I should like you as a companion, unless I were your companion; therefore I must judge of what I should do, by seeing what others do in the same circumstances."

"Oh, pray don't, ma'am! for then you would not love me either.—And yet I think you would love me; for I hope that I am as ready to oblige, and as good-natured as—"

"Yes, Cecilia, I don't doubt but what you would be very good-natured to me, but I am afraid that I should not like you unless you were good-tempered too."

"But, ma'am, by good-natured I mean good-tempered—it's all the same thing."

"No, indeed, I understand by them two very different things: you are good-natured, Cecilia, for you are desirous to oblige, and serve your companions; to gain them praise, and save them from blame; to give them pleasure, and relieve them from pain; but Leonora is good-tempered, for she can bear with their foibles, and acknowledge her own; without disputing about the right, she sometimes yields to those who are in the wrong; in short, her temper is perfectly good, for it can bear and forbear."

"I wish that mine could!" said Cecilia, sighing.

"It may," replied Mrs. Villars, "but it is not wishes alone which can improve us in any thing: turn the same exertion and perseverance which have won you the prize today to this object, and you will meet with the same success; perhaps not on the first, the second, or the third attempt, but depend upon it that you will at last: every new effort will weaken your bad habits, and strengthen your good ones. But you must not expect to succeed all at once: I repeat it to you, for habit must be counteracted by habit. It would be as extravagant in us to expect that all our faults could be destroyed by one punishment, were it ever so severe, as it was in the Roman emperor we were reading of a few days ago to wish that all the heads of his enemies were upon one neck, that he might cut them off at a blow."[8]

Here Mrs. Villars took Cecilia by the hand, and they began to walk home. Such was the nature of Cecilia's mind, that when any object was forcibly impressed on her imagination, it caused a temporary suspension of her reasoning faculties. Hope was too strong a stimulus for her spirits; and when fear did take possession of her mind, it was attended with total debility: her vanity was now as much mortified, as in the morning it had been elated. She walked on with Mrs. Villars in silence, until they came under the shade of the elm-tree walk, and then, fixing her eyes upon Mrs. Villars, she stopped short—"Do you think, madam," said she, with hesitation, "Do you think, madam, that I have a bad heart?"

"A bad heart, my dear! why, what put that into your head?"

"Leonora said that I had, ma'am, and I felt ashamed when she said so."

"But, my dear, how can Leonora tell whether your heart be good or bad?—However, in the first place, tell me what you mean by a bad heart."

"Indeed I do not know what is meant by it, ma'am; but it is something which every body hates."

"And why do they hate it?"

"Because they think that it will hurt them, ma'am, I believe: and that those who have bad hearts, take delight in doing mischief; and that they never do any body any good but for their own ends."

"Then the best definition which you can give me of a bad heart, is that it is some constant propensity to hurt others, and to do wrong for the sake of doing wrong."

"Yes, ma'am, but that is not all neither; there is still something else meant: something which I cannot express—which, indeed, I never distinctly understood; but of which, therefore, I was the more afraid."

"Well then, to begin with what you do understand, tell me, Cecilia, do you really think it possible to be wicked merely for the love of wickedness?——No human being becomes wicked all at once; a man begins by doing wrong because it is, or because he thinks it for his interest; if he continue to do so, he must conquer his sense of shame, and lose his love of virtue. But how can you, Cecilia, who feel such a strong sense of shame, and such an eager desire to improve, imagine that you have a bad heart?"

"Indeed, madam, I never did, until every body told me so, and then I began to be frightened about it: this very evening, ma'am, when I was in a passion, I threw little Louisa's strawberries away; which, I am sure, I was very sorry for afterwards; and Leonora and every body cried out that I had a bad heart—but I am sure I was only in a passion."

"Very likely.—And when you are in a passion, as you call it, Cecilia, you see that you are tempted to do harm to others: if they do not feel angry themselves, they do not sympathise with you; they do not perceive the motive which actuates you, and then they say that you have a bad heart—I dare say, however, when your passion is over, and when you recollect yourself, you are very sorry for what you have done and said, are not you?"

"Yes, indeed, madam—very sorry."

"Then make that sorrow of use to you, Cecilia, and fix it steadily in your thoughts, as you hope to be good and happy, that if you suffer yourself to yield to your passion upon every trifling occasion, anger and its consequences will become familiar to your mind; and, in the same proportion, your sense of shame will be weakened, till what you began with doing from sudden impulse, you will end with doing from habit and choice: and then you would indeed, according to our definition, have a bad heart."

"Oh, madam! I hope—I am sure I never shall."

"No, indeed, Cecilia; I do, indeed, believe that you never will; on the contrary, I think that you have a very good disposition; and what is of infinitely more consequence to you, an active desire of improvement; show me that you have as much perseverance as you have candour, and I shall not despair of your becoming every thing that I could wish."

Here Cecilia's countenance brightened, and she ran up the steps in almost as high spirits as she ran down them in the morning.

"Good night to you, Cecilia," said Mrs. Villars as she was crossing the hall.

"Good night to you, madam," said Cecilia; and she ran up stairs to bed.

She could not go to sleep, but she lay awake, reflecting upon the events of the preceding day, and forming resolutions for the future; at the same time considering that she had resolved, and resolved without effect, she wished to give her mind some more powerful motive: ambition she knew to be its most powerful incentive.

"Have I not," said she to herself, "already won the prize of application, and cannot that same application, procure me a much higher prize?—Mrs. Villars said, that if the prize had been promised to the most amiable, it would not have been given to me: perhaps it would not yesterday—perhaps it might not tomorrow; but that is no reason that I should despair of ever deserving it."

In consequence of this reasoning Cecilia formed a design of proposing to her companions, that they should give a prize, the first of the ensuing month (the first of June) to the most amiable.

Mrs. Villars applauded the scheme, and her companions adopted it with the greatest alacrity.

"Let the prize," said they, "be a bracelet of our own hair;" and instantly their shining scissors were produced, and each contributed a lock of their hair. They formed the most beautiful gradation of colours, from the palest auburn to the brightest black. Who was to have the honour of plaiting them was now the question.

Caroline begged that she might, as she could plait very neatly, she said.

Cecilia, however, was equally sure that she could do it much better; and a dispute would inevitably have ensued, if Cecilia, recollecting herself just as her colour rose to scarlet, had not yielded— yielded, with no very good grace indeed, but as well as could be expected for the first time. For it is habit which confers ease; and without ease, even in moral actions, there can be no grace.

The bracelet was plaited in the neatest manner by Caroline, finished round the edge with silver twist, and on it was worked in the smallest silver letters this motto, TO THE MOST AMIABLE. The moment it was completed, every body begged to try it on: it fastened with little silver clasps, and as it was made large enough for the eldest girls, it was too large for the youngest; of this they bitterly complained, and unanimously entreated that it might be cut to fit them.

"How foolish!" exclaimed Cecilia; "don't you perceive, that if any of you win it, you have nothing to do but to put the clasps a little further from the edge; but, if we get it, we can't make it larger."

"Very true," said they; "but you need not have called us foolish, Cecilia!"

It was by such hasty and unguarded expressions as these, that Cecilia offended: a slight difference in the manner makes a very material one in the effect; Cecilia lost more love by general petulance, than she could gain by the greatest particular exertions.

How far she succeeded in curing herself of this defect, how far she became deserving of the bracelet, and to whom the bracelet was given, shall be told in the History of the First of June.

The first of June was now arrived, and all the young competitors were in a state of the most anxious suspense. Leonora and Cecilia continued to be the foremost candidates; their quarrel had never been finally adjusted, and their different pretensions now retarded all thoughts of a reconciliation. Cecilia, though she was capable of acknowledging any of her faults in public before all her companions, could not humble herself in private to Leonora; Leonora was her equal, they were her inferiors; and submission is much easier to a vain mind, where it appears to be voluntary, than when it is the necessary tribute to justice or candour. So strongly did Cecilia feel this truth, that she even delayed making any apology, or coming to any explanation with Leonora, until success should once more give her the palm.

If I win the bracelet to-day, said she to herself, I will solicit the return of Leonora's friendship; it will be more valuable to me than even the bracelet; and at such a time, and asked in such a manner, she surely cannot refuse it to me. Animated with this hope of a double triumph, Cecilia canvassed with the most zealous activity: by constant attention and exertion she had considerably abated the violence of her temper, and changed the course of her habits. Her powers of pleasing were now excited, instead of her abilities to excel; and if her talents appeared less brilliant her character was acknowledged to be more amiable, so great an influence upon our manners and conduct have the objects of our ambition.—Cecilia was now, if possible, more than ever desirous of doing what was right, but she had not yet acquired sufficient fear of doing wrong. This was the fundamental error of her mind: it arose in a great measure from her early education.

Her mother died when she was very young; and though her father had supplied her place in the best and kindest manner, he had insensibly infused into his daughter's mind a portion of that enterprising, independent spirit, which he justly deemed essential to the character of her brother: this brother was some years older than Cecilia, but he had always been the favourite companion of her youth: what her father's precepts inculcated, his example enforced, and even Cecilia's virtues consequently became such as were more estimable in a man, than desirable in a female.

All small objects, and small errors, she had been taught to disregard as trifles; and her impatient disposition was perpetually leading her into more material faults; yet her candour in confessing these, she had been suffered to believe was sufficient reparation and atonement.

Leonora, on the contrary, who had been educated by her mother in a manner more suited to her sex, had a character and virtues more peculiar to a female: her judgment had been early cultivated, and her good sense employed in the regulation of her conduct; she had been habituated to that restraint which, as a woman, she was to expect in life, and early accustomed to yield; complaisance in her seemed natural and graceful.

Yet, notwithstanding the gentleness of her temper, she was in reality more independent than Cecilia; she had more reliance upon her own judgment, and more satisfaction in her own approbation: though far from insensible to praise, she was not liable to be misled by the indiscriminate love of admiration: the uniform kindness of her manner, the consistency and equality of her character, had fixed the esteem and passive love of her companions.

By passive love we mean that species of affection which makes us unwilling to offend, rather than anxious to oblige; which is more a habit than an emotion of the mind. For Cecilia her companions felt active love, for she was active in showing her love to them.

Active love arises spontaneously in the mind, after feeling particular instances of kindness, without reflection on the past conduct or general character; it exceeds the merits of its object, and is connected with a feeling of generosity rather than with a sense of justice.

Without determining which species of love is the most flattering to others, we can easily decide which is the most agreeable feeling to our own minds; we give our hearts more credit for being generous than for being just; and we feel more self-complacency, when we give our love voluntarily, than when we yield it as a tribute which we cannot withhold. Though Cecilia's companions might not know all this in theory, they proved it in practice; for they loved her in a much higher proportion to her merits, than they loved Leonora.

Each of the young judges were to signify their choice, by putting a red or a white shell into a vase prepared for the purpose. Cecilia's colour was red, Leonora's white. In the morning nothing was to be seen but these shells, nothing talked of but the long-expected event of the evening. Cecilia, following Leonora's example, had made it a point of honour not to enquire of any individual her vote, previously to their final determination.

They were both sitting together in Louisa's room; Louisa was recovering from the measles: every one, during her illness, had been desirous of attending her; but Leonora and Cecilia were the only two that were permitted to see her, as they alone had had the distemper. They were both assiduous in their care of Louisa; but Leonora's want of exertion to overcome any disagreeable feelings of sensibility, often deprived her of presence of mind, and prevented her from being so constantly useful as Cecilia. Cecilia, on the contrary, often made too much noise and bustle with her officious assistance, and was too anxious to invent amusements, and procure comforts for Louisa, without perceiving, that illness takes away the power of enjoying them.

As she was sitting in the window in the morning, exerting herself to entertain Louisa, she heard the voice of an old pedlar, who often used to come to the house. Down stairs she ran immediately to ask Mrs. Villars's permission to bring him into the hall.

Mrs. Villars consented, and away Cecilia ran to proclaim the news to her companions; then first returning into the hall, she found the pedlar just unbuckling his box, and taking it off his shoulders. "What would you be pleased to want, miss," said he, "I've all kinds of tweezer-cases, rings, and lockets of all sorts," continued he, opening all the glittering drawers successively.

"Oh!" said Cecilia, shutting the drawer of lockets which tempted her most, "these are not the things which I want; have you any china figures, any mandarins?"

"Alack-a-day, miss, I had a great stock of that same china ware, but now I'm quite out of them kind of things; but I believe," said he, rummaging in one of the deepest drawers, "I believe I have one left, and here it is."

"Oh, that is the very thing! What's its price?"

"Only three shillings, ma'am."—Cecilia paid the money, and was just going to carry off the mandarin, when the pedlar took out of his great coat pocket a neat mahogany case: it was about a foot long, and fastened at each end by two little clasps; it had, besides, a small lock in the middle.

"What is that?" said Cecilia, eagerly.

"It's only a china figure, miss, which I am going to carry to an elderly lady, who lives nigh hand, and who is mighty fond of such things."

"Could you let me look at it?"

"And welcome, miss," said he, and opened the case.

"Oh goodness! how beautiful!" exclaimed Cecilia.

It was a figure of Flora, crowned with roses, and carrying a basket of flowers in her hand.[9] Cecilia contemplated it with delight. "How I should like to give this to Louisa," said she to herself; and at last, breaking silence, "Did you promise it to the old lady?"

"Oh no, miss; I didn't promise it, she never saw it; and if so be that you'd like to take it, I'd make no more words about it."

"And how much does it cost?"

"Why, miss, as to that, I'll let you have it for half-a-guinea."

Cecilia immediately produced the box in which she kept her treasure, and, emptying it upon the table, she began to count the shillings: alas! There were but six shillings. "How provoking!" said she, "then I can't have it—where's the mandarin? Oh I have it," said she, taking it up, and looking at it with the utmost disgust; "is this the same that I had before?"

"Yes, miss, the very same," replied the pedlar, who, during this time, had been examining the little box, out of which Cecilia had taken her money: it was of silver.

"Why, ma'am," said he, "since you've taken such a fancy to the piece, if you've a mind to make up the remainder of the money, I will take this here little box, if you care to part with it."

Now this box was a keep-sake from Leonora to Cecilia. "No," said Cecilia, hastily, blushing a little, and stretching out her hand to receive it.

"Oh, miss!" said he, returning it carelessly, "I hope there's no offence; I meant but to serve you, that's all; such a rare piece of china-work has no cause to go a begging;" added he, putting the Flora deliberately into the case, then turning the key with a jerk he let it drop into his pocket, and lifting up his box by the leather straps, he was preparing to depart.

"Oh, stay one minute!" said Cecilia, in whose mind there had passed a very warm conflict during the pedlar's harangue. "Louisa would so like this Flora," said she, arguing with herself; "besides, it would be so generous in me to give it to her, instead of that ugly mandarin; that would be doing only common justice, for I promised it to her, and she expects it. Though, when I come to look at this mandarin, it is not even so good as her's was; the gilding is all rubbed off, so that I absolutely must buy this for her. Oh yes, I will, and she will be so delighted! and then every body will say it is the prettiest thing they ever saw, and the broken mandarin will be forgotten for ever."

Here Cecilia's hand moved, and she was just going to decide. "Oh! but stop," said she to herself, "consider, Leonora gave me this box, and it is a keepsake; however, now we have quarrelled, and I dare say that she would not mind my parting with it: I'm sure that I should not care, if she was to give away my keepsake, the smelling-bottle, or the ring, which I gave her; so what does it signify? Besides, is it not my own, and have I not a right to do what I please with it?"

At this dangerous instant for Cecilia, a party of her companions opened the door; she knew that they came as purchasers, and she dreaded her Flora's becoming the prize of some higher bidder. "Here," said she hastily, putting the box into the pedlar's hand, without looking at it; "take it, and give me the Flora." Her hand trembled, though she snatched it impatiently; she ran by, without seeming to mind any of her companions—she almost wished to turn back.

Let those who are tempted to do wrong by the hopes of future gratification, or the prospect of certain concealment and impunity, remember, that unless they are totally depraved, they bear in their own hearts a monitor, who will prevent their enjoying what they have ill obtained.

In vain Cecilia ran to the rest of her companions, to display her present, in hopes that the applause of others would restore her own self-complacency; in vain she saw the Flora pass in due pomp from hand to hand, each vying with the other in extolling the beauty of the gift, and the generosity of the giver. Cecilia was still displeased with herself, with them, and even with their praise; from Louisa's gratitude, however, she yet expected much pleasure, and immediately she ran up stairs to her room.

In the mean time Leonora had gone into the hall to buy a bodkin; she had just broken hers. In giving her change, the pedlar took out of his pocket, with some halfpence, the very box which

Cecilia had sold to him. Leonora did not in the least suspect the truth, for her mind was above suspicion and, besides, she had the utmost confidence in Cecilia. "I should like to have that box," said she, "for it is like one of which I was very fond."

The pedlar named the price, and Leonora took the box: she intended to give it to little Louisa.

On going to her room she found her asleep, and she sat down softly by her bed-side. Louisa opened her eyes.

"I hope I didn't disturb you," said Leonora.

"Oh no; I didn't hear you come in; but what have you got there?"

"It is only a little box; would you like to have it? I bought it on purpose for you, as I thought perhaps it would please you; because it's like that which I gave Cecilia."

"Oh yes! That out of which she used to give me Barbary drops: I am very much obliged to you; I always thought *that* exceedingly pretty, and this, indeed, is as like it as possible. I can't unscrew it; will you try?"

Leonora unscrewed it.

"Goodness!" exclaimed Louisa, "this must be Cecilia's box; look, don't you see a great 'L' at the bottom of it?"

Leonora's colour changed. "Yes," she replied calmly, "I see that; but it is no proof that it is Cecilia's; you know that I bought this box just now of the pedlar."

"That may be," said Louisa; "but I remember scratching that 'L' with my own needle, and Cecilia scolded me for it too: do go and ask her if she has lost her box—do," repeated Louisa, pulling her by the ruffle, as she did not seem to listen.

Leonora indeed did not hear, for she was lost in thought; she was comparing circumstances which had before escaped her attention: she recollected, that Cecilia had passed her, as she came into the hall without seeming to see her, but had blushed as she passed. She remembered, that the pedlar appeared unwilling to part with the box, and was going to put it again into his pocket with the halfpence: "and why should he keep it in his pocket, and not show it with his other things?"—Combining all these circumstances, Leonora had no longer any doubt of the truth; for though she had honourable confidence in her friends, she had too much penetration to be implicitly credulous.—"Louisa," she began, but at this instant she heard a step, which, by its quickness, she knew to be Cecilia's, coming along the passage.—"If you love me, Louisa," said Leonora, "say nothing about the box."

"Nay, but why not? I dare say she has lost it."

"No, my dear, I'm afraid she has not." Louisa looked surprised.

"But I have reasons for desiring you not to say any thing about it."

"Well then, I won't, indeed."

Cecilia opened the door, came forward smiling, as if secure of a good reception, and, taking the Flora out of the case, she placed it on the mantle-piece, opposite to Louisa's bed. "Dear, how beautiful," cried Louisa, starting up.

"Yes," said Cecilia, "and guess who it's for?"

"For me, perhaps!" said the ingenuous Louisa.

"Yes, take it, and keep it for my sake: you know that I broke your mandarin."

"Oh! but this is a great deal prettier, and larger than that."

"Yes, I know it is; and I meant that it should be so; I should only have done what I was bound to do, if I had only given you a mandarin."

"Well, and that would have been enough, surely: but what a beautiful crown of roses! and then that basket of flowers! they almost look as if I could smell them:—dear Cecilia! I'm very much obliged to you, but I won't take it by way of payment for the mandarin you broke; for I'm sure you could not help that; and, besides, I should have broken it myself by this time. You shall give it to me entirely, and I'll keep it as long as I live as your keepsake."

Louisa stopped short and coloured. The word keepsake recalled the box to her mind, and all the train of ideas which the Flora had banished.—"But," said she, looking up wistfully in Cecilia's face, and holding the Flora doubtfully, "did you—"

Leonora, who was just quitting the room, turned her head back, and gave Louisa a look, which silenced her.

Cecilia was so infatuated with her vanity, that she neither perceived Leonora's sign, nor Louisa's confusion, but continued showing off her present, by placing it in various situations, till at length she put it into the case, and, laying it down with an affected carelessness upon the bed, "I must go now, Louisa". "Good bye,"

said she, running up, and kissing her; "but I'll come again presently." Then, clapping the door after her, she went.

But, as soon as the fermentation of her spirits subsided, the
sense of shame, which had been scarcely felt when mixed with
so many other sensations, rose uppermost in her mind. "What!"
said she to herself, "is it possible that I have sold what I promised
to keep for ever? and what Leonora gave me! and I have concealed
it too, and have been making a parade of my generosity. Oh what
would Leonora, what would Louisa, what would every body think
of me, if the truth were known?"

Humiliated and grieved by these reflections, Cecilia began to
search in her own mind for some consoling idea. She began to
compare her conduct with the conduct of others of her own age;
and at length, fixing her comparison upon her brother George, as
the companion of whom, from her infancy, she had been habit-
ually the most emulous, she recollected, that an almost similar
circumstance had once happened to him, and that he had not
only escaped disgrace, but had acquired glory by an intrepid confession of his fault. Her father's words to her brother, on the occasion, she also perfectly recollected.

"Come to me, George," he said, holding out his hand, "you are
a generous, brave boy: they who dare to confess their faults will
make great and good men."

These were his words; but Cecilia, in repeating them to herself, forgot to lay that emphasis on the word 'men', which would
have placed it in contradistinction to the word 'women'. But
she willingly believed that the observation extended equally
to both sexes, and flattered herself that she should exceed her
brother in merit, if she owned a fault, which she thought that it
would be so much more difficult to confess. "Yes, but," said she,
stopping herself, "how can I confess it? This very evening, in a
few hours, the prize will be decided; Leonora or I shall win it:
I have now as good a chance as Leonora, perhaps a better; and
must I give up all my hopes? All that I have been labouring for
this month past? Oh, I never can;—if it were but to-morrow, or
yesterday, or any day but this, I would not hesitate; but now I
am almost certain of the prize, and if I win it—well, why then
I will—I think, I will tell all—yes I will; I am determined," said
Cecilia.

Here a bell summoned them to dinner; Leonora sat opposite to her, and she was not a little surprised to see Cecilia look so gay and unconstrained. "Surely," said she to herself, "if Cecilia had done this, that I suspect, she would not, she could not look as she does." But Leonora little knew the cause of her gaiety; Cecilia was never in higher spirits, or better pleased with herself, than when she had resolved upon a sacrifice or a confession.

"Must not this evening be given to the most amiable? Whose then will it be?" All eyes glanced first at Cecilia, and then at Leonora. Cecilia smiled; Leonora blushed. "I see that it is not yet decided," said Mrs. Villars; and immediately they ran up stairs, amidst confused whisperings.

Cecilia's voice could be distinguished far above the rest. "How can she be so happy," said Leonora to herself; "Oh Cecilia, there was a time, when you could not have neglected me so!—when we were always together, the best of friends and companions; our wishes, tastes, and pleasures the same! Surely she did once love me," said Leonora; "but now she is quite changed, she has even sold my keepsake; and she would rather win a bracelet of hair from girls whom she did not always think so much superior to Leonora, than have my esteem, my confidence, and my friendship, for her whole life: yes, for her whole life, for I am sure she will be an amiable woman: oh! that this bracelet had never been thought of, or, that I were certain of her winning it; for I am sure that I do not wish to win it from her: I would rather, a thousand times rather, that we were as we used to be, than have all the glory in the world: and how pleasing Cecilia can be, when she wishes to please!—how candid she is!—how much she can improve herself!—Let me be just, though she has offended me:—she is wonderfully improved within this last month; for one fault, and that against myself, should I forget all her merits?"

As Leonora said these last words, she could but just hear the voices of her companions; they had left her alone in the gallery—she knocked softly at Louisa's door—"Come in," said Louisa, "I'm not asleep; oh," said she, starting up with the Flora in her hand, the instant that the door was opened; "I'm so glad you are come, Leonora, for I did so long to hear what you were all making such a noise about—have you forgot that the bracelet——"

"Oh yes! is this the evening?"

"Well, here's my white shell for you, I've kept it in my pocket this fortnight; and though Cecilia did give me this Flora, I still love you a great deal better."

"I thank you, Louisa," said Leonora, gratefully, "I will take your shell, and I shall value it as long as I live; but here is a red one, and if you wish to show me that you love me, you will give this to Cecilia; I know that she is particularly anxious for your preference, and I am sure that she deserves it."

"Yes, if I could I would choose both of you—but you know I can only choose which I like the best."

"If you mean, my dear Louisa," said Leonora, "that you like me the best, I am very much obliged to you; for, indeed, I wish you to love me; but it is enough for me to know it in private; I should not feel the least more pleasure at hearing it in public, or in having it made known to all my companions, especially at a time when it would give poor Cecilia a great deal of pain."

"But why should it give her pain? I don't like her for being jealous of you."

"Nay, Louisa, surely you don't think Cecilia jealous; she only tries to excel, and to please: she is more anxious to succeed than I am, it is true, because she has a great deal more activity, and perhaps more ambition; and it would really mortify her to lose this prize; you know, that she proposed it herself; it has been her object for this month past, and I am sure she has taken great pains to obtain it."

"But, dear Leonora, why should you lose it?"

"Indeed, my dear, it would be no loss to me; and if it were, I would willingly suffer it for Cecilia; for, though we seem not to be such good friends as we used to be, I love her very much, and she will love me again; I'm sure she will; when she no longer fears me as a rival, she will again love me as a friend."

Here Leonora heard a number of her companions running along the gallery. They all knocked hastily at the door, calling "Leonora! Leonora! Will you never come? Cecilia has been with us this half hour."

Leonora smiled, "Well, Louisa," said she, smiling. "Will you promise me?"

"Oh, I'm sure by the way they speak to you, that they won't give you the prize!" said the little Louisa; and the tears started into her eyes.

"They love me, though, for all that; and as for the prize, you know who I wish to have it."

"Leonora! Leonora!" called her impatient companions; "don't you hear us? what are you about?"

"Oh she never will take any trouble about any thing," said one of the party, "let's go away!"

"Oh go! go! make haste!" cried Louisa; "don't stay, they are so angry. I will, I will, indeed!"

"Remember, then, that you have promised me," said Leonora, and she left the room. During all this time Cecilia had been in the garden with her companions. The ambition which she had felt to win the first prize, the prize of superior talents, and superior application, was not to be compared to the absolute anxiety which she now expressed to win this simple testimony of the love and approbation of her equals and rivals.

To employ her exuberant activity, she had been dragging branches of lilacs and laburnums, roses, and sweet briar, to ornament the bower in which her fate was to be decided. It was excessively hot, but her mind was engaged, and she was indefatigable. She stood still, at last, to admire her works; her companions all joined in loud applause; they were not a little prejudiced in her favour, by the great eagerness which she expressed to win their prize, and by the great importance which she seemed to affix to the preference of each individual. At last, "where is Leonora?" cried one of them, and immediately, as we have seen, they ran to call her.

Cecilia was left alone; overcome with heat, and too violent exertion, she had hardly strength to support herself; each moment appeared to her intolerably long: she was in a state of the utmost suspense, and all her courage failed her, even hope forsook her, and hope is a cordial which leaves the mind depressed and enfeebled. "The time is now come," said Cecilia, "in a few moments all will be decided.—In a few moments! goodness! how much do I hazard! If I should not win the prize, how shall I confess what I have done? How shall I beg Leonora to forgive me? I who hoped to restore my friendship to her as an honour!—They are gone to see for her—the moment she appears I shall be forgotten—what shall—what shall I do?" said Cecilia, covering her face with her hands.

Such was her situation, when Leonora, accompanied by her companions, opened the hall-door; they most of them ran forward to Cecilia. As Leonora came into the bower, she held out her hand to Cecilia—"we are not rivals, but friends, I hope," said she: Cecilia clasped her hand, but she was in too great agitation to speak.

The table was now set in the arbour; the vase was now placed in the middle. "Well!" said Cecilia, eagerly, "who begins?" Caroline, one of her friends, came forward first and then all the others successively.—Cecilia's emotion was hardly conceivable. "Now they are all in!—count them, Caroline!"

"One, two, three, four; the numbers are both equal."

There was a dead silence.

"No, they are not," exclaimed Cecilia, pressing forward and putting a shell into the vase—"I have not given mine, and I give it to Leonora." Then snatching the bracelet, "it is yours, Leonora," said she, "take it, and give me back your friendship." The whole assembly gave an universal clap, and shout of applause.

"I cannot be surprised at this from you, Cecilia," said Leonora; "and do you then still love me as you used to do?"

"Oh Leonora! stop! don't praise me; I don't deserve this," said she, turning to her loudly applauding companions; "you will soon despise me—oh, Leonora, you will never forgive me!—I have deceived you—I have sold——"

At this instant Mrs. Villars appeared—the crowd divided—she had heard all that passed from her window.

"I applaud your generosity, Cecilia," said she, "but I am to tell you that in this instance it is unsuccessful: you have it not in your power to give the prize to Leonora—it is yours—I have another vote to give you—you have forgotten Louisa."

"Louisa! But surely, ma'am, Louisa loves Leonora better than she does me?"

"She commissioned me, however," said Mrs. Villars, "to give you a red shell; and you will find it in this box."

Cecilia started, and turned as pale as death—it was the fatal box.

Mrs. Villars produced another box—she opened it—it contained the Flora;—"and Louisa also desired me," said she, "to return you this Flora"—she put it into Cecilia's hand—Cecilia trembled so that she could not hold it; Leonora caught it.

"Oh madam! Oh Leonora!" exclaimed Cecilia; "now I have no hope left: I intended, I was just going to tell——"

"Dear Cecilia," said Leonora, "you need not tell it me, I know it already, and I forgive you with all my heart."

"Yes, I can prove to you," said Mrs. Villars, "that Leonora has forgiven you: it is she who has given you the prize; it was she who persuaded Louisa to give you her vote. I went to see her a little while ago, and perceiving, by her countenance, that something was the matter, I pressed her to tell me what it was.

"'Why, madam,' said she, 'Leonora has made me promise to give my shell to Cecilia; now I don't love Cecilia half so well as I do Leonora; besides, I would not have Cecilia think I vote for her because she gave me a Flora.' Whilst Louisa was speaking," continued Mrs. Villars, "I saw this silver box lying on the bed; I took it up, and asked, if it was not yours, and how she came by it.

"'Indeed, madam,' said Louisa, 'I could have been almost certain that it was Cecilia's; but Leonora gave it me, and she said that she bought it of the pedlar, this morning; if any body else had told me so, I could not have believed them, because I remembered the box so well; but I can't help believing Leonora.'

"'But did not you ask Cecilia about it?' said I.

"'No, madam,' replied Louisa, 'for Leonora forbad me.'

"I guessed her reason. 'Well,' said I, 'give me the box, and I will carry your shell in it to Cecilia.'

"'Then, madam," said she, 'if I must give it her, pray do take the Flora, and return it to her first, that she may not think it is for that I do it.'"

"Oh, generous Louisa!" exclaimed Cecilia; "but indeed, Leonora, I cannot take your shell."

"Then, dear Cecilia, accept of mine instead of it; you cannot refuse it, I only follow your example; as for the bracelet," added she, taking Cecilia's hand, "I assure you I don't wish for it; and you do, and you deserve it."

"No," said Cecilia, "indeed I do not deserve it; next to you surely Louisa deserves it best."

"Louisa! oh yes, Louisa," exclaimed every body with one voice.

"Yes," said Mrs. Villars, "and let Cecilia carry the bracelet to her; she deserves that reward. For one fault I cannot forget all your merits, Cecilia; nor, I am sure, will your companions."

"Then, surely, not your best friend," said Leonora, kissing her.

Every body present was moved—they looked up to Leonora with respectful and affectionate admiration.

"Oh, Leonora, how I love you! and how I wish to be like you!" exclaimed Cecilia; "to be as good, as generous!"

"Rather wish, Cecilia," interrupted Mrs. Villars, "to be as just; to be as strictly honourable, and as invariably consistent."

"Remember that many of our sex are capable of great efforts, of making what they call great sacrifices to virtue, or to friendship; but few treat their friends with habitual gentleness, or uniformly conduct themselves with prudence and good sense."

'Lazy Lawrence'

In the pleasant valley of Ashton there lived an elderly woman of the name of Preston; she had a small neat cottage, and there was not a weed to be seen in her garden. It was upon her garden that she chiefly depended for support: it consisted of strawberry beds, and one small border for flowers. The pinks and roses she tied up in nice nosegays, and sent either to Clifton or Bristol to be sold; as to her strawberries, she did not send them to market, because it was the custom for numbers of people to come from Clifton, in the summer time, to eat strawberries and cream at the gardens in Ashton.[10]

Now the widow Preston was so obliging, active, and good humoured, that every one who came to see her was pleased. She lived happily in this manner for several years; but, alas! One autumn she fell sick, and, during her illness, every thing went wrong; her garden was neglected, her cow died, and all the money which she had saved was spent in paying for medicines. The winter passed away, while she was so weak that she could earn but little by her work; and, when the summer came, her rent was called for, and the rent was not ready in her little purse as usual. She begged a few months delay, and they were granted to her; but at the end of that time there was no resource but to sell her horse Lightfoot. Now Lightfoot, though perhaps he had seen his best days, was a very great favourite: in his youth he had always carried the dame to market behind her husband; and it was now her little son Jem's turn to ride him. It was Jem's business to feed Lightfoot, and to take care of him; a charge which he never neglected, for, besides being a very good natured, he was a very industrious boy.

"It will go near to break my Jem's heart," said dame Preston to herself, as she sat one evening beside the fire stirring the embers, and considering how she had best open the matter to her son, who stood opposite to her, eating a dry crust of bread very heartily for supper.

"Jem," said the old woman, "what, ar't hungry?"

"That I am, brave and hungry!"

"Aye! No wonder, you've been brave hard at work—Eh?"

"Brave hard! I wish it was not so dark, mother, that you might just step out and see the great bed I've dug; I know you'd say it was no bad day's work—and, oh mother! I've good news; Farmer Truck will give us the giant-strawberries, and I'm to go for 'em tomorrow morning, and I'll be back afore breakfast."

"God bless the boy! How he talks !—Four mile there, and four mile back again, afore breakfast."

"Aye, upon Lightfoot you know, mother, very easily; mayn't I?"

"Aye, child!"

"Why do you sigh, mother?"

"Finish thy supper, child."

"I've done!" cried Jem, swallowing the last mouthful hastily, as if he thought he had been too long at supper—"and now for the great needle; I must see and mend Lightfoot's bridle afore I go to bed."—To work he set, by the light of the fire, and the dame having once more stirred it, began again with "Jem, dear, does he go lame at all now?"—"What, Light-foot! Oh la, no, not he!—never was so well of his lameness in all his life—he's grown quite young again, I think, and then he's so fat he can hardly wag."—"God bless him—that's right—we must see, Jem, and keep him fat."

"For what, mother?"

"For Monday fortnight at the fair. He's to be——sold!"

"Lightfoot!" cried Jem, and let the bridle fall from his hand; "and *will* mother sell Lightfoot?"

"*Will*; no: but I *must*, Jem."

"Must; who says you *must?* Why *must* you, mother?"

"I must, I say, child—Why must not I pay my debts honestly—and must not I pay my rent; and was not it called for long and long ago; and have not I had time; and did not I promise to pay it for certain Monday fortnight, and am not I two guineas short— and where am I to get two guineas?[11] So what signifies talking, child?" said the widow, leaning her head upon her arm, "Lightfoot *must* go."

Jem was silent for a few minutes—"Two guineas; that's a great, great deal.—If I worked, and worked, and worked ever so hard, I could no ways earn two guineas *afore* Monday fortnight—could I, mother?"

"Lord help thee, no; not an' work thyself to death."

"But I could earn something, though, I say," cried Jem proudly; "and I *will* earn *something*—if it be ever so little, it will be *something*—and I shall do my very best; so I will."

"That I'm sure of, my child," said his mother, drawing him towards her and kissing him; "you were always a good industrious lad, *that* I will say afore your face or behind your back;—but it won't do now—Lightfoot *must* go."

Jem turned away, struggling to hide his tears, and went to bed without saying a word more. But he knew that crying would do no good, so he presently wiped his eyes, and lay awake, considering what he could possibly do to save the horse.—"If I get ever so little," he still said to himself, "it will be *something*; and who knows but Landlord might then wait a bit longer? And we might make it all up in time; for a penny a day might come to two guineas in time."

But how to get the first penny was the question—Then he recollected, that one day, when he had been sent to Clifton to sell some flowers, he had seen an old woman with a board beside her covered with various sparkling stones, which people stopped to look at as they passed, and he remembered that some people bought the stones, and paid twopence, another threepence, and another sixpence for them; and Jem heard her say that she got them amongst the neighbouring rocks: so he thought that if he tried he might find some too, and sell them as she had done.[12]

Early in the morning he wakened full of this scheme, jumped up, dressed himself, and, having given one look at poor Lightfoot in his stable, set off to Clifton in search of the old woman, to inquire where she found her sparkling stones. But it was too early in the morning, the old woman was not at her seat; so he turned back again disappointed.—He did not waste his time waiting for her, but saddled and bridled Lightfoot, and went to Farmer Truck's for the giant-strawberries. A great part of the morning was spent in putting them into the ground; and, as soon as that was finished, he set out again in quest of the old woman, who, to his great joy, he spied sitting at her corner of the street with her board before her. But this old woman was deaf and cross; and when at last Jem made her hear his questions, he could get no answer from her, but that she found the fossils where he would never find any more. "But can't I look where you looked?"—"Look away, nobody hinders you," replied the old woman; and these were the only words she would say.—Jem was not, however, a boy to be easily discouraged; he went to the rocks, and walked slowly along, looking at all the stones as he passed. Presently he came to a place where a number of men were at work loosening some large rocks, and one amongst the workmen was stooping down looking for something very eagerly; Jem ran up, and asked if he could help him. "Yes," said the man, "you can; I've just dropped amongst this heap of rubbish a fine piece of crystal that I got to-day."—"What kind of a looking thing is it?" said Jem. "White, and like glass," said the man, and went on working whilst Jem looked very carefully over the heap of rubbish for a great while. "Come," said the man, "it's gone for ever, don't trouble yourself any more, my boy."—"It's no trouble; I'll look a little longer; we'll not give it up so soon," said Jem; and, after he had looked a little longer, he found the piece of crystal. "Thank'ee," said the man, "you are a fine little industrious fellow." Jem, encouraged by the tone of voice in which the man spoke this, ventured to ask him the same questions which he had asked the old woman. "One good turn deserves another," said the man; "we are going to dinner just now, and shall leave off work— wait for me here, and I'll make it worth your while."

Jem waited; and, as he was very attentively observing how the workmen went on with their work, he heard somebody near him give a great yawn, and, turning round, he saw stretched upon the grass, beside the river, a boy about his own age, who he knew very well went in the village of Ashton by the name of Lazy Lawrence: a name which he most justly deserved, for he never did any thing from morning till night; he neither worked nor played, but sauntered or lounged about restless and yawning. His father was an alehouse keeper, and, being generally drunk, could take no care of his son, so that Lazy Lawrence grew every day worse and worse. However, some of the neighbours said that he was a good-natured poor fellow enough, and would never do any one harm but himself; whilst others, who were wiser, often shook their heads, and told him that idleness was the root of all evil.

"What, Lawrence!" cried Jem to him, when be saw him lying upon the grass—"what, are you asleep?"—"Not quite."—"Are you awake?"—"Not quite."—"What are you doing there?"—"Nothing."—"What are you thinking of?"—"Nothing."—"What makes you lie there?"—"I don't know—because I can't find any body to play with me today—Will you come and play?"—"No, I can't; I'm busy."—"Busy," cried Lawrence, stretching himself, "you are always busy—I would not be you for the world, to have so much to do always."—"And I," said Jem laughing, "would not be you for the world, to have nothing to do." So they parted, for the workman just then called Jem to follow him.—He took him home to his own house, and showed him a parcel of fossils, which he had gathered, he said, on purpose to sell, but had never had time yet to sort them. He set about it however now, and having picked out those which he judged to be the best, he put them in a small basket, and gave them to Jem to sell, upon condition that he should bring him half of what he got. Jem, pleased to be employed, was ready to agree to what the man proposed, provided his mother had no objection to it. When he went home to dinner, he told his mother his scheme, and she smiled and said he might do as he pleased, for she was not afraid of his being from home. "You are not an idle boy," said she, "so there is little danger of your getting into any mischief."

Accordingly Jem that evening took his stand, with his little basket, upon the bank of the river, just at the place where people land from a ferry-boat, and where the walk turns to the Wells, where numbers of people perpetually pass to drink the waters.[13] He chose his place well, and waited almost all evening, offering his fossils with great assiduity to every passenger; but not one person bought any. "Holla!" cried some sailors, who had just rowed a boat to land, "bear a hand here, will you my little fellow! And carry these parcels for us into yonder house." Jem ran down immediately for the parcels, and did what he was asked to do so quickly, and with so much good will, that the master of the boat took notice of him, and, when he was going away, stopped to ask him what he had got in his little basket; and when he saw that they were fossils, he immediately told Jem to follow him, for that he was going to carry some shells he had brought from abroad to a lady in the neighbourhood who was making a grotto.[14] "She will very likely buy your stones into the bargain: come along, my lad; we can but try."

The lady lived but a very little way off, so that they were soon at her house. She was alone in her parlour, and was sorting a bundle of feathers of different colours: they lay on a sheet of pasteboard upon a window-seat, and it happened that as the sailor was bustling round the table to show off his shells, he knocked down the sheet of pasteboard, and scattered all the feathers.[15] The lady looked very sorry, which Jem observing, he took the opportunity, whilst she was busy looking over the sailor's bag of shells, to gather together all the feathers, and sort them according to their different colours, as he had seen them sorted when he first came into the room.

"Where is the little boy you brought with you? I thought I saw him here just now."—"And here I am, ma'am," cried Jem, creeping from under the table with some few remaining feathers which he had picked from he carpet; "I thought," added he, pointing to the others, "I had better be doing something than standing idle, ma'am." She smiled, and, pleased with his activity and simplicity, began to ask him several questions; such as, who he was, where he lived, what employment he had, and how much a day he earned by gathering fossils. "This is the first day I ever tried," said Jem; "I never sold any yet, and, if you don't buy 'em now, ma'am, I'm afraid nobody else will, for I've asked every body else."—"Come then," said the lady, laughing, "if that is the case, I think I had better buy them all." So emptying all the fossils out of his basket, she put half a crown into it. Jem's eyes sparkled with joy. "Oh, thank you, ma'am," said he, "I will be sure and bring you as many more to-morrow."—"Yes, but I don't promise you," said she, "to give you half a crown to-morrow."—"But, perhaps, though you don't promise it, you will."—"No," said the lady, "do not deceive yourself; I assure you that I will not. *That,* instead of encouraging you to be industrious, would teach you to be idle." Jem did not quite understand what she meant by this, but answered, "I'm sure I don't wish to be idle; what I want is to earn something every day, if I knew how: I'm sure I don't wish to be idle. If you knew all, you'd know I did not."—"How do you mean, *if I knew all?*"—"Why I mean, if you knew about Lightfoot."—"Who's Lightfoot?"—"Why, mammy's horse; and so he is," added Jem, looking out of the window; "I must make haste home and feed him, afore it get dark; he'll wonder what's gone with me."—"Let him wonder a few minutes longer," said the lady, "and tell me the rest of your story."—"I've no story, ma'am, to tell, but as how mammy says he must go to the fair Monday fortnight to be sold, if she can't get the two guineas for her rent; and I should be main sorry to part with him, for I love him, and he loves me; so I'll work for him, I will, all I can: to be sure, as mammy says, I have no chance, such a little fellow as I am, of earning two guineas afore Monday fortnight."—"But are you in earnest willing to work?" said the lady; "You know there is a great deal of difference between picking up a few stones, and working steadily every day, and all day long."—"But," said Jem, "I would work every day, and all day long."—"Then," said the lady, "I will give you work. Come here to-morrow morning, and my gardener will set you to weed the shrubberies, and I will pay you six-pence a day. Remember you must be at the gates by six o'clock." Jem bowed, thanked her, and went away. It was late in the evening, and he was impatient to get home to feed Lightfoot; yet he recollected that he had promised the man who had trusted him to sell the fossils that he would bring him half of what he got for them; so he thought that he had better go to him directly: and away he went, running along by the water side about a quarter of a mile, till he came to the man's house. He was just come home from work, and was surprised when Jem showed him the half crown, saying, "Look what I got for the stones: you are to have half, you know."—"No," said the man, when he had heard his story, "I shall not take half of that; it was given to you. I expected but a shilling at the most, and the half of that is but sixpence, and that I'll take.—Wife! Give the lad two shillings, and take this half crown." So his wife opened an old glove, and took out two shillings; and the man, as she opened the glove, put in his fingers, and took out a little silver penny.—"There, he shall have that into the bargain for his honesty.—Honesty is the best policy.—There's a lucky penny for you, that I've kept ever since I can remember."—"Don't you ever go to part with it, do ye hear!" cried the woman. "Let him do what he will with it, wife," said the man. "But," argued the wife, "another penny would do just as well to buy gingerbread, and that's what it will go for."—"No, that it shall not, I promise you," said Jem; and so he ran away home, fed Lightfoot, stroked him, went to bed, jumped up at five o'clock in the morning, and went singing to work as gay as a lark.

Four days he worked every day and all day long, and the lady every evening, when she came out to walk in her gardens, looked at his work. At last she said to her gardener, "This little boy works very hard."—"Never had so good a little boy about the grounds," said the gardener; "he's always at his work let me come by when I will, and he has got twice as much done as another would do; yes, twice as much ma'am; for look here—he began at this here rose bush, and now he's got to where you stand, ma'am; and here is the day's work that t'other boy, and he's three years older too, did today—I say, measure Jem's fair, and it's twice as much, I'm sure."—"Well," said the lady to her gardener, "show me how much is a fair good day's work for a boy of his age."—"Come at six o'clock, and go at six? Why, about this much, ma'am," said the gardener, marking off a piece of the border with his spade. "Then, little boy," said the lady "so much shall be your task every day; the gardener will mark it off for you: and when you've done, the rest of the day you may do what you please." Jem was extremely glad of this; and the next day he had finished his task by four o'clock; so that he had all the rest of the evening to himself. Jem was as fond of play as any little boy could be, and, when he was at it, played with all the eagerness and gaiety imaginable: so as soon as he had finished his task, fed Lightfoot, and put by the six-pence he had earned that day, he ran to the play-ground in the village, where he found a party of boys playing, and amongst them Lazy Lawrence, who indeed was not playing, but lounging upon a gate with his thumb in his mouth. The rest were playing at cricket. Jem joined them, and was the merriest and most active amongst them; till, at last, when quite out of breath with running, he was obliged to give up to rest himself, and sat down upon the stile, close to the gate on which Lazy Lawrence was swinging. "And why don't you play, Lawrence?" said he.—"I'm tired," said Lawrence.—"Tired of what?"—"I don't know well what tires me; grandmother says I'm ill, and I must take something—I don't know what ails me."—"Oh, pugh! Take a good race, one, two, three, and away, and you'll find yourself as well as ever. Come, run—one, two, three, and away!"—"Ah, no, I can't run indeed," said he, hanging back heavily; you know I can play all day long if I like it, so I don't mind play as you do, who have only one hour for it."—"So much the worse for you. Come now, I'm quite fresh again, will you have one game at ball; do."—"No, I tell you I can't; I'm as tired as if I had been working all day long as hard as a horse."—"Ten times more," said Jem, "for I have been working all day long as hard as a horse, and yet you see I'm not a bit tired; only a little out of breath just now."—"That's very odd," said Lawrence, and yawned, for want of some better answer; then taking out a handful of halfpence—"See what I got from father to-day, because I asked him just at the right time, when he had drank a glass or two; then I can get any thing I want out of him—see! A penny, two-pence, three-pence, four-pence—there's eight-pence in all; would not you be happy if you had *eight-pence?*"—"Why, I don't know," said Jem laughing, "for you don't seem happy, and you *have eight-pence.*"—"That does not signify though—I'm sure you only say that because you envy me—you don't know what it is to have eight-pence—you never had more than two-pence or three-pence at a time in all your life." Jem smiled. "Oh, as to that," said he, "you are mistaken, for I have at this very time more than two-pence, three-pence, or eight-pence either; I have—let me see—stones, two shillings; then five day's work, that's five six-pences, that's two shillings and six-pence, in all makes four shilling and six-pence, and my silver penny, is four and seven-pence—Four and seven-pence!"—"You have not!" said Lawrence, roused so as absolutely to stand upright. "Four and seven-pence! Have you? Show it me, and then I'll believe you."—"Follow me then," cried Jem, "and I'll soon make you believe me; come."—"Is it far?" said Lawrence, following half running, half hobbling, till he came to the stable, where Jem showed him his treasure. "And how did you come by it? Honestly?"—"*Honestly?* To be sure I did; I earned it all."—"Lord bless me, earned it! Well, I've a great mind to work; but then it's such hot weather; besides grandmother says I'm not strong enough yet for hard work; and besides I know how to coax daddy out of money when I want it, so I need not work.—But four and seven-pence; let's see, what will you do with it all?"—"That's a secret," said Jem, looking great. "I can guess; I know what I'd do with it if it was mine—First, I'd buy pockets full of gingerbread; then I'd buy ever so many apples and nuts; don't you love nuts? I'd buy nuts enough to last me from this time to Christmas, and I'd make little Newton crack 'em for me, for that's the worst of nuts, there's the trouble of cracking 'em."—"Well, you never deserve to have a nut."—"But you'll give me some of yours," said Lawrence in a fawning tone, for he thought it easier to coax than to work—you'll give me some of your good things, won't you."—"I shall not have any of those good things," said Jem. "Then what will you do with all your money?"—"Oh, I know very well what to do with it; but, as I told you, that's a se-cret, and I shan't tell it any body—Come now, let's go back and play—their game's up, I dare say."—Lawrence, went back with him full of curiosity, and out of humour with himself and his eight-pence.—"If I had four and seven-pence," said he to himself, "I certainly should be happy!"

The next day, as usual Jem jumped up before six o'clock and went to his work, whilst Lazy Lawrence sauntered about without knowing what to do with himself. In the course of two days he laid out six-pence of his money in apples and gingerbread, and as long as these lasted he found himself well received by his com-panions; but at length the third day he spent his last halfpenny, and when it was gone, unfortunately some nuts tempted him very much, but he had no money to pay for them; so he ran home to coax his father, as he called it. When he got home, he heard his father talking very loud, and at first he thought he was drunk; but when he opened the kitchen door, he saw that he was not drunk but angry.

"You lazy dog!" cried he, turning suddenly upon Lawrence, and gave him such a violent box on the ear as made the light flash from his eyes; "You lazy dog! See what you've done for me—look!—Look, look, I say!" Lawrence looked as soon as he came to the use of his senses, and, with fear, amazement, and remorse, beheld at least a dozen bottles burst, and the fine Worcestershire cider streaming over the floor. "Now, did not I order you three days ago to carry these bottles to the cellar; and did not I charge you to wire the corks? Answer me, you lazy rascal; did not I?"—"Yes," said Lawrence, scratching his head. "And why was not it done? I ask you," cried his father with renewed anger, as another bottle burst at the moment. "What do you stand there for, you lazy brat? Why don't you move? I say—No, no," catching hold of him, "I believe you can't move; but I'll make you." And he shook him, till Lawrence was so giddy he could not stand. "What had you to think of? What had you to do all day long, that you could not carry my cider, my Worcestershire cider, to the cellar when I bid you? But go, you'll never be good for any thing, you are such a lazy rascal—get out of my sight!" So saying, he pushed him out of the house door, and Lawrence sneaked off, seeing that this was no time to make his petition for halfpence.

The next day he saw the nuts again, and, wishing for them more than ever, went home in hopes that his father, as he said to himself, would be in a better humour. But the cider was still fresh in his recollection, and the moment Lawrence began to whisper the word "halfpenny" in his ear, his father swore, with a loud oath, "I will not give you a halfpenny, no, not a farthing, for a month to come; if you want money, go work for it; I've had enough of your laziness—Go work!" At these terrible words Lawrence burst into tears, and, going to the side of a ditch, sat down and cried for an hour; and, when he had cried till he could cry no more, he exerted himself so far as to empty his pockets, to see whether there might not happen to be one halfpenny left; and, to his great joy, in the farthest corner of his pocket one halfpenny was found. With this he proceeded to the fruit woman's stall. She was busy weighing out some plums, so he was obliged to wait; and, whilst he was waiting, he heard some people near him talking and laughing very loud. The fruit woman's stall was at the gate of an inn-yard; and peeping through the gate in this yard, Lawrence saw a postillion and a stable-boy about his own size playing at pitch-farthing.[16] He stood by watching them for a few minutes. "I begun but with one halfpenny," cried the stable-boy with an oath, "and now I've got two-pence!" added he, jingling the half-pence in his waistcoat pocket. Lawrence was moved at the sound, and said to himself, "If *I* begin with one halfpenny, I may end like him with having two-pence; and it is easier to play at pitch-farthing than to work." So he stepped forward, presenting his halfpenny, offering to toss up with the stable-boy, who, after looking him full in the face, accepted the proposal, and threw his halfpenny into the air, "Head or tail!" cried he. "Head," replied Lawrence, and it came up head. He seized the penny, surprised at his own success, and would have gone instantly to have laid it out in nuts; but the stable-boy stopped him, and tempted him to throw again. This time he lost; he threw again and won; and so he went on, sometimes losing, but most frequently winning, till half the morning was gone. At last, however, he chanced to win twice running, and, finding himself master of three halfpence, said he would play no more. The stable-boy, grumbling, swore he would have his revenge another time, and Lawrence went and bought the nuts. "It is a good thing," said he to himself, "to play at pitch-farthing: the next time I want a halfpenny I'll not ask my father for it, nor go to work neither." Satisfied with this resolution, he sat down to crack his nuts at his leisure, upon the horse-block in the inn-yard. Here, whilst he eat, he overheard the conversation of the stable-boys and postillions. At first their shocking oaths and loud wrangling frightened and shocked him; for Lawrence, though a *lazy*, had not yet learned to be a *wicked*, boy. But, by degrees, he was accustomed to their swearing and quarrelling, and took a delight and interest in their disputes and battles. As this was an amusement which he could enjoy without any sort of exertion on his part, he soon grew so fond of it, that every day he returned to the stable-yard, and the horse block became his constant seat. Here he found some relief from the insupportable fatigue of doing nothing, and here, hour after hour, with his elbows on his knees, and his head on his hands, he sat the spectator of wickedness. Gaming, cheating, and lying, soon became familiar to him; and, to complete his ruin, he formed a sudden and close intimacy with the stable-boy with whom he had first began to game—a very bad boy. The consequences of this intimacy we shall presently see. But it is now time to inquire what little Jem has been doing all this while.

One day, after he had finished his task, the gardener asked him to stay a little while, to help him to carry some geranium pots into the hall. Jem, always active and obliging, readily stayed from play, and was carrying in a heavy flower-pot, when his mistress crossed the hall. "What a terrible litter," said she, "you are making here—why don't you wipe your shoes upon the mat?" Jem turned round to look for the mat, but he saw none. "Oh," said the lady, recollecting herself, "I can't blame you, for there is no mat."— "No, ma'am," said the gardener, "nor I don't know when, if ever, the man will bring home those mats you bespoke, ma'am."—"I am very sorry to hear that," said the lady, "I wish we could find somebody who would do them; if he can't—I should not care what sort of mats they were, so that one could wipe one's feet on them." Jem, as he was sweeping away the litter, when he heard these last words, said to himself, "perhaps I could make a mat?" And all the way home, as he trudged along whistling, he was thinking over a scheme for making mats, which, however bold it may appear, he did not despair of executing, with patience and industry. Many were the difficulties which his *"prophetic eye"* foresaw; but he felt within himself that spirit, which spurs men on to great enterprises, and makes them "trample on impossibilities."[17]

He recollected, in the first place, that he had seen Lazy Lawrence, whilst he lounged upon the gate, twist a bit of heath into different shapes, and he thought, that if he could find some way of plaiting heath firmly together, that it would make a very pretty green soft mat, which would do very well for one to wipe one's shoes on. About a mile from his mother's house, on the common which Jem rode over when he went to Farmer Truck's for the giant strawberries, he remembered to have seen a great quantity of this heath; and, as it was now only six o'clock in the evening, he knew that he should have time to feed Lightfoot, stroke him, go to the common, return, and make one trial of his skill before he went to bed.

Lightfoot carried him swiftly to the common, and there Jem gathered as much of the heath as he thought he should want. But, what toil! What time! What pains did it cost him, before he could make any thing like a mat! Twenty times he was ready to throw aside the heath, and give up his project from impatience of repeated disappointments. But still he persevered. Nothing *truly great* can be accomplished without toil and time. Two hours he worked before he went to bed. All his play hours the next day he spent at his mat; which, in all, made five hours of fruitless attempts.—The sixth, however, repaid him for the labours of the other five; he conquered his grand difficulty of fastening the heath substantially together, and at length completely finished a mat, which far surpassed his most sanguine expectations. He was extremely happy—sung, danced round it—whistled—looked at it again and again, and could hardly leave off looking at it when it was time to go to bed. He laid it by his bed-side, that he might see it the moment he wakened in the morning.

And now came the grand pleasure of carrying it to his mistress. She looked full as much surprised, as he expected, when she saw it, and when she heard who made it. After having duly admired it, she asked him how much he expected for his mat. "Expect!—Nothing, ma'am," said Jem; "I meant to give it you, if you'd have it; I did not mean to sell it. I made it at my play hours, and I was very happy making it; and I'm very glad too, that you like it; and if you please to keep it, ma'am—that's all."—"But that's not all," said the lady. "Spend your time no more in weeding in my garden, you can employ yourself much better; you shall have the reward of your ingenuity as well as of your industry. Make as many more such mats as you can, and I will take care and dispose of them for you."—"Thank'ee, ma'am," said Jem, making his best bow, for he thought by the lady's looks that she meant to do him a favour, though he repeated to himself, " 'Dispose of them'; what does that mean?"

The next day he went to work to make more mats, and he soon learned to make them so well and quickly, that he was surprised at his own success. In every one he made he found less difficulty, so that, instead of making two, he could soon make four, in a day. In a fortnight he made eighteen. It was Saturday night when he finished, and he carried, at three journeys, his eighteen mats to his mistress's house: piled them all up in the hall, and stood with his hat off, with a look of proud humility, beside the pile, waiting for his mistress's appearance. Presently a folding door, at one end of the hall, opened, and he saw his mistress, with a great many gentlemen and ladies, rising from several tables.

"Oh! There is my little boy, and his mats," cried the lady; and, followed by all the rest of the company, she came into the hall. Jem modestly retired whilst they looked at his mats; but in a minute or two his mistress beckoned to him, and, when he came into the middle of the circle, he saw that his pile of mats had disappeared. "Well," said the lady smiling, "what do you see that makes you look so surprised?"—"That all my mats are gone," said Jem; "but you are very welcome."—"Are we!" said the lady; "well take up your hat, and go home then, for you see that it is getting late, and you know Lightfoot will wonder what's become of you." Jem turned round to take up his hat, which he had left on the floor.

But how his countenance changed! The hat was heavy with shillings. Every one who had taken a mat had put in two shillings; so that for the eighteen mats he had got thirty-six shillings. "Thirty-six shillings!" said the lady; "five and seven pence I think you told me you had earned already—how much does that make? I must add, I believe, one other six-pence to make out your two guineas."—"Two guineas!" exclaimed Jem, now quite conquering his bashfulness, for at the moment he forgot where he was, and saw nobody that was by. "Two guineas!" cried he, clapping his hands together.—"Oh, Lightfoot!—Oh, mother!" Then, recollecting himself, he saw his mistress, whom he now looked up to quite as a friend. "Will *you* thank them all," said he, scarcely daring to glance his eye round upon the company, "will *you* thank 'em, for you know I don't know how to thank 'em *rightly*." Every body thought, however, that they had been thanked *rightly*.

"Now we won't keep you any longer—only," said his mistress, "I have one thing to ask you, that I may be by when you show your treasure to your mother."—"Come, then," said Jem, "come with me now."—"Not now," said the lady laughing, "but I will come to Ashton to-morrow evening; perhaps your mother can find me a few strawberries."

"That she will," said Jem; "I'll search the garden myself." He now went home, but felt it a great restraint to wait till to-morrow evening before he told his mother. To console himself he flew to the stable: "Lightfoot, you're not to be sold to-morrow! Poor fellow!" said he, patting him, and then could not refrain from counting out his money. Whilst he was intent upon this, Jem was startled by a noise at the door: somebody was trying to pull the latch. It opened, and there came in Lazy Lawrence, with a boy in a red jacket, who had a cock under his arm. They started when they got into the middle of the stable, and when they saw Jem, who had been at first hidden by the horse.

"We—we—we came"—stammered Lazy Lawrence—"I mean, I came to—to—to—" "To ask you," continued the stable-boy in a bold tone, "whether you will go with us to the cock-fight on

Monday? See, I've a fine cock here, and Lawrence told me you were a great friend of his, so I came."

Lawrence now attempted to say something in praise of the pleasures of cock-fighting, and in recommendation of his new companion. But Jem looked at the stable-boy with dislike, and a sort of dread; then turning his eyes upon the cock with a look of compassion, said in a low voice to Lawrence, "Shall you like to stand by and see its eyes pecked out?"—"I don't know," said Lawrence, "as to that; but they say a cock-fight's a fine sight, and it's no more cruel in me to go than another; and a great many go; and I've nothing else to do, so I shall go."—"But I have something else to do," said Jem, laughing, "so I shall not go."—"But," continued Lawrence, "you know Monday is the great Bristol fair, and one must be merry then, of all days in the year."—"One day in the year, sure, there's no harm in being merry," said the stable-boy. "I hope not," said Jem; "for I know, for my part, I am merry every day in the year."—"That's very odd," said Lawrence; "but I know, for my part, I would not for all the world miss going to the fair, for at least it will be something to talk of for half a year after—come, you'll go, won't you."—"No," said Jem, still looking as if he did not like to talk before the ill-looking stranger. "Then what will you do with all your money?"—"I'll tell you about that another time," whispered Jem; "and don't you go to see that cock's eyes pecked out; it won't make you merry, I'm sure."—"If I had any thing else to divert me," said Lawrence, hesitating and yawning.—"Come," cried the stable-boy, seizing his stretching arm, "come along," cried he; and, pulling him away from Jem, upon whom he cast a look of extreme contempt, "leave him alone, he's not the sort."— "What a fool you are," said he to Lawrence, the moment he got him out of the stable, "you might have known he would not go— else we should soon have trimmed him out of his four and seven-pence. But how came you to talk of four and seven-pence; I saw in the manger a hat full of silver."—"Indeed!" exclaimed Lawrence. "Yes, indeed—but why did you stammer so when we first got in? You had like to have blown us all up."—"I was so ashamed," said Lawrence, hanging down his head. "Ashamed! But you must not talk of shame now you are in for it, and I shan't let you off: you owe us half a crown, recollect, and I must be paid to-night; so see and get the money some how or other." After a considerable pause he added, "I'll answer for it he'd never miss half a crown out of all that silver."—"But to steal," said Lawrence, drawing back with horror—"I never thought I should come to that—and from poor Jem too—the money that he has worked so hard for too."—"But it is not stealing; we don't mean to steal; only to borrow it: and, if we win, as we certainly shall, at the cock-fight, pay it back again, and he'll never know any thing of the matter; and what harm will it do him? Besides, what signifies talking, you can't go to the cock-fight, or the fair either, if you don't; and I tell ye we don't mean to steal it; we'll pay it again Monday night." Lawrence made no reply, and they parted without his coming to any determination.

Here let us pause in our story—we are almost afraid to go on—the rest is very shocking—our little readers will shudder as they read. But it is better that they should know the truth, and see what the idle boy came to at last.

In the dead of the night Lawrence heard somebody tap at his window. He knew well who it was, for this was the signal agreed upon between him and his wicked companion. He trembled at the thoughts of what he was about to do, and lay quite still, with his head under the bed-clothes, till he heard the second tap. Then he got up, dressed himself, and opened his window. It was almost even with the ground. His companion said to him, in a hollow voice, "Are you ready?" He made no answer, but got out of the window and followed. When he got to the stable, a black cloud was just passing over the moon, and it was quite dark. "Where are you?" whispered Lawrence, groping about, "where are you? Speak to me."—"I am here; give me your hand." Lawrence stretched out his hand. "Is that your hand?" said the wicked boy, as Lawrence laid hold of him; "how cold it felt."—"Let us go back," said Lawrence; "it is time yet."—"It is no time to go back," replied the other opening the door; "you've gone too far now to go back:" and he pushed Lawrence into the stable.——"Have you found it—take care of the horse—have you done?—what are you about?—make haste, I hear a noise," said the stable-boy, who watched at the door. "I am feeling for the half crown, but I can't find it."—"Bring all together." He brought Jem's broken flower-pot, with all the money in it, to the door.

The black cloud was now passed over the moon, and the light shone full upon them. "What do we stand here for?" said the stable-boy, snatching the flower-pot out of Lawrence's trembling hands, and pulled him away from the door. "Good God!" cried Lawrence, "you won't take all—you said you'd only take half a crown, and pay it back on Monday—you said you'd only take half a crown!"—"Hold your tongue," replied the other walking on, deaf to all remonstrances—"if I am to be hanged ever, it sha'n't be for half a crown," Lawrence's blood ran cold in his veins, and he felt as if all his hair stood on end. Not another word passed. His accomplice carried off the money, and Lawrence crept, with all the horrors of guilt upon him, to his restless bed. All night he was starting from frightful dreams; or else, broad awake, he lay listening to every small noise, unable to stir, and scarcely daring to breathe—tormented by that most dreadful of all kinds of fear, that fear which is the constant companion of an evil conscience. He thought the morning would never come; but when it was day, when he heard the birds sing, and saw every thing look cheerful as usual, he felt still more miserable. It was Sunday morning, and the bell rang for church. All the children of the village, dressed in their Sunday clothes, innocent and gay, and little Jem, the best and gayest amongst them, went flocking by his door to church. "Well, Lawrence," said Jem, pulling his coat as he passed, and saw Lawrence leaning against his father's door, "what makes you look so black!"—"I?" said Lawrence starting, "why do you say that I look black?"—"Nay, then," said Jem, "you look white enough, now, if that will please you; for you're turned as pale as death."—"Pale!" replied Lawrence, not knowing what he said; and turned abruptly away, for he dared not stand another look of Jem's; conscious that guilt was written in his face, he shunned every eye. He would now have given the world to have thrown off the load of guilt which lay upon his mind; he longed to follow Jem, to fall upon his knees, and confess all; dreading the moment when Jem should discover his loss, Lawrence dared not stay at home, and not knowing what to do, or where to go, he mechanically went to his old haunt at the stable-yard, and lurked thereabouts all day with his accomplice, who tried in vain to quiet his fears and raise his spirits, by talking of the next day's cock-fight. It was agreed, that, as soon as the dusk of the evening came on, they should go together into a certain lonely field, and there divide their booty.

In the mean time Jem, when he returned from church, was very full of business, preparing for the reception of his mistress, of whose intended visit he had informed his mother; and, whilst she was arranging the kitchen and their little parlour, he ran to search the strawberry-beds. "Why, my Jem, how merry you are today!" said his mother when he came in with the strawberries, and was jumping about the room playfully. "Now keep those spirits of yours, Jem, till you want 'em, and don't let it come upon you all at once. Have it in mind that to-morrow's fair day, and Lightfoot must go. I bid farmer Truck call for him tonight; he said he'd take him along with his own, and he'll be here just now— and then I know how it will be with you, Jem!"—"So do I!" cried Jem, swallowing his secret with great difficulty, and then tumbling head over heels four times running. A carriage passed the window and stopped at the door. Jem ran out; it was his mistress. She came in smiling, and soon made the old woman smile too, by praising the neatness of every thing in the house. But we shall pass over, however important they were deemed at the time, the praises of the strawberries, and of "my grandmother's china plate." Another knock was heard at the door. "Run, Jem," said his mother, "I hope it's our milk-woman with cream for the lady." No; it was farmer Truck come for Lightfoot. The old woman's countenance fell. "Fetch him out, dear," said she, turning to her son; but Jem was gone; he flew out to the stable the moment he saw the flap of farmer Truck's great-coat. "Sit ye down, farmer," said the old woman, after they had waited about five minutes in expectation of Jem's return. "You'd best sit down, if the lady will give you leave; for he'll not hurry himself back again. My boy's a fool, madam, about that there horse." Trying to laugh, she added, "I knew how Lightfoot and he would be loath enough to part—he won't bring him out till the last minute; so do sit ye down, neighbour." The farmer had scarcely sat down, when Jem, with a pale wild countenance, came back. "What's the matter!" said his mistress. "God bless the boy!" said his mother, looking at him quite frightened, whilst he tried to speak, but could not. She went up to him, and then leaning his head against her, he cried, "It's gone!— it's all gone!" and, bursting into tears, he sobbed as if his little heart would break. "What's gone, love?" said his mother. "My two guineas—Lightfoot's two guineas. I went to fetch 'em to give you, mammy; but the broken flower-pot that I put them in, and all's gone!—quite gone!" repeated he, checking his sobs. "I saw them safe last night, and was showing 'em to Lightfoot, and I was so glad to think I had earned them all myself; and I thought how surprised you'd look, and how glad you'd be, and how you'd kiss me, and all!"

His mother listened to him with the greatest surprise, whilst his mistress stood in silence, looking first at the old woman, and then at Jem with a penetrating eye, as if she suspected the truth of his story, and was afraid of becoming the dupe of her own compassion. "This is a very strange thing!" said she gravely. "How came you to leave all your money in a broken flower-pot in the stable? How came you not to give it to your mother to take care of?"— "Why, don't you remember," said Jem, looking up in the midst of his tears; "why, don't you remember you your own self bid me not tell her about it till you were by?"—"And did you not tell her?"— "Nay, ask mammy," said Jem, a little offended; and, when afterwards the lady went on questioning him in a severe manner, as if she did not believe him, he at last made no answer. "Oh, Jem! Jem! Why don't you speak to the lady?" said his mother. "I have spoke, and spoke the truth," said Jem proudly, "and she did not believe me."

Still the lady, who had lived too long in the world to be without suspicion, maintained a cold manner, and determined to wait the event without interfering, saying only, that she hoped the money would be found; and advised Jem to have done crying. "I have done," said Jem, "I shall cry no more." And as he had the greatest command over himself, he actually did not shed another tear, not even when the farmer got up to go, saying, he could wait no longer.—Jem silently went to bring out Lightfoot.—The lady now took her seat where she could see all that passed at the open parlour window.—The old woman stood at the door, and several idle people of the village, who had gathered round the lady's carriage examining it, turned about to listen. In a minute or two Jem appeared, with a steady countenance, leading Lightfoot; and, when he came up, without saying a word, put the bridle into farmer Truck's hand. "He *has been* a good horse," said the farmer. "He *is* a good horse!" cried Jem, and threw his arm over Lightfoot's neck, hiding his own face as he leaned upon him.

At this instant a party of milkwomen went by; and one of them having set down her pail, came behind Jem, and gave him a pretty smart blow upon the back.—He looked up.—"And don't you know me?" said she. "I forget," said Jem; "I think I have seen your face before, but I forget."—"Do you so? And you'll tell me just now," said she, half opening her hand, "that you forget who gave you this, and who charged you not to part with it too." Here she quite opened her large hand, and on the palm of it appeared Jem's silver penny. "Where?" exclaimed Jem seizing it, "oh, where did you find it? And have you?—Oh, tell me, have you got the rest of my money?"—"I know nothing of your money—I don't know what you would be at," said the milkwoman. "But where, pray, pray tell me where, did you find this?"—"With them that you gave it to, I suppose," said the milkwoman, turning away suddenly to take up her milk-pail. But now Jem's mistress called to her through the window, begging her to stop, and joining in his entreaties to know how she came by the silver penny.

"Why, madam," said she, taking up the corner of her apron, "I came by it in an odd way too—You must know my Betty is sick, so I come with the milk myself, tho' it's not what I'm used to; for my Betty—you know my Betty," said she, turning round to the old woman, "my Betty serves you, and she's a tight and stirring lassy, ma'am, I can assure—" "Yes, I don't doubt it," said the lady impatiently; "but about the silver penny?"—"Why, that's true; as I was coming along all alone, for the rest came round, and I came a short cut across yon field—No, you can't see it, madam, where you stand—but if you were here—" "I see it—I know it," said Jem, out of breath with anxiety. "Well—well—I rested my pail upon the stile, and sets me down a while, and there comes out of the hedge—I don't know well how, for they startled me so I'd like to have thrown down my milk—two boys, one about the size of he," said she, pointing to Jem, "and one a matter taller, but ill-looking like, so I did not think to stir to make way for them, and they were like in a desperate hurry: so, without waiting for the stile, one of 'em pulled at the gate, and when it would not open (for it was tied with a pretty stout cord) one of 'em whips out with his knife and cuts it——

"Now have you a knife about you, Sir?" continued the milk-woman to the farmer. He gave her his knife.

"Here now, ma'am, just sticking as it were here, between the blade and the haft, was the silver penny. He took no notice, but when he opened it, out it falls; still he takes no heed but cuts the cord, as I said before, and through the gate they went, and out of sight in half a minute I picks up the penny, for my heart misgave me that it was the very one husband had had a long time, and had given against my voice to he," pointing to Jem; "and I charged him not to part with it; and, ma'am, when I looked I knew it by the mark, so I thought I would show it to *he,*" again pointing to Jem, "and let him give it back to those it belongs to."—"It belongs to me," said Jem, "I never gave it to any body—but—" "But," cried the farmer, "those boys have robbed him—it is they who have all his money."—"Oh, which way did they go?" cried Jem, "I'll run after them."

"No, no," said the lady, calling to her servant; and she desired him to take his horse and ride after them. "Aye," added farmer Truck, "do you take the road, and I'll take the field-way, and I'll be bound we'll have 'em presently."

Whilst they were gone in pursuit of the thieves the lady, who was now thoroughly convinced of Jem's truth, desired her coachman would produce what she had ordered him to bring with him that evening. Out of the boot of the carriage the coachman immediately produced a new saddle and bridle.

How Jem's eyes sparkled when the saddle was thrown upon Lightfoot's back! "Put it on your horse yourself, Jem," said the lady—"it is yours."

Confused reports of Lightfoot's splendid accoutrements, of the pursuit of thieves and of the fine and generous lady who was standing at dame Preston's window, quickly spread through the village, and drew every body from their houses. They crowded round Jem to hear the story. The children especially, who were all fond of him, expressed the strongest indignation against the thieves. Every eye was on the stretch; and now some, who had run down the lane, came back shouting, "Here they are, they've got the thieves!"

The footman on horseback carried one boy before him; and the farmer, striding along, dragged another. The latter had on a red jacket, which little Jem immediately recollected, and scarcely dared lift his eyes to look at the boy on horseback. "Good God!"

said he to himself, "it must be—yet surely it can't be Lawrence!" The footman rode on as fast as the people would let him. The boy's hat was slouched, and his head hung down, so that nobody could see his face.

At this instant there was a disturbance in the crowd. A man who was half drunk, pushed his way forwards, swearing that nobody should stop him; that he had a right to see and he would see. And so he did; for, forcing through all resistance, he staggered up to the footman just as he was lifting down the boy he had carried before him. "I *will*—I tell you I *will* see the thief!" cried the drunken man, pushing up the boy's hat.—It was his own son.— "Lawrence!" exclaimed the wretched father. The shock sobered him at once, and he hid his face in his hands.

There was an awful silence. Lawrence fell on his knees, and in a voice that could scarcely be heard made a full confession of all the circumstances of his guilt. "Such a young creature so wicked! What could put such wickedness into your head?"—"Bad company," said Lawrence. "And how came you—what brought you into bad company!"—"I don't know—except it was idleness." While this was saying, the farmer was emptying Lazy Lawrence's pockets; and when the money appeared, all his former companions in the village looked at each other with astonishment and terror. Their parents grasped their little hands closer, and cried, "Thank God! He is not my son—how often, when he was little, we used, as he lounged about, to tell him that idleness was the root of all evil."

As for the hardened wretch his accomplice, every one was impatient to have him sent to gaol. He had put on a bold, insolent countenance, till he heard Lawrence's confession; till the money was found upon him; and he heard the milk-woman declare, that she would swear to the silver penny which he had dropped. Then he turned pale, and betrayed the strongest signs of fear. "We must take him before the justice," said the farmer, "and he'll be lodged in Bristol gaol. "Oh!" said Jem, springing forwards when Lawrence's hands were going to be tied, "Let him go—won't you—can't you let him go?"—"Yes, madam! for mercy's sake," said Jem's mother to the lady, "think what a disgrace to his family to be sent to gaol." His father stood by wringing his hands in an agony of despair. "It's all my fault," cried he; "I brought him up in *idleness*."—"But he'll never be idle any more," said Jem; "won't you speak for him, ma'am?"—"Don't ask the lady to speak for him," said the farmer; "it's better he should go to bridewell now, than to the gallows by and by."

Nothing more was said, for every body felt the truth of the farmer's speech. Lawrence was sent to bridewell for a month, and the stable boy was transported to Botany Bay.[18]

During Lawrence's confinement, Jem often visited him and carried him such little presents as he could afford to give; and Jem could afford to be *generous,* because he was *industrious.* Lawrence's heart was touched by his kindness, and his example struck him so forcibly, that, when his confinement was ended, he resolved to set immediately to work; and, to the astonishment of all who knew him, soon became remarkable for industry: he was found early and late at his work, established a new character, and for ever lost the name of *Lazy Lawrence.*

'Waste Not, Want Not; or, Two Strings to Your Bow'

Mr. Gresham, a Bristol merchant, who had, by honourable industry and economy, accumulated a considerable fortune, retired from business to a new house, which he had built upon the Downs, near Clifton.[19] Mr. Gresham, however, did not imagine, that a new house, alone, could make him happy: he did not propose, to live in idleness and extravagance; for such a life would have been equally incompatible with his habits and his principles. He was fond of children, and as he had no sons, he determined to adopt one of his relations. He had two nephews, and he invited both of them to his house, that he might have an opportunity of judging of their dispositions, and of the habits which they had acquired.

Hal and Benjamin, Mr. Gresham's nephews, were about ten years old; they had been educated very differently: Hal was the son of the elder branch of the family; his father was a gentleman, who spent rather more than he could afford; and Hal, from the example of the servants in his father's family, with whom he had passed the first years of his childhood, learned to waste more of everything than he used.[20] He had been told, that "gentlemen should be above being careful and saving"; and he had unfortunately imbibed a notion, that extravagance is the sign of a generous, and economy of an avaricious disposition.

Benjamin*, on the contrary, had been taught habits of care and foresight: his father had but a very small fortune, and was

---

* Benjamin, so called from Dr. Benjamin Franklin.

anxious, that his son should early learn, that œconomy ensures independence, and sometimes puts it in the power of those who are not very rich to be very generous.[21]

The morning after these two boys arrived at their uncle's, they were eager to see all the rooms in the house. Mr. Gresham accompanied them, and attended to their remarks, and exclamations.

"Oh! What an excellent motto!"—exclaimed Ben, when he read the following words, which were written in large characters, over the chimney-piece, in his uncle's spacious kitchen—

WASTE NOT, WANT NOT.

"Waste not, want not!" repeated his cousin Hal, in rather a contemptuous tone;—"I think it looks stingy to servants; and no gentleman's servants, cooks especially, would like to have such a mean motto always staring them in the face."

Ben, who was not so conversant as his cousin in the ways of cooks and gentlemen's servants, made no reply to these observations.

Mr. Gresham was called away whilst his nephews were looking at the other rooms in the house. Some time afterwards, he heard their voices in the hall.

"Boys," said he, "what are you doing there?"

"Nothing, sir," said Hal; "you were called away from us; and we did not know which way to go."

"And have you nothing to do?" said Mr. Gresham.

"No, sir! nothing," answered Hal, in a careless tone, like one who was well content with the state of habitual idleness.

"No, sir, nothing!" replied Ben, in a voice of lamentation.

"Come," said Mr. Gresham, "if you have nothing to do, lads, will you unpack these two parcels for me?"

The two parcels were exactly alike, both of them well tied up with good whip-cord.—Ben took his parcel to a table, and, after breaking off the sealing wax, began carefully to examine the knot, and then to untie it. Hal stood still, exactly in the spot where the parcel was put into his hands, and tried first at one corner, and then at another, to pull the string off by force: "I wish these people wouldn't tie up their parcels so tight, as if they were never to be undone," cried he, as he tugged at the cord; and he pulled the knot closer instead of loosening it.

"Ben! Why, how did ye get yours undone, man?—What's in your parcel?—I wonder what is in mine. I wish I could get this string off—I must cut it."

"Oh, no," said Ben, who now had undone the last knot of his parcel, and who drew out the length of string with exultation, "don't cut it, Hal—look what a nice cord this is, and your's is the same; it's a pity to cut it; '*Waste not, want not!*' you know."

"Pooh!" said Hal, "what signifies a bit of packthread?"

"It is whip-cord," said Ben.

"Well, whip-cord! What signifies a bit of whip-cord! You can get a bit of whip-cord twice as long as that for two-pence; and who cares for two-pence! Not I, for one! So here it goes," cried Hal, drawing out his knife; and he cut the cord, precipitately, in sundry places.

"Lads! Have you undone the parcels for me?" said Mr. Gresham, opening the parlour door as he spoke.

"Yes, sir," cried Hal; and he dragged off his half cut, half entangled string—"here's the parcel."

"And here's my parcel, uncle; and here's the string," said Ben.

"You may keep the string for your pains," said Mr. Gresham.

"Thank you, sir," said Ben: "what an excellent whip-cord it is!"

"And you, Hal,"—continued Mr. Gresham—"you may keep your string too, if it will be of any use to you."

"It will be of no use to me, thank you, sir," said Hal.

"No, I am afraid not, if this be it," said his uncle, taking up the jagged, knotted remains of Hal's cord.

A few days after this, Mr. Gresham gave to each of his nephews a new top.

"But how's this," said Hal; "these tops have no strings;—what shall we do for strings?"

"I have a string that will do very well for mine," said Ben; and he pulled out of his pocket the fine, long smooth string, which had tied up the parcel. With this he soon set up his top, which spun admirably well.

"Oh, how I wish I had but a string," said Hal: "What shall I do for a string?—I'll tell you what; I can use the string that goes round my hat!"

"But then," said Ben, "what will you do for a hat-band?"

"I'll manage to do without one," said Hal: and he took the string off his hat for his top.—It soon was worn through; and he split his top by driving the peg too tightly into it. His cousin Ben let him set up his the next day; but Hal was not more fortunate or more careful when he meddled with other people's things than when he managed his own. He had scarcely played half an hour before he split it, by driving in the peg too violently.

Ben bore this misfortune with good humour—"Come," said he, "it can't be helped: but give me the string, because *that* may still be of use for something else."

It happened some time afterwards, that a lady, who had been intimately acquainted with Hal's mother at Bath, that is to say, who had frequently met her at the card-table during the winter, now arrived at Clifton. She was informed by his mother, that Hal was at Mr. Gresham's; and her sons, who were friends of his, came to see him, and invited him to spend the next day with them.

Hal joyfully accepted the invitation. He was always glad to go out to dine, because it gave him something to do, something to think of, or, at least, something to say.—Besides this, he had been educated to think it was a fine thing, to visit fine people; and Lady Diana Sweepstakes (for that was the name of his mother's acquaintance), was a very fine lady; and her two sons intended to be very *great* gentlemen.

He was in a prodigious hurry when these young gentlemen knocked at his uncle's door the next day; but just as he got to the hall door, little Patty called to him from the top of the stairs, and told him, that he had dropped his pocket handkerchief.

"Pick it up, then, and bring it to me quick, can't you child," cried Hal, "for Lady Di's sons are waiting for me."

Little Patty did not know any thing about Lady Di's sons; but as she was very good-natured, and saw that her cousin Hal was, for some reason or other, in a desperate hurry, she ran down stairs as fast as she possibly could, towards the landing place, where the handkerchief lay;—but, alas! before she reached the handkerchief, she fell, rolled down a whole flight of stairs, and, when her fall was at last stopped by the landing place, she did not cry, but she writhed, as if she was in great pain.

"Where are you hurt, my love?" said Mr. Gresham, who came instantly, on hearing the noise of some one falling down stairs. "Where are you hurt, my dear?"

"Here, papa," said the little girl, touching her ankle, which she had decently covered with her gown; "I believe I'm hurt here, but not much," added she, trying to rise; "only it hurts me when I move."

"I'll carry you; don't move then," said her father; and he took her up in his arms.

"My shoe, I've lost one of my shoes," said she.

Ben looked for it upon the stairs, and he found it sticking in a loop of whipcord, which was entangled round one of the banisters. When this cord was drawn forth, it appeared that it was the very same jagged, entangled piece, which Hal had pulled off his parcel. He had diverted himself with running up and down stairs, whipping the banisters with it, as he thought he could convert it to no better use; and, with his usual carelessness, he at last left it hanging just where he happened to throw it when the dinner bell rang. Poor little Patty's ankle was terribly sprained, and Hal reproached himself for his folly, and would have reproached himself longer, perhaps, if Lady Di Sweepstake's sons had not hurried him away.

In the evening, Patty could not run about as she used to do but she sat upon the sofa, and she said that "She did not feel the pain of her ankle *so much*, whilst Ben was so good as to play at *jack-straws* with her."

"That's right, Ben; never be ashamed of being good-natured to those who are younger and weaker than your self," said his uncle, smiling at seeing him produce his whip-cord, to indulge his little cousin with a game at her favourite cat's-cradle.[22] "I shall not think you one bit less manly, because I see you playing at cat's cradle with a little child of six years old."

Hal, however, was not precisely of his uncle's opinion; for when he returned in the evening, and saw Ben playing with his little cousin, he could not help smiling contemptuously, and asked if he had been playing at cat's-cradle all night. In heedless manner he made some inquiries after Patty's sprained ankle, and then he ran on to tell all the news he had heard at Lady Diana Sweepstake's— news which he thought would make him appear a person of vast importance.

"Do you know, uncle—Do you know, Ben," said he—"there's to be the most *famous* doings, that ever were heard of upon the

Downs here, the first day of next month, which will be in a fort-night, thank my stars! I wish the fortnight was over; I shall think of nothing else, I know, till that happy day comes!"

Mr. Gresham inquired, why the first of September was to be so much happier than any other day in the year.

"Why," replied Hal, "Lady Diana Sweepstakes, you know, is a *famous* rider, and archer, and *all that*."

"Very likely," said Mr. Gresham soberly;—"but what then?"

"Dear uncle!" cried Hal, "but you shall hear. There's to be a race upon the Downs the first of September, and after the race there's to be an archery meeting for the ladies, and Lady Diana Sweepstakes is to be one of them. And after the ladies have done shooting—now, Ben, comes the best part of it!—we boys are to have our turn, and Lady Di is to give a prize, to the best marksman amongst us, of a very handsome bow and arrow! Do you know I've been practising already, and I'll show you to-morrow, as soon as it comes home, the *famous* bow and arrow, that Lady Diana has given me: but, perhaps," added he, with a scornful laugh, "you like a cat's cradle better than a bow and arrow."

Ben made no reply to this taunt at the moment; but the next day, when Hal's new bow and arrow came home, he convinced him, that he knew how to use it very well.

"Ben," said his uncle, "you seem to be a good marksman, though you have not boasted of yourself. I'll give you a bow and arrow, and, perhaps, if you practise, you may make yourself an archer before the first of September; and, in the mean time, you will not wish the fortnight to be over, for you will have something to do."

"Oh, sir," interrupted Hal, "but if you mean, that Ben should put in for the prize, he must have a uniform."

"Why *must* he?" said Mr. Gresham.

"Why, sir, because every body has—I mean every body that's any body;—Lady Diana was talking about the uniform all dinner time, and it's settled all about it, except the buttons; the young Sweepstakes are to get theirs made first for patterns: they are to be white, faced with green; and they'll look very handsome, I'm sure; and I shall write to mamma to-night, as Lady Diana bid me, about mine; and I shall tell her, to be sure, to answer my letter, without fail, by return of the post and then, if mamma makes no objection, which I know she won't, because she never thinks much about expense, and all that—then I shall bespeak my uniform, and get it made by the same tailor, that makes for Lady Diana and the young Sweepstakes."

"Mercy upon us!" said Mr. Gresham, who was almost stunned by the rapid vociferation, with which this long speech about a uniform was pronounced. "I don't pretend to understand these things," added he, with an air of simplicity; "but we will inquire, Ben, into the necessity of the case; and if it is necessary—or if you think it necessary, that you should have a uniform—why—I'll give you one."

"*You*, uncle!—Will you *indeed*?" exclaimed Hal with amazement painted in his countenance. "Well, that's the last thing in the world I should have expected!—You are not at all the sort of person I should have thought would care about a uniform; and now I should have supposed, you'd have thought it extravagant, to have a coat on purpose only for one day; and I'm sure Lady Diana Sweepstakes thought as I do; for when I told her of that motto over your kitchen chimney, WASTE NOT, WANT NOT, she laughed, and said, that I had better not talk to you about uniforms; and that my mother was the proper person to write to about my uniform: but I'll tell Lady Diana, uncle, how good you are, and how much she was mistaken."

"Take care how you do that," said Mr. Gresham; "for perhaps the Lady was not mistaken."

"Nay, did not you say, just now, you would give poor Ben a uniform?"

"I said, I would, if he thought it necessary to have one."

"Oh, I'll answer for it, he'll think it necessary," said Hal, laughing, "because it is necessary."

"Allow him, at least, to judge for himself," said Mr. Gresham.

"My dear uncle, but I assure you," said Hal, earnestly, "there's no judging about the matter, because really, upon my word, Lady Diana said distinctly that her sons were to have uniforms, white faced with green, and a green and white cockade in their hats."

"Maybe so," said Mr. Gresham, still with the same look of calm simplicity, "put on your hats, boys, and come with me. I know a gentleman, whose sons are to be at this archery meeting; and we will inquire into all the particulars from him. Then, after we have seen him (it is not eleven o'clock yet), we shall have time enough to walk on to Bristol, and choose the cloth for Ben's uniform, if it is necessary."

"I cannot tell what to make of all he says," whispered Hal, as he reached down his hat; "do you, think, Ben, he means to give you this uniform, or not?"

"I think," said Ben, "that he means to give me one, if it is necessary or, as he said, if I think it is necessary."

"And that, to be sure, you will; won't you? Or else you'll be a great fool, I know, after all I've told you. How can any one in the world know so much about the matter, as *I*, who have dined with Lady Diana Sweepstakes but yesterday, and heard all about it, from beginning to end; and as for this gentleman, that we are going to, I'm sure, if he knows any thing about the matter, he'll say exactly the same as I do."

"We shall hear," said Ben, with a degree of composure, which Hal could by no means comprehend, when a uniform was in question.

The gentleman, upon whom Mr. Gresham called, had three sons, who were all to be at this archery meeting; and they unanimously assured him, in the presence of Hal and Ben, that they had never thought of buying uniforms for this grand occasion, and that, amongst the number of their acquaintance, they knew of but three boys, whose friends intended to be at such an *unnecessary* expense. Hal stood amazed.—"Such are the varieties of opinion upon all the grand affairs of life," said Mr. Gresham, looking at his nephews—"What amongst one set of people you hear asserted to be absolutely necessary, you will hear, from another set of people is quite unnecessary—All that can be done, my dear boys, in these difficult cases, is to judge for yourselves, which opinions, and which people, are the most reasonable."

Hal, who had been more accustomed to think of what was fashionable, than of what was reasonable, without at all considering the good sense of what his uncle said to him, replied, with childish petulance, "Indeed, sir, I don't know what other people think; but I only know what Lady Diana Sweepstakes said."

The name of Lady Diana Sweepstakes, Hal thought, must impress all present with respect: he was highly astonished, when, as he looked round, he saw a smile of contempt upon every one's countenance; and he was yet further bewildered, when he heard her spoken of as a very silly, extravagant, ridiculous woman, whose opinion no prudent person would ask upon any subject, and whose example was to be shunned, instead of being imitated.

"Aye, my dear Hal," said his uncle, smiling at his look of amazement, "these are some of the things that young people must learn from experience. All the world do not agree in opinion about characters: you will hear the same person admired in one company, and blamed in another; so that we must still come round to the same point, *Judge for yourself.*"

Hal's thoughts were, however, at present, too full of the uniform, to allow his judgment to act with perfect impartiality. As soon as their visit was over, and all the time they walked down the hill from Prince's Buildings towards Bristol, he continued to repeat nearly the same arguments, which he had formerly used, respecting necessity, the uniform, and Lady Diana Sweepstakes.[23]

To all this Mr. Gresham made no reply; and longer had the young gentleman expatiated upon the subject which had strongly seized upon his imagination, had not his senses been forcibly assailed at this instant by the delicious odours and tempting sight of certain cakes and jellies in a pastry-cook's shop.

"Oh, uncle," said he, as his uncle was going to turn the corner to pursue the road to Bristol, "look at those jellies," pointing to a confectioner's shop, "I must buy some of those good things; for I've got some half-pence in my pocket."

"Your having half-pence in your pocket is an excellent reason for eating," said Mr. Gresham, smiling.

"But I really am hungry," said Hal; "you know, uncle, it is a good while since breakfast."

His uncle, who was desirous to see his nephews act without restraint, that he might judge of their characters, bid them do as they pleased.

"Come, then, Ben, if you've any half-pence in your pocket."

"I'm not hungry," said Ben.

"I suppose *that* means, that you've no half-pence," said Hal, laughing, with the look of superiority, which he had been taught to think *the rich* might assume towards those, who were convicted either of poverty or economy.

"Waste not, want not," said Ben to himself. Contrary to his cousin's surmise, he happened to have two penny-worth of half-pence actually in his pocket.

At the very moment Hal stepped into the pastry-cook's shop, a poor industrious man with a wooden leg, who usually sweeps the dirty corner of the walk which turns at this spot to the Wells,[24] held his hat to Ben, who, after glancing his eye at the petitioner's well-worn broom, instantly produced his two-pence. "I wish I had more half-pence for you, my good man," said he; "but I've only two-pence."

Hal came out of Mr. Millar's, the confectioner's shop, with a hat-full of cakes in his hand.

Mr. Millar's dog was sitting on the flags before the door; and he looked up, with a wistful, begging eye, at Hal, who was eating a queen-cake.

Hal, who was wasteful even in his good-nature, threw a whole queen-cake to the dog, who swallowed it for a single mouthful.

"There goes two-pence in the form of a queen-cake," said Mr. Gresham.

Hal next offered some of his cakes to his uncle and cousin; but they thanked him, and refused to eat any, because, they said, they were not hungry; so he ate and ate, as he walked along, till at last he stopped, and said, "This bun tastes so bad after the queen-cakes, I can't bear it!" and he was going to fling it from him into the river.

"Oh, it is a pity to waste that good bun; we may be glad of it yet," said Ben; "give it to me, rather than throw it away."

"Why, I thought you said you were not hungry," said Hal.

"True, I am not hungry now; but that is no reason why I should never be hungry again."

"Well, there is the cake for you, take it; for it has made me sick; and, I don't care what becomes of it."

Ben folded the refuse bit of his cousin's bun in a piece of paper, and put it into his pocket.

"I'm beginning to be exceeding tired, or sick, or something," said Hal, "and as there is a stand of coaches somewhere here-abouts, had not we better take a coach, instead of walking all the way to Bristol?"

"For a stout archer," said Mr. Gresham, "you are more easily tired, than one might have expected. However, with all my heart;

let us take a coach; for Ben asked me to show him the cathedral yesterday; and I believe I should find it rather too much for me to walk so far, though I am not sick with eating good things."

"*The cathedral!*" said Hal, after he had been seated in the coach about a quarter of an hour, and had somewhat recovered from his sickness—"The cathedral! Why, are we only going to Bristol to see the cathedral!—I thought we came out to see about a uniform."

There was a dullness, and melancholy kind of stupidity, in Hal's countenance, as he pronounced these words like one wakening from a dream, which made both his uncle and cousin burst out a laughing.

"Why," said Hal, who was now piqued, "I'm sure you *did* say, uncle, you would go to Mr.—'s. to choose the cloth for the uniform."

"Very true; and so I will," said Mr. Gresham; "but we need not make a whole morning's work, need we, of looking at a piece of cloth?—Cannot we see a uniform and a cathedral both in one morning?"

They went first to the cathedral. Hal's head was too full of the uniform, to take any notice of the painted window, which immediately caught Ben's unembarrassed attention. He looked at the large stained figures on the gothic window; and he observed their coloured shadows on the floor and walls.[25]

Mr. Gresham, who perceived that he was eager on all subjects to gain information, took this opportunity of telling him several things about the lost art of painting on glass, gothic arches, &c. which Hal thought extremely tiresome.

"Come! come! we shall be late indeed," said Hal; "surely you've looked long enough, Ben, at this blue and red window."

"I'm only thinking about these coloured shadows," said Ben.

"I can show you, when we go home, Ben," said his uncle, "an entertaining paper upon such shadows."[†][26]

"Hark!" cried Ben, "did you hear that noise?"

They all listened and they heard a bird singing, in the cathedral.

"It's our old robin, sir," said the lad, who had opened the cathedral door for them.

[†] Vide Priestly's History of Vision, chapter on Coloured Shadows.

"Yes," said Mr. Gresham, "there he is, boys—look—perched upon the organ: he often sits there, and sings, whilst the organ is playing."—"And," continued the lad who showed the cathedral, "he has lived here these many, many winters[‡]; they say, he is fifteen years old; and he is so tame, poor fellow, that, if I had a bit of bread, he'd come down, and feed in my hand."

"I've a bit of a bun here," cried Ben, joyfully, producing the remains of the bun which Hal but an hour before would have thrown away. "Pray let us see the poor robin eat out of your hand."

The lad crumbled the bun, and called to the robin, who fluttered and chirped, and seemed rejoiced at the sight of the bread; but yet he did not come down from his pinnacle on the organ.

"He is afraid of *us*," said Ben; "he is not used to eat before strangers, I suppose."

"Ah, no, sir," said the young man, with a deep sigh, "that is not the thing: he is used enough to eat afore company; time was, he'd have come down for me, before ever so many fine folks, and have eat his crumbs out of my hand, at my first call; but, poor fellow, it's not his fault now: he does not know me now, sir, since my accident, because of this great black patch."

The young man put his hand to his right eye, which was covered with a huge black patch.

Ben asked what *accident* he meant; and the lad told him, that, but a few weeks ago, he had lost the sight of his eye by the stroke of a stone, which reached him as he was passing under the rocks at Clifton, unluckily, when the workmen were blasting.[27]

"I don't mind so much for myself sir," said the lad; "but I can't work so well now, as I used to do before my accident, for my old mother, who has had a stroke of the palsy; and I've a many little brothers and sisters, not well able yet to get their own livelihoods though they be as willing, as willing can be."

"Where does your mother live?" said Mr. Gresham.

"Hard by, sir, just close to the church here: it was *her*, that always had the showing of it to strangers, till she lost the use of her poor limbs."

[‡] This is true. [*Editor's note:* Presumably Edgeworth draws here upon her own experiences while in Clifton.]

"Shall we, may we, uncle, go that way?—This is the house; is not it?" said Ben, when they went out of the cathedral.

They went into the house: it was rather a hovel than a house; but, poor as it was, it was as neat as misery could make it.

The old woman was sitting up in her wretched bed, winding worsted; four meagre, ill-clothed, pale children, were all busy, some of them sticking pins in papers for the pin-maker, and others sorting rags for the paper-maker.

"What a horrid place it is," said Hal, sighing, "I did not know there were such shocking places in the world. I've often seen terrible-looking, tumble-down places, as we drove through the town in mamma's carriage; but then I did not know who lived in them; and I never saw the inside of any of them. It is very dreadful, indeed, to think that people are forced to live in this way. I wish mamma would send me some more pocket-money, that I might do something for them. I had half-a-crown but," continued he, feeling in his pockets, "I'm afraid I spent the last shilling of it this morning, upon those cakes that made me sick. I wish I had my shilling now, I'd give it to these poor people."

Ben, though he was all this time silent, was as sorry as his talkative cousin for all these poor people. But there was some difference between the sorrow of these two boys. Hal, after he was again seated in the hackney-coach, and had rattled through the busy streets of Bristol for a few minutes, quite forgot the spectacle of misery, which he had seen; and the gay shops in Wine-street, and the idea of his green and white uniform wholly occupied his imagination.[28]

"Now for our uniforms," cried he, as he jumped eagerly out of the coach, when his uncle stopped at the woollen-draper's door.

"Uncle," said Ben, stopping Mr. Gresham before he got out of the carriage, "I don't think a uniform is at all necessary for me. I'm very much obliged to you; but I would rather not have one. I have a very good coat; and I think it would be waste."

"Well, let me get out of the carriage, and we will see about it," said Mr. Gresham; "perhaps the sight of the beautiful green and white cloth, and the epaulettes (have you ever considered the epaulettes?) may tempt you to change your mind."

"O no," said Ben, laughing; "I shall not change my mind."

The green cloth, and the white cloth, and the epaulettes, were produced, to Hal's infinite satisfaction. His uncle took up a pen, and calculated for a few minutes; then, showing the back of the letter, upon which he was writing, to his nephews, "Cast up these sums, boys," said he, "and tell me whether I am right."

"Ben, do you do it," said Hal, a little embarrassed; "I am not quick at figures."

Ben *was*, and he went over his uncle's calculation very expeditiously.

"It is right, is it?" said Mr. Gresham.

"Yes, sir, quite right."

"Then by this calculation, I find I could, for less than half the money your uniforms would cost, purchase for each of you boys a warm great coat, which you will want, I have a notion, this winter upon the downs."

"O, sir," said Hal, with an alarmed look; "but it is not winter *yet*; it is not cold weather *yet*. We shan't want great coats *yet*."

"Don't you remember how cold we were, Hal, the day before yesterday, in that sharp wind, when we were flying our kite upon the Downs; and winter will come, though it is not come yet. I am sure, I should like to have a good warm great coat very much."

Mr. Gresham took six guineas out of his purse; and he placed three of them before Hal, and three before Ben.

"Young gentlemen," said he, "I believe your uniforms would come to about three guineas a-piece. Now I will lay out this money for you, just as you please. Hal, what say you?"

"Why, sir," said Hal, "a great coat is a good thing, to be sure; and then, after the great coat, as you said it would only cost half as much as the uniform, there would be some money to spare, would not there?"

"Yes, my dear, about five and twenty shillings."

"Five and twenty shillings!—I could buy and do a great many things, to be sure, with five and twenty shillings: but then, *the thing is*, I must go without the uniform, if I have the great coat."

"Certainly," said his uncle.

"Ah!" said Hal, sighing, as he looked at the epaulette, "uncle, if you would not be displeased, if I choose the uniform—."

"I shall not be displeased at your choosing whatever you like best," said Mr. Gresham.

"Well, then, thank you, sir; I think I had better have the uniform, because, if I have not the uniform now directly, it will be of no use to me, as the archery meeting is the week after next, you know; and as to the great coat, perhaps, between this time and the *very* cold weather, which, perhaps, won't be till Christmas, papa will buy a great coat for me; and I'll ask mamma to give me some pocket-money to give away, and she will, perhaps."

To all this conclusive, conditional reasoning, which depended upon *perhaps*, three times repeated, Mr. Gresham made no reply; but he immediately bought the uniform for Hal, and desired that it should be sent to Lady Diana Sweepstakes' sons' tailor, to be made up. The measure of Hal's happiness was now complete.

"And how am I to lay out the three guineas for you, Ben?" said Mr. Gresham; "speak, what do you wish for first?"

"A great coat, uncle, if you please."

Mr. Gresham bought the coat; and, after it was paid for, five and twenty shillings of Ben's three guineas remained.

"What next, my boy," said his uncle.

"Arrows, uncle, if you please: three arrows."

"My dear, I promised you a bow and arrows."

"No, uncle, you only said a bow."

"Well, I meant a bow and arrows. I'm glad you are so exact, however. It is better to claim less than more than what is promised. The three arrows you shall have. But, go on; how shall I dispose of these five and twenty shillings for you?"

"In clothes, if you will be so good, uncle, for that poor boy, who has the great black patch on his eye."

"I always believed," said Mr. Gresham, shaking hands with Ben, "that economy and generosity were the best friends, instead of being enemies, as some silly, extravagant people would have us think them. Choose the poor blind boy's coat, my dear nephew, and pay for it. There's no occasion for my praising you about the matter: your best reward is in your own mind, child; and you want no other, or I'm mistaken. Now jump into the coach, boys, and let's be off. We shall be late, I'm afraid," continued he, as the coach drove on; "but I must let you stop, Ben, with your goods, at the poor boy's door."

When they came to the house, Mr. Gresham opened the coach-door, and Ben jumped out with his parcel under his arm.

"Stay, stay! You must take me with you," said his pleased uncle; "I like to see people made happy, as well as you do."

"And so do I too!" said Hal; "let me come with you. I almost wish my uniform was not gone to the tailor's, so I do."

And when he saw the look of delight and gratitude, with which the poor boy received the clothes, which Ben gave him; and when he heard the mother and children thank him, Hal sighed, and said, "Well, I hope mamma will give me some more pocket-money soon."

Upon his return home, however, the sight of the *famous* bow and arrow, which Lady Diana Sweepstakes had sent him, recalled to his imagination all the joys of his green and white uniform; and he no longer wished, that it had not been sent to the tailor's.

"But I don't understand, cousin Hal, said little Patty, why you call this bow a *famous* bow: you say *famous* very often; and I don't know exactly what it means—a *famous* uniform—*famous* doings— I remember you said there are to be *famous* doings, the first of September, upon the Downs—What does *famous* mean?"

"O, why *famous* means—Now don't you know what *famous* means?—It means—It is a word that people say—It is the fashion to say it—It means—it means *famous*."

Patty laughed, and said, "*This* does not explain it to me."

"No," said Hal, "nor can it be explained: if you don't understand it, that's not my fault: every body but little children, I suppose, understands it; but there's no explaining *those sort* of words, if you don't *take them* at once. There's to be *famous* doings upon the Downs, the first of September; that is, grand, fine.—In short, what does it signify talking any longer, Patty, about the matter?—Give me my bow; for I must go out upon the Downs, and practise."

Ben accompanied him with the bow and the three arrows, which his uncle had now given to him; and, every day, these two boys went out upon the Downs, and practised shooting with indefatigable perseverance. Where equal pains are taken, success is usually found to be pretty nearly equal. Our two archers, by constant practice, became expert marksmen; and, before the day of trial, they were so exactly matched in point of dexterity, that it was scarcely possible to decide which was superior.

The long-expected first of September at length arrived. "What sort of a day is it?" was the first question that was asked by Hal and Ben, the moment that they wakened.

The sun shone bright but there was a sharp and high wind.

"Ha!" said Ben, "I shall be glad of my good great coat to-day; for I've a notion it will be rather cold upon the Downs, especially when we are standing still, as we must, whilst all the people are shooting."

"O, never mind! I don't think I shall feel it cold at all," said Hal, as he dressed himself in his new green and white uniform; and he viewed himself with much complacency.

"Good morning to you, uncle; how do you do?" said he, in a voice of exultation, when he entered the breakfast-room.

How do you do? seemed rather to mean, How do you like me in my uniform?

And his uncle's cool, "Very well, thank you, Hal," disappointed him, as it seemed only to say, "Your uniform makes no difference in my opinion of you."

Even little Patty went on eating her breakfast much as usual, and talked of the pleasure of walking with her father to the Downs, and of all the little things which interested her, so that Hal's epaulettes were not the principal object in any one's imagination but his own.

"Papa," said Patty, "as we go up the hill where there is so much red mud, I must take care to pick my way nicely; and I must hold up my frock, as you desired me; and perhaps you will be so good, if I am not troublesome to lift me over the very bad place where there are no stepping-stones. My ankle is entirely well, and I'm glad of that, or else I should not be able to walk so far as to the Downs. How good you were to me, Ben, when I was in pain, the day I sprained my ankle: you played at jack straws, and at cat's cradle, with me—Oh, that puts me in mind—Here are your gloves, which I asked you that night to let me mend. I've been a great while about them, but are not they very neatly mended, papa?— Look at the sewing."

"I am not a very good judge of sewing, my dear little girl," said Mr. Gresham, examining the work with a close and scrupulous eye; "but, in my opinion, here is one stitch, that is rather too long; the white teeth are not quite even."

"Oh, papa, I'll take out that long tooth in a minute," said Patty, laughing: "I did not think that you would have observed it so soon."

"I would not have you trust to my blindness," said her father, stroking her head fondly: "I observe every thing. I observe, for instance, that you are a grateful little girl, and that you are glad to be of use to those, who have been kind to you; and for this I forgive you the long stitch."

"But it's out, it's out, papa," said Patty, "and the next time your gloves want mending, Ben, I'll mend them better."

"They are very nice, I think," said Ben, drawing them on; "and I am much obliged to you; I was just wishing I had a pair of gloves to keep my fingers warm to-day, for I never can shoot well when my hands are numbed. Look, Hal—you know how ragged these gloves were; you said they were good for nothing but to throw away; now look, there's not a hole in them," said he, spreading his fingers.

"Now is it not very extraordinary," said Hal to himself, "that they should go on so long talking about an old pair of gloves, without saying scarcely a word about my new uniform! Well, the young Sweepstakes and Lady Diana will talk enough about it; that's one comfort."

"Is not it time, to think of setting out, sir?" said Hal to his uncle. "The company, you know, are to meet at the Ostrich at twelve, and the race to begin at one, and Lady Diana's horses, I know, were ordered to be at the door at ten."

Mr. Stephen, the butler, here interrupted the hurrying young gentleman in his calculations—"There's a poor lad, sir, below, with a great black patch on his right eye, who is come from Bristol, and wants to speak a word with the young gentlemen, if you please. I told him, they were just going out with you, but he says he won't detain them above half a minute."

"Show him up, show him up," said Mr. Gresham.

"But I suppose," said Hal, with a sigh, "that Stephen mistook, when he said the young *gentlemen*; he only wants to see Ben, I dare say; I'm sure he has no reason to want to see me. Here he comes— Oh, Ben, he is dressed in the new coat you gave him," whispered Hal, who was really a good-natured boy, though extravagant. "How much better he looks than he did in the ragged coat! Ah! He looked at you first, Ben;—and well he may!"

The boy bowed, without any cringing servility, but with an open, decent freedom in his manner, which expressed that he had been obliged, but that he knew his young benefactor was not thinking of the obligation. He made as little distinction as possible between his bows to the two cousins.

"As I was sent with a message, by the clerk of our parish, to Redland chapel,[29] out on the Downs, to-day, sir," said he to Mr. Gresham, "knowing your house lay in my way, my mother, sir, bid me call, and make bold to offer the young gentlemen two little worsted balls that she has worked for them," continued the lad, pulling out of his pocket two worsted balls worked in green and orange-coloured stripes: "They are but poor things, sir, she bid me to say, to look at, but, considering she has but one hand to work with, and *that* her left hand, you'll not despise 'em, we hopes."

He held the balls to Ben and Hal.—"They are both alike, gentlemen," said he; "if you'll be pleased to take 'em, they're better than they look, for they bound higher than your head; cut the cork round for the inside myself, which was all I could do."

"They are nice balls, indeed; we are much obliged to you," said the boys as they received them, and they proved them immediately. The balls struck the floor with a delightful sound, and rebounded higher than Mr. Gresham's head. Little Patty clapped her hands joyfully: but now a thundering double rap at the door was heard.

"The master Sweepstakes, sir," said Stephen, "are come for Master Hal; they say, that all the young gentlemen who have archery uniforms are to walk together, in a body, I think they say, sir; and they are to parade along the Well-walk, they desired me to say, sir, with a drum and fife, and so up the hill by Prince's Place,[30] and all to go upon the Downs together, to the place of meeting. I am not sure I'm right, sir, for both the young gentlemen spoke at once, and the wind is very high at the street door, so that I could not well make out all they said; but I believe this is the sense of it."

"Yes, yes," said Hal, eagerly, "it's all right; I know that is just what was settled the day I dined at Lady Diana's; and Lady Diana and a great party of gentlemen are to ride—"

"Well, that is nothing to the purpose," interrupted Mr. Gresham, "Don't keep these Master Sweepstakes waiting; decide—do you choose to go with them, or with us?"

"Sir—uncle—sir, you know, since all the *uniforms* agreed to go together—"

"Off with you, then, Mr. Uniform, if you mean to go," said Mr. Gresham.

Hal ran down stairs in such a hurry, that he forgot his bow and arrows.—Ben discovered this, when he went to fetch his own; and the lad from Bristol, who had been ordered by Mr. Gresham to eat his breakfast, before he proceeded to Redland chapel, heard Ben talking about his cousin's bow and arrows.

"I know," said Ben, "he will be sorry not to have his bow with him, because here are the green knots tied to it, to match his cockade; and he said, that the boys were all to carry their bows, as part of the show."

"If you'll give me leave, sir," said the poor Bristol lad, "I shall have plenty of time; and I'll run down to the Well-walk after the young gentleman, and take him his bow and arrows."

"Will you? I shall be much obliged to you," said Ben; and away went the boy with the bow that was ornamented with green ribands.

The public walk leading to the Wells was full of company. The windows of all the houses in St. Vincent's parade were crowded with well-dressed ladies, who were looking out in expectation of the archery procession. Parties of gentlemen and ladies, and a motley crowd of spectators, were seen moving backwards and forwards, under the rocks, on the opposite side of the water. A barge, with coloured streamers flying, was waiting to take up a party, who were going upon the water. The bargemen rested upon their oars, and gazed with broad faces of curiosity upon the busy scene, that appeared on the public walk.

The archers and archeresses were now drawn up on the flags under the semi-circular piazza just before Mrs. Yearsley's library.[31] A little band of children, who had been mustered by Lady Diana Sweepstakes' *spirited exertions*, closed the procession. They were now all in readiness. The drummer only waited for her ladyship's signal; and the archers' corps only waited for her ladyship's word of command to march.

"Where are your bow and arrows, my little man?" said her Ladyship to Hal, as she reviewed her Lilliputian regiment. "You can't march, man, without your arms!"

Hal had dispatched a messenger for his forgotten bow, but the messenger returned not; he looked from side to side in great distress—"O, there's my bow coming, I declare!" cried he—look, I see the bow and the ribands;—look now, between the trees, Charles Sweepstakes, on the Hotwell-walk;—it is coming!"

"But you've kept us all waiting a confounded time," said his impatient friend.

"It is that good-natured poor fellow from Bristol, I protest, that has brought it me; I'm sure I don't deserve it from him," said Hal to himself, when he saw the lad with the black patch on his eye running, quite out of breath, towards him with his bow and arrow.

"Fall back, my good friend, fall back," said the military lady, as soon as he had delivered the bow to Hal; "I mean, stand out of the way, for your great patch cuts no figure amongst us. Don't follow so close, now, as if you belonged to us, pray."

The poor boy had no ambition to partake the triumph; he *fell back* as soon as he understood the meaning of the lady's words. The drum beat, the fife played, the archers marched, the spectators admired. Hal stepped proudly, and felt as if the eyes of the whole universe were upon his epaulettes, or upon the facings of his uniform; whilst all the time he was considered only as part of a show. The walk appeared much shorter than usual, and he was extremely sorry, that Lady Diana, when they were half way up the hill leading to Prince's Place, mounted her horse, because the road was dirty, and all the gentlemen and ladies, who accompanied her, followed her example. "We can leave the children to walk, you know," said she to the gentleman who helped her to mount her horse. "I must call to some of them, though, and leave orders when they are to *join*."

She beckoned; and Hal, who was foremost, and proud to show his alacrity, ran on to receive her Ladyship's orders. Now, as we have before observed, it was a sharp and windy day; and though Lady Diana Sweepstakes was actually speaking to him, and looking at him, he could not prevent his nose from wanting to be blowed: he pulled out his handkerchief, and out rolled the new ball, which had been given to him just before he left home, and which, according to his usual careless habits, he had stuffed into his pocket in his hurry. "O, my new ball!" cried he, as he ran after it. As he stooped to pick it up, he let go his hat, which he had hitherto held on with anxious care; for the hat, though it had a fine green and white cockade, had no band or string round it. The string, as we may recollect, our wasteful hero had used in spinning his top. The hat was too large for his head without this band; a sudden gust of wind blew it off—Lady Diana's horse started, and reared. She was a *famous* horsewoman and sat him to the admiration of all beholders; but there was a puddle of red clay and water in this spot, and her ladyship's uniform-habit was a sufferer by the accident.

"Careless brat!" said she. "Why can't he keep his hat upon his head?"

In the mean time, the wind blew the hat down the hill, and Hal ran after it, amidst the laughter of his kind friends, the young Sweepstakes, and the rest of the little regiment. The hat was lodged, at length, upon a bank. Hall pursued it: he thought this bank was hard, but alas! The moment he set his foot upon it, the foot sunk. He tried to draw it back, his other foot slipped and he fell prostrate, in his green and white uniform, into the treacherous bed of red mud. His companions, who had halted upon the top of the hill, stood laughing spectators of his misfortune.

It happened that the poor boy with the black patch upon his eye, who had been ordered by Lady Diana to "*fall back*," and to "*keep at a distance*," was now coming up the hill; and the moment he saw our fallen hero, he hastened to his assistance. He dragged poor Hal, who was a deplorable spectacle, out of the red mud; the obliging mistress of a lodging-house, as soon as she understood that the young gentleman was nephew to Mr. Gresham, to whom she had formerly let her house, received Hal, covered as he was with dirt.

The poor Bristol lad hastened to Mr. Gresham's for clean stockings and shoes for Hal. He was unwilling to give up his uniform; it was rubbed and rubbed, and a spot here and there was washed out; and he kept continually repeating—"When it's dry it will all brush off; when it's dry, it will all brush off, won't it?"—But soon the fear of being too late at the archery-meeting began to balance the dread of appearing in his stained habiliments; and he now as anxiously repeated, whilst the woman held the wet coat to the fire, "Oh, I shall be too late; indeed, I shall be too late; make haste, it will never dry; hold it nearer—nearer to the fire: I shall lose my turn to shoot; oh, give me the coat; I don't mind how it is, if I can but get it on."

Holding it nearer and nearer to the fire dried it quickly, to be sure, but it shrunk it also; so that it was no easy matter to get the coat on again. However, Hal, who did not see the red splashes, which, in spite of all these operations, were too visible upon his shoulders, and upon the skirt of his white coat, behind, was pretty well satisfied to observe, that there was not one spot upon the facings. "Nobody," said he, "will take notice of my coat behind, I dare say. I think it looks as smart almost as ever!"—and under this persuasion our young archer resumed his bow—with green ribands now no more!—and he pursued his way to the Downs.

All his companions were far out of sight. "I suppose," said he to his friend with the black patch—"I suppose my uncle and Ben had left home, before you went for the shoes and stockings for me?"

"O, yes, sir; the butler said they had been gone to the Downs a matter of a good half hour or more."

Hal trudged on as fast as he possibly could. When he got upon the Downs, he saw numbers of carriages, and crowds of people, all going towards the place of meeting, at the Ostrich. He pressed forwards; he was at first so much afraid of being late, that he did not take notice of the mirth his motley appearance excited in all beholders. At length he reached the appointed spot. There was a great crowd of people: in the midst, he heard Lady Diana's loud voice, betting upon some one, who was just going to shoot at the mark.

"So then the shooting is begun, is it?" said Hal. "Oh, let me in; pray let me into the circle: I'm one of the archers—I am, indeed; don't you see my green and white uniform?"

"Your red and white uniform, you mean," said the man to whom he addressed himself; and the people, as they opened a passage for him, could not refrain from laughing at the mixture of dirt and finery, which he exhibited. In vain, when he got into the midst of the formidable circle, he looked to his friends, the young Sweepstakes, for their countenance and support: they were amongst the most unmerciful of the laughers. Lady Diana also seemed more to enjoy than to pity his condition. "Why could not you keep your hat upon your head, man?" said she, in her masculine tone. "You have been almost the ruin of my poor uniform-habit; but thank God, I've escaped rather better than you have.—Don't stand there, in the middle of the circle, or you'll have an arrow in your eyes just now, I've a notion."

Hal looked round, in search, of better friends—"Oh, where's my uncle? Where's Ben?" said he. He was in such confusion, that, amongst the number of faces, he could scarcely distinguish one from another; but he felt somebody at this moment pull his elbow, and, to his great relief, he heard the friendly voice and saw the good-natured face of his cousin Ben.

"Come back; come behind these people," said Ben; "and put on my great coat; here it is for you."

Right glad was Hal to cover his disgraced uniform with the rough great coat, which he had formerly despised. He pulled the stained, drooping cockade out of his unfortunate hat; and he was now sufficiently recovered from his vexation, to give an intelligible account of his accident to his uncle and Patty, who anxiously inquired what had detained him so long, and what had been the matter. In the midst of the history of his disaster, he was just proving to Patty, that his taking the hat-band to spin his top had nothing to do with his misfortune; and he was at the same time endeavouring to refute his uncle's opinion, that the waste of the whip-cord, that tied the parcel, was the original cause of all his evils, when he was summoned to try his skill with his *famous* bow.

"My hands are numbed, I can scarcely feel," said he, rubbing them, and blowing upon the ends of his fingers.

"Come, come," cried young Sweepstakes, "I'm within one inch of the mark; who'll go nearer, I shall like to see. Shoot away, Hal; but first understand our laws; we settled them before you came upon the green. You are to have three shots, with your own bow and your own arrows; and nobody's to borrow or lend under pretence of other bows being better or worse, or under any pretence.— Do you hear, Hal?"

This young gentleman had good reasons for being so strict in these laws, as he had observed, that none of his companions had such an excellent bow as he had provided for himself. Some of the boys had forgotten to bring more than one arrow with them, and by his cunning regulation, that each person should shoot with their own arrows, many had lost one or two of their shots.

"You are a lucky fellow; you have your three arrows," said young Sweepstakes. "Come, we can't wait while you rub your fingers, man—shoot away!"

Hal was rather surprised at the asperity, with which his friend spoke. He little knew how easily acquaintance, who call themselves friends, can change, when their interest comes in the slightest degree in competition with their friendship. Hurried by his impatient rival, and with his hands so much benumbed, that he could scarcely feel how to fix the arrow in the string, he drew the bow. The arrow was within a quarter of an inch of Master Sweepstakes' mark, which was the nearest that had yet been hit. Hal seized his second arrow—"If I have any luck," said he—But just as he pronounced the word *luck*, and as he bent his bow, the string broke in two, and the bow fell from his hands.

"There, it's all over with you," cried Master Sweepstakes, with a triumphant laugh.

"Here's my bow for him, and welcome," said Ben.

"No, no, sir; that is not fair; that's against the regulation. You may shoot with your own bow, if you choose it; or you may not, just as you think, proper; but you must not lend it, sir."

It was now Ben's turn to make his trial. His first arrow was not successful. His second was exactly as near as Hal's first.

"You have but one more," said Master Sweepstakes:—"now for it!"

Ben, before he ventured his last arrow, prudently examined the string of his bow; and, as he pulled it to try its strength, it cracked.

Master Sweepstakes clapped his hands with loud exultations, and insulting laughter. But his laughter ceased, when our provident hero calmly drew from his pocket an excellent piece of whip-cord.

"The everlasting whip-cord, I declare!" exclaimed Hal, when he saw that it was the very same, that had tied up the parcel.

"Yes," said Ben, as he fastened it to his bow, "I put it into my pocket today, on purpose, because I thought I might happen to want it."

He drew his bow the third and last time.

"O, papa," cried little Patty, as the arrow hit the mark, "it's the nearest; is not it the nearest?"

Master Sweepstakes, with anxiety, examined the hit. There could be no doubt. Ben was victorious! The bow, the prize bow, was now delivered to him; and Hal as he looked at the whip-cord, exclaimed, "How *lucky* this whip-cord has been to you, Ben!"

"It is *lucky*, perhaps, you mean, that he took care of it," said Mr. Gresham.

"Aye," said Hal, "very true; he might well say, 'Waste not, want not;' it is a good thing to have two strings to one's bow."

'The Good Aunt'

Charles Howard was left an orphan when he was very young: his father had dissipated a large fortune, and lost his life in a duel, about some *debt of honour*, which had been contracted at the gaming-table. Without fortune, and without friends, this poor boy would probably have lived and died in wretchedness, but for the humanity of his good aunt, Mrs. Frances Howard. This lady possessed a considerable fortune, which, in the opinion of some of her acquaintance, was her highest merit: others respected her as the branch of an ancient family: some courted her acquaintance because she was visited by the best company in town: and many were ambitious of being introduced to her because they were sure of meeting at her house several of those distinguished literary characters, who throw a radiance upon all who can contrive to get within the circle of their glories. Some few, some very few of Mrs. Howard's acquaintance, admired her for her real worth, and merited the name of friends.

She was a young and cheerful woman, when she first undertook the education of her little nephew: she had the courage to resist the allurements of dissipation, or all that by her sex are usually thought allurements. She had the courage, at six and twenty, to apply herself seriously to the cultivation of her understanding; she educated herself, that she might be able to fulfil the important duty of educating a child. Hers was not the foolish fondness of a foolish aunt; she loved her nephew, and she wished to educate him, so that her affection might increase, instead of diminishing, as he grew up. By associating early pleasure with reading, little Charles soon became fond of it; he was never forced to read books which he did not understand: his aunt used, when he was very young, to read aloud to him any thing entertaining, that she met with; and whenever she perceived, by his eye, that his attention was not fixed, she stopped. When he was able to read fluently to himself, she selected for him passages from books, which she thought would excite his curiosity to know *more*; and she was not in a hurry to cram him with knowledge, but rather anxious to prevent his growing appetite for literature from being early satiated.—She always encouraged him to talk to her freely about what he read, and to tell her when he did not like any of the books which she gave him. She conversed with him with so much kindness and cheerfulness; she was so quick at perceiving his latent meaning, and she was so gentle and patient when she reasoned with him, that he loved to talk to her better than to any body else; nor could little Charles ever thoroughly enjoy any pleasure without her sympathy.

The conversation of the sensible, well-informed people who visited Mrs. Howard, contributed to form her nephew's taste. A child may learn as much from conversation as from books; not so many historic facts, but as much instruction. Greek and Latin were the grand difficulties. Mrs. Howard did not understand Greek and Latin; nor did she, though a woman, set too high or too low a value upon the learned languages. She was convinced, that a man might be a great scholar, without being a man of sense; she was also persuaded that a man of sense might be a good scholar. She knew that, whatever abilities her nephew might possess, he could not be upon a footing with other men in the world, without possessing that species of knowledge, which is universally expected from gentlemen, as an essential proof of their having received a liberal education; nor did she attempt to undervalue the pleasures of classic taste, merely because she was not qualified to enjoy them: she was convinced, by the testimony of men of candour and judgment, that a classical taste is a source of real enjoyment, and she wished her nephew's literary pleasures to have as extensive a range as possible.

To instruct her nephew in the learned languages, she engaged a good scholar and a man of sense: his name—for a man is nothing

without a name—was Russell*.[32] Little Charles did not at first
relish Latin; he used sometimes to come from his Latin lessons
with a very dull, stupefied face, which gradually brightened into
intelligence, after he had talked for a few minutes with his aunt.
Mrs. Howard, though pleased to perceive that he was fond of her,
had not the weakness to sacrifice his permanent advantage to
her transient gratification. One evening Charles came running
up-stairs to his aunt, who was at tea; several people happened to
be present. "I have done with Mr. Russell, and my Latin, ma'am,
thank goodness—now may I have the elephant, and the camel, or
the bear and her cubs, that you marked for me last night?"

The company laughed at this speech of Charles; and a silly
lady—for even Mrs. Howard could not make all her acquaintance
wise—a silly lady whispered to Charles, "I've a notion, if you'd
tell the truth, now, that you like the bear and her cubs a great deal
better than you do Latin and Mr. Russell."

"I like the bear a great deal better than I do Latin, to be sure,"
said the boy; "but as for Mr. Russell—why, I think," added he,
encouraged by the lady's smiles, "I think I like the bear better
than Mr. Russell."

The lady laughed affectedly at this sally.

"I am sure," continued Charles, fancying that every person present was delighted with his wit, "I am sure, at any rate, I like the
learned pig fifty times better than Mr. Russell!"[33]

The judicious lady burst into a second fit of laughter.
Mrs. Howard looked very grave. Charles broke from the lady's
caresses, and, going up to his aunt, timidly looking up in her face,
said, "Am I a fool?"

"You are but a child," said Mrs. Howard; and, turning away
from him, she desired the servant, who waited at tea, to let
Mr. Russell know, that she desired the *honour* of his company.—
Mrs. Holloway, for that was the silly lady's name, at the words,
"honour of his company," resumed her gravity, but looked round,
to see what the rest of the company thought.

---

* RUSSELL—This name is chosen for that of a good tutor, because it was
the name of Mr. Edgeworth's tutor, at Oxford. Mr. Russell was also tutor to
the late Mr. Day. He was respected, esteemed, and beloved, in no common
degree by both by Mr. Day and Mr. Edgeworth.

"Give me leave, Mr. Russell," said Mrs. Howard, as soon as he came into the room, "to introduce you to a gentleman, for whose works, I know, you have a great esteem." The gentleman was a celebrated traveller, just returned from abroad, whose conversation was as much admired as his writings.

The conversation now took a literary turn. The traveller being polite, as well as entertaining, drew out Mr. Russell's knowledge and abilities. Charles now looked up to his tutor with respect.—Children have sufficient penetration, to discover the opinions of others by their countenance and manner, and their sympathy is quickly influenced by the example of those around them. Mrs. Howard led the traveller to speak of what he had seen in different countries—of natural history—of the beaver, and the moose deer, and the humming-bird, that is scarcely larger than an humble bee; and the mocking-bird, that can imitate the notes of all other birds.[34]—Charles *niched* himself into a corner of the sofa, upon which the gentlemen were sitting, and grew very attentive.—He was rather surprised to perceive, that his tutor was as much entertained with the conversation as he was himself.

"Pray, sir," said Mrs. Howard to the traveller, "is it true, that the humming-bird is a passionate little animal?—Is the story told by the author of the Farmer's Letters true?"

"What story?" said Charles, eagerly.

"Of a humming-bird, that flew into a fury with a flower, and tore it to pieces, because it could not get the honey out of it all at once."[35]

"Oh, ma'am," said little Charles, peeping over his tutor's shoulders, "will you show me that?—Have you got the book, *dear* aunt?"

"It is Mr. Russell's book," said his aunt.

"Your book?" cried Charles, "what, and do you know all about animals, and those sorts of entertaining things, as well as Latin?—And can you tell me, then, what I want very much to know, how they catch the humming-bird?"

"They shoot it."

"Shoot it! But what a large hole they must make in its body and beautiful feathers! I thought you said its whole body was no bigger than a bee—an humble bee."

"They make no hole in its body—they shoot it without ruffling even its feathers."

"How, how?" cried Charles, fastening upon his tutor, whom he now regarded no longer as a mere man of Latin.

"They charge the gun with water," said Mr. Russell, "and the poor little humming-bird is stunned by the discharge."

The conversation next turned upon the entertaining chapter on instinct, in Dr. Darwin's Zoonomia. Charles did not understand all that was said, for the gentlemen did not address themselves to him. He never listened to what he did not understand; but he was very quick at hearing whatever was within the limits of his comprehension. He heard of the tailor-bird, that uses its long bill as a needle, to sew the dead and the living leaf together, of which it makes its light nest, lined with feathers and gossamer:—of the fish called the old soldier, who looks out for the empty shell of some dead animal, and fits this armour upon himself:—of the Jamaica spider, who makes himself a house under ground, with a door and hinges, which door the spider and all the members of his family take care to shut after them, whenever they go in and out.[36]

Little Charles, as he sat eagerly attentive in his corner of the sofa, heard of the trumpet of the common gnat[†], and of its proboscis, which serves at once for an awl, a saw, and a pump.[37]

"Are there any more such things," exclaimed Charles, "in these books?"

"A great many," said Mr. Russell.

"I'll read them all," cried Charles, starting up—"May I? May not I, aunt?"

"Ask Mr. Russell," replied his aunt: "he, who is obliged to give you the pain of learning what is tiresome, should have the pleasure of rewarding you with entertaining books. Whenever he asks me for Dr. Darwin and St. Pierre, you shall have them. We are both of one mind. We know, that learning Latin is not the most amusing occupation in the world, but still it must be learned."

"Why," said Charles, modestly, "you don't understand Latin, aunt, do you?"

[†] St. Pierre, Études de la Nature.

"No," said Mrs. Howard, "but I am a woman, and it is not thought necessary that a woman should understand Latin; nor can I explain to you, at your age, why it is expected that a gentleman should: but here are several gentlemen present; ask them, whether it be not necessary, that a gentleman should understand Latin and Greek?"

Charles gathered all the opinions, and especially that of the entertaining traveller.

Mrs. Holloway, the silly lady, during that part of the conversation from which she might have acquired some knowledge, had retired to the farther end of the room, to a game at trictrac, with an obsequious chaplain.[38] Her game being finished, she came up to hear what the crowd round the sofa could be talking about; and hearing Charles ask the opinions of the gentlemen about the necessity of learning Latin, she nodded sagaciously at Mrs. Howard, and, by way of making up for former errors, said to Charles, in the most authoritative tone:—

"Yes, I can assure you, Mr. Charles, I am quite of the gentlemen's opinion, and so is every body—and this is a point upon which I have some right to speak; for my Augustus, who is only a year and seven months older than you are, sir, is one of the best scholars of his age, I am told, in England. But then, to be sure, it was flogged into him well at first, at a public school, which, I understand, is the best way of making good scholars."

"And the best way of making boys love literature?" said Mrs. Howard.

"Certainly, certainly," said Mrs. Holloway, who mistook Mrs. Howard's tone of inquiry for a tone of assertion, a tone more familiar to her—"Certainly, ma'am, I knew you would come round to my notions at last. I'm sure my Augustus must be fond of his Latin, for never in the vacations did I ever catch him with any English book in his hand!"

"Poor boy," said Charles, with unfeigned compassion.

"And when, my dear Mrs. Howard," continued Mrs. Holloway, laying her hand upon Mrs. Howard's arm, with a yet untasted pinch of snuff between her fingers, "when will you send Mr. Charles to school?"

"Oh, aunt, don't send me away from you—Oh, sir! Mr. Russell, try me—I will do my very *very* best, without having it flogged into me, to learn Latin—only try me."

"Dear sir, I really beg your pardon," said Mrs. Holloway to Mr. Russell, "I absolutely only meant to support Mrs. Howard's opinion for the sweet boy's good—and I thought I saw you go out of the room, or somebody else went out, whilst I was at trictrac. But I'm convinced, a private tutor may do wonders at the same time, and if my Augustus prejudiced me in favour of public education, you'll excuse a mother's partiality.—Besides, I make it a rule never to interfere in the education of my boys. Mr. Holloway is answerable for them, and, if he prefer public schools to a private tutor, you must be sensible, sir, it would be very wrong in me, to set my poor judgment in opposition to Mr. Holloway's opinion."

Mr. Russell bowed: for when a lady claims a gentleman's assent to a series of inconsistent propositions, what answer can he make but—a bow? Mrs. Holloway's carriage was now at the door, and, without troubling herself any farther about the comparative merits of public and private education, she departed.

When Mrs. Howard was left alone with her nephew, she seized the moment, while his mind was yet warm, to make a lasting impression. Charles, instead of going to Buffon's account of the elephant, which he was very impatient to read, sat down resolutely to his Latin lesson.[39] Mrs. Howard looked over his shoulder, and when he saw her smile of approbation, he said, "Then you won't send me away from you?"

"Not unless you oblige me to do so," said his aunt: "I love to have you with me, and I will try for one year, whether you have energy enough to learn what is disagreeable to you, without——"

"Without its being flogged into me," said Charles—"you shall see."

This boy had a great deal of energy and application. The Latin lessons were learned very perfectly; and, as he did not spend above an hour a day at them, he was not disgusted with application. His general taste for literature, and his fund of knowledge, increased rapidly from year to year, and the activity of his mind promised continual improvement. His attachment to Mrs. Howard increased as he grew up, for she never claimed any gratitude from her pupil, or exacted from him any of those little observances, which women sometimes consider as essential proofs of affection. She knew, that these minute attentions are particularly irksome to boys, and that they are by no means the natural expressions of their feelings.

She had sufficient strength of mind, to be secure in the possession of those qualities, which merit esteem and love, and to believe, that the child, whom she had educated, had a heart and understanding, that must feel and appreciate her value.

When Charles Howard was about thirteen, an event happened, which changed his prospects in life. Mrs. Howard's large fortune was principally derived from an estate in the West Indies, which had been left to her by her grandfather. She did not particularly wish to be the proprietor of slaves, and from the time that she came to the management of her own affairs, she had been desirous to sell her West India property. Her agent represented to her, that this could not be done without considerable loss. From year to year the business was delayed, till at length a gentleman, who had a plantation adjoining to hers, offered to purchase her estate. She was neither one of those ladies, who, jealous of their free-will, would rather *act for themselves*, that is to say, follow their own whims in matters of business, than consult men who possess the requisite information; nor was she so ignorant of business, or so indolent, as to be at the mercy of any designing agent or attorney. After consulting proper persons, and after exerting a just proportion of her own judgment, she concluded her bargain with the West Indian. Her plantation was sold to him, and all her property was shipped for her on board *The Lively Peggy*.——— Mr. Alderman Holloway, husband to the silly Mrs. Holloway, was one of the trustees appointed by her grandfather's will.—The alderman, who was supposed to be very knowing in all worldly concerns, sanctioned the affair with his approbation. The lady was at this time rich, and Alderman Holloway applauded her humanity in having stipulated for the liberty and *provision grounds* of some old negroes upon her plantation; he even suggested to his son Augustus, that this would make a very pretty, proper subject for a copy of verses, to be addressed to Mrs. Howard.[40] The verses were written in elegant Latin, and the young gentleman was proceeding with some difficulty in his English translation of them, when they were suppressed by parental authority.—The alderman changed his opinion as to the propriety of the argument of this poem: the reasons, which worked upon his mind were never distinctly expressed; they may, however, be deduced from the perusal of the following letter:—

To Mrs. Frances Howard.

"DEAR MADAM;

"Sorry am I to be under the disagreeable necessity of communicating to you, thus abruptly, the melancholy news of the loss of 'The Lively Peggy,' with your valuable consignment on board, *viz.*—Sundry puncheons of rum, and hogsheads of sugar, in which commodities (as usual) your agent received the purchase-money of your late fine West India estate. I must not, however reluctantly, omit to mention the casket of your grandmother's jewels, which I now regret was sent by this opportunity.—'Tis an additional loss——some thousands, I apprehend.

"The captain of the vessel I have just seen, who was set on shore, on the 15th ultimo, on the coast of Wales; his mate mutinied, and, in conspiracy with the crew, have run away with the vessel.

"I have only to add, that Mrs. Holloway and my daughter Angelina sincerely unite with me in compliments and condolence; and I shall be happy if I can be of any service in the settlement of your affairs.

"Mrs Holloway desires me to say, she would do herself the honour of waiting upon you to-morrow, but is setting out for Margate.[41]

"I am, dear madam,

"Your most obed. and humble servant,

"A. T. Holloway."

"P.S. Your agent is much to blame for neglecting to insure."

Mrs. Howard, as soon as she had perused this epistle, gave it to her nephew, who was reading in the room with her, when she received it. He showed more emotion on reading it than she had done. The coldness of the alderman's letter seemed to strike the boy more than the loss of a fortune—"And this is a friend!" he exclaimed with indignation.

"No, my love," said Mrs. Howard, with a calm smile, "I never thought Mr. Holloway any thing more than a common acquaintance—I hope—I am sure I have chosen *my friends* better."

Charles fixed an eager, inquiring eye upon his aunt, which seemed to say, "Did you mean to call me one of your friends?" and then he grew very thoughtful.

"My dear Charles," said the aunt, after nearly a quarter of an hour's silence, "may I know what you have been thinking of all this time?"

"Thinking of, ma'am!" said Charles, starting from his reverie— "of a great many things—of all you have done for me—of—of what I could do—I don't mean now; for I know I am a child, and can do nothing—I don't mean *nothing*.—I shall soon be a man, and then I can be a physician, or a lawyer, or something.— Mr. Russell told me the other day, that if I applied myself, I might be whatever I pleased. What would *you* wish me to be, ma'am?— Because that's what I will be—if I can."

"Then I wish you to be what you are."

"Oh, madam," said Charles, with a look of great mortification, "but that's nothing. Won't you make me of some use to you?—But I beg your pardon, I know you can't think about me just now.— Good night," said he, and hurried out of the room.

The news of the loss of the Lively Peggy, with all the particulars mentioned in Alderman Holloway's letter, appeared in the next day's newspapers, and in the succeeding paper appeared an advertisement of Mrs. Howard's house in Portman Square, of her plate, china, furniture, books, &c.[42]—She had never in affluence disdained economy.—She had no debts; not a single tradesman was a sufferer by her loss. She had always lived within her annual income; and though her generous disposition had prevented her from hoarding money, she had a small sum in the funds, which she had prudently reserved for any unforeseen exigence. She had also a few diamonds, which had been her mother's, which Mr. Carat, the jeweller, who had new set them, was very willing to purchase.[43] He waited upon Mrs. Howard, in Portman Square, to complete the bargain.

The want of sensibility, which Charles showed when his aunt was parting with her jewels to Mr. Carat, would have infallibly ruined him in the opinion of most ladies. He took the trinkets up, one by one, without ceremony, and examined them, asking his aunt and the jeweller questions about the use and value of diamonds—about the working of the mines of Golconda—about the shining of diamonds in the dark, observed by the children of Cogi Hassan, the rope-maker, in the Arabian Tales—about the experiment of Francis the First upon *melting* of diamonds and rubies.[44]

Mr. Carat was a Jew, and, though extremely cunning, profoundly ignorant.

"Dat king wash very grand fool, beg his majesty's pardon," said the Jew, with a shrewd smile; "but kings know better now-a-days. Heaven bless dere majesties!"

Charles had a great mind to vindicate the philosophic fame of Francis the First, but a new idea suddenly started into his head.— "My dearest aunt," cried he, stopping her hand as she was giving her diamond earrings to Mr. Carat—"stay, my dearest aunt, one instant, till I have seen whether this is a good day for selling diamonds."

"O my dear young gentleman, no day in the Jewish calendar more proper for de purchase," said the Jew.

"For the purchase, yes," said Charles, "but for the sale?"

"My love," said his aunt, "surely you are not so foolish as to think there are lucky and unlucky days."

"No, I don't mean any thing about lucky and unlucky days," said Charles, running up to consult the barometer, "but what I mean is not foolish indeed: in some book I've read that the dealers in diamonds buy them, when the air is light; and sell them, when it is heavy, if they can; because their scales are so nice that they vary with the change in the atmosphere. Perhaps I may not remember exactly the words, but that's the sense, I know; I'll look for the words; I know whereabouts to find them." He jumped upon a chair, to get down the book.

"But, master Charles," said the Jew, with a show of deference, "I will not pretend to make a bargain with you—I see you know a great deal more than I of dese traffics."

To this flattery Charles made no answer, but continued looking for the passage he wanted in his book.

Whilst he was turning over the leaves, a gentleman, a friend of Mrs. Howard, who had promised her to meet Mr. Carat, came in. He was the gentleman formerly mentioned by the name of *the traveller*: he was a good judge of diamonds, and, what is better, he was a good judge of the human heart and understanding. He was much pleased with Charles's ready recollection of the little knowledge he possessed, with his eagerness to make that knowledge of use to his aunt, and more with his perfect simplicity and integrity; for Charles, after a moment's thought, turned to the Jew, and said,

"But the day that is good for my aunt must be bad for you. The buyers and sellers should each have fair play.—Mr. Carat, your weights should be diamonds, and then the changes in the weight of the air would not signify one way or the other‡."[45]

Mr. Carat smiled at this speech, but, suppressing his contempt for the young gentleman, only observed, that he should most certainly follow Mr. Charles's advice, whenever he *wash* rich enough to have diamonds for weights.

The traveller drew from his pocket a small book, took a pen, and wrote in the title-page of it,—*For one who will make a good use of it,*—and, with Mrs. Howard's permission, he gave the book to her nephew.

"I do not believe," said the gentleman, "that there is at present another copy in England: I have just got this from France by a private hand."

The sale of his aunt's books appeared to Charles a much more serious affair than the parting with her diamonds. He understood something of the value of books, and he took a sorrowful leave of many, which he had read, and of many more, which he had intended to read. Mrs. Howard selected a few for her own use, and she allowed her nephew to select as many for himself as she had done. He observed that there was a beautiful edition of Shakspeare, which he knew his aunt liked particularly, but which she did not keep, reserving instead of it Smith's Wealth of Nations, which would in a few years, she said, be very useful to him.[46] He immediately offered his favourite Etudes de la Nature, to redeem the Shakspeare; but Mrs. Howard would not accept of it, because she justly observed, that she could read Shakspeare *almost* as well without its being in such a beautiful binding. Her readiness to part with all the luxuries to which she had been for many years accustomed, and the freedom and openness, with which she spoke of all her affairs to her nephew, made a great impression upon his mind.

Those are mistaken, who think that young people cannot be interested in such things; if no mystery be made of the technical parts of business, young people easily learn them, and they early

---

‡ This observation was literally made by a boy of ten years of age.

take an interest in the affairs of their parents, instead of learning to separate their own views from those of their friends.[47] Charles, young as he was, at this time, was employed by his aunt frequently to copy, and sometimes to write letters of business for her. He drew out a careful inventory of all the furniture before it was disposed of; he took lists of all the books and papers; and at this work, however tiresome, he was indefatigable, because he was encouraged by the hope of being useful. This ambition to be useful had been early excited in his mind.

When Mrs. Howard had settled her affairs, she took a small neat house near Westminster school[§], for the purpose of a boarding-house for some of the Westminster boys.[48] This plan she preferred, because it secured an independent means of support, and at the same time enabled her, in some measure, to assist in her nephew's education, and to enjoy his company. She was no longer able to afford a sufficient salary to a well-informed private tutor; therefore, she determined to send Charles to Westminster School; and, as he would board with her, she hoped to unite, by this scheme, as much as possible, the advantages of a private and of a public education. Mr. Russell desired still to have the care of Mrs. Howard's nephew; he determined to offer himself as a tutor at Westminster School; and, as his acquirements were well known to the literary world, he was received with eagerness.

"My dear boy," said Mrs. Howard to her nephew, when he first went to Westminster School, "I shall not trouble you with a long chapter of advice; do you remember that answer of the oracle, which seemed to strike you so much the other day, when you were reading the life of Cicero?"

"Yes," said Charles, "I recollect it—I shall never forget it. When Cicero asked how he should arrive at the height of glory, the oracle answered, 'By making his own genius, and not the opinion of the people, the guide of his life.' "[49]

"Well," said Mrs. Howard, smiling, "if I were your oracle, and you were to put the same question to me, I think I should make you nearly the same answer: except that I should change the word genius into good sense; and, instead of *the people,* I should say *the world*, which, in general, I think, means all *the silly people*

---

§ See the account of Mrs. C. Ponten, in Gibbon's Life.

of one's acquaintance.—Farewell: now go to the Westminster world."

Westminster was quite a new world to young Howard. The bustle and noise, at first, astonished his senses, and almost confounded his understanding; but he soon grew accustomed to the din, and familiarized to the sight of numbers. At first, he thought himself much inferior to all his companions, because practice had given them the power of doing many things with ease, which to him appeared difficult, merely because he had not been used to them. In all their games and plays, either of address or force, he found himself foiled. In a readiness of repartee, and a certain ease and volubility of conversation, he perceived his deficiency; and though he frequently was conscious that his ideas were more just, and his arguments better, than those of his companions, yet he could not, at first, bring out his ideas to advantage, or manage his arguments, so as to stand his ground against the mixed raillery and sophistry of his school-fellows. He had not yet the tone of his new society, and he was as much at a loss, as a traveller in a foreign country, before he understands the language of a people who are vociferating round about him. As fast, however, as he learned to translate the language of his companions into his own, he discovered that there was not so much meaning in their expressions as he had been inclined to imagine, whilst they had remained unintelligible: but he was good humoured and good natured, so that, upon the whole, he was much liked, and even his inferiority, in many little trials of skill, was, perhaps, in his favour. He laughed with those that laughed at him, let them triumph in his awkwardness, but still persisted in new trials, till at last, to the great surprise of the spectators, he succeeded. He learned, by perseverance, the mysteries of trap ball and marbles.

The art of boxing cost him more than all the rest; but, as he was neither deficient in courage of mind, nor activity of body, he did not despair of acquiring the *necessary* skill in this noble science: necessary, we say, for Charles had not been a week at Westminster, before he was made sensible of the necessity of practising this art in his own defence. He had yet a stronger motive; he found it necessary for the defence of one who looked up to him for protection.

There was, at this time, at Westminster, a little boy, of the name of Oliver, a Creole, lively, intelligent, open hearted, and affectionate in the extreme, but rather passionate in his temper, and adverse to application. His *literary* education had been strangely neglected before he came to school, so that his ignorance of the common rudiments of spelling, reading, grammar, and arithmetic, made him the laughing-stock of Westminster School. The poor boy felt inexpressible shame and anguish; his cheek burned with blushes, when every day, in the public class, he was ridiculed and disgraced; but his dark complexion, perhaps, prevented those blushes from being noticed by his companions, otherwise they certainly would have suppressed, or would have endeavoured to repress some of their insulting peals of laughter. He suffered no complaint or tear to escape him in public; but his book was sometimes blistered with the tears that fell when nobody saw them: what was worse than all the rest, he found insurmountable difficulties, at every step, in his grammar. He was unwilling to apply to any of his more learned companions for explanations or assistance.—He began to sink into despair of his own abilities, and to imagine that he must for ever remain, what indeed he was every day called, a dunce. He was usually flogged three times a week. Day after day brought no relief, either to his bodily or mental sufferings; at length his honest pride yielded, and he applied to one of the elder scholars for help. The boy to whom he applied was Augustus Holloway, Alderman Holloway's son, who was acknowledged to be one of the best Latin scholars at Westminster. He readily helped Oliver in his exercises, but he made him pay most severely for this assistance, by the most tyrannical usage; and, in all his tyranny, he thought himself fully justifiable, because little Oliver, beside his other misfortunes, had the misfortune to be a fag.

There may be—though many schoolboys will, perhaps, think it scarcely possible—there may be, in the compass of the civilised world, some persons, so barbarously ignorant, as not to know what is meant by the term fag. To these it may be necessary to explain, that at some English schools it is the custom, that all little boys, when they first go to school, should be under the dominion of the elder boys. These little boys are called fags, and are forced to wait upon and obey their master-companions. Their duties vary in different schools. I have heard of its being customary, in some places, to make use of a fag regularly in the depth of winter instead of a warming-pan, and to send the shivering urchin through ten or twenty beds successively to take off the chill of cold for their luxurious masters. They are expected in most schools to run of all the elder boys' errands, to be ready at their call, and to do all their high behests. They must never complain of being tired, or their complaints will, at least, never be regarded, because, as the etymology of the word implies, it is their business to be tired. The substantive *fag* is not to be found in Dr. Johnson's Dictionary; but the verb to fag is there a verb active, from fatigo, Latin, and is there explained to mean, "to grow weary, to faint with weariness." This is all the satisfaction we can, after the most diligent research, afford the curious and learned reader upon the subject of *fags* in general.

In particular, Mr. Augustus Holloway took great delight in teasing his fag, little Oliver. One day it happened, that young Howard and Holloway were playing at nine-pins together, and little Oliver was within a few yards of them, sitting under a tree, with a book upon his knees, anxiously trying to make out his lesson. Holloway, whenever the nine-pins were thrown down, called to Oliver, and made him come from his book, and set them up again; this he did repeatedly, in spite of Howard's remonstrances, who always offered to set up the nine-pins, and who said it teased the poor little fellow, to call him every minute from what he was about.

"Yes," said Holloway, "I know it teases him, that I see plain enough, by his running so fast back to his *form*, like a hare—there he is, *squatting* again: halloo! halloo! come, start again here," cried Holloway, "you haven't done yet; bring me the bowl, halloo!"

Howard did not at all enjoy the diversion of hunting the poor boy about in this manner, and he said, with some indignation, "How is it possible, Holloway, that the boy can get his lesson, if you interrupt him every instant?"

"Pooh, what signifies his foolish lesson?"

"It signifies a great deal to him," replied Howard; "you know what he suffered this morning, because he had not learned it,"

"Suffered! Why, what did he suffer?" said Holloway, upon whose memory the sufferings of others made no very deep impression. "Oh, ay, true, you mean he was flogged; more shame for him!— Why did not he mind and get his lesson better?"

"I had not time to understand it rightly," said Oliver, with a deep sigh; "and I don't think I shall have time today either."

"More shame for you," repeated Holloway; "I'll lay any bet on earth, I get all you have to get in three minutes."

"Ah, you, to be sure," said Oliver, in a tone of great humiliation; "but then you know what a difference there is between you and me."

Holloway misunderstood him; and, thinking he meant to allude to the difference in their age, instead of the difference of their abilities, answered, sharply,

"When I was your age, do you think I was such a dunce as you are, pray?"

"No, that I am sure you never were," said Oliver; "but, perhaps, you had some good father or mother, or somebody, who taught you a little, before you came to school."

"I don't remember any thing about that," replied Holloway; "I don't know who was so good as to teach me, but I know I was so good as to learn fast enough, which is a goodness, I've a notion, some folks will never have to boast of—so trot, and fetch the bowl for me, do you hear, and set up the nine-pins. You've sense enough to do that, have not you? And as for your lesson, I'll drive that into your head, by and by, if I can," added he, rapping with his knuckles upon the little boy's head.

"As to my lesson," said the boy, putting aside his head from the insulting knuckles, "I had rather try and make it out by myself, if I can."

"If you can!" repeated Holloway, sneering; "but we all know you can't."

"Why can't he, Mr. Holloway?" exclaimed Howard, with a raised voice—for he was no longer master of his indignation— "Why can't he?" repeated Holloway, looking round upon Howard, with a mixture of surprise and insolence, "you must answer that question yourself, Mr. Howard, I say he can't."

"And I say he can, and he shall," replied Howard; "and he *shall* have time to learn; he's willing, and, I'll answer for it, able to learn; and he shall not be called a dunce; and he shall have time; and he shall have justice."

"Shall! shall! shall!" retorted Holloway, vociferating with a passion of a different sort from Howard's: "Pray, sir, who allowed you to say shall to me—and how dare you to talk in this *here* style to me, about justice?—and what business have you, I should be glad to know, to interfere between me and my fag? What right have you to him, or his time either? And if I choose to call him a dunce forty times a day, what then? He is a dunce, and he will be a dunce to the end of his days, I say, and who is there thinks proper to contradict me?"

"I," said Howard, firmly, "and I'll do more than contradict you; I'll prove that you are mistaken. Oliver, bring your book to me."

"Oliver, stir at your peril!" cried Holloway, clenching his fist with a menacing gesture: "nobody shall give any help to my fag but myself, sir," added he to Howard.

"I am not going to help him, I am only going to prove to him that he may do it without your help," said Howard.

The little boy sprang forward, at these words, for his book; but his tormentor caught hold of him, and, pulling him back, said, "He's my fag! Do you recollect, sir, he's my fag?"

"Fag or no fag," cried Howard, "you shall not make a slave of him."

"I will! I shall! I will," cried Holloway, worked up to the height of tyrannical fury; "I will make a slave of him, if I choose it—a negro-slave, if I please!"

At the sound of "negro-slave", the little Creole burst into tears: Howard sprang forward to free him from his tyrant's grasp: Holloway struck Howard a furious blow, which made him stagger backwards.

"Ay," said Holloway, "learn to stand your ground, and fight, before you meddle with me, I advise you."

Holloway was an experienced pugilist, and he knew that Howard was not; but before his defiance had escaped his lips, he felt his blow returned, and a battle ensued. Howard fought with all his *soul*; but the *body* has something to do, as well as the soul, in the art of boxing, and his body was not yet a match for his adversary's. After receiving more blows than Holloway, perhaps, could have borne, Howard was brought to the ground.

"Beg my pardon, and promise never to interfere between me and my fag any more," said Holloway, standing over him triumphant; "ask my pardon."

"Never," said the fallen hero; "I'll fight you again, in the same cause, whenever you please; I can't have a better cause," and he struggled to rise.

Several boys had, by this time, gathered round the combatants, and many admired the fortitude and spirit of the vanquished, though it is extremely difficult to boys, if not to men, to sympathize with the beaten. Every body called out, that Howard had had enough, for that night; and though he was willing to have renewed the battle, his adversary was withheld by the omnipotence of public opinion. As to the cause of the combat, some few inquired into its merits, but many more were content with seeing the fray, and with hearing, vaguely, that it began about Howard's having interfered with Holloway's fag in an impertinent manner.

Howard's face was so much disfigured, and his clothes were so much stained with blood, that he did not wish to present himself such a deplorable spectacle before his aunt; besides, no man likes to be seen, especially by a woman, immediately after he has been beaten; therefore, he went directly to bed as soon as he got home, but desired, that one of his companions, who boarded at Mrs. Howard's, would, if his aunt inquired for him at supper, tell her "that he had been beaten in a boxing-match, but hoped to be more expert after another lesson or two." This lady did not show her tenderness to her nephew, by wailing over his disaster: on the contrary, she was pleased to hear, that he had fought in so good a cause.

The next morning, as soon as Howard went to school, he saw little Oliver watching eagerly for him.

"Mr. Howard—Charles," said he, catching hold of him, "I've one word to say; let him call me dunce, or slave, or negro, or what he will, don't you mind any more about me; I can't bear to see it," said the affectionate child; "I'd rather have the blows myself, only I know I could not bear them as you did."

Oliver turned aside his head, and Howard, in a playful voice, said, "Why, my little Oliver, I did not think you were such a coward; you must not make a coward of me."

No sooner did the boys go out to play, in the evening, than Howard called to Oliver, in Holloway's hearing, and said, "If you want any assistance from me, remember, I'm ready."

"You may be ready, but you are not able," cried Holloway, "to give him any assistance—therefore, you'd better be quiet; remember last night."

"I do remember it perfectly," said Howard, calmly.

"And do you want any more?—Come, then, I'll tell you what, I'll box with you every day, if you please, and when you have conquered *me*, you shall have my fag all to yourself, if you please—but, till then, you shall have nothing to do with him."

"I take you at your word," said Howard, and a second battle began. As we do not delight in fields of battle, or hope to excel, like Homer, in describing variety of wounds,[50] we shall content ourselves with relating, that after five pitched battles, in which Oliver's champion received bruises of all shapes and sizes, and of every shade of black, blue, green, and yellow, his unconquered spirit still maintained the justice of his cause, and with as firm a voice as at first he challenged his constantly victorious antagonist to a sixth combat.

"I thought you had learned by this time," said the successful pugilist, "that Augustus Holloway is not to be conquered by one of *woman breed.*"[51] To this taunt Howard made no reply; but whether it urged him to superior exertion, or whether the dear-bought experience of the five preceding days had taught him all the caution, that experience only can teach, we cannot determine; but, to the surprise of all the spectators, and to the lively joy of Oliver, the redoubted Holloway was brought, after an obstinate struggle, fairly to the ground. Every body sympathized with the generous victor, who immediately assisted his fallen adversary to rise, and offered his hand in token of reconciliation. Augustus Holloway, stunned by his fall, and more by his defeat, returned from the field of battle, as fast as the crowd would let him, who stopped him continually with their impertinent astonishment and curiosity; for though the boasted unconquerable hero had pretty evidently received a black eye, not one person would believe it without looking close in his face; and many would not trust the information of their own senses, but pressed to hear the news confirmed by the reluctant lips of the unfortunate Augustus. In the mean time, little Oliver, a fag no longer, exulting in his liberty, clapped his joyful hands, sang, and capered round his deliverer.—"And now," said he, fixing his grateful, affectionate eyes upon Howard, "you will suffer no more for me, and, if you'll let me, I'll be your fag. Do, will you? Pray let me! I'll run of your errands, before you can say one, two, three, and away; only whistle for me," said he, whistling, "and I'll hear you, wherever I am. If you only hold up your finger, when you want me, I'm sure I shall see it; and I'll always set up your nine-pins, and fly for your ball, let me be doing what I will. May I be your fag?"

"Be my *friend*," said Howard, taking Oliver in his arms, with emotion which prevented him from articulating any other words. The word "friend" went to the little Creole's heart, and he clung to Howard in silence. To complete his happiness, little Oliver this day obtained permission to board at Mrs. Howard's, so that he was now constantly to be with his protector.—Howard's friendship was not merely the sudden enthusiasm of a moment; it was the steady persevering choice of a manly mind, not the caprice of a school-boy. Regularly, every evening, Oliver brought his books to his friend, who never was too busy to attend to him. Oliver was delighted to find that he understood Howard's manner of explaining himself: his own opinion of himself rose with the opinion which he saw his instructor had of his abilities. He was convinced that he was not doomed to be a dunce for life; his ambition was rekindled; his industry was encouraged by hope, and rewarded by success. He no longer expected daily punishment, and that worst of all punishments, disgrace. His heart was light, his spirits rose, his countenance brightened with intelligence, and resumed its natural vivacity: to his masters and his companions he appeared a new creature. "What has inspired you?" said one of his masters to him one day, surprised at the rapid development of his understanding:—"What has inspired you?"

"My good genius," said the little boy, pointing to Howard.

Howard had some merit in giving up a good deal of his time to Oliver, because he knew the value of time, and he had not quite so much as he wished for himself. The day was always too short for him; every moment was employed; his active mind went from one thing to another, as if it did not know the possibility of idleness, and as if he had no idea of any recreation, but in a change of employment. Not that he was always poring over books, but his mind was active, let him be about what he would; and, as his exertions were always voluntary, there was not that opposition in his mind, between the ideas of play and work, which exists so strongly in the minds of those school-boys, who are driven to their tasks by fear, and who escape from them to that delicious exercise of their free will, which they call play.

"Constraint, that sweetens liberty,"

often gives a false value to its charms, or rather a false idea to its nature.—Idleness, ennui, noise, mischief, riot, and a nameless train of mistaken notions of pleasure, are often classed, in a young man's mind, under the general head of *liberty.*[52]

Mr. Augustus Holloway, who is necessarily recalled to our recollection, when we want to personify an ill-educated young man, was, in the strictest sense of the word, a school-boy—a clever school-boy—a good scholar—a good historian—he wrote a good hand—read with fluency—declaimed at a public exhibition of Westminster orators with no bad grace and emphasis, and had always extempore words, if not extempore sense, at command. But still he was but a school-boy. His father thought him a man, and more than a man. Alderman Holloway prophesied to his friends, that his son Augustus would be one of the first orators in England. He was in a hurry to have him ready to enter college, and had a borough secure for him at the proper age.[53] The proper age, he regretted, that parliament had fixed to twenty-one; for the alderman was impatient to introduce his young statesman to the house, especially as he saw honours, perhaps a title, in the distant perspective of his son's advancement.

Whilst this vision occupied the father's imagination, a vision of another sort played upon the juvenile fancy of his son: a vision— of a gig; for, though Augustus was but a school-boy, he had very manly ideas—if those ideas be manly, which most young men have. Lord Rawson, the son of the Earl of Marryborough, had lately appeared to Augustus in a gig. The young Lord Rawson had lately been a school-boy at Westminster like Augustus: he was now master of himself and three horses at college. Alderman Holloway had lent the Earl of Marryborough certain monies, the interest of which the Earl scrupulously paid in civility. The alderman valued himself upon being a shrewd man; he looked to one of the earl's boroughs as a security for his principal, and, from long-sighted political motives, encouraged an intimacy between the young nobleman and his son. It was one of those useful friendships, one of those fortunate connexions, which some parents consider as the peculiar advantage of a public school. Lord Rawson's example already powerfully operated upon his young friend's mind, and this intimacy was most likely to have a decisive influence upon the future destiny of Augustus. Augustus was the son of an alderman—Lord Rawson was two years older than Holloway—had left school—had been at college—had driven both a curricle and a barouche, and who had gone through all the gradations of coachmanship—was a man, and had *seen the world.* How many things to excite the ambition of a school-boy!—Augustus was impatient for the moment when he might "be what he admired." The drudgery of Westminster, the confinement, the ignominious appellation of *a boy,* were all insupportable to this *young man.* He had obtained from his father a promise, that he should leave school in a few months; but these months appeared to him an age. It was rather a misfortune to Holloway, that he was so far advanced in his Latin and Greek studies, for he had the less to do at school; his school business quickly dispatched, his time hung upon his hands. He never thought of literature as an amusement for his leisure hours; he had no idea of improving himself farther in general science and knowledge. He was told, that his education was *nearly* at an end; he believed it was *quite* finished, and he was glad of it, and glad it was so well over. In the idle time, that hung upon his hands during this intermediate state at Westminster, he heartily regretted, that he could not commence his manly career by learning to *drive*—to drive a curricle. Lord Rawson had carried him down to the country, the last summer vacation, in his *dog-cart,* driven *randem-tandem.*[54] The reins had touched his fingers. The whip had been committed to his hand, and he longed for a repetition of these pleasures. From the windows of the house in Westminster, where he boarded, Holloway at every idle moment lolled, to enjoy a view of every carriage, and of every coachman that passed.

Mr. Supine, Mr. Holloway's tutor, used, at these leisure moments, to employ himself with practising upon the German flute, and was not sorry to be relieved from his pupil's conversation. Sometimes it was provoking to the amateur in music, to be interrupted by the exclamations of his pupil; but he kept his eyes steadily upon his music-book, and contented himself with recommending a difficult passage, when Mr. Holloway's raptures about horses, and coachmanship, and driving well in hand, offended his musical ear. Mr. Supine was, both from nature and fashion, indolent; the trouble of reproving or of guiding his pupil, was too much for him; besides, he was sensible, that the task of watching, contradicting, and thwarting a young gentleman, at Mr. Holloway's time of life, would have been productive of the most disagreeable scenes of altercation, and could possibly have no effect upon the gentleman's character, which, he presumed, was perfectly well formed at this time. Mr. and Mrs. Holloway were well satisfied with his improvements. Mr. Supine was on the best terms imaginable with the whole family, and thought it his business to keep himself *well* with his pupil; especially as he had some secret hope, that, through Mr. Holloway's interest with Lord Rawson, and through Lord Rawson's influence with a young nobleman, who was just going abroad, he might be invited as a travelling companion in a tour upon the continent. His taste for music and painting had almost raised him to the rank of a connoisseur: an amateur he modestly professed himself, and he was frequently stretched in elegant ease, upon a sofa, already in reverie in Italy, whilst his pupil was conversing out of the window, in no very elegant dialect, with the driver of a stage-coach in the neighbourhood. Young Holloway was almost as familiar with this coachman as with his father's groom, who, during his visits at home, supplied the place of Mr. Supine, in advancing his education. The stage-coachman so effectually wrought upon the ambition of Augustus, that his desire to learn *to drive* became uncontrollable. The coachman, partly by entreaties, and partly by the mute eloquence of a crown, was prevailed upon to promise, that, if Holloway could manage it without his tutor's knowledge, he should ascend to the honours of the box, and at least have the satisfaction of *seeing some good driving*.

Mr. Supine was soon invited to a private concert, at which Mrs. Holloway was expected, and at which her daughter, miss Angelina Holloway, was engaged to perform. Mr. Supine's judicious applause of this young lady's execution was one of his greatest recommendations to the whole family, at least to the female part of it: he could not, therefore, decline an invitation to this concert. Holloway complained of a sore throat, and desired to be excused from accompanying his tutor, adding, with his usual politeness, that "music was the greatest bore in nature, and especially Angelina's music." For the night of the concert Holloway had arranged his plan with the stage-coachman. Mr. Supine dressed, and then practised upon the German flute, till towards nine o'clock in the evening. Holloway heard the stage-coach rattling through the street, whilst his tutor was yet in the middle of a long concerto; the coachman was to stop at the public-house, about ten doors off, to take up parcels and passengers, and there he was to wait for Holloway; but he had given him notice that he could not wait many minutes.

"You may practise the rest, without book, in the chair, as you are going to——street, *quite at your ease*, Mr. Supine," said Holloway to his tutor.

"Faith, so I can, and I'll adopt your idea, for it's quite a novel thing, and may take, if the fellows will only carry one steady. Good night, I'll mention your sore throat *properly* to Mrs. Holloway."

No sooner were the tutor and his German flute safely raised upon the chairmen's shoulders, than his pupil recovered from his sore throat, ran down to the place where the stage was waiting, seized the stage-coachman's down-stretched hand, sprang up, and seated himself triumphantly upon the coach-box.[55]

"Never saw a cleverer fellow," said the coachman; "now we are off."

"Give me the reins then!" said Holloway.

"Not till we are out o'town," said the coachman: "when we get off the stones, we'll see a little of your driving."

When they got on the turnpike road, Holloway impatiently seized the reins, and was as much gratified by this coachman's praises of his driving, as ever he had been by the applauses he had received for his Latin verses.[56] A taste for vulgar praise is the most dangerous taste a young man can have; it not only leads him into vulgar company, but it puts him entirely in the power of his companions, whoever they may happen to be. Augustus Holloway, seated beside a coachman, became, to all intents and purposes, a coachman himself; he caught, and gloried in catching, all his companion's slang, and with his language, caught all his ideas. The coachman talked with rapture of some young gentleman's horses, whom he had lately seen; and said that, if he was a gentleman, there was nothing he should pride himself so much upon as his horses. Holloway, as he was a gentleman, determined to have the finest horses, that could be had for money, as soon as he should become his own master.

"And then," continued the coachman, "if I was a gentleman born, I'd never be shabby in the matters of wages and perquisites to them, that be to look after my horses, seeing that horses can't be properly looked after for nothing."

"Certainly not," agreed the young gentleman:—"my friend, Lord Rawson, I know, has a prodigious smart groom, and so will I, all in good time."

"To be sure," said the coachman, "but it was not in regard to grooms I was meaning, so much as in regard to a coachman, which, I take it, is one of the first persons to be considered in a really grand family, seeing how great a trust is placed in him (mind, sir, if you please, the turn at the corner, it's rather sharp); seeing how great a trust is placed in him, as I was observing, a good coachman's worth his weight in gold."

Holloway had not leisure to weigh the solidity of this observation, for the conversation was now interrupted by the sound of a post-chaise, which drove rapidly by.

"The job and four!" exclaimed the coachman, with as many oaths "as *the occasion required.*"

"Why did you let it pass us?" And with enthusiasm, which forgot all ceremony, he snatched the whip from his young companion, and, seizing the reins, drove at a furious rate. One of the chaise postillions luckily dropped his whip; they passed the job and four; and the coachman, having redeemed his honour, resigned once more the reins to Holloway, upon his promising not to let the job and four get ahead of them. The postillions were not without ambition; the men called to each other, and to their horses; the horses caught some portion of their masters' spirit, and began to gain upon the coach. The passengers in the coach put out their heads, and female voices screamed in vain. All these terrors increased the sport; till at length, at a narrow part of the road, the rival coachman and postillions hazarded every thing for precedency. Holloway was desperate in proportion to his ignorance; the coachman attempted to snatch the reins, but, missing his grasp, he shortened those of the off-hand horse, and drew them the wrong way; the coach ran upon a bank, and was overturned. Holloway was dismayed and silent; the coachman poured forth a torrent of abuse, sparing neither friend nor foe; the complaints of the female passengers were so incoherent, and their fears operated so much upon their imagination, that, in the first moments of confusion, each asserted, that she had broken either an arm or a leg, or fractured her skull.

The moon, which had shone bright in the beginning of the evening, was now under a cloud, and the darkness increased the impatience of the various complainers; at length, a lantern was brought from the turnpike-house, which was near the spot where the accident happened. As soon as the light came, the ladies looked at each other, and after they had satisfied themselves, that no material injury had been done to their clothes, and that their faces were in no way disfigured, they began to recover from their terrors, and were brought to allow, that all their limbs were in good preservation, and that they had been too hasty in declaring that their skulls were fractured. Holloway laughed loudly at all this, and joined in all the wit of the coachman upon the occasion. The coach was lifted up, the passengers got in, the coachman and Holloway mounted the box, when, just as they were setting off, the coachman heard a voice crying to him to stop. He listened, and the voice, which seemed to be that of a person in great pain, again called for assistance.

"It's the mulatto woman," said the coachman; "we forgot her in the bustle.[57] Lend me hold of the lantern, and stand at the horses' heads, whilst I see after her," added the coachman, addressing himself to the man, who had come from the turnpike-house.

"I sha'n't stir for a *mulatto*, I promise you," said Holloway, brutally: "she was on the top of the coach; wasn't she? She must have had a fine hoist!"

The poor woman was found to be much hurt; she had been thrown from the top of the coach into a ditch, which had stones at the bottom of it. She had not been able to make herself heard by any body, whilst the ladies' loud complaints continued; nor had she been able long to call for any assistance, for she had been stunned by her fall, and had not recovered her senses for many minutes. She was not able to stand, but when the coachman held her up, she put her hand to her head, and, in broken English, said, she felt too ill to travel farther that night.

"You shall have an inside place, if you'll pluck up your heart; and you'll find yourself better with the motion of the coach."

"What, is she hurt?—The mulatto woman—I say, coachy, make haste," cried Holloway, "I want to be off."

"So do I," said the coachman, "but we are not likely to be off yet; here's this here poor woman can't stand, and is all over bruises, and won't get into the inside of the coach, though I offered her a place."

Holloway, who imagined, that the sufferings of all, who were not so rich as himself, could be *bought off* for money, pulled out a handful of silver, and leaning from the coach-box, held it towards the fainting woman,—"Here's a shilling for every bruise at least, my good woman :"—but the woman did not hear him, for she was very faint. The coachman was forced to carry her to the turnpike-house, where he left her; telling the people of the house, that a return chaise would call for her, in an hour's time, and would carry her either to the next stage, or back to town, whichever she pleased. Holloway's diversion for the rest of the night was spoiled, not because he had too much sympathy with the poor woman, who was hurt, but because he had been delayed so long by the accident, that he lost the pleasure of driving into the town of * * * * *. He had intended to have gone the whole stage, and to have returned in the job and four. This scheme had been arranged before he set out by his friend the coachman; but the postillions in the job and four, having won the race, and made the best of their way, had now returned, and met the coach about two miles from the turnpike-house.

"So," said Holloway, "I must descend, and get home before Mr. Supine wakens from his first sleep."

Holloway called at the turnpike-house, to inquire after the mulatto; or, rather, one of the postillions stopped, as he had been desired by the coachman, to take her up to town, if she was able to go that night.

The postillion, after he had spoken to the woman, came to the chaise-door, and told Holloway "that he could hardly understand what she said; she spoke, she talked such outlandish English; and that he could not make out where she wanted to be carried to."

"Ask the name of some of her friends in town," cried Holloway, "and don't let her keep us here all night."

"She has no friends, as I can find," replied the postillion, "nor acquaintance neither."

"Well, whom does she belong to, then?"

"She belongs to nobody, she's quite a stranger in these parts, and doesn't know no more than a child where to go in all London; she only knows the Christian name of an old gardener, where she lodged, she says."

"What would she have us to do with her, then?" said Holloway. "Drive on, for I shall be late."

The postillion, more humane than Holloway, exclaimed, "No, master, no!—it's a sin to leave her upon the road this ways, though she's no Christian, as we are; poor copper-coloured soul! I was once a stranger myself in *Lon'on*, without a sixpence to bless myself, so I know what it is, master."

The good-natured postillion returned to the mulatto woman. "Mistress," said he, "I'd fain see ye safe home, if you could but think of the t'other name of that gardener, that you mentioned lodging with, because there be so many Pauls in London town, that I should never find your Paul, as you don't know neither the name of his street,—but I'll tell ye now all the streets I'm acquainted with, and that's a many; do you stop me, mistress, when I come to the right; for you're sadly bruised, and I won't see ye left this ways on the road."

He then named several streets; the mulatto woman stopped him at one name, which she recollected to be the name of the street in which the gardener lived. The woman at the turnpike-house, as soon as she heard the street in which he lived named, said she knew this gardener; that he had a large garden about a mile off, and that he came from London early almost every morning, with his cart, for garden-stuff for the market; she advised the mulatto woman to stay where she was that night, and to send to ask the gardener to come on to the turnpike-house for her, in the morning. The postillion promised to go to the gardener's "by the first break of day"; the woman raised her head to bless him, and the impatient Holloway loudly called to him to return to his horses, swearing that he would not give him one farthing for himself, if he did not.

The anxiety, which Holloway felt to escape detection, kept him in pain; but Holloway never measured or estimated his pleasures and his pains, therefore he never discovered, that, even upon the most selfish calculation, he had paid too dear for the pleasure of sitting upon a coach-box for one hour.

It was two o'clock in the morning before the chaise arrived in town, when he was set down at the house at which the stagecoach put up, walked home, got in at his bed-chamber window—his bed-chamber was upon the ground-floor;—Mr. Supine was fast asleep, and his pupil triumphed in his successful *frolic*.

Whilst Holloway, in his dreams, was driving again, and again overturning stage-coaches, young Howard, in his less manly dreams, saw Dr. B., the head master of Westminster School, advancing toward him, at a public examination, with a prize medal in his hand, which turned, Howard thought, as he looked upon it, first into the face of his aunt, smiling upon him; then into a striking likeness of his tutor, Mr. Russell, who also smiled upon him; and then changed into the head of little Oliver, whose eyes seemed to sparkle with joy. Just at the instant Howard awoke, and, opening his eyes, saw Oliver's face close to him, laughing heartily.

"Why," exclaimed Oliver, "you seized my head with both your hands, when I came to waken you, what could you be dreaming of, Charles?"

"I dreamed, I took you for a medal, and I was right glad to have hold of you," said Howard, laughing; "but I shall not get my medal by dreaming about it. What o'clock is it? I shall be ready in half a second."

"Ay," said Oliver, "I won't tell you what o'clock it is till you're dressed: make haste; I have been up this half hour, and I've got every thing ready, and I've carried the little table, and all your books, and the pen and ink, and all the things, out to our seat; and the sun shines upon it, and every thing looks cheerful, and you'll have a full hour to work, for it's only half after five."

At the back of Mrs. Howard's house there was a little garden; at the end of the garden was a sort of root-house, which Oliver had cleaned out, and which he dignified by the title of *the Seat*.[58]

There were some pots of geraniums and myrtles kept in it, with Mrs. Howard's permission, by a gardener, who lived next door to her, and who frequently came to work in her garden. Oliver watered the geraniums, and picked off the dead leaves, whilst Howard was writing at the little table, which had been prepared for him. Howard had at this time two grand works in hand, on which he was enthusiastically intent; he was translating the little French book, which the traveller had given to him; and he was writing *an essay for a prize.* The young gentlemen at Westminster were engaged in writing essays for a periodical paper, and Dr. B. had promised to give a prize medal as the reward for that essay, which he, and a jury of critics, to be chosen from among the boys themselves, should pronounce to be the best composition.

"I won't talk to you, I won't interrupt you," said Oliver to Howard, "but only answer me one question: what is your essay about?"

Howard put his finger upon his lips, and shook his head.

"I assure you, I did not look, though I longed to peep at it this morning before you were up. Pray, Charles, do you think *I* shall ever be able to write essays?"

"To be sure," said Howard, "why not?"

"Ah," said Oliver, with a sigh, "because I've no genius, you know."

"But," said Howard, "have not you found out, that you could do a great many things, that you thought you could not do?"

"Ay, thank you for that: but then you know, those are the sort of things, which can be done without genius."

"And what *are* the things," replied Howard, "which cannot be done without genius?"

"Oh, a great, *great* many, I believe," said Oliver; "you know Holloway said so."

"But we are not forced to believe it, because Holloway said so, are we? Besides, a *great many things* may mean any thing, buckling your shoes, or putting on your hat, for instance."

Oliver laughed at this, and said, "These, to be sure, are not the sort of things that can't be done without genius."

"What are the sort of things?" repeated Howard. "Let us, now I've the pen in my hand, make a list of them."

"Take a longer bit of paper."

"No, no, the list will not be so very long, as you think it will. What shall I put first?—make haste, for I'm in a hurry."

"Well—writing, then—writing, I am sure, requires genius."

"Why?"

"Because I never could write, and I've often tried and tried to write something, but I never could; because I've no genius for it."

"What did you try to write?" said Howard.

"Why, letters," said Oliver; "my uncle, and my aunt, and my two cousins, desired I would write to them regularly once a fort-night; but I never can make out a letter, and I'm always sorry when letter-writing day comes: and if I sit thinking and thinking, for ever so long, I can find nothing to say. I used always to beg *a beginning* from somebody; but then, when I've got over the begin-ning, that's only three or four lines, and if I stretch it out ever so much, it won't make a whole letter, and what can I put in the mid-dle? There's nothing but that *I am well, and hope they are all well;* or else, *that I am learning Latin, as you desired, dear uncle, and am forward in my English.*

"The end I can manage well enough, because there's duty and love to send to every body: and about *the post is just going out, and believe me to be, in haste, your dutiful and affectionate nephew.* But then," continued little Oliver, "this is all nonsense, I know, and I'm ashamed to write such bad letters: now your pen goes on, scratch, scratch, scratch, the moment you sit down to it, and you can write three pages of a nice, long, good letter, whilst I am writ-ing *'My dear uncle John,'* and that's what I call having a genius for writing. I wonder how you came by it; could you write good letters when you were of my age?"

"I never wrote any letters at your age," said Howard.

"Oh, how happy you must have been! But then, if you never learned, how comes it that you can write them now? How can you always find something to say?"

"I never write, but when I have something to say, and you know, when you had something to say last post about Easter holi-days, your pen, Oliver, went scratch, scratch, scratch, as fast as any body's."

"So it did," cried Oliver; "but then, the thing is, I'm forced to write, when I've nothing about the holidays to say."

"Forced?"

"Yes, because I'm afraid my uncle and cousins should be angry if I didn't write."

"I'm sure I'm much obliged," said Howard, "to my dear aunt, who never forced me to write: she always said, 'never write, Charles, but when you like it': and I never did. When I had any thing to say, that is, any thing to describe, or any reasons to give, upon any subject, or any questions to ask, which I very much wished to have answered, then, you know, I could easily write, because I had nothing to do, but to write down just the words which I should have said, if I had been speaking."

"But I thought writing was quite a different thing from speaking, because, in writing, there must be sentences, and long sentences, and fine sentences, such as there are in books."

"In *some* books," said Howard, "but not in all."

"Besides," continued Oliver, "one person's speaking is quite different from another person's speaking. Now I believe, I make use of a great number of odd words, and vulgar expressions, and bad English, which I learned from being with the servants, I believe, at home. You have never talked to servants, Charles, I dare say, for you have not one of their words."

"No," said Charles, "never, and my aunt took a great deal of pains, to prevent me from hearing any of their conversation; therefore it was impossible that I should catch—"

Here the conversation was interrupted by the appearance of old Paul, the gardener.

"So, Paul," cried little Oliver, "I've been doing your work for you, this morning; I've watered all the geraniums, and put the Indian corn in the sun; what kept you so late in your bed this fine morning, Paul? Fie, Paul!"

"You would not say fie, master," replied Paul, "if you knew how early I had been out of my bed this morning: I was abroad afore sun-rise, so I was, master."

"And why didn't you come to work then, Paul? You shall not have the watering-pot till you tell me: don't look so grave about it; you know you must smile when I please, Paul."

"I can't smile, just now, master," said old Paul; but he smiled, and then told Oliver, that "the reason he could not smile was, that he was a little sick at heart, with just coming from the sight of a poor soul who had been sadly bruised by a fall from the top of the stage, which was overturned last night. She was left all night at the *pike*, and as she had no other friends, she sent for me by a return chay-boy,[59] and I went for her, and brought her home in my covered cart, to my good woman, which she liked, with good reason, better, ten to one, than the stage. And she's terribly black and blue, and does not seem quite right in her head, to my fancy."

"I wish we could do something for her," said Howard. "As soon as Mr. Russell is up, I'll ask him to go with us to see her. We will call as we go by to school this morning."

"But, master," said the gardener, "I should warn ye before hand, that mayhap you mayn't pity her so much, for she's rather past her best days; and bad must have been her best, for she's swarthy, and not like one of this country; she comes from over the seas, and they call her a—a—not quite a negro."

"A mulatto!—I like her the better," cried Oliver, "for my nurse was a mulatto. I'll go and waken Mr. Russell this instant, for I'm sure he'll not be angry." He ran away to Mr. Russell, who was not angry at being awakened, but dressed himself *almost* as expeditiously as Oliver wished, and set out immediately with his pupils, delighted to be the companion of their benevolent schemes, instead of being the object of their fear and hatred. Tutors may inspire affection, even though they have the misfortune to be obliged to teach Greek and Latin[¶].[60]

When the boys arrived at the gardener's they found the poor mulatto woman lying upon a bed, in a small close room, which was so full of smoke, when they came in, that they could hardly breathe; the little window, that let in but a glimmering light, could not, without difficulty, be opened. The poor woman made but few complaints; she appeared to be most concerned at the thoughts of being a burden to the good old gardener and his wife. She said, that she had not been long in England, that she came to London in hopes of finding a family, who had been very kind to her in her youth; but that, after inquiry at the house where they formerly lived, she could hear nothing of them. After

---

¶ Vide Dr. Johnson's assertions to the contrary, in Mrs. Piozzi's Anecdotes.

a great deal of trouble, she discovered that a West India gentleman, who had known her abroad, was now at Bath; but she had
spent the last farthing of her money, and she was, therefore,
unable to undertake the journey. She had brought over with her,
she said, some foreign seeds of flowers, which her young mistress
used to be fond of when she was a child, which she had kept
till hunger obliged her to offer them to a gardener, for a loaf of
bread. The gardener, to whom she offered them, was old Paul,
who took compassion upon her distress, lodged her for a week,
and, at last paid for an outside place for her upon the Bath coach.
There was such an air of truth and simplicity in this woman,
that Mr. Russell, more experienced than his pupils, believed her
story, at once, as implicitly as they did, "Oh," exclaimed little
Oliver, "I have but this half crown for her; I wish Holloway had
but paid me my half-guinea; I'll ask him for it again to-day; and
will you come with us here again, this evening, Mr. Russell, that
I may bring it then?"

Mr. Russell and Howard hired the room, for a fortnight, in
which the mulatto woman was now lying; and paid old Paul, the
gardener, for it; promising, at the same time, to supply her with
food. The gardener's wife, at the poor woman's earnest request,
promised, that, as soon as she was able to sit up, she would get her
some coarse plain work to do.

"But," said Oliver, "how can she see to work in this smoke? I'm
sure it makes my eyes water so, that I can hardly bear it, though I
have been in it scarcely ten minutes."

"I wish," exclaimed Howard, turning to Mr. Russell, "that this
chimney could be cured of smoking."

"Oh, well-a-day," said the gardener, "we must put up with it as
it is, for I've had doctors to it, at one time or another, that have
cost me a power of money: but, after all, it's as bad as ever, and my
good dame never lights a fire in it this fine spring weather; how-
somever, she," pointing to the mulatto woman, "is so chilly, coming from a country, that, by all accounts, is a hot-house, compared
with ours, that she can't sleep o' nights, or live o' days, without a
small matter of fire, which she's welcome to; though, you see, it
almost fills the house with smoke."

Howard, during the gardener's speech, had been trying to recollect, where it was, that he had lately seen some essay upon smoky

chimneys; and he suddenly exclaimed, "It was in Dr. Franklin's works; was it not, Mr. Russell?"[61]

"What?" said Mr. Russell, smiling.

"That essay upon smoky chimneys, which I said I would skip over, the other day, because I had nothing to do with it; and I thought I should not understand. Don't you remember telling me, sir, that I had better not skip it, because it might, some time or other, be useful to me? I wish I could get the book now, I would take pains to understand it, because, perhaps, I might find out how this poor man's chimney might be cured of smoking; as for his window, I know how that can be easily mended, because I once watched a man who was hanging some windows for my aunt—I'll get some sash line."

"Do you recollect what o'clock it is, my good friend?" said Mr. Russell, holding out his watch to Howard. "We cannot wait till you are perfect master of the theory of smoky chimneys, and the practice of hanging windows; it is time that we should be gone." Mr. Russell spoke this with an air of raillery, as he usually did, when he was particularly pleased.

As they were going away, Oliver earnestly repeated his request, that Mr. Russell would come again in the evening, that he might have an opportunity of giving the poor woman his half-guinea. Mr. Russell promised him that he would; but he at the same time added, "All charity, my dear Oliver, does not consist in giving money; it is easy for a man to put his hand in his pocket and take out a few shillings, to give any person in distress."

"I wish," said Oliver, "I was able to do more! What can I do? I'll think of something. Howard, will you think of something that I can do? But I must see about my Latin lesson first, for I had not time to look it over this morning, before I came out."

When they got back, the business of the day for some hours suspended all thoughts of the mulatto woman; but in the first interval of leisure, Oliver went in search of Mr. Holloway, to ask for his half-guinea. Holloway had a crowd of his companions round him, whom he seemed to be entertaining with some very diverting story, for they were laughing violently when little Oliver first came up to them; but they no sooner perceived him, than all their merriment suddenly ceased. Holloway first lowered his voice into a whisper, and then observing, that Oliver still stood his ground, he asked him, in his usual peremptory tone, what might be his business? Oliver drew him aside, and asked him to pay him *the* half-guinea. "*The* half-guinea?" repeated Holloway: "man, you talk of *the* half-guinea, as if there was but one half-guinea in the world; you shall have *the* half-guinea, for I hate to be dunned——stay, I believe I have no *half* a guinea about me; you can't give me two half-guineas for a guinea, can ye?"[62]

"Me!"

"Well, then, you must wait till I can get change."

"Must I wait? But I really want it for a particular reason, this evening; I wish you could give it me now, you know you promised; but I don't like putting people in mind of their promises, and I would not ask you about the money, only that I really want it."

"Want it!—nonsense; what can you want money for, such a little chap as you? I'll lay you any wager, your *particular reason*, if the truth was told, is, that you can't resist the tart-woman."

"I *can* resist the tart-woman," cried Oliver proudly; "I have a much better use for my money; but I don't want to boast, neither; only, Holloway, do give me the half-guinea; shall I run and ask somebody to give you two half-guineas for a guinea?"

"No, no, I'll not be dunned into paying you. If you had not asked me for it, I should have given it you to-night; but since you could not trust to my honour, you'll please to wait till to-morrow morning."

"But I did trust to your honour for a whole month."

"A month; a great while, indeed; then trust to it a day longer, and if you ask me for the money to-morrow, you sha'n't have it till the next day; I'll teach you not to be such a little dun; nobody, that has any spirit, can bear to be dunned, particularly for such small sums. I thought you had been above such meanness, or, I promise you, I should never have borrowed your half-guinea," added Holloway; and he left his unfortunate creditor, to reflect upon the new ideas of *meanness* and *spirit*, which had been thus artfully thrown out.

Oliver was roused from his reflections by his friend Howard. "Mr. Russell is ready to go with us to the gardener's again," said Howard, "have you a mind to come?"

"A great mind; but I am ashamed, for I've not got my half-guinea, which I lent." Here his newly-acquired fear of meanness checked Oliver, and, without complaining of his creditor's want of punctuality, he added—"but I should like to see the poor woman, though, for all that."

They set out, but stopped in their way at a bookseller's, where Howard inquired for that essay of Dr. Franklin's on smoky chimneys, which he was impatient to see. This bookseller was well acquainted with Mr. Russell; Howard had promised to give the bookseller the translation, of the little French book which we formerly mentioned; and the bookseller, on his part, was very obliging in furnishing Howard with any books he wanted.

Howard was deep in the essay on smoky chimneys, and examining the references in the print belonging to it, whilst Mr. Russell was looking over the prints in the Encyclopedia, with little Oliver. They were all so intent upon what they were about, that they did not perceive the entrance of Holloway and Mr. Supine. Mr. Supine called in merely to see what Mr. Russell could be looking at, with so much appearance of interest. The indolent are always curious, though they will not always exert themselves, even to gratify their curiosity.

"Only the Encyclopedia prints," said Supine, looking over Mr. Russell's shoulder; "I thought you had got something new,"

"Only smoky chimneys," exclaimed Holloway, looking over Howard's shoulder, "what upon earth, Howard, can you find so entertaining in smoky chimneys? Are you turned chimney-doctor, or chimney-sweeper? This will be an excellent thing for Lord Rawson, won't it, Mr. Supine? We'll tell it to him on Thursday; it will be a good joke for us, for half the day.—Pray, Doctor Charles Howard," continued the wit, with mock solemnity, "do you go up the chimneys yourself?"

Howard took this raillery with so much good humour, that Holloway looked quite disappointed, and Mr. Supine, in a careless tone, cried, "I take it reading such things as these will scarcely improve your style, sir; will they, think ye, Mr. Russell?"

"I am not sure," replied Mr. Russell, "that Mr. Howard's *first* object, in reading, is to improve his style; but," added he, turning to the title-page, and pointing to Franklin's name, "you, perhaps, did not know——"

"Oh, Dr. Franklin's works," interrupted Supine, "I did not see the name before; to be sure I must bow down to *that*."

Having thus easily satisfied Mr. Supine's critical scruples by the authority of a name, Mr. Russell rose to depart, as he perceived that there was no chance of getting rid of the idlers.

"What are you going to do with yourself, Russell?" said Mr. Supine; "we'll walk with you, if you are for walking, this fine evening; only don't let's walk like penny post-men."

"But he's in a hurry," said Oliver; "he's going to see a poor woman."

"A *poor* woman!" said Supine, "down this close lane too!"

"Oh, let's see all that's to be seen," whispered Holloway, "ten to one we shall get some diversion out of it; Russell's a quiz worth studying, and Howard's his ditto."

They came to the gardener's house. Holloway's high spirits suddenly subsided, when he beheld the figure of the mulatto woman.

"What's the matter?" said Oliver, observing that he started; "why did you start so?"

"Tell Howard I want to speak one word with him, this instant, in the street; bid him come out to me," whispered Holloway; and he hastily retreated before the poor woman saw his face.

"Howard," cried Holloway, "I sent for you, to tell you a great secret."

"I'm sorry for it," said Charles, "for I hate secrets."

"But you can keep a secret, man, can't you?"

"If it were necessary, I hope I could; but I'd rather not hear——"

"Pooh, nonsense," interrupted Holloway, "you must hear it; I'll trust to your honour; and, besides, I have not a moment to stand shilly shally; I've got a promise from my father, to let me go down, this Easter, with Lord Rawson, to Marryborough, in his dog-cart, *randem-tandem*, you know."

"I did not know it, indeed," said Charles; "but what then?"

"Why, then, you see, I must be upon my good behaviour, and you would not do such an ill-natured trick as to betray me?"

"Betray you! I don't know what you mean," said Howard, astonished.

Holloway now briefly told him his stage-coach adventure, and concluded by saying, he was afraid that the mulatto woman should recollect either his face or voice, and should *blow him*.[63]

"And what," said Howard, shocked at the selfishness which Holloway showed—"and what do you want me to do? Why do you tell me all this?"

"Because," said Holloway, "I thought, if you heard what the woman said, when she saw me, you would have got it all out of her, to be sure; therefore I thought it best to trust you with my secret, and so put you upon honour with me. All I ask of you is, to hold your tongue about my—my—my frolic, and just make some excuse for my not going into the room again, where the mulatto woman is: you may tell Supine, if he asks what's become of me, that I'm gone to the music shop, to get some new music for him: that will keep him quiet.—Good bye."

"Stay," cried Howard, "I promise you only not to betray you; I will not make any false excuses."

"You are the greatest quiz, you are the most confounded prig, that ever existed: I tell you, I am going to the music shop:—I trust to your honour.—Lord Rawson, I know, will call me a fool for trusting to the honour of a quiz."[64]

Howard stood for a few minutes fixed to the spot, after Holloway left him; the words "quiz" and "prig" he had not heard without emotion: but his good sense quickly recovered him, and he dared to abide by his own ideas of honour, even though Lord Rawson might call it the honour of a quiz.

When Howard returned to the room where the mulatto woman lay, he expected to be questioned by Mr. Supine about Holloway's sudden departure; but this gentleman was not in the habit of paying great attention to his pupil's motions. He took it for granted, that Holloway had escaped, because he did not wish to be called upon for a charitable subscription; from the same fear, Mr. Supine affected unusual absence of mind, whilst Mr. Russell talked to the mulatto woman, and at length, professing himself unable to endure any longer the smell of smoke, he pushed his way into the street. "Mr. Holloway, I suppose," said he, "has taken himself home, very wisely, and I shall follow him: we make it a rule, I think, to miss one another; but to keep a young man in leading-strings would be a great *bore*—we're upon the best footing in the world together: as to the rest—"

New difficulties awaited Holloway. He got home some time before Mr. Supine, and found his friend, the stage-coachman, waiting for him with a rueful face.

"Master," said, he, "here's a sad job: there was a parcel lost last night, in the confusion of the overturn of the coach; and I must make it good, for it's booked, and it's booked to the value of five guineas, for it was a gold muslin gown, that a lady was very particular about—and, master, I won't peach if you'll pay; but as for losing my place, or making up five guineas afore Saturday, it's what I can't take upon me to do."

Holloway was much dismayed at this news; he now began to think he should pay too dear for his frolic. The coachman persisted in his demand. Mr. Supine appeared at the corner of the street, and his pupil was forced to get rid immediately of the coachman, by a promise, that the money should be ready on Saturday. When Holloway made this promise, he was not master of two guineas in the world; how to procure the whole sum was now the question. Alderman Holloway, with the hope of exciting in his son's mind a love for literature, made it a practice to reward him with *solid gold,* whenever he brought home any certificate of his scholarship. Holloway had lately received five guineas from his father, for an approved copy of Latin verses; and the alderman had promised to give him five guineas more if he brought home the medal, which was to be the reward for the best essay in the periodical paper, which the Westminster boys were now writing. Holloway, though he could write elegant Latin verses, had not any great facility in English composition; he, consequently, according to the usual practice of little minds, undervalued a talent, which he did not possess. He had ridiculed the scheme of writing an English periodical paper, and had loudly declared, that he did not think it worth his while to write English. His opinion was, however, somewhat changed, by his father's promised reward; and the stage-coachman's impatience for his money, now impelled Holloway to exertion. He began to write his essay late on Friday evening; the medal was to be given on Saturday morning; so that there could not be much time for revisal and corrections. Corrections he affected to disdain, and piqued himself upon the rapidity with which he wrote. "Howard," said he, when they met, to deliver in their compositions, "you have been three weeks writing your essay; I ran mine off in three hours and a quarter."

Mr. Holloway had not considered, that what is written with ease is not always read with ease. His essay was written with such a careless superfluity of words, and such a lack of ideas appeared in the performance, that the judges unanimously threw it aside, as unworthy of their notice. "Gentlemen," cried Dr. B., coming forward among the anxious crowd of expectants, "which of you owns this motto? It is from Dr. Darwin's Botanic Garden.

> "'Hear it, ye Senates, hear this truth sublime,
> He who allows oppression shares the crime.**' "[65]

"It's his!—It's his!—It's his!" exclaimed little Oliver, clapping his hands; "It's Howard's, sir."

Dr. B., pleased with this grateful little boy's honest joy, put the medal into his hands, without speaking, and Oliver ran with it to his friend. "Only," said he, "only let me be by, when you show it to your aunt."

How much the pleasure of success is increased by the sympathy of our friends! The triumph of a school-boy over his competitors is sometimes despicable; but Howard's joy was not of this selfish and puerile sort. All the good passions had stimulated him to exertion, and he was rewarded by his own generous feelings. He would not have exchanged the delight which he saw in his little friend Oliver's face, the approving smile of his aunt, and the proud satisfaction Mr. Russell expressed at the sight of his medal, for all the solid gold which Alderman Holloway deemed the highest reward of literature.

Alderman Holloway was filled with indignation, when he heard, from Mr. Supine, that his son's essay had been rejected with contempt. The young gentleman was also much surprised at the decision of the judges; and his tutor, by way of pleasing his pupil's friends, hesitated not to hint, that there "certainly was great injustice done to Mr. Augustus Holloway's talents." The subject was canvassed at a turtle dinner, at the alderman's.[66] "There shall not be injustice done to my Augustus," said the irritated father, wisely encouraging his Augustus in all his mean feelings. "Never mind 'em all, my boy; you have a father, you may thank Heaven, who *can* judge for himself, and *will*; you shall not be the loser by Dr. B.'s, or Doctor Any Body's injustice; I'll make it up to you, my boy; in the mean time, join us in a bumper of port. Here's to Dr. B.'s better judgment; wishing him his health and happiness these Easter holidays, and a *new pair of spectacles,*—hey, Mr. Supine!"

** Botanic Garden, vol. ii.

This well-chosen toast was drunk with much applause and laughter by the company. The alderman insisted upon having his Augustus's essay produced in the evening. Holloway had now ample satisfaction, for the whole company were unanimous in their plaudits, after Mr. Supine had read two or three sentences: the alderman, to confirm his own critical judgment, drew out his purse, and counting out ten bright guineas, presented them, with a look of high self-satisfaction, to his son. "Here, Augustus, my boy," said he; "I promised you five guineas if you brought me home the prize medal, but I now present you with ten, to make you the amends you so richly deserve, for not having got their medal. Thank God, I am able to afford it, and I hope," added the alderman, looking round, and laughing, "I hope I'm as good a patron of the *belles lettres* as the head doctor of Westminster himself."

Holloway's eyes sparkled with joy at the sight of the glittering bribe. He began some speech in reply, in which he compared his father to Mecænas,[67] but being entangled in a sentence, in which the nominative case had been too long separated from the verb, he was compelled to pause abruptly.—Nevertheless, the alderman rubbed his hands with exultation; and "Hear him ! Hear him!—Hear your member!" was vociferated by all the friends of the young orator.—"Well, really," concluded his mother, to the ladies, who were complimenting her upon her son's performance, "it was not a bad speech, considering he had nothing to say!"

Lord Rawson, who was one of the company, now congratulated his friend in a whisper—"You've made a good job of it to-day, Augustus," said he; "solid pudding's better than empty praise. We're going," continued his Lordship, to the alderman, "to try my new horses in my barouche this evening"; and he pulled Augustus with him out of the room.

"There they go," said the prudent father, delighted with his own son's being the chosen friend of a nobleman—"there they go, arm in arm, a couple of rare ones—we shall have fine work with them, I foresee, when Augustus gets to college—but young men of spirit must not be curbed like common boys—we must make allowances—I have been young myself.—Hey, Mr. Supine?"

"Certainly, sir," said the obsequious tutor; "and you still have all the sprightliness of youth—and my ideas of education square completely with yours."

According to Alderman Holloway's ideas of education, the holidays were always to be made a season of complete idleness and dissipation, to relieve his son from his school studies. It was his great delight, to contrast the pleasures of home with the hardships of school, and to make his son compare the indulgence of a father with the severity of a school-master. How he could expect an education to succeed, which he sedulously endeavoured to counteract, it may be difficult for any rational person to conceive.

After Lord Rawson and Holloway had enjoyed the pleasures of driving a barouche and a dog-cart, *randem-tandem,* and had conversed about dogs and horses, till they had nothing left to say to each other, his Lordship proposed stepping in to Mr. Carat, the jeweller's shop, to look at some new watches: his Lordship said, he was tired of his own watch, for he had had it six months. Mr. Carat was not in the way, when they first went in. One of the young men, who attended in the shop, said, "that his master was extremely busy, in settling some accounts with a captain of a ship, who was to leave England in a few days."

"Don't tell me of settling accounts," cried Lord Rawson, "I hate the sound of settling accounts; run and tell Mr. Carat that Lord Rawson is here, and must speak to him this instant, for I'm in a desperate hurry."

A quarter of an hour elapsed before the impatient lord could be obeyed; during this time, his Lordship and Holloway rummaged over every thing in the shop.—A pretty bauble to hang to his watch caught his Lordship's fancy. His Lordship happened to have no money in his pocket.—"Holloway," said he, "my good fellow, you've ten guineas in your pocket, I know; do lend me them here." Holloway, rather proud of his riches, lent his ten guineas to his noble friend with alacrity; but a few minutes afterward recollected that he should want five of them, that very night, to pay the poor stage-coachman. His recollection came too late, for after Lord Rawson had paid three or four guineas for his trinket, he let the remainder of the money down, with an absent nonchalance, into his pocket. "We'll settle—I'll pay you, Holloway, to-morrow morning, you know."

Holloway, from false shame, replied, "Oh, very well." And at this instant Mr. Carat entered the shop, bowing and apologizing to his Lordship for having been busy.

"I'm always, to be sure, in a very great hurry," cried Lord Rawson; "I never have a minute, that I can call my own. All I wanted, though, just now, was to tell you, that I could not settle any thing—you understand—till we come back from Marryborough. I go down there to-morrow."

The Jew bowed with unlimited acquiescence, assuring his Lordship, that he should ever wait his perfect convenience. As he spoke, he glanced an inquiring eye upon Holloway.

"Mr. Holloway, the eldest, the only son of Alderman Holloway; rich as a Jew! And he'll soon leave Westminster," whispered Lord Rawson to the Jew. "Holloway," continued he, turning to his friend, "give me leave to introduce Mr. Carat to you. You may," added his Lordship, lowering his voice, "find this Jew a useful friend, some time or other, my lad. He's my man in all money jobs."

The Jew and the school-boy seemed equally flattered and pleased by this introduction; they were quickly upon familiar terms with one another; and Mr. Carat, who was willing that such an acquaintance should begin in the most advantageous and agreeable manner on his part, took the young gentleman, with an air of mystery and confidence, into a little room behind the shop; there he produced a box full of old fashioned second-hand trinkets, and, without giving Holloway time to examine them, said, that he was going to make a lottery of these things. "If I had any young favourite friends," continued the wily Jew, "I should give them a little whisper in the ear, and bid them try their fortune; they never will have a finer opportunity." He then presented a hand-bill, drawn up in a style which even Messrs. Goodluck and Co. need not have disdained to admire.[68] The youth was charmed with the composition. The Jew made him a present of a couple of tickets for himself, and gave him a dozen more, to distribute amongst his companions at Westminster. Holloway readily undertook to distribute the tickets, upon condition that he might have a list of the prizes in the lottery. "If they don't see a list of the prizes," said he, "not a soul will put in."

The Jew took a pen immediately, and drew up a captivating list of prizes.

Holloway promised to copy it, because Mr. Carat said, his hand must not appear in the business, and it must be conducted with

the strictest secrecy, because "the law," added the Jew, "has a little jealousy of these sort of things—government likes none but
licensed lotteries, young gentleman."

"The law! I don't care what the law likes," replied the school-
boy; "if I break the law, I hope I'm rich enough to pay the forfeit,
or my father will pay for me, which is better still."

To this doctrine the Jew readily assented, and they parted, mutu-
ally satisfied with each other. It was agreed, that Lord Rawson
should drive his friend to Marryborough the next Tuesday, and that
he should return on Wednesday, with Holloway, to Westminster,
on purpose that he might meet Mr. Carat there, who was then to
deliver the prizes.

"I'll lay you a bet," cried Lord Rawson, as he left the Jew's, "that
you'll have a prize yourself. Now are you not obliged to me for
introducing you to Carat?"

"Yes, that I am," replied Holloway; "it's easier to put into the lottery than to write Latin verses and English essays. I'll puzzle and
bore myself no more with those things, I promise my father."

"Who does, after they've once left school, I want to know?" said
his noble friend. "I'm sure I've forgot all I ever learned from Latin
and Greek fellows; you know they tell just for nothing when one
gets into the world. I make it a principle never to talk of books, for
nobody does, you know, that has any thing else to talk of. None
but quizzes and quozzes ever came out with any thing of that sort.
Now, how they'd stare at Marryborough, Holloway, if you were to
begin sporting some of your Horace and Virgil!"

The dashing, yet bashful school-boy, with much emotion,
swore that he cared as little for Horace and Virgil as his Lordship
did. Holloway was really an excellent scholar, but he began to be
heartily ashamed of it in his Lordship's company, and prudently
resolved to adopt the principles he had just heard; to forget as fast
as possible all he had learned; never to talk of books; and to con-
ceal both his knowledge and his abilities, lest *they should stare at
him at Marryborough.*

The lottery tickets were easily disposed of amongst the young
gentlemen at Westminster. As young men can seldom calculate,
they are always ready to trust to their individual good fortune,
and they are, consequently, ever ready to put into any species of
lottery.

"Look here!" cried little Oliver, showing a lottery ticket to Howard; "look what Holloway has just offered to give me, instead of half a guinea, which he owes me. I told him I would just run and ask your advice. Shall I accept of it?"

"I would advise you not," answered Howard; "you are sure of your half-guinea, and you have only a chance of getting any thing in the lottery."

"Oh, but then I've a chance of such a number of fine things! You have not seen the list of prizes. Do you know there's a watch amongst them? Now, suppose my ticket should come up a prize, and that I should get a watch for my half-guinea!—A real watch!— A watch that would *go*!—A watch that I should wind up myself every night! Oh, Charles! Would not that be a good bargain for my half-guinea? I'm sure you have not read the list of prizes, have you?"

"No; I have not," said Howard; "have you seen the list of blanks?"

"Of blanks! No," said Oliver, with a changed countenance; "I never thought of the blanks."

"And yet in most lotteries there are many more blanks than prizes, you know."

"Are there? Well, but I hope I shall not have a blank," said Oliver.

"So every body hopes, but some people must be disappointed."

"Yes," said the little boy, pausing—"but then some people must win, and I have as good a chance as another, have not I?"

"And do you know what the chance against your winning is? Once I had a great mind, as you have now, Oliver, to put into a lottery. It was just after my aunt lost all her fortune, and I thought that, if I were to get the twenty thousand pound prize, I could give it to her."

"Ah, that is so like you! I'll give my watch (if I get it, I mean) to somebody. I'll give it to the mulatto woman, because she is poor. No; I'll give it to you, because you are the best, and I love you the best, and I am more obliged to you than to any body in the world, for you have taught me more; and you have taught me as I was never taught before, without laughing at, or scolding, or frightening, or calling me blockhead, or dunce; and you have made me think a great deal better of myself; and I am always happy when I'm with you; and I'm quite another creature since you came to school. I hope you'll never leave school whilst I am here," cried Oliver.

"But you have quite forgot the lottery," said Howard, smiling, and much touched by his little friend's simplicity and enthusiasm.

"O, the lottery! Ay," said Oliver, "you were telling me something about yourself, do go on."

"I once thought, as you do now, that it would be a charming thing to put into a lottery."

"Well, and did you win?"

"No."

"Did you lose?"

"No."

"How then?"

"I did not put into the lottery, for I was convinced that it was a foolish way of spending money."

"If you think it's foolish or wrong," said Oliver, "I'll have nothing to do with this lottery."

"I don't want to govern you by my opinion," said Howard; "but if you have patience to attend to all the reasons that convinced me, you will be able to judge, and form an opinion for yourself. You know I must leave school some time or other, and then——"

"Well, don't talk of that, but tell me all the reasons, quick."

"I can't tell them so very quickly," said Howard, laughing; "when we go home this evening, I'll ask my aunt to look for the passage in Smith's Wealth of Nations, which she showed me."[69]

"Oh!" interrupted Oliver, with a sigh, "*Smith's Wealth* of what? That's a book, I'm sure, I shall never be able to understand; is it not that great large book that Mr. Russell reads?"

"Yes."

"But I shall never understand it."

"Because it's a large book?"

"No," said Oliver, smiling, "but because I suppose it's very difficult to understand."

"Not what I've read of it: but I have only read passages here and there. That passage about lotteries, I think, you would understand, because it is so plainly written."

"I'll read it, then," said Oliver, "and try; and in the meantime I'll go and tell Holloway that I had rather not put into the lottery, till I know whether it's right or not."

Holloway flew into a violent passion with little Oliver when he went to return his lottery ticket. He abused and ridiculed Howard for his interference, and succeeded so well in raising a popular cry that the moment Howard appeared on the play-ground, a general hiss, succeeded by a deep groan, was heard.—Howard recollected the oracle's answer to Cicero, and was not dismayed by the voice of the multitude.[70] Holloway threw down half a guinea, to pay Oliver, and muttered to himself, "I'll make you remember this, Mr. Oliver."

"I'll give this half-guinea to the mulatto woman, and that's much better than putting it into a lottery, Charles!" said the little boy; and as soon as the business of the day was done, Oliver, Howard, and Mr. Russell, took their usual evening's walk towards the gardener's house.

"Ay, come in!" cried old Paul, "come in! God bless you all! I don't know which is the best of you. I've been looking out of my door this quarter of an hour for ye," said he, as soon as he saw them, "and I don't know when I've been idle a quarter of an hour afore. But I've put on my best coat, though it's not Sunday, and wife has treated *her* to a dish of tea, and she's up and dressed; the mulatto woman, I mean, and quite hearty again. Walk in, walk in; it will do your hearts good to see her; she's so grateful too, though she can't speak good English, which is her only fault, poor soul; but we can't be born what we like, or she would have been as good an Englishman as the best of us. Walk in, walk in!—And the chimney does not smoke, master, no more than I do; and the window opens too; and the paper's up, and looks beautiful. God bless ye, God bless ye! Walk in."—Old Paul, whilst he spoke, had stopped the way into the room; but at length he recollected that they could not *walk in* whilst he stood in the door-way, and he let them pass.

The little room was no longer the smoky, dismal, miserable place which it was formerly. It was neatly papered; it was swept clean; there was a cheerful fire, which burned quite clearly; the mulatto woman was cleanly dressed, and, rising from her work, she clasped her hands together with an emotion of joyful gratitude, which said more than any words could have expressed.

This room was not papered, nor was the chimney cured of smoking, nor was the woman clad in new clothes, by magic. It was all done by human means; by the industry and abilities of a benevolent boy.

The translation of the little French book, which Howard had completed, procured him the means of doing good. The bookseller to whom he offered it was both an honest man, and a good judge of literary productions, Mr. Russell's name also operated in his pupil's favour, and Howard received ten guineas for his translation.

Oliver was impatient for an opportunity to give his half-guinea, which he had held in his hand, till it was quite warm. "Let me look at that pretty thimble of yours," said he, going up to the mulatto woman, who had now taken up her work again; and, as he playfully pulled off the thimble, he slipped his half-guinea into her hand; then he stopped her thanks, by running on to a hundred questions about her thimble. "What a strange thimble! How came you by such a thimble? Was it given to you? Did you buy it? What's the use of this screw round the inside of the rim of it? Do look at it, Charles!"

The thimble was, indeed, remarkable; and it seemed extraordinary, that such a one should belong to a poor woman, who had lately been in great distress.

"It is gold," said Mr. Russell, examining it, "and very old gold."

The mulatto woman sighed; and as she put the thimble upon her finger again, said, that she did not know whether it was gold or not; but she had a great value for it: that she had had it a great many years; that it had been given to her by the best friend she had ever had.

"Tell me about that best friend," said Oliver; "I like to hear about best friends."

"She was a very good friend indeed; though she was but young, scarcely bigger than yourself, at the time she gave me this thimble: she was my young mistress; I came all the way from Jamaica on purpose to find her out, and in hopes to live with her in my elder days."

"Jamaica!" cried Howard—"Jamaica!" cried Oliver, in the same breath, "what was her name?"

"Frances Howard."

"My aunt!" exclaimed Howard.

"I'll run and tell her; I'll run and bring her here, this instant!" said Oliver. But Mr. Russell caught hold of him, and detained him, whilst they farther questioned the woman. Her answers were perfectly consistent and satisfactory. She said, that her mistress's estate, in Jamaica, had been sold, just before she left the island; that some of the old slaves had been set at liberty, by orders, which came, she understood, in her mistress's last letter; and that, amongst the rest, she had been freed: that she had heard say, that her good mistress had desired the agent to give her also some little *provision ground*, upon the plantation, but that this had never been done; and that she had sold all the clothes and little things she possessed, to raise money to pay for her passage to England, hoping to find her mistress in London. She added, that the agent had given her a direction to her mistress; but that she had, in vain, applied at the house, and at every house in the same street. "Show us the direction, if you have it," said Mr. Russell. The woman said, she had kept it very carefully; but now it was almost worn out. The direction was, however, still legible upon the ragged bit of paper, which she produced—*To Mrs. Frances Howard, Portman Square, London.* The instant Mr. Russell was satisfied, he was as expeditious as Oliver himself; they all three went home immediately to Mrs. Howard: she had, some time before, been confined to her room by a severe toothache. "You promised me, aunt," said her nephew, "that as soon as you were well enough, you would go to old Paul's with us, to see our poor woman; can you go this evening?"

"Oh do! Do, pray; I'm sure you won't catch cold," said Oliver; "for we have a very particular reason for wishing you to go."

"There is a sedan chair at the door," said Mr. Russell, "if you are afraid, madam, of catching cold."

"I am not rich enough to go out in sedan chairs," interrupted Mrs. Howard; "nor prudent enough, I am afraid, to stay at home."

"Oh! Thank you," said Oliver, who had her clogs ready in his hands; "now you'll see something that will surprise you."

"Then take care you don't tell me what it is, before I see it," said Mrs. Howard.

Oliver, with some difficulty, held his tongue during the walk, and contented himself with working off his *superfluous animation*, by jumping over every obstacle in his way.

The meeting between the poor mulatto woman and her mistress was as full of joy and surprise, as little Oliver had expected; and this is saying a great deal, for where much is expected, there is usually much disappointment; and very sympathetic people are often angry with others, for not being as much astonished, or as much delighted, as they think the occasion requires.

When Mrs. Howard returned home, she found a letter had been left for her, from the marquis of——, who was, at this time, high in power. It is well known, that a watchful eye is kept upon every rising genius, in the great seminaries of public education in England. A young man, at Westminster or Eton, who distinguishes himself for abilities, is not distinguished only by his masters and his companions, but by those who see in him the writer or the orator of a future day. Howard's prize essay appeared as well in print, as it had done in manuscript. The names of the boys, who received public premiums at Westminster, were sent, by particular desire, to the marquis of——; and with them Dr. B. sent the little essay, which, he thought, would do Howard credit. He was not mistaken in his judgment. The marquis of——, who possessed the "prophetic eye of taste,"[71] in his answer to Dr. B.'s note, said many civil things of the performance, and begged to know, if there were any thing in his power, which might be done for the lady, who had so well conducted Mr. C. Howard's education; a lady, who, as he understood, had lately met with unmerited misfortunes. His Lordship's letter concluded with a hint, that the place of a housekeeper for one of the king's palaces, an eligible situation, was then vacant, and that a handsome salary would be secured, &c.

Howard's joy, at the perusal of this letter, was heightened by the delight, which he saw painted in his aunt's countenance. She was a woman rather in the habit of repressing her emotions; therefore her sensibility commanded respect, as well as sympathy. "My dear boy! my dear nephew! my dear friend!" said she, "from this moment forward, remember, we are upon equal terms; and I rejoice at it: let me never hear more from you of *obligations* and *gratitude:* you have repaid, amply repaid me for all."

"No, no; I never can; I never wish," interrupted Howard. But so many ideas, and so many grateful feelings rushed upon his mind, that he could not explain farther what he wished, or what he did not wish.

"You can't speak, I perceive," said Mrs. Howard; "but we know, you can write : so sit down and write *your* answer to Lord——'s letter, and I will write *mine*."

"Must there be two answers?" said Howard.

"Not if you approve of mine?"

"That I am sure I shall," said Howard.

Mrs. Howard's letter was quickly written. She expressed, with much propriety, her sense of the honour which had been conferred upon her nephew; but she declined, decidedly, the favour intended for herself.

"Why? May I ask why, my dear aunt," said young Howard, "do you send this answer? Is it not right for you to accept, what it is so right in Lord————to offer? Is it not generous and noble," continued he, with enthusiasm——"is it not generous and noble in those, who have wealth and power, to make so good a use of it? I don't mean to call it generous and noble in Lord————to praise my essay," said Howard, recollecting himself; "but surely what is said of *you*, ma'am, in his letter, is very handsome: and you always told me, that you did not love that kind of pride, which will not receive any obligation."

"Nor do I," answered Mrs. Howard; "nor do I now act from that kind of pride : but you do not know enough of the world, to feel the nature of this obligation ; you do not perceive, that you would hereafter be called upon, probably in honour and gratitude, to return this obligation for me."

"I should, I hope, be grateful for it," said Howard; "but how could I return it? I should wish to return it if I could."

"Perhaps not in the manner it would be expected," replied his aunt. "At all events, I should think myself unjustifiable, if I were tacitly to pledge you, young as you are, to any party, or to any public leader of a party. Whenever you go into public life, if that should ever be your choice, you will surely wish to have perfect liberty to act, as your unbiassed judgement and integrity shall direct?"

"Certainly," said Howard.

"Then," said his aunt, smiling, "seal my letter, and keep your *unbiassed judgement*. You will understand all this much better some years hence."

The letter was accordingly sealed and sent.[72]

*   *   *

The day, which Mr. Augustus Holloway imagined would bring him such complete felicity—the day on which Lord Rawson had promised to call for him in his dog-cart, and to drive him down *randem-tandem,* to Marryborough—was now arrived. His Lordship, in his dog-cart, was at the door; and Holloway, in high spirits, was just going to get into the carriage, when some one pulled his coat, and begged to speak a few words with him. It was the stage-coachman, who was absolutely in distress for the value of the lost parcel, which Holloway had promised him should be punctually paid: but Holloway, now that his excursion to Marryborough was perfectly secure, thought but very little of the poor coachman's difficulties; and though he had the money, which he had raised by the lottery tickets, in his pocket, he determined to keep that for his amusements during the Easter holidays. "You must wait till I come back from Marryborough; I can't possibly speak to you now; I can't possibly, you see, keep Lord Rawson waiting. Why didn't you call sooner? I'm not at all convinced that any parcel was lost."

"I'll show you the books—it's booked, sir," said the man, eagerly.

"Well, well, this is not a time to talk of booking. I'll be with you in an instant, my Lord," cried Holloway to Lord Rawson, who was all impatience to *be off.* But the coachman would not quit his hold. "I'm sorry to come to that, master," said he. "As long as we were both upon honour together, it was very well; but, if you break squares with me,[73] being a gentleman, and rich, you can't take it ill, I being a poor man, and my place and all at stake, if I take the shortest way to get my own; I must go to Dr. B., your master, for justice, if you won't give it me without my peaching," said the coachman.

"I'll see you again to-morrow morning," said Holloway, alarmed; "we come up to town again to-morrow."

"To-morrow won't do," said the coachman; "I shall lose my place and my bread to-day. I know how to trust to young gentlemen's 'to-morrows'."

A volley of oaths from lord Rawson again summoned his companion. At this instant Mr. Russell, young Howard, and little Oliver, came up the street, and were passing into Westminster School, when Holloway stopped Howard, who was the last of the party. "For Heaven's sake," said he, in a whisper, "do settle for me with this confounded dun of a coachman! I know you are rich; your bookseller told me so; pay five guineas for me to him, and you shall have them again to-morrow, there's a good fellow. Lord Rawson's waiting; good bye."

"Stay, stay," said Howard, who was not so easily to be drawn into difficulties by a moment's weakness, or by the want of a moment's presence of mind; "I know nothing of this business; I have other uses for my money; I cannot pay five guineas for you, Holloway."

"Then let it alone," cried Holloway, with a brutal execration; and he forcibly broke from the coachman, shook hands with his tutor, Mr. Supine, who was talking to Lord Rawson about the varnish of his gig, jumped into the carriage, and was whirled away from all reflection in a moment, by his noble companion.

The poor coachman entreated Howard to stay one instant, to hear him. He explained the business to him, and reproached himself bitterly for his folly. "I'm sure I thought," said he, "I was sure of a gentleman's honour; and young gentlemen ought to be above not paying handsome for their frolics, if they must have frolics; and a frolic's one thing, and cheating a poor man like me is another; and he had like to have killed a poor mulatto woman, too, by the overturn of the coach, which was all his doings."

"The woman is got very well, and is very well off now," interrupted Howard; "you need say nothing about that."

"Well, but my money, I must say about *that*," said the coachman. Here Howard observed, that Mr. Supine had remained at the door in a lounging attitude, and was quite near enough to overhear their conversation. Howard, therefore, to avoid exciting his attention by any mysterious whispers, walked away from the coachman; but in vain; he followed. "I'll peach," said he; "I must in my own defence."

"Stay till to-morrow morning," said Howard. "Perhaps you'll be paid then."

The coachman, who was a good-natured fellow, said, "Well, I don't like making mischief among young gentlemen, I will wait till to-morrow, but not a day more, master, if you'd go down on your knees to me."

Mr. Supine, whose curiosity was fully awake, called to the coachman the moment Howard was out of hearing, and tried, by various questions, to draw the secret from him. The words, *"over-turn of the coach—mulatto woman"* and the sentence, which the irritated coachman had pronounced in a raised voice, *"that young gentlemen should be above not paying handsome for their frolics,"* had reached Mr. Supine's attentive ear, before Howard had been aware that the tutor was a listener. Nothing more could Mr. Supine draw, however, from the coachman, who now felt himself *upon hon-our,* having promised Howard not to *peach* till the next morning. Difficulties stimulated Mr. Supine's curiosity; but he remained for the present satisfied in the persuasion, that he had discovered *a fine frolic* of the immaculate Mr. Charles Howard; his own pupil he did not suspect upon this occasion. Holloway's whisperings with the coachman had ended the moment Mr. Supine appeared at the door, and the tutor had in the same moment been so struck with the beautiful varnish of Lord Rawson's dog-cart, that his pupil might have whispered longer, without rousing his attention. Mr. Supine was further confirmed in his mistake about Howard, from the recollection of the mulatto woman, whom he had seen at the gardener's; he knew that she had been hurt by a fall from a stage-coach. He saw Howard much interested about her. All this he joined with what he had just overheard about *a frolic,* and he was rejoiced at the idea of implicating in this business Mr. Russell, whom he disliked.

Mr. Supine, having got rid of his pupil, went immediately to Alderman Holloway's, where he had a general invitation to din-ner. Mrs. Holloway approved of her son's tutor, full as much for his love of gossiping, as for his musical talents; Mr. Supine con-stantly supplied her with news and anecdotes; upon the present occasion, he thought that his story, however imperfect, would be eagerly received, because it concerned Howard.

Since the affair of the prize essay, and the medal, Mrs. Holloway had taken a dislike to young Howard, whom she considered as the enemy of her dear Augustus. No sooner had she heard Mr. Supine's blundering information, than, without any farther examination, she took the whole for granted: eager to repeat the anecdote to Mrs. Howard, she instantly wrote a note to her, saying that she would drink tea with her that evening. Many apologies were added in the note, for Mrs. Holloway's not having waited upon Mrs. Howard since her return from Margate.

When Mrs. Holloway, attended by Mr. Supine, went, in the evening, to Mrs. Howard's, they found with her Mrs. B., the lady of Dr. B., the master of Westminster School.

"Is not this an odd rencontre?" whispered Mrs. Holloway to Mr. Supine, as she drew him to a recessed window, commodious for gossiping; "I shall be called a tell-tale, I know, at Westminster; but I shall tell our story, notwithstanding. I would keep any other boy's secret; but Howard is such a saint: and I hate saints."

A knock at the door interrupted Mrs. Holloway; she looked out of the window. "Oh, here he comes, up the steps," continued she, "after his sober evening promenade, and *his* Mr. Russell with— and, I declare, the mulatto woman with him. Now for it!"

Howard entered the room, went up to his aunt, and said, in a low voice, "Ma'am, poor Cuba is come; she is rather tired with walking, and she is gone to rest herself in the front parlour."

"Her lameness, though," pursued little Oliver, who followed Howard into the room, "is almost well. I just asked her how high she thought the coach was from which she was—"

A look from Howard made Oliver stop short; for though he did not understand the full meaning of it, he saw it was designed to silence him. Howard was afraid of betraying Holloway's secret to Mr. Supine or to Mrs. Holloway; his aunt sent him out of the room with some message to Cuba, which gave Mrs. Holloway an opportunity of opening her business.

"Pray," said she, "might I presume to ask—for I perceive the young gentleman has some secret to keep from me, which he may have good reasons for—may I, just to satisfy my own mind, presume to ask whether, as her name leads one to guess, your Cuba, Mrs. Howard, is a mulatto woman?"

Surprised by the manner of the question, Mrs. Howard coldly replied, "Yes, madam—a mulatto woman."

"And she is lame, I think, sir, you mentioned?" persisted the curious lady, turning to little Oliver.

"Yes, she's a little lame still; but she will soon be quite well."

"Oh ! Then her lameness *came,* I presume, from an accident, sir, and not from her birth?"

"From an accident, ma'am."

"Oh! An accident—a fall—a fall from a coach—from a stage-coach, perhaps," continued Mrs. Holloway, smiling significantly at Mr. Supine: "you take me for a conjuror, young gentleman, I see by your astonishment," continued she to Oliver; "but a little bird told me the whole story; and I see Mrs. Howard knows how to keep a secret as well as myself."

Mrs. Howard looked for an explanation.

"Nay," said Mrs. Holloway, "you know best, Mrs. Howard; but as we're all *out of school* now, I shall not be afraid to mention such a little affair, even before the doctor's lady; for, to be sure, she would never let it reach the doctor's ears."

"Really, ma'am," said Mrs. Howard, "you puzzle me a little; I wish you would explain yourself; I don't know what it is that you would not have reach the doctor's ears."

"You don't?—well, then, your nephew must have been very clever, to have kept you in the dark; mustn't he, Mr. Supine?"

"I always, you know, thought the young gentleman very *clever,* ma'am," said Mr. Supine, with a malicious emphasis.

Mrs. Howard's colour now rose, and, with a mixture of indignation and anxiety, she pressed both Mr. Supine and Mrs. Holloway to be explicit. "I hate mysteries!" said she. Mrs. Holloway still hung back, saying, it was a tender point; and hinting, that it would lessen her esteem and confidence, in one most dear to her, to hear the whole truth.

"Do you mean Howard, ma'am?" exclaimed little Oliver: "Oh, speak! Speak! it's impossible Charles Howard can have done any thing wrong."

"Go for him, my dear," said Mrs. Howard, resuming her composure; "let him be present. I hate mysteries."

"But, my dear Mrs. Howard," whispered Mrs. Holloway, "you don't consider; you'll get your nephew into a shocking scrape; the story will infallibly go from Mrs. B. to Dr. B. You are warm, and don't consider consequences."

"Charles," said Mrs. Howard to her nephew, the moment he appeared, "from the time you were five years old, till this instant, I have never known you tell a falsehood; I should, therefore, be very absurd, as well as very unjust, if I were to doubt your integrity. Tell me—have you got into any difficulties? I would rather hear of them from yourself, than from any body else. Is there any mystery about overturning a stage-coach, that you know of, and that you have concealed from me?"

"There is a mystery, ma'am, about overturning a stage-coach," replied Howard, in a firm tone of voice; "but when I assure you that it is no mystery of mine—nothing in which I have myself any concern, I am sure that you will believe me, my dear aunt; and that you will press me no farther."

"Not a word farther, not a frown farther," said his aunt, with a smile of entire confidence; in which Mr. Russell joined, but which appeared incomprehensible to Mr. Supine.

"Very satisfactory indeed!" said that gentleman, leaning back in the chair; "I never heard any thing more satisfactory to my mind!"

"Perfectly satisfactory, upon my word!" echoed Mrs. Holloway; but no looks, no innuendoes, could now disturb Mrs. Howard's security, or disconcert the resolute simplicity, which appeared in her nephew's countenance. Mrs. Holloway, internally devoured by curiosity, was compelled to submit in silence. This restraint soon became so irksome to her, that she shortened her visit as much as she decently could.

In crossing the passage, to go to her carriage, she caught a glimpse of the mulatto woman, who was going into a parlour. Resolute, at all hazards, to satisfy herself, Mrs. Holloway called to the retreating Cuba—began, by asking some civil questions about her health; then spoke of the accident she had lately met with; and, in short, by a skilful cross-examination, drew her whole story from her. The gratitude with which the poor woman spoke of Howard's humanity was by no means pleasing to Mr. Supine.

"Then it was not he who overturned the coach?" said Mrs. Holloway.

The woman eagerly replied, "Oh no, madam!" and proceeded to draw, as well as she could, a description of the youth who had been mounted upon the coach-box: she had seen him only by the light of the moon, and afterwards by the light of a lantern; but she recollected his figure so well, and described him so accurately, that Mr. Supine knew the picture instantly, and Mrs. Holloway whispered to him, "Can it be Augustus?"

"Mr. Holloway !—Impossible !—I suppose——"

But the woman interrupted him by saying that she recollected to have heard the young gentleman called by that name by the coachman.

The mother and the tutor were nearly alike confounded by this discovery. Mrs. Holloway got into her carriage, and, on their way home, Mr. Supine represented, that he should be ruined for ever with the alderman, if this transaction came to his knowledge; that, in fact, it was a mere boyish frolic; but that the alderman might not consider it in that light, and would, perhaps, make Mr. Augustus feel his serious displeasure. The foolish mother, out of mistaken good nature, at length promised to be silent upon the subject. But, before he slept, Alderman Holloway heard the whole story. The footman, who had attended the carriage, was at the door when Mrs. Holloway was speaking to the mulatto woman, and had listened to every word that was said. This footman was in the habit of telling his master, when he attended him at night, all the news which he had been able to collect in the day. Mr. Supine was no favourite of his; because, whenever the tutor came to the house, he gave a great deal of trouble, being too indolent to do any thing for himself, and yet not sufficiently rich, or sufficiently generous, to pay the usual premiums for the active civility of servants. This footman was not sorry to have an opportunity of repeating any story that might injure Mr. Supine with his master. Alderman Holloway heard it under the promise of concealing the name of the person who had given him the information, and resolved to discover the truth of the affair the next day, when he was to visit his son at Westminster.

But we must now return to Mrs. Howard's. We mentioned that Mrs. B. spent the evening with her. Dr. B., soon after Mrs. Holloway went away, called to take his lady home: he had been engaged to spend the evening at a card assembly; but, as he was a man who liked agreeable conversation better than cards, he had made his escape from a rout, to spend half an hour with Mr. Russell and Mrs. Howard. The doctor was a man of various literature; able to appreciate others, he was not insensible to the pleasure of seeing himself appreciated. Half an hour passes quickly in agreeable conversation: the doctor got into an argument, concerning the propriety of the distinction made by some late metaphysical writers, between imagination and fancy. Thence he was led to some critical remarks upon Warton's beautiful Ode to Fancy;[74] then to the never-ending debate upon original genius; including also the doctrine of hereditary temper and dispositions, which the doctor warmly supported, and which Mrs. Howard coolly questioned.

In the midst of their conversation, they were suddenly interrupted by a groan. They all looked round, to see whence it came. It came from little Oliver. He was sitting at a little table at the farther end of the room, reading so intently in a large book, that he saw nothing else: a long unsnuffed candle, with a perilous fiery summit to its black wick, stood before him, and his left arm embraced a thick china jar, against which he leaned his head. There was, by common consent, a general silence in the room, whilst every one looked at Oliver, as at a picture. Mrs. Howard moved gently round behind his chair, to see what he was reading; the doctor followed her. It was the account of the execution of two rebel Koromantyn negroes, related in Edwards's History of the West Indies[††].[75] To try whether it would interrupt Oliver's deep attention, Mrs. Howard leaned over him, and snuffed his dim candle; but the light was lost upon him, he did not feel the obligation. Dr. B. then put his hand upon the jar, which he pulled from Oliver's embrace. "Be quiet! I must finish this!" cried Oliver, still holding fast the jar, and keeping his eyes upon the book. The doctor gave a second pull at the jar, and the little boy made an impatient push with his elbow; then casting his eye upon the large hand, which pulled the jar, he looked up, surprised, in the doctor's face.

The nice china jar, which Oliver had held so sturdily, was very precious to him. His uncle had just sent him two jars of fine West-India sweetmeats. One of these he had shared with his companions: the other he had kept, to give to Mrs. Howard, who had once said, in his hearing, that she was fond of West-India sweetmeats. She accepted Oliver's little present. Children sometimes feel as

---

[††] Vol. ii. p. 57, second edition.

much pleasure in giving away sweetmeats, as in eating them; and Mrs. Howard too well understood the art of education, even in trifles, to deny to grateful and generous feelings their natural and necessary exercise. A child can show gratitude and generosity only in trifles.

"Are these *all* the sweetmeats that you have left, Oliver?" said Mrs. Howard.

"Yes, all."

"Was not Rousseau wrong, Dr. B.," said Mrs. Howard, "when he asserted, that no child ever gives away *his last mouthful* of any thing good?"[76]

"Of any thing *good*!" said the doctor, laughing; "when I have tasted these sweetmeats, I shall be a better judge."

"You shall taste them this minute, then," said Mrs. Howard; and she rang for a plate, whilst the doctor, to little Oliver's great amusement, exhibited various pretended signs of impatience, as Mrs. Howard deliberately untied the cover of the jar. One cover after another she slowly took off; at length the last transparent cover was lifted up: the doctor peeped in; but lo! Instead of sweetmeats there appeared nothing but paper. One crumpled roll of paper after another Mrs. Howard pulled out; still no sweetmeats. The jar was entirely stuffed with paper, to the very bottom. Oliver was silent with amazement.

"The sides of the jar are quite clean," said Howard.

"But the inside of the paper that covered it is stained with sweetmeats," said Dr. B.

"There must have been sweetmeats in it lately," said Mrs. Howard, "because the jar smells so strongly of sweetmeats."

Amongst the pieces of crumpled paper, which had been pulled out of the jar, Dr. B. espied one, on which there appeared some writing: he looked it over.

"Humph! What have we here? What's this? What can this be about a lottery?—tickets, price half a guinea—prizes—gold watch!—silver ditto—chased tooth-pick case—buckles—knee-buckles—What is all this?—April 10th, 1797—the drawing to begin—prices to be delivered at Westminster School, by Aaron Carat, jeweller? Hey, young gentlemen," cried Dr. B., looking at Oliver and Charles, "do you know any thing of this lottery?"

"I have no concern in it, sir, I assure you," said Howard.

"Nor I, thank goodness—I mean, thank you, Charles," exclaimed Oliver; "for you hindered me from putting into the lottery; how very lucky I was to take your advice!"

"How very wise, you should say, Oliver," said Dr. B. "I must inquire into this business; I must find out who ordered these things from Mr. Aaron Carat. There shall be no lotteries, no gaming at Westminster School, whilst I have power to prevent it. To-morrow morning I'll inquire into this affair; and to-morrow morning we shall also know, my little fellow, what became of your sweetmeats."

"Oh, never mind *that*," cried the good natured Oliver; "don't say any thing, pray, sir, about my sweetmeats: I don't mind about them; I know already—I guess, now, who took them; therefore you need not ask; I dare say it was only meant for a joke."

Dr. B. made no reply; but deliberately folded up the paper, which he had been reading; put it into his pocket, and soon after took his leave.

* * *

Lord Rawson was one of those young men, who measure their own merit and felicity by the number of miles, which their horses can go in a day; he undertook to drive his friend up from Marryborough to Westminster, a distance of forty miles, in six hours. The arrival of his Lordship's gig was a signal, for which several people were in waiting at Westminster School. The stage-coachman was impatiently waiting to demand his money from Holloway. Mr. Carat, the jeweller, was arrived, and eager to settle with Mr. Holloway about the lottery; he had brought the prizes in a small case, to be delivered, upon receiving from Holloway, the money for all the tickets of which he had disposed. Dr. B. was waiting for the arrival of Mr. Holloway, as he had determined to collect all his pupils together, and to examine into the lottery business. Little Oliver was also watching for Holloway, to prevent mischief, and to assure him of forgiveness about the sweetmeats.

Lord Rawson's dog-cart arrived: Holloway saw the stage-coachman as he alighted, and, abruptly turning from him, shook hands with little Oliver, saying, "You look as if you had been waiting for me."

"Yes," said Oliver; "but I can't say what I want to say, before every body."

"I'll wait upon you presently," said Holloway, escaping from the coachman. As he crossed the hall, he descried Mr. Carat, and a crowd of boys surrounding him, crying, "Mr. Carat's come—he has brought the prizes—he's brought the prizes! He'll show them all as soon as you've settled with him." Holloway called to the Jew; but little Oliver insisted upon being heard first.

"You must hear me; I have something to say to you about the prizes; about the lottery."

The words arrested Holloway's attention; he followed Oliver; heard with surprise and consternation the history of the paper which had been found in the jar, by Dr. B. "I've done for myself, now, faith!" he exclaimed; "I suppose the doctor knows all about the hand *I* have in the lottery."

"No," replied Oliver, "he does not."

"Why, *you* must have known it, and did not he question you and Howard?"

"Yes; but when we told him that we had nothing to do with it, he did not press us farther."

"You are really a noble little fellow," exclaimed Holloway, "to bear me no malice for the many ill turns I have done you: this last has fallen upon myself, as ill luck would have it: but before we go any farther—your sweetmeats are safe in the press, in my room; I didn't mean to steal them; only to plague you, child:—but you have your revenge now."

"I don't want any revenge, indeed," said Oliver, "for I'm never happy when I've quarrelled with any body: and even when people quarrel with me, I don't feel quite sure that I'm in the right, which makes me uncomfortable; and, besides, I don't want to find out that they are quite in the wrong; and that makes me uncomfortable the other way. After all, quarrelling and bearing malice are very disagreeable things, somehow or other. Don't you, when you have made it up with people, and shaken hands, Holloway—don't you feel quite light, and ready to jump again? So shake hands, if you are not above shaking hands with such a little boy as I am; and I shall never think again about the sweetmeats, or old *fag* times."

Holloway could not help feeling touched. "Here's my hand," cried he, "I'm sorry I've tormented you so often; I'll never plague you any more. But now—I don't know what upon earth to do. Where's Charles Howard? If he can't help me, I'm undone. I have got into more scrapes than I can get out of, I know. I wish I could see Howard."

"I'll run and bring him to you; he's the best person at knowing what should be done—at least for me, I know, that ever I saw."

Holloway abruptly began, as soon as Howard came up to him: "Howard," said he, "you know this plaguey lottery business—but you don't know half yet: here's Carat come to be paid for his tickets; and here's that dunning stage-coachman sticks close to me for his five guineas; and not one farthing have I upon earth."

"Not a farthing! But you don't mean that you have not the money for Mr. Carat?"

"But I *do* though."

"Why, you cannot have spent it since yesterday morning?"

"No; but I have lost half and lent half; and the half that I have lent is gone for ever, I am afraid, as much as that which I lost."

"Whom did you lend the money to? How did you lose it?"

"I lost part to Sir John O'Shannon, last night, at billiards—more fool I to play, only because I wanted to cut a figure amongst those fine people at Marryborough. I wonder my father lets me go there; I know I sha'n't go back there this Easter, unless Lord Rawson makes me an apology, I can tell him. I've as good a right to be upon my high horse as he has; for though his father's an earl, my father's a great deal richer, I know; and has lent him a great deal of money, too, and that's the only reason he's civil to us; but I can tell him—"

Here Howard brought the angry Holloway from his high horse, by asking what all this had to do with Mr. Carat, who was waiting to be paid?

"Why, don't I explain to you," said Holloway, "that I lent *him*—Lord Rawson, I mean—all the money I had left yesterday, and I couldn't get it out of him again, though I told him my distress about the stage-coachman? Did you ever know any thing so selfish? Did you ever know any thing so shabby? So shameful? And then to make me his butt, as he did last night at supper, because there were two or three dashing young men by; I think more of *that* than all the rest. Do you know, he asked me to eat custard with my apple pie, just to point me out for an alderman's son; and when I only differed from him about Captain Shouldham's pup-py's ears, Lord Rawson asked how I should know any thing about dog's ears? Just to put me in mind that I was a school-boy; but I'll never go to Marryborough any more, unless he begs my pardon. I've no notion of being an humble friend; but it does not signify being in a passion about it now," continued Holloway. "What I want you, Howard, to do for me is just to think; for I can't think at present, I'm in such a hurry, with all these things coming across me at once. What can I do to find money for the stage-coachman and for Mr. Carat? Why, both together come to fifteen guineas— And what can I do about Dr. B.? And do you know, my father is coming here this very morning? How shall I manage? He'd never forgive me: at least he'd not give me any money, for I don't know how long, if these things were to come out. What would you advise me to do?"

Howard, with his usual honest policy, advised Holloway at once to tell all the circumstances to his father. Holloway was at first much alarmed at this proposal, and insisted upon it that this method would not *do at all* with the alderman, though it might do very well with such a woman as Mrs. Howard. At length, however, overcome, partly by the arguments, and partly by the persuasion of his new adviser, Holloway determined upon his confession.

Alderman Holloway arrived, and was beginning to talk to Dr. B. of his son's proficiency in his studies, when the young gentleman made his appearance, with a countenance extremely embarrassed and agitated. The sight of Dr. B. deprived Holloway of courage to speak. The doctor fixed his penetrating eye upon the pale culprit, who immediately stopped short in the middle of the room, stam-mering out—"I came to speak, sir—I had something to say to my father, sir—I came, if you please, to speak to my father, sir." To Holloway's utter astonishment, Dr. B.'s countenance and manner suddenly changed at these words; all his severity vanished; and, with a look and voice the most encouraging, he led the abashed youth towards his father.

"You came to speak to your father, sir? Speak to him then with-out fear, without reserve: you will certainly find in a father your most indulgent friend.[77] I'll leave you together."

This opening of the case by Dr. B. was of equal advantage both to the father and to the son. Alderman Holloway, though without literature, was not without understanding: his affection for his son made him quickly comprehend the good sense of the doctor's hint. The alderman was not *surprised* by the story of the over-turn of the stage-coach, because he had heard it before from his footman. But the lottery transaction with the Jew—and, above all, with the loss and loan of so much money to his friend, Lord Rawson, struck him with some astonishment; yet he commanded his temper, which was naturally violent; and, after a constrained silence, he begged his son to summon Mr. Supine. "At least," cried the alderman, "I've a right to be in a passion with that careless, indolent, dilettante puppy, whom I've been paying all this while for taking such care of you. I wish I had hold of his German flute at this instant. You are very right, Augustus, to come like a man, and tell me all these things; and now I must tell you, that some of them I had heard of before. I wish I had that Jew, that Mr. Carat of yours, here! And that stage-coachman, who had the impertin-ence to take you out with him at night. But it's all Mr. Supine's fault—and mine, for not choosing a better tutor for you. As to Lord Rawson, I can't blame you either much for that, for I encour-aged the connexion, I must own. I'm glad you have quarrelled with him, however; and pray look out for a better friend as fast as possible; you were very right to tell me all these things; on that consideration, and that only, I'll lend my hand to getting you out of these scrapes."

"For that," cried Holloway, "I may thank Howard, then; for he advised and urged me to tell you all this at once."

"Call him; let me thank him," said the alderman; "he's an excel-lent young man then—call him."

Dr. B. now entered the room with little Oliver.

When Holloway returned with Howard, he beheld the stage-coachman standing silent on one side of his father; Mr. Carat, the Jew, on the other side, jabbering an unintelligible vindica-tion of himself; whilst Dr. B. was contemplating the box of lottery prizes, which lay open upon the table. Mr. Supine, leaning against the chimney-piece, appeared in the attitude of an Antinous in despair.[78]

"Come, my little friend," said Dr. B. to Oliver, "you did not put into the lottery, I understand. Choose from amongst these things whatever you please. It is better to trust to prudence than fortune, you see. Mr. Howard, I know that I am rewarding you, at this instant, in the manner you best like, and best deserve."

There was a large old-fashioned chased gold toothpick-case, on which Oliver immediately fixed his eye. After examining it very carefully, he made it his choice, in preference to anything in the box. As soon as the doctor delivered it to him, Oliver, without waiting to hear his own praise, or yet to hear his friend Howard's, pushed his way hastily out of the room; whilst the alderman, with all the eloquence of which he was master, expressed his gratitude to Howard for the advice which he had given his son. "Cultivate this young gentleman's friendship," added he, turning to Holloway: "he has not a title; but even *I*, Augustus, am now ready to acknowledge he is worth twenty Lord Rawsons. Had he a title, he would grace it; and that's as much as I can say for any man."

The Jew, all this time, stood in the greatest trepidation; he trembled lest the alderman should have him taken up and committed to gaol for his illegal, unlicensed lottery. He poured forth as many protestations as his knowledge of the English language could afford, of the purity of his intentions; and, to demonstrate his disinterestedness, began to display the trinkets in his prize-box, with a panegyric upon each. Dr. B. interrupted him, by paying for the toothpick-case, which he had bought for Oliver. "Now, Mr. Carat," said the doctor, "you will please to return, in the first place, the money you have received for your *illegal* lottery tickets."

The word *illegal*, pronounced in a tremendous tone, operated instantaneously upon the Jew; his hand, which had closed upon Holloway's guineas, opened; he laid the money down upon the table; but mechanically seized his box of trinkets, which he seemed to fear would be the next seized, as forfeits. No persons are so apprehensive of injustice and fraud, as those who are themselves dishonest. Mr. Carat, bowing repeatedly to Alderman Holloway, shuffled toward the door, asking if he might now depart; when the door opened with such a force, as almost to push the retreating Jew upon his face.

Little Oliver, out of breath, burst into the room, whispered a few words to Dr. B. and Alderman Holloway, who answered, "*He* may come in;" and a tall, stout man, an officer from Bow Street, immediately entered. "There's your man, sir," said the alderman, pointing to the Jew—"there is Mr. Carat." The man instantly seized

Mr. Carat, producing a warrant from Justice——, for apprehending the Jew, upon suspicion of his having in his possession certain valuable jewels, the property of Mrs. Frances Howard.

Oliver was eager to explain. "Do you know, Howard," said he, "how all this came about? Do you know your aunt's gone to Bow Street, and has taken the mulatto woman with her, and Mr. Russell is gone with her—and she thinks—and *I* think, she'll certainly have her jewels, her grandmother's jewels, that were left in Jamaica."

"How? But how?" exclaimed Howard.

"Tell us how?" cried everybody at once.

"Why," said Oliver, "by the tooth-pick case. The reason I chose that tooth-pick case out of the Jew's box was, because it came into my head, the minute I saw it, that the mulatto woman's curious thimble—you remember her thimble, Howard—would just fit one end of it. I ran home, with Mr. Russell, and tried it, and the thimble screwed on as nicely as possible; and the chasing, as Mr. Russell said, and the colour of the gold, matched exactly. Oh! Mrs. Howard was so surprised, when we showed it to her—so astonished to see this tooth-pick case in England, for it had been left, she said, with all her grandmother's diamonds, and *things,* in Jamaica."

"Yes," interrupted Howard; "I remember my aunt told us, when you asked her about Cuba's thimble, that she gave it to Cuba, when she was a child, and that it belonged to some old trinket—Go on."

"Well, where was I?—Oh, then, as soon as she saw the tooth-pick case, she asked how it had been found; and I told her all about the lottery and Mr. Carat; then she and Mr. Russell consulted, and away they went, with Cuba, in a coach, and all the rest you know; and I wish I could hear the end of it!"

"And so you shall, my good little fellow; we'll all go together to hear the Jew's examination; you shall go with me in my coach to Bow Street," said Alderman Holloway.

"This is a holiday," cried Dr. B., who was much interested in hearing the event of this business, and he begged to have a seat, as well as Oliver, in the alderman's coach. Howard and Holloway ran for their hats, and they were all impatience for the coming of the hackney-coach, which the Bow Street officer had sent for at Mr. Carat's request.

In the midst of their bustle, the poor stage-coachman, who had waited with uncommon patience in the hopes that Alderman Holloway would at last recollect him, pressed forward, and petitioned to be paid his five guineas for the lost parcel. "I have lost my place already," said he, "and the little goods I have will be seized this day, for the value of that unlucky parcel, master."

The alderman put his hand slowly into his purse; but just when he had pulled out five guineas, a servant came into the room, to inform Dr. B., that a sailor was waiting in the hall, who desired to speak, directly, about something of consequence, to the stage-coachman.

Dr. B., who imagined that the sailor might have something to do with the business in question, ordered that he might be shown into the room.

"I wants one Gregory Giles, a stage-coachman, if such a one be here amongst ye, gentlefolks, and nobody else," cried the sailor, producing a parcel wrapped up in brown paper.

"It's my very parcel!" exclaimed the stage-coachman; "I am Gregory Giles! God bless your honest heart!—Where did ye find it?—Give it me!"

The sailor said he had found it in a dry ditch on the Bath road, a little beyond the first turnpike going out of town; that he had inquired at the turnpike-house; had heard that the stage had been overturned a few days before, and that a parcel had been lost, about which the coachman had been in great trouble; that he had gone directly to the inn where the coach put up; had traced the coachman from place to place; and was heartily glad he had found him at last.

"Thank'ee, with all my heart," said the coachman, "for all the trouble you've been at; and here's the crown reward that I offered for it, and my thanks into the bargain."

"No, no," said the honest sailor, pushing back the money, "I won't take any thing from a poor fellow like myself; put your silver into your pocket; I hear you lost your place already, by that parcel. There was a great talk at the turnpike-house, about your losing your place, for giving some young gentleman a lift.—Put up your money."

Young Howard, struck with this sailor's honesty and good nature, proposed a subscription for him, and began by putting down half a guinea himself. All the young gentlemen, who had just received the half guineas for their lottery tickets, were present, and eager to bestow some of their money to better purpose. Holloway had no money to give.

The sailor received the money from Howard, with a single nod of his head by way of thanks. "I'm not a main speechifier, masters; but I'm thankful; and you, master, who were foremost, most of all, I wish you may roll in his majesty's coin before you die yourself, so I do!"

The hackney-coach was now come to the door for Mr. Carat, and every body hurried off as fast as possible.

"Where are they all steering to?" said the sailor. The stage-coachman told him all that he had heard of the matter. "I'll be in their wake, then," cried the sailor; "I shall like to see the Jew upon his court-martial; I was choused[79] once by a Jew myself." He got to Bow Street as soon as they did.

The first thing Howard learned was, that the jewels, which had been all found at Mr. Carat's, precisely answered the description which his aunt had given of them. The Jew was in the utmost consternation: finding that the jewels were positively sworn to, he declared, upon his examination, that he had bought them from a captain of a ship; that he had paid the full value for them; and that, at the time he purchased them, he had no suspicion of their having been fraudulently obtained. This defence appearing evidently evasive, the magistrates who examined Mr. Carat informed him that, unless he could produce the person from whom he had bought the jewels, he must be committed to Newgate for receiving stolen goods. Terrified at this sentence, the Jew, though he had at first asserted that he knew nothing of the captain from whom he had received the diamonds, now acknowledged that he actually lodged at his house.

"Hah!" exclaimed Holloway, "I remember, the day that I and Lord Rawson called at your house, you were settling accounts, your foreman told us, with a captain of a ship, who was to leave England in a few days: it's well he's not off."

An officer was immediately sent to Mr. Carat's, in quest of this captain: but there were great apprehensions, that he might have escaped at the first alarm of the search for the jewels. Fortunately, however, he had not been able to get off, as two constables had been stationed at Mr. Carat's house. The officer from Bow Street found him in his own bed-chamber, rummaging a portmanteau for some papers, which he wanted to burn. His papers were seized, and carried along with him before the magistrate.

Alderman Holloway knew the captain the moment he was brought into the room, though his dress and whole appearance were very different from what they had been, when he had waited upon the alderman, some months before this time, with a dismal, plausible story of his own poverty and misfortunes. He had then told him that his mate and he had had a quarrel upon the voyage from Jamaica; that the mate knew what a valuable cargo he had on board; that just when they got in sight of land, the crew rose upon him; the mate seized him, and by force put him into a boat, and set him ashore.

The discovery of the jewels at Mr. Carat's at once overturned the captain's whole story: cunning people often insert something in their narration, to make it better, which ultimately tends to convict them of falsehood. The captain having now no other resource, and having the horrors of imprisonment, and the certainty of condemnation upon a public trial full before him, threw himself, as the only chance that remained for him, upon Mrs. Howard's mercy; confessed, that all that he had told her before was false; that his mate and he had acted in concert; that the rising of the crew against him had been contrived between them; that he had received the jewels, when he was set ashore, for his immediate share of the booty; and that the mate had run the ship off to *Charlestown*[80] to sell her cargo. According to agreement, the captain added, he was to have had a share in the cargo; but the mate had *cheated him* of that; he had never heard from him, or of him, he would take his oath, from the day he was set ashore, and knew nothing of him or the cargo.

"Avast, friend, by your leave," cried the honest sailor, who had found the stage-coachman's parcel—"avast, friend, by your leave," said he, elbowing his way between Alderman Holloway and his next neighbour, and getting clear into the middle of the circle—"I know more of this matter, *my lord*, or please your worship, which is much the same thing, than any body here! And I'm glad on't, mistress," continued the tar, pulling a quid of tobacco out of his mouth, and addressing himself to Mrs. Howard: then turning to the captain, "Wasn't *she* the *Lively Peggy,* pray?—It's no use tacking. Wasn't your mate one John Matthews, pray? And hadn't she a great patch in the starboard side of her mainsail, I want to know?—Captain, your face tells truth, in spite of your teeth."

The captain instantly grew pale, and trembled; on which the sailor turned abruptly from him, and went on with his story. "Mistress," said he, "though I'm a loser by it, no matter. The Lively Peggy and her cargo are safe and sound in Plymouth, at this very time being, and we have her mate in limbo, curse him. We made a prize of him, coming from America, for he was under French colours, and a fine prize we thought we'd made. But her cargo belongs to a British subject; and there's an end to our prize money: no matter for that. There was an ugly look with Matthews, from the first; and I found, the day we took her, something odd in the look of her stern. The rascals had done their best to paint over her name; but *I*, though no great scholar, made a shift to spell the Lively Peggy through it all. We have the mate in limbo at Plymouth: but it's all come out, without any more to do; and, mistress, I'll get you her bill of lading in a trice, and I give ye joy with all my heart—you, I should say, master," said he, nodding at Howard, "for the gentlewoman's your kin, I've made out; God bless you both! I told you you'd roll in his majesty's coin afore you went to *Davy's locker,*[81] and so you will, thank my stars."

Alderman Holloway, a man used to business, would not indulge himself in a single compliment upon this occasion, till he had cautiously searched the captain's papers. The bill of lading, which had been sent with the Lively Peggy from Jamaica, was found amongst them; it was an exact list, corresponding precisely with that, which Mrs. Howard's agent had sent her by post, of the consignment shipped after the sale of her plantation. The alderman, satisfied, after counting the puncheons of rum and hogsheads of sugar, turned to Mrs. Howard, and shook hands with her, with a face of mercantile congratulation, declaring that "she was now as good a woman as ever she had been, and need never desire to be better."

"My dear Oliver," cried Howard, "this is all owing to you: *you* discovered——"

No, no, no!" interrupted Oliver, precipitately: "all that I did was accident; all that you did was not accident. You first made me love you, by teaching me that I was not a blockhead, and by freeing me from——"

"*A tyrant,* you were going to say," cried Holloway, colouring deeply; "and, if you had, you'd have said the truth. I thought, Howard, *afterward,* that you were a brave fellow for taking his part, I confess.—But, Oliver, I thought you had forgiven me for all these things."

"Forgiven! Oh yes, to be sure," cried little Oliver; "I wasn't thinking of myself, or you either; I was only thinking of Howard's good nature; and then," continued he, "Howard was just as good to the mulatto woman as he was to me—Wasn't he, Cuba?"

"That he was!" replied the poor woman, and looking at Mrs. Howard, added, "Massa's *heart* as good as hers."

"And his *head's* as good as his heart, which makes it all better still," continued Oliver, with enthusiasm. "Mr. Russell, you know how hard he worked at that translation, to earn money to support poor Cuba, and to paper the room, and to pay the bricklayer for the smoky chimney: these things were not done by accident, were they? Though it was by accident, that I happened to observe Cuba's curious thimble."

"There are some people," interrupted Mr. Russell, "who, by accident, never observe any thing. We will not allow you, Oliver, to call your quick habit of observation accident; your excellent capacity will——"

"*My* excellent capacity," repeated Oliver, with unfeigned surprise; "why, you know, I get by rote slower than anybody in the world."

"You may," said Dr. B., "notwithstanding, have an excellent capacity; much may be learned without books; much more with books, Oliver; but, for your comfort, you need not learn them by rote."

"I'm glad of it, heartily," cried Oliver; "but this put something out of my head that I was in a great hurry to say—Oh, one other thing about *accident.* It was not *accident,* but it was Howard's sense, in persuading me not to put into the lottery, that was the very cause of Dr. B.'s giving me the choice of all the things in the Jew's box—was it not?"

"Well, Oliver, we are ready to allow all you want us to perceive, in one word, that your friend Howard *has not been educated by accident,*" said Dr. B., looking at Mrs. Howard.

The Jew and the captain of the Lively Peggy were now left in the hands of the law. The sailor was properly rewarded. Mr. Russell was engaged to superintend the education of Holloway. He succeeded, and was presented by the alderman with a living in Surrey. Mr. Supine never visited Italy, and did not meet with any consolation, but in his German flute. Howard continued eager to improve himself; nor did he imagine that, the moment he left school, and parted from his tutor, his education was finished; and that his books were, "like past misfortunes," good for nothing, but to be forgotten. His love for literature he found one of the first pleasures of his life; nor did he, after he came into the possession of a large fortune, find that his habits of constant occupation lessened his enjoyments, for he was never known to yawn at a window upon a rainy morning!

Little Oliver's understanding rapidly improved; his affection for his friend Howard increased as he grew up, for he always remembered that Howard was the first person who discovered that he was not a dunce. Mrs. Howard had the calm satisfaction of seeing an education well finished, which she had well begun; and she enjoyed, in her nephew's friendship, esteem, and unconstrained gratitude, all the rewards which her good sense, firmness, and benevolence had so well deserved.

'The Grateful Negro'

In the island of Jamaica there lived two planters, whose methods of managing their slaves were as different as possible. Mr. Jefferies considered the negroes as an inferior species, incapable of gratitude, disposed to treachery, and to be roused from their natural indolence only by force;[82] he treated his slaves, or rather suffered his overseer to treat them, with the greatest severity.

Jefferies was not a man of a cruel, but of a thoughtless and extravagant temper. He was of such a sanguine disposition, that he always calculated upon having a fine season, and fine crops on his plantation; and never had the prudence to make allowance for unfortunate accidents: he required, as he said, from his overseer, produce and not excuses.

Durant, the overseer, did not scruple to use the most cruel and barbarous methods* of forcing the slaves to exertions beyond their strength.[83] Complaints of his brutality, from time to time, reached his master's ears; but though Mr. Jefferies was moved to momentary compassion, he shut his heart against conviction: he hurried away to the jovial banquet, and drowned all painful reflections in wine.

---

* The Negro Slaves—A fine drama, by Kotzebue. It is to be hoped that such horrible instances of cruelty are not now to be found in nature. Bryan Edwards, in the History of Jamaica, says that most of the planters are humane; but he allows that some facts can be cited in contradiction of this assertion.

He was this year much in debt; and, therefore, being more than usually anxious about his crop, he pressed his overseer to exert himself to the utmost.

The wretched slaves upon his plantation thought themselves still more unfortunate when they compared their condition with that of the negroes on the estate of Mr. Edwards. This gentleman treated his slaves with all possible humanity and kindness. He wished that there was no such thing as slavery in the world; but he was convinced, by the arguments of those who have the best means of obtaining information, that the sudden emancipation of the negroes would rather increase than diminish their miseries.[84] His benevolence, therefore, confined itself within the bounds of reason. He adopted those plans for the amelioration of the state of the slaves which appeared to him the most likely to succeed without producing any violent agitation or revolution.[†] For instance, his negroes had reasonable and fixed daily tasks; and when these were finished, they were permitted to employ their time for their own advantage or amusement. If they chose to employ themselves longer for their master, they were paid regular wages for their extra work.[85] This reward, for as such it was considered, operated most powerfully upon the slaves. Those who are animated by hope can perform what would seem impossibilities to those who are under the depressing influence of fear.[86] The wages which Mr. Edwards promised, he took care to see punctually paid.

He had an excellent overseer, of the name of Abraham Bayley, a man of a mild but steady temper, who was attached not only to his master's interests but to his virtues; and who, therefore, was more intent upon seconding his humane views than upon squeezing from the labour of the negroes the utmost produce.[87] Each negro had, near his cottage, a portion of land, called his provision-ground; and one day in the week was allowed for its cultivation.

It is common in Jamaica for the slaves to have provision-grounds, which they cultivate for their own advantage; but it too often happens that, when a good negro has successfully improved his little spot of ground, when he has built himself a house, and

---

[†] History of the West Indies, from which these ideas are adopted—not stolen.

begins to enjoy the fruits of his industry, his acquired property is seized upon by the sheriff's officer for the payment of his master's debts;[‡] he is forcibly separated from his wife and children, dragged to public auction, purchased by a stranger, and perhaps sent to terminate his miserable existence in the mines of Mexico; excluded for ever from the light of heaven! And all this without any crime or imprudence on his part, real or pretended. He is punished because his master is unfortunate.[88]

To this barbarous injustice the negroes on Mr. Edwards's plantation were never exposed. He never exceeded his income; he engaged in no wild speculations; he contracted no debts; and his slaves, therefore, were in no danger of being seized by a sheriff's officer: their property was secured to them by the prudence as well as by the generosity of their master.

One morning, as Mr. Edwards was walking in that part of his plantation which joined to Mr. Jefferies' estate, he thought he heard the voice of distress at some distance. The lamentations grew louder and louder as he approached a cottage, which stood upon the borders of Jefferies' plantation.

This cottage belonged to a slave of the name of Caesar, the best negro in Mr. Jefferies' possession.[89] Such had been his industry and exertion that, notwithstanding the severe tasks imposed by Durant, the overseer, Caesar found means to cultivate his provision-ground to a degree of perfection nowhere else to be seen on this estate. Mr. Edwards had often admired this poor fellow's industry, and now hastened to inquire what misfortune had befallen him.

When he came to the cottage, he found Caesar standing with his arms folded, and his eyes fixed upon the ground. A young and beautiful female negro was weeping bitterly, as she knelt at the feet of Durant, the overseer, who, regarding her with a sullen aspect, repeated, "He must go. I tell you, woman, he must go. What signifies all this nonsense?"

At the sight of Mr. Edwards, the overseer's countenance suddenly changed, and assumed an air of obsequious civility. The poor woman retired to the farther corner of the cottage, and

---

[‡] See an eloquent and pathetic passage on this subject in the History of the West Indies, v.ii p.153, second edition. [This footnote is omitted in editions from 1832 onwards.]

continued to weep. Caesar never moved. "Nothing is the matter, sir," said Durant, "but that Caesar is going to be sold. That is what the woman is crying for. They were to be married; but we'll find Clara another husband, I tell her; and she'll get the better of her grief, you know, sir, as I tell her, in time."

"Never! never!" said Clara.

"To whom is Caesar going to be sold; and for what sum?"

"For what can be got for him," replied Durant, laughing; "and to whoever will buy him. The sheriff's officer is here, who has seized him for debt, and must make the most of him at market."

"Poor fellow!" said Mr. Edwards; "and must he leave this cottage which he has built, and these bananas which he has planted?"

Caesar now for the first time looked up, and fixing his eyes upon Mr. Edwards for a moment, advanced with an intrepid rather than an imploring countenance, and said, "Will you be my master? Will you be her master? Buy both of us. You shall not repent of it. Caesar will serve you faithfully."

On hearing these words, Clara sprang forward, and clasping her hands together, repeated, "Caesar will serve you faithfully."

Mr. Edwards was moved by their entreaties, but he left them without declaring his intentions. He went immediately to Mr. Jefferies, whom he found stretched on a sofa, drinking coffee. As soon as Mr. Edwards mentioned the occasion of his visit, and expressed his sorrow for Caesar, Jefferies exclaimed, "Yes, poor devil! I pity him from the bottom of my soul. But what can I do? I leave all those things to Durant. He says the sheriff's officer has seized him; and there's an end of the matter. You know money must be had. Besides, Caesar is not worse off than any other slave sold for debt. What signifies talking about the matter, as if it were something that never happened before! Is not it a case that occurs every day in Jamaica?"

"So much the worse," replied Mr. Edwards.

"The worse for them, to be sure," said Jefferies. "But, after all, they are slaves, and used to be treated as such; and they tell me the negroes are a thousand times happier here, with us, than they ever were in their own country."[90]

"Did the negroes tell you so themselves?"

"No; but people better informed than negroes have told me so; and, after all, slaves there must be; for indigo, and rum, and sugar, we must have."

"Granting it to be physically impossible that the world should exist without rum, sugar, and indigo, why could they not be produced by freemen as well as by slaves?[91] If we hired negroes for labourers, instead of purchasing them for slaves, do you think they would not work as well as they do now? Does any negro, under the fear of the overseer, work harder than a Birmingham journeyman, or a Newcastle collier, who toil for themselves and their families?"

"Of that I don't pretend to judge. All I know is that the West India planters would be ruined if they had no slaves, and I am a West India planter."

"So am I: yet I do not think they are the only people whose interest ought to be considered in this business."

"Their interests, luckily, are protected by the laws of the land; and though they are rich men, and white men, and freemen, they have as good a claim to their rights as the poorest black slave on any of our plantations."[92]

"The law, in our case, seems to make the right; and the very reverse ought to be done—the right should make the law."

"Fortunately for us planters, we need not enter into such nice distinctions. You could not, if you would, abolish the trade. Slaves would be smuggled into the islands."

"What, if nobody would buy them! You know that you cannot smuggle slaves into England. The instant a slave touches English ground he becomes free.[93] Glorious privilege! Why should it not be extended to all her dominions? If the future importation of slaves into these islands were forbidden by law, the trade must cease. No man can either sell or possess slaves without its being known: they cannot be smuggled like lace or brandy."

"Well, well!" retorted Jefferies, a little impatiently, "as yet the law is on our side. I can do nothing in this business, nor you neither."

"Yes, we can do something; we can endeavour to make our negroes as happy as possible."

"I leave the management of these people to Durant."

"That is the very thing of which they complain; forgive me for speaking to you with the frankness of an old acquaintance."

"Oh! You can't oblige me more: I love frankness of all things! To tell you the truth, I have heard complaints of Durant's severity; but I make it a principle to turn a deaf ear to them, for I know nothing can be done with these fellows without it. You are partial to negroes; but even you must allow they are a race of beings naturally inferior to us. You may in vain think of managing a black as you would a white. Do what you please for a negro, he will cheat you the first opportunity he finds. You know what their maxim is: 'God gives black men what white men forget.' "[94]

To these common-place desultory observations Mr. Edwards made no reply; but recurred to poor Caesar, and offered to purchase both him and Clara, at the highest price the sheriff's officer could obtain for them at market. Mr. Jefferies, with the utmost politeness to his neighbour, but with the most perfect indifference to the happiness of those whom he considered of a different species from himself, acceded to this proposal. Nothing could be more reasonable, he said; and he was happy to have it in his power to oblige a gentleman for whom he had such a high esteem.

The bargain was quickly concluded with the sheriff's officer; for Mr. Edwards willingly paid several dollars more than the market price for the two slaves. When Caesar and Clara heard that they were not to be separated, their joy and gratitude were expressed with all the ardour and tenderness peculiar to their different characters. Clara was an Eboe, Caesar a Koromantyn negro: the Eboes are soft, languishing, and timid; the Koromantyns are frank, fearless, martial, and heroic.[95]

Mr. Edwards carried his new slaves home with him, desired Bayley, his overseer, to mark out a provision-ground for Caesar, and to give him a cottage, which happened at this time to be vacant.

"Now, my good friend," said he to Caesar, "you may work for yourself, without fear that what you earn may be taken from you; or that you should ever be sold, to pay your master's debts.[96] If he does not understand what I am saying," continued Mr. Edwards, turning to his overseer, "you will explain it to him."

Caesar perfectly understood all that Mr. Edwards said; but his feelings were at this instant so strong that he could not find expression for his gratitude: he stood like one stupified! Kindness was new to him; it overpowered his manly heart; and, at hearing the words "my good friend," the tears gushed from his eyes: tears which no torture could have extorted! Gratitude swelled in his bosom; and he longed to be alone, that he might freely yield to his emotions.

He was glad when the conch-shell sounded to call the negroes to their daily labour, that he might relieve the sensations of his soul by bodily exertion. He performed his task in silence; and an inattentive observer might have thought him sullen.

In fact, he was impatient for the day to be over, that he might get rid of a heavy load which weighed upon his mind.

The cruelties practised by Durant, the overseer of Jefferies' plantation, had exasperated the slaves under his dominion.

They were all leagued together in a conspiracy, which was kept profoundly secret. Their object was to extirpate every white man, woman, and child, in the island. Their plans were laid with consummate art; and the negroes were urged to execute them by all the courage of despair.

The confederacy extended to all the negroes in the island of Jamaica, excepting those on the plantation of Mr. Edwards. To them no hint of the dreadful secret had yet been given; their countrymen, knowing the attachment they felt to their master, dared not trust them with these projects of vengeance. Hector, the negro who was at the head of the conspirators, was the particular friend of Caesar, and had imparted to him all his designs. These friends were bound to each other by the strongest ties. Their slavery and their sufferings began in the same hour: they were both brought from their own country in the same ship. This circumstance alone forms, amongst the negroes, a bond of connexion not easily to be dissolved. But the friendship of Caesar and Hector commenced even before they were united by the sympathy of misfortune; they were both of the same nation, both Koromantyns.[97] In Africa they had both been accustomed to command; for they had signalized themselves by superior fortitude and courage. They respected each other for excelling in all which they had been taught to consider as virtuous; and with them revenge was a virtue!

Revenge was the ruling passion of Hector: in Caesar's mind it was rather a principle instilled by education. The one considered it as a duty, the other felt it as a pleasure. Hector's sense of injury was acute in the extreme; he knew not how to forgive. Caesar's sensibility was yet more alive to kindness than to insult. Hector would sacrifice his life to extirpate an enemy. Caesar would devote himself for the defence of a friend; and Caesar now considered a white man as his friend.

He was now placed in a painful situation. All his former friendships, all the solemn promises by which he was bound to his companions in misfortune, forbade him to indulge that delightful feeling of gratitude and affection, which, for the first time, he experienced for one of that race of beings whom he had hitherto considered as detestable tyrants—objects of implacable and just revenge!

Caesar was most impatient to have an interview with Hector, that he might communicate his new sentiments, and dissuade him from those schemes of destruction which he meditated. At midnight, when all the slaves except himself were asleep, he left his cottage, and went to Jefferies' plantation, to the hut in which Hector slept. Even in his dreams Hector breathed vengeance. "Spare none! Sons of Africa, spare none!" were the words he uttered in his sleep, as Caesar approached the mat on which he lay. The moon shone full upon him. Caesar contemplated the countenance of his friend, fierce even in sleep. "Spare none! Oh, yes! There is one that must be spared. There is one for whose sake all must be spared."

He wakened Hector by this exclamation. "Of what were you dreaming?" said Caesar.

"Of that which, sleeping or waking, fills my soul—revenge! Why did you waken me from my dream? It was delightful. The whites were weltering in their blood! But silence! we may be overheard."

"No; every one sleeps but ourselves," replied Caesar. "I could not sleep, without speaking to you on—a subject that weighs upon my mind. You have seen Mr. Edwards?"

"Yes. He that is now your master."

"He that is now my benefactor—my friend!"

"Friend! Can you call a white man friend?" cried Hector, starting up with a look of astonishment and indignation.

"Yes," replied Caesar, with firmness. "And you would speak, ay, and would feel, as I do, Hector, if you knew this white man. Oh, how unlike he is to all of his race, that we have ever seen! Do not turn from me with so much disdain. Hear me with patience, my friend."

"I cannot," replied Hector, "listen with patience to one who between the rising and the setting sun can forget all his resolutions, all his promises; who by a few soft words can be so wrought upon as to forget all the insults, all the injuries he has received from this accursed race; and can even call a white man friend!"

Caesar, unmoved by Hector's anger, continued to speak of Mr. Edwards with the warmest expressions of gratitude; and finished by declaring he would sooner forfeit his life than rebel against such a master. He conjured Hector to desist from executing his designs; but all was in vain. Hector sat with his elbows fixed upon his knees, leaning his head upon his hands, in gloomy silence.

Caesar's mind was divided between love for his friend and gratitude to his master: the conflict was violent and painful. Gratitude at last prevailed: he repeated his declaration, that he would rather die than continue in a conspiracy against his benefactor!

Hector refused to except him from the general doom. "Betray us if you will!" cried he, "Betray our secrets to him whom you call your benefactor; to him whom a few hours have made your friend! To him sacrifice the friend of your youth, the companion of your better days, of your better self! Yes, Caesar, deliver me over to the tormentors: I can endure more than they can inflict. I shall expire without a sigh, without a groan. Why do you linger here, Caesar? Why do you hesitate? Hasten this moment to your master; claim your reward for delivering into his power hundreds of your countrymen! Why do you hesitate? Away! The coward's friendship can be of use to none. Who can value his gratitude? Who can fear his revenge?"

Hector raised his voice so high, as he pronounced these words, that he wakened Durant, the overseer, who slept in the next house. They heard him call out suddenly, to inquire who was there: and Caesar had but just time to make his escape, before Durant appeared. He searched Hector's cottage; but finding no one, again retired to rest. This man's tyranny made him constantly suspicious: he dreaded that the slaves should combine against him; and he endeavoured to prevent them by every threat and every stratagem he could devise, from conversing with each other.

They had, however, taken their measures, hitherto, so secretly, that he had not the slightest idea of the conspiracy which was forming in the island. Their schemes were not yet ripe for execution; but the appointed time approached. Hector, when he coolly reflected on what had passed between him and Caesar, could not help admiring the frankness and courage with which he had avowed his change of sentiments. By this avowal, Caesar had in feet exposed his own life to the most imminent danger, from the vengeance of the conspirators; who might be tempted to assassinate him who had their lives in his power. Notwithstanding the contempt with which, in the first moment of passion, he had treated his friend, he was extremely anxious that he should not break off all connexion with the conspirators. He knew that Caesar possessed both intrepidity and eloquence; and that his opposition to their schemes would perhaps entirely frustrate their whole design. He therefore determined to use every possible means to bend him to their purposes.

He resolved to have recourse to one of those persons§[98] who, amongst the negroes, are considered as sorceresses. Esther, an

---

§ The enlightened inhabitants of Europe may, perhaps, smile at the superstitious credulity of the negroes, who regard those ignorant beings called *Obeah* people with the most profound respect and dread; who believe that they hold in their hands the power of good and evil fortune, of health and sickness, of life and death. The instances which are related of their power over the minds of their countrymen are so wonderful that none but the most unquestionable authority could make us think them credible. The following passage from Edwards's History of the West Indies is inserted to give an idea of this strange infatuation.

"In the year 1760, when a very formidable insurrection of the Koromantyn or Gold Coast negroes broke out, in the parish of St. Mary, and spread through almost every other district of the island, an old Koromantyn negro, the chief instigator and oracle of the insurgents in that parish, who had administered the fetish, or solemn oath, to the conspirators, and furnished them with a magical preparation, which was to render them invulnerable, was fortunately apprehended, convicted, and hung up, with all his feathers and trumperies about him; and his execution struck the insurgents with a general panic, from which they never afterwards recovered. The examinations, which were taken at that period, first opened the eyes of the public to the very dangerous tendency of the *Obeah* practices; and gave birth to the law, which was then enacted, for their suppression and punishment; but neither the terror of this law, the strict investigation which has since been made after the professors of Obi, old Koromantyn negress, had obtained by her skill in poisonous herbs, and her knowledge of venomous reptiles, a high reputation amongst her countrymen. She soon taught them to believe her to be possessed of supernatural powers; and she then worked their imagination to what pitch and purpose she pleased.

---

nor the many examples of those, who from time to time have been hanged or transported, have hitherto produced the desired effect. A gentleman, on his returning to Jamaica, in the year 1775, found that a great many of his negroes had died during his absence; and that, of such as remained alive, at least one half were debilitated, bloated, and in a very deplorable condition. The mortality continued after his arrival; and two or three were frequently buried in one day; others were taken ill, and began to decline under the same symptoms. Every means were tried, by medicine and the most careful nursing, to preserve the lives of the feeblest; but, in spite of all his endeavours, this depopulation went on for a twelvemonth longer, with more or less intermission, and without his being able to ascertain the real cause, though the *Obeah* practice was strongly suspected, as well by himself as by the doctor, and other white persons upon the plantation; as it was known to have been very common in that part of the island, and particularly among the negroes of the *Popaw* or *Popo* country. Still he was unable to verify his suspicions; because the patients constantly denied their having any thing to do with persons of that order, or any knowledge of them. At length, a negress, who had been ill for some time, came and informed him that, feeling it was impossible for her to live much longer, she thought herself bound in duty, before she died, to impart a very great secret, and acquaint him with the true cause of her disorder; in hopes that the disclosure might prove the means of stopping that mischief, which had already swept away such a number of her fellow-slaves. She proceeded to say that her step-mother, a woman of the *Popo* country, above eighty years old, but still hale and active, had *put Obi upon her;* as she had upon those who had lately died; and that the old woman had practised *Obi* for as many years past as she could remember. The other negroes of the plantation no sooner heard of this impeachment than they ran in a body to their master, and confirmed the truth of it. **** Upon this he repaired directly, with six white servants, to the old woman's house; and, forcing open the door, observed the whole inside of the roof, which was of thatch, and every crevice of the wall, stuck with the implements of her trade, consisting of rags, feathers, bones of cats, and a thousand other articles. **** The house was instantly pulled down; and, with the whole of its contents, committed to the flames, amidst the general acclamations of all his other negroes. **** From the moment of her departure, his negroes seemed all to be animated with new spirits; and the malady spread no farther among them. The total of his losses, in the course of about fifteen years preceding the discovery, and imputable solely to the *Obeah practice*, he estimates, at least, at one hundred negroes."

She was the chief instigator of this intended rebellion. It was she who had stimulated the revengeful temper of Hector almost to phrensy. She now promised him that her arts should be exerted over his friend; and it was not long before he felt their influence. Caesar soon perceived an extraordinary change in the countenance and manner of his beloved Clara. A melancholy hung over her, and she refused to impart to him the cause of her dejection. Caesar was indefatigable in his exertions to cultivate and embellish the ground near his cottage, in hopes of making it an agreeable habitation for her; but she seemed to take no interest in anything. She would stand beside him immoveable, in a deep reverie; and when he inquired whether she was ill, she would answer no, and endeavour to assume an air of gaiety: but this cheerfulness was transient; she soon relapsed into despondency. At length, she endeavoured to avoid her lover, as if she feared his farther inquiries.

Unable to endure this state of suspense, he one evening resolved to bring her to an explanation. "Clara," said he, "you once loved me: I have done nothing, have I, to forfeit your confidence?"

"I once loved you!" said she, raising her languid eyes, and looking at him with reproachful tenderness; "and can you doubt my constancy? Oh, Caesar, you little know what is passing in my heart! You are the cause of my melancholy!"

She paused, and hesitated, as if afraid that she had said too much: but Caesar urged her with so much vehemence, and so much tenderness, to open to him her whole soul, that, at last, she could not resist his eloquence. She reluctantly revealed to him that secret of which she could not think without horror. She informed him that, unless he complied with what was required of him by the sorceress Esther, he was devoted to die. What it was that Esther required of him, Clara knew not: she knew nothing of the conspiracy. The timidity of her character was ill-suited to such a project; and every thing relating to it had been concealed from her with the utmost care.

When she explained to Caesar the cause of her dejection, his natural courage resisted these superstitious fears; and he endeavoured to raise Clara's spirits. He endeavoured in vain: she fell at his feet, and with tears, and the most tender supplications, conjured him to avert the wrath of the sorceress by obeying her commands whatever they might be!

"Clara," replied he, "you know not what you ask!"

"I ask you to save your life!" said she. "I ask you, for my sake, to save your life, while yet it is in your power!"

"But would you to save my life, Clara, make me the worst of criminals? Would you make me the murderer of my benefactor?"

Clara started with horror!

"Do you recollect the day, the moment, when we were on the point of being separated for ever, Clara? Do you remember the white man's coming to my cottage? Do you remember his look of benevolence—his voice of compassion? Do you remember his generosity? Oh! Clara, would you make me the murderer of this man?"

"Heaven forbid!" said Clara. "This cannot be the will of the sorceress!"

"It is," said Caesar. "But she shall not succeed, even though she speaks with the voice of Clara. Urge me no farther; my resolution is fixed. I should be unworthy of your love if I were capable of treachery and ingratitude."

"But, is there no means of averting the wrath of Esther?" said Clara. "Your life——"

"Think, first, of my honour," interrupted Caesar. "Your fears deprive you of reason. Return to this sorceress, and tell her that I dread not her wrath. My hands shall never be imbrued in the blood of my benefactor. Clara! Can you forget his look when he told us that we should never more be separated?"

"It went to my heart," said Clara, bursting into tears. "Cruel, cruel Esther! Why do you command us to destroy such a generous master?"

The conch sounded to summon the negroes to their morning's work. It happened this day, that Mr. Edwards, who was continually intent upon increasing the comforts and happiness of his slaves, sent his carpenter, while Caesar was absent, to fit up the inside of his cottage; and when Caesar returned from work, he found his master pruning the branches of a tamarind tree that overhung the thatch. "How comes it, Caesar," said he, "that you have not pruned these branches?"

Caesar had no knife. "Here is mine for you," said Mr. Edwards. "It is very sharp," added he, smiling; "but I am not one of those masters who are afraid to trust their negroes with sharp knives."

These words were spoken with perfect simplicity: Mr. Edwards had no suspicion, at this time, of what was passing in the negro's mind. Caesar received the knife without uttering a syllable; but no sooner was Mr. Edwards out of sight than he knelt down, and, in a transport of gratitude, swore that, with this knife, he would stab himself to the heart sooner than betray his master!

The principle of gratitude conquered every other sensation. The mind of Caesar was not insensible to the charms of freedom: he knew the negro conspirators had so taken their measures, that there was the greatest probability of their success. His heart beat high at the idea of recovering his liberty: but he was not to be seduced from his duty, not even by this delightful hope; nor was he to be intimidated by the dreadful certainty that his former friends and countrymen, considering him as a deserter from their cause, would become his bitterest enemies. The loss of Hector's esteem and affection was deeply felt by Caesar. Since the night that the decisive conversation relative to Mr. Edwards passed, Hector and he had never exchanged a syllable.

This visit proved the cause of much suffering to Hector, and to several of the slaves on Jefferies' plantation. We mentioned that Durant had been awakened by the raised voice of Hector. Though he could not find any one in the cottage, yet his suspicions were not dissipated; and an accident nearly brought the whole conspiracy to light. Durant had ordered one of the negroes to watch a boiler of sugar: the slave was overcome by the heat, and fainted. He had scarcely recovered his senses when the overseer came up, and found that the sugar had fermented, by having remained a few minutes too long in the boiler. He flew into a violent passion, and ordered that the negro should receive fifty lashes. His victim bore them without uttering a groan; but, when his punishment was over, and when he thought the overseer was gone, he exclaimed, "It will soon be our turn!"

Durant was not out of hearing. He turned suddenly, and observed that the negro looked at Hector when he pronounced these words, and this confirmed the suspicion that Hector was carrying on some conspiracy. He immediately had recourse to that brutality which he considered as the only means of governing black men: Hector and three other negroes were lashed unmercifully; but no confessions could be extorted.

Mr. Jefferies might perhaps have forbidden such violence to be used, if he had not been at the time carousing with a party of jovial West Indians, who thought of nothing but indulging their appetites in all the luxuries that art and nature could supply. The sufferings which had been endured by many of the wretched negroes to furnish out this magnificent entertainment were never once thought of by these selfish epicures. Yet so false are the general estimates of character, that all these gentlemen passed for men of great feeling and generosity! The human mind, in certain situations, becomes so accustomed to ideas of tyranny and cruelty, that they no longer appear extraordinary or detestable: they rather seem part of the necessary and immutable order of things.

Mr. Jefferies was stopped, as he passed from his dining-room into his drawing-room, by a little negro child, of about five years old, who was crying bitterly. He was the son of one of the slaves who were at this moment under the torturer's hand. "Poor little devil!" said Mr. Jefferies, who was more than half intoxicated. "Take him away; and tell Durant, some of ye, to pardon his father—if he can."

The child ran, eagerly, to announce his father's pardon; but he soon returned, crying more violently than before. Durant would not hear the boy; and it was now no longer possible to appeal to Mr. Jefferies, for he was in the midst of an assembly of fair ladies; and no servant belonging to the house dared to interrupt the festivities of the evening. The three men, who were so severely flogged to extort from them confessions, were perfectly innocent: they knew nothing of the confederacy; but the rebels seized the moment when their minds were exasperated by this cruelty and injustice, and they easily persuaded them to join the league. The hope of revenging themselves upon the overseer was a motive sufficient to make them brave death in any shape.

Another incident, which happened a few days before the time destined for the revolt of the slaves, determined numbers who had been undecided. Mrs. Jefferies was a languid beauty, or rather a languid fine lady who had been a beauty, and who spent all that part of the day which was not devoted to the pleasures of the table, or to reclining on a couch, in dress. She was one day extended on a sofa, fanned by four slaves, two at her head and two at her feet, when news was brought that a large chest, directed to her, was just arrived from London.[99]

This chest contained various articles of dress of the newest fashions. The Jamaica ladies carry their ideas of magnificence to a high pitch: they willingly give a hundred guineas for a gown, which they perhaps wear but once or twice. In the elegance and variety of her ornaments, Mrs. Jefferies was not exceeded by any lady in the island, except by one who had lately received a cargo from England. She now expected to outshine her competitor, and desired that the chest should be unpacked in her presence.

In taking out one of the gowns, it caught on a nail in the lid, and was torn. The lady, roused from her natural indolence by this disappointment to her vanity, instantly ordered that the unfortunate female slave should be severely chastised. The woman was the wife of Hector; and this fresh injury worked up his temper, naturally vindictive, to the highest point. He ardently longed for the moment when he might satiate his vengeance.

The plan the negroes had laid was to set fire to the canes, at one and the same time, on every plantation; and when the white inhabitants of the island should run to put out the fire, the blacks were to seize this moment of confusion and consternation to fall upon them, and make a general massacre. The time when this scheme was to be carried into execution was not known to Caesar; for the conspirators had changed their day, as soon as Hector told them that his friend was no longer one of the confederacy. They dreaded he should betray them; and it was determined that he and Clara should both be destroyed, unless they could be prevailed upon to join the conspiracy.

Hector wished to save his friend; but the desire of vengeance overcame every other feeling. He resolved, however, to make an attempt, for the last time, to change Caesar's resolution.

For this purpose, Esther was the person he employed: she was to work upon his mind by means of Clara. On returning to her cottage one night, she found suspended from the thatch one of those strange fantastic charms with which the Indian sorceresses terrify those whom they have proscribed.[100] Clara, unable to conquer her terror, repaired again to Esther, who received her first in mysterious silence; but, after she had implored her forgiveness for the past, and with all possible humility conjured her to grant her future protection, the sorceress deigned to speak. Her commands were that Clara should prevail upon her lover to meet her, on this awful spot, the ensuing night.

Little suspecting what was going forward on the plantation of Jefferies, Mr. Edwards that evening gave his slaves a holiday. He and his family came out at sunset, when the fresh breeze had sprung up, and seated themselves under a spreading palm-tree, to enjoy the pleasing spectacle of this negro festival. His negroes were all well clad; their turbans were of the gayest colours, and their merry countenances suited the gaiety of their dress. While some were dancing, and some playing on the tambourine, others appeared amongst the distant trees, bringing baskets of avocado pears, grapes, and pine-apples, the produce of their own provision-grounds; and others were employed in spreading their clean trenchers, or the calabashes, which served for plates and dishes.[101] The negroes continued to dance and divert themselves till late in the evening. When they separated and retired to rest, Caesar, recollecting his promise to Clara, repaired secretly to the habitation of the sorceress. It was situated in the recess of a thick wood. When he arrived there, he found the door fastened; and he was obliged to wait some time before it was opened by Esther.

The first object he beheld was his beloved Clara, stretched on the ground, apparently a corpse! The sorceress had thrown her into a trance by a preparation of deadly nightshade.[102] The hag burst into an infernal laugh, when she beheld the despair that was painted in Caesar's countenance. "Wretch!" cried she, "you have defied my power: behold its victim!"

Caesar, in a transport of rage, seized her by the throat: but his fury was soon checked.

"Destroy me," said the fiend, "and you destroy your Clara. She is not dead: but she lies in the sleep of death, into which she has been thrown by magic art, and from which no power but mine can restore her to the light of life. Yes! Look at her, pale and motionless! Never will she rise from the earth, unless, within one hour, you obey my commands. I have administered to Hector and his companions the solemn fetish oath, at the sound of which every negro in Africa trembles! You know my object."

"Fiend, I do!" replied Caesar, eyeing her sternly; "but, while I have life, it shall never be accomplished."

"Look yonder!" cried she, pointing to the moon; "in a few minutes that moon will set: at that hour Hector and his friends will appear. They come armed—armed with weapons which I shall steep in poison for their enemies. Themselves I will render invulnerable. Look again!" continued she; "if my dim eyes mistake not, yonder they come. Rash man, you die if they cross my threshold."

"I wish for death," said Caesar. "Clara is dead!"

"But you can restore her to life by a single word."

Caesar, at this moment, seemed to hesitate.

"Consider! Your heroism is vain," continued Esther. "You will have the knives of fifty of the conspirators in your bosom, if you do not join them; and, after you have fallen, the death of your master is inevitable. Here is the bowl of poison, in which the negro knives are to be steeped. Your friends, your former friends, your countrymen, will be in arms in a few minutes; and they will bear down every thing before them—Victory, Wealth, Freedom, and Revenge, will be theirs."

Caesar appeared to be more and more agitated. His eyes were fixed upon Clara. The conflict in his mind was violent; but his sense of gratitude and duty could not be shaken by hope, fear, or ambition; nor could it be vanquished by love. He determined, however, to appear to yield. As if struck with panic, at the approach of the confederate negroes, he suddenly turned to the sorceress, and said, in a tone of feigned submission, "It is in vain to struggle with fate. Let my knife, too, be dipt in your magic poison."

The sorceress clapped her hands with infernal joy in her countenance. She bade him instantly give her his knife, that she might plunge it to the hilt in the bowl of poison, to which she turned with savage impatience. His knife was left in his cottage; and, under pretence of going in search of it, he escaped. Esther promised to prepare Hector and all his companions to receive him with their ancient cordiality on his return. Caesar ran with the utmost speed along a by-path out of the wood, met none of the rebels, reached his master's house, scaled the wall of his bedchamber, got in at the window, and wakened him, exclaiming, "Arm—arm yourself, my dear master! Arm all your slaves! They will fight for you, and die for you; as I will the first. The Koromantyn yell of war will be heard in Jefferies' plantation this night![103] Arm—arm yourself, my dear master, and let us surround the rebel leaders while it is yet time. I will lead you to the place where they are all assembled, on condition that their chief, who is my friend, shall be pardoned."

Mr. Edwards armed himself and the negroes on his plantation, as well as the whites: they were all equally attached to him.[104] He followed Caesar into the recesses of the wood.

They proceeded with all possible rapidity, but in perfect silence, till they reached Esther's habitation: which they surrounded completely, before they were perceived by the conspirators.

Mr. Edwards looked through a hole in the wall; and, by the blue flame of a caldron, over which the sorceress was stretching her shrivelled hands, he saw Hector and five stout negroes standing, intent upon her incantations. These negroes held their knives in their hands, ready to dip them into the bowl of poison. It was proposed, by one of the whites, to set fire immediately to the hut; and thus to force the rebels to surrender. The advice was followed; but Mr. Edwards charged his people to spare their prisoners. The moment the rebels saw that the thatch of the hut was in flames, they set up the Koromantyn yell of war, and rushed out with frantic desperation.

"Yield! You are pardoned, Hector," cried Mr. Edwards, in a loud voice.

"You are pardoned, my friend!" repeated Caesar. Hector, incapable at this instant of listening to any thing but revenge, sprang forwards, and plunged his knife into the bosom of Caesar. The faithful servant staggered back a few paces: his master caught him in his arms. "I die content," said he. "Bury me with Clara."

He swooned from loss of blood as they were carrying him home; but when his wound was examined, it was found not to be mortal. As he recovered from his swoon, he stared wildly round him, trying to recollect where he was, and what had happened. He thought that he was still in a dream, when he saw his beloved Clara standing beside him. The opiate, which the pretended sorceress had administered to her, had ceased to operate; she wakened from her trance just at the time the Koromantyn yell commenced. Caesar's joy!—We must leave that to the imagination.

In the mean time, what became of the rebel negroes, and Mr. Edwards?

The taking the chief conspirators prisoners did not prevent the negroes upon Jefferies' plantation from insurrection. The moment they heard the war-whoop, the signal agreed upon, they rose in a body; and, before they could be prevented, either by the whites on the estate, or by Mr. Edwards's adherents, they had set fire to the overseer's house, and to the canes. The overseer was the principal object of their vengeance—he died in tortures, inflicted by the hands of those who had suffered most by his cruelties. Mr. Edwards, however, quelled the insurgents before rebellion spread to any other estates in the island. The influence of his character, and the effect of his eloquence upon the minds of the people, were astonishing: nothing but his interference could have prevented the total destruction of Mr. Jefferies and his family, who, as it was computed, lost this night upwards of fifty thousand pounds. He was never afterwards able to recover his losses, or to shake off his constant fear of a fresh insurrection among his slaves. At length, he and his lady returned to England, where they were obliged to live in obscurity and indigence. They had no consolation in their misfortunes but that of railing at the treachery of the whole race of slaves. Our readers, we hope, will think that at least one exception may be made, in favour of THE GRATEFUL NEGRO.

March, 1802.

Notes

1. Editions published in and after 1803 omit these first two paragraphs.
2. Editions published in and after 1803 omit the details of the explanation given by the mother.
3. Adaptation of first two lines of an English folk ballad, 'The Banks of the Sweet Primroses'.
4. A simple portable device to facilitate drawing in perspective is described, with two diagrams showing the machine, in the chapter on mechanics in Edgeworth's *Practical Education*, 2 vols (London: J. Johnson, 1798), II, 462.
5. Cecilia may be mischievously named after the heroine of Fanny Burney's novel of that name, published in 1782 to great acclaim; Edgeworth admired Burney's *Evelina*, but her father forbade her to read *Cecilia* when it first appeared, fearing that it would divert her talents into novel-writing rather than the serious work he hoped she would produce. Edgeworth reused the name for a leading character in her last fiction for adults, *Helen* (1834): this later Cecilia is also impetuous and misled by her desire to please others. Leonora is, Marilyn Butler conjectures, based upon Edgeworth's own school friend, Fanny Robinson: but Butler suggests that she is really a cipher for 'the woman Maria wanted to be, and felt she was not—secure, strong in herself, and (emotionally most essential of all) greatly valued by the tight-knit domestic circle round her. By the time Maria was a schoolgirl, [...] that dominant characteristic of hers, what her father was to call her "inordinate desire to be beloved", had already been born out of her sensation that she was not loved enough' (Marilyn Butler, *Maria Edgeworth: A Literary Biography* (Oxford: Clarendon Press, 1972), 150, 154). It seems probable that Edgeworth was also thinking of her first stepmother, Honora, in the naming of the schoolgirl in 'The Bracelets' and the heroine of her later novel, *Leonora* (1806). Honora, who was dignified, impressively intelligent and scrupulously just, inspired lasting respect in Maria Edgeworth and was idealized by Richard Lovell Edgeworth: the daughter he loved most uncomplicatedly was named after her.
6. *Mandarin*: a type of ornament popular in the late eighteenth century, typically made of porcelain, representing a seated figure in traditional Chinese costume, with a head that continues to nod after being shaken.
7. *Threading-the-needle*: a game in which a number of children join hands and the player at the end of the string passes between the last two at the other end, the rest following.

8. *Roman emperor*: see 'Cajus Caesar Caligula', chapter 30 of Suetonius, *The Twelve Caesars*, trans. by Robert Graves (Harmondsworth: Penguin Books, 1957), 169.

9. Flora was the Roman goddess of flowers and of spring. Her festival was the Floralia, associated with 1 May.

10. Ashton is located just to the south-west of Bristol. Clifton is across the Avon gorge, close to the centre of Bristol.

11. The British currency system at this time was of pounds (£), shillings (s) and pence (d). There were 20 shillings in a pound sterling and 12 pence in a shilling. A guinea was 21 shillings, a crown 5 shillings. It is difficult to offer an estimate of what an eighteenth-century guinea would be worth today, but the figures (and Jem's doubts as to whether he could earn two guineas in a fortnight) can be placed in perspective by the consideration that late eighteenth-century craftworkers might earn 10 or 12 shillings a week in the west of England; London journeymen might earn 15 to 20 shillings a week. A month's supply of tea and sugar for a family of six cost 2s.6d; a good pair of breeches cost between 10s. and 12s. (Richard D. Altick, *The English Common Reader* (Chicago & London: University of Chicago Press, 1957), 51–2).

12. Fossil-collecting had become very fashionable by the late eighteenth and early nineteenth centuries.

13. *The Wells*: Bristol Hotwell was a summer spa resort, site of a warm water spring and adjacent pump-rooms built in the late seventeenth century. It was less than two miles from Ashton to the Wells.

14. Marilyn Butler points out that there was, and still is, a grotto in the grounds of an early eighteenth-century house in Clifton belonging to the Goldney family (General Introduction, vol. 1, *Novels and Selected Works of Maria Edgeworth*, 12 vols (London: Pickering & Chatto, 1999/2003), LXXVI). The grotto was constructed between 1737 and 1764 and incorporates shells, fossils, quartz and rock crystal.

15. Making screens and other decorative items out of feathers was a fashionable female pastime in the late eighteenth century. See William Cowper's poem about the Bluestocking Elizabeth Montagu's featherwork, 'On Mrs. Montagu's Feather Hangings' (1788).

16. *Pitch-farthing*: a farthing was worth a quarter of a penny. Pitch-farthing, or pitch and toss, was a game of combined skill and chance, in which coins were pitched at a mark, and then chucked at a hole by the player who came nearest the mark, who won all that landed in the hole.

17. Alexander Pope uses the phrase 'prophetic eye' in his translation of the *Odyssey* (1725–6), Book I, l.261. William Pitt (the Elder), 1st Earl of Chatham, is said to have declared his intention to 'trample upon impossibilities'; Edgeworth attributes the words to him in her *Essay on Irish Bulls* (1802), in *Novels and Selected Works of Maria Edgeworth*, I, 131.

18. A bridewell is a prison for petty offenders, derived from St Bride's Well in the City of London, the site of a sixteenth-century house of correction. The first Bridewell, established in a former royal palace in

1553, was a place of punishment for the disorderly poor. In 1797, 34 of its prisoners were disorderly apprentices. 'Botany Bay' was a synonym for penal transportation by 1795, but originally connoted the penal colony established close to Botany Bay in New South Wales, Australia, to which convicts were sent from 1788 onward.

19. The name 'Gresham' has connections with business and with the founding of educational establishments: Sir John Gresham (1495–1556), Lord Mayor of London in 1547, founded Gresham's School in Norfolk in 1555; his nephew, Sir Thomas Gresham (c.1518–79), financier and philanthropist, was an extremely successful merchant, and founded the Royal Exchange and Gresham College in London, an institution offering public lectures. The Downs (Clifton Down and Durdham Down) cover a large area north of Clifton, on the edge of Bristol.

20. Hal is probably named after Henry, Prince of Wales, as portrayed in Shakespeare, *Henry IV Part I*, in which he appears as an irresponsible, fun-loving youth, nicknamed Hal.

21. Benjamin Franklin (1706–90), American revolutionary and scientist, co-author of the Declaration of Independence (1775). From 1732 he published a very successful almanac, *Poor Richard*, the preface to which, 'The Way to Wealth', was much reprinted and his best-known work in his lifetime. His 'Advice to a Young Tradesman' (1748) advocates industry, frugality, and the avoidance of profligate use of time and money.

22. *Jack-straws* and *cat's cradle*: jack-straws, or spillikins, is a game in which a set of straws, or strips of ivory, bone, or wood, are thrown together in a heap on a table; players have to extract each piece singly without disturbing the rest of the heap. Cat's cradle is a game played with a piece of packthread with its ends tied together to form a loop. Players have to take turns creating symmetrical shapes out of the cord, using their fingers to twist and hold the cord taut, alternately lifting the cord from each other's fingers to create new shapes.

23. Prince's Buildings, also known as Prince of Wales Crescent, was built in the late eighteenth century in Clifton, a fashionable district of Bristol. The Edgeworth family had lodgings there in 1791–3.

24. See note 13, 'Lazy Lawrence'.

25. Bristol Cathedral, founded as the Abbey of St Augustine in 1148, is the major example of a 'Hall Church' in Britain and the only one of its kind in England. The windows include some fine examples of mediaeval stained glass.

26. Joseph Priestley, *The History and Present State of Discoveries Relating to Vision, Light, and Colours*, 2 vols (London: C. Bathurst, 1772). Priestley describes the comte de Buffon's observations upon green and blue shadows (II, 438–9), in the midst of a chapter on coloured shadows and the colour of clouds and the sky (Period VI, chapter III).

27. Black Rock Quarry and the Great Quarry are sited in the sides of the Avon Gorge that runs through Bristol: they were sources of dolomite and limestone.

28. Wine Street was one of Bristol's main shopping streets.
29. Redland Chapel, completed in 1743, was in a rural location just to the north-west of Bristol in the late eighteenth century; now it is within the city itself.
30. Well Walk, Prince's Place and St. Vincent's Parade were all close to the fashionable tree-lined promenade leading to Hotwell House.
31. Ann Yearsley (1756–1806), poet and protégée of Hannah More until a breach over money. When More discovered her, Yearsley (a milk-woman by trade) was close to destitution. She started a circulating library at the Colonnade, Bristol Hotwells, in 1793, helped by Thomas Beddoes, among others, who married Maria Edgeworth's sister, Anna, in 1794, having met her while the family were at Clifton. Edgeworth discusses Yearsley's quarrel with More indignantly in a letter to her Aunt Ruxton in December 1791.
32. Richard Lovell Edgeworth recalls his 'excellent tutor Mr. Russell', of Corpus Christi, Oxford, in his *Memoirs* (1820; 2nd edition, 2 vols, London: R. Hunter; Baldwin, Cradock & Joy, 1821), associating him with 'the pleasure I then felt, from the consciousness of intellectual improvement' (I, 86).
33. The learned pig, which appeared to be able to count and spell, was a sensation in London in the mid 1780s.
34. *Moose-deer*: elk.
35. J. Hector St. John [de Crèvecoeur], *Letters from an American Farmer* (London: Thomas Davies & Lockyer Davis, 1783), 243.
36. Erasmus Darwin, *Zoonomia; or, The Laws of Organic Life*, 2 vols (1794; 2nd edition, London: J. Johnson, 1796). Volume 1, section XVI is on instinct: see subsections XIII, XIV and XV for the descriptions of the animals paraphrased here.
37. Bernardin de Saint-Pierre, *Studies of Nature* (1784), translated by Henry Hunter, 3 vols (2nd edition, London: C. Dilly, 1799): Study VII (I, 294–5).
38. *Trictrac* is a game similar to backgammon.
39. See *Buffon's Natural History, Abridged* (Dublin: P. Wogan, P. Byrne, A. Grueber et al., 1791): chapter XVI has a long section on the elephant.
40. Edgeworth does not footnote the italicized words, but is probably alluding to Bryan Edwards's discussion of provision-grounds, and in particular to the passage in which Edwards attacks the hardship that results when slaves are sold to defray their masters' debts. The provision-ground, argues Edwards, as 'the creation of [a slave's] own industry, and the staff of his existence, affords him not only support, but the means also of adding something to the mere necessaries of life' (Edwards, *The History, Civil and Commercial, of the British Colonies in the West Indies*, 2 vols (2nd edition, London: John Stockdale, 1794), II, 154). Edgeworth's footnoted references to Edwards in both 'The Good Aunt' and 'The Grateful Negro' are to this edition (the *History* was first published in 1793).

41. Margate was a fashionable seaside resort, situated on the south coast in East Kent within easy reach of London.

42. Portman Square is a prestigious square just north of Oxford Street in central London. It was the home of Elizabeth Montagu, a prominent Bluestocking.

43. See Edgar Rosenberg on Carat as an anti-semitic stereotype: *From Shylock to Svengali* (Stanford CA: Stanford University Press, 1960), 54–8; and Frank Felsenstein, *Anti-Semitic Stereotypes* (Baltimore & London: Johns Hopkins University Press 1995), chapter 4, for a general discussion of the Jewish stereotypes on which Edgeworth draws. In 1815, an American Jewish woman, Rachel Mordecai Lazarus, wrote to Edgeworth reproving her for the representation of Mr. Carat in 'The Good Aunt', and other anti-semitic characters in her tales for children and young people: see *The Education of the Heart: The Correspondence of Rachel Mordecai Lazarus and Maria Edgeworth*, ed. by Edgar E. MacDonald (Chapel Hill: University of North Carolina Press, 1977), 6. As part of her response, Edgeworth wrote her novel about anti-Jewish prejudice, *Harrington* (1817), intended as an act of reparation and atonement. See 'Introduction' (especially 7–10), *Harrington*, ed. by Susan Manly (Peterborough, Ontario: Broadview Press, 2004), for a discussion of *Harrington* in relation to the anti-semitism of *Moral Tales*.

44. Golkonda, near Hyderabad in India, was famed for its diamond mines. 'The Story of Cogia Hassan Alhabbal' is related in the *Arabian Tales*, which were first translated into English from Antoine Galland's French translation in 1706: see the 7th edition of 1728–30 (London: J. Osborn and T. Longman), X, 138–XI, 27 for the full tale. A letter from Richard Lovell Edgeworth to his daughter in November 1779, when she was not quite eleven years old, begins an 'Arabian fable' and challenges her to finish it (Edgeworth Papers, National Library of Ireland, MS 10/166/7/15). She later included an innovative reworking of an Arabian tale in *Popular Tales*, 'Murad the Unlucky'; for a discussion of this, see 'Introduction', *Oriental Tales*, ed. by Robert L. Mack (Oxford & New York: Oxford University Press, 1992), xi–xlvi. An experiment involving the melting of diamonds by means of sunlight and a strong lens was carried out in the presence of the grand duke of Tuscany in 1694; the experiment was supposedly repeated in 1760 with diamonds and rubies by Francis Stephen of Lorraine, afterwards the Hapsburg Emperor Francis I, in Vienna, as recorded by Jean-Étienne Guettard.

45. Edgeworth relates an anecdote about her younger brother Sneyd making this observation in Chapter XXI, on memory and invention, in *Practical Education* (1798): see vol. 11 in *Novels and Selected Works of Maria Edgeworth*, ed. by Susan Manly (London: Pickering & Chatto, 2003), 332.

46. Adam Smith, *The Wealth of Nations* (1776). One of Richard Lovell Edgeworth's first acts on recalling Maria Edgeworth to the family

circle in Edgeworthstown, aged 14, was to give her a copy of Smith's *Wealth of Nations*: it discusses education as well as political economy, and was a formative influence on her thought.

47. Edgeworth echoes section 92 in John Locke, *Some Thoughts Concerning Education* (London: A. & J. Churchill, 1693), 108–9: Locke urges parents to discuss their business affairs openly with their children as they grow closer to adulthood, treating them as friends rather than holding them at a distance.

48. Edgeworth draws on Edward Gibbon's *Life* for the character of her 'good aunt' and her nephew. Like Edgeworth's Charles, Gibbon disliked learning Greek and Latin. See *Miscellaneous Works of Edward Gibbon, Esquire, with Memoirs of his Life and Writings, Composed by Himself*, 2 vols (London: A. Strahan, T. Cadell & W. Davies, 1796), I, 24, 29–30.

49. Plutarch, *Lives*, 11 vols, trans. by Bernadotte Perrin (Cambridge, MA & London: Harvard University Press/William Heinemann, Loeb Classical Library, 1919), VII, 93.

50. Homer gives detailed and anatomically accurate descriptions of many different wounds inflicted in battle in the *Iliad*.

51. If this is an allusion to *Macbeth*, Act IV.i.96–7—the witches' prophecy that 'none of woman born/Shall harm Macbeth'—it suggests that Augustus does not know the play, which is in keeping with his disdain for English literature as opposed to Greek and Latin authors.

52. Edgeworth discusses the ideas of play and work in chapter II of *Practical Education*: see 40–2 (2003). The line of poetry is a paraphrase of Thomas Gray's 'Ode on a Distant Prospect of Eton College', ll. 33–4.

53. *Enter college ... a borough secure for him*: The alderman is keen for Augustus to matriculate as a student at Oxford or Cambridge, and then to take up a position in Parliament, via election to a pocket borough, a constituency in which the election of political representatives was controlled by one person or family—in this case the Holloway family. Pocket boroughs were increasingly regarded as corrupt, and were eventually abolished by the Reform Acts of 1832 and 1867.

54. A curricle is a light two-wheeled carriage, drawn by two horses abreast; a barouche is a four-wheeled carriage with a half-head behind that can be raised or lowered, a seat for the driver, and seats inside for two couples to sit facing one another. A dog-cart is an open carriage with two transverse seats back to back, the rear seat originally converting into a box for dogs. To drive 'randem-tandem' means to drive a two-wheeled vehicle with two horses in harness, one in front of the other.

55. *Chairmen's shoulders*: Mr Supine is travelling by sedan chair, a mode of transport that became fashionable in the seventeenth century, and continued to be used until the early nineteenth century in cities such as London and Bath. The advantage of the sedan chair was that it

could be carried through narrow passageways and even into buildings; it also afforded its passenger complete privacy.

56. *Turnpike road*: a road on which turnpikes (spiked barriers) were erected for the collection of tolls; hence, a main road or highway maintained by a toll levied on cattle and wheeled vehicles.

57. *Mulatto*: a person with one white, one black parent, or otherwise of mixed race.

58. *Root-house*: an outbuilding for storing root vegetables; alternatively, an ornamental building made principally of tree-roots. It is probably the former in this case.

59. *Chay-boy*: vulgar corruption of chaise-boy.

60. Johnson thought that forcing a child to learn Greek and Latin 'cramps and warps many a mind, which if left more at liberty would have been respectable in some way'. Hester Lynch Piozzi, *Anecdotes of the Late Samuel Johnson, During the Last Twenty Years of his Life* (Dublin: Moncrieffe, White, Byrne et al., 1786), 218.

61. Benjamin Franklin, *Observations on the Causes and Cure of Smoky Chimneys* (London: John Debrett & J. Sewell, 1787).

62. *Dunned*: pursued for a debt.

63. *Blow*: used as slang for giving someone's game away.

64. *Quiz* (or later, quoz): an odd or ridiculous-looking person.

65. Erasmus Darwin, *The Botanic Garden, a Poem*, 2 vols (4th edition, London: J. Johnson, 1799), *The Loves of the Plants* (1789), II, Canto III, ll. 457–8.

66. *Turtle-dinner*: this was an expensive treat, the kind of meal that would be offered to potential political or business associates to curry favour. In 1805, a turtle-dinner cost two guineas, a substantial amount of money.

67. Gaius Maecenas (c.70–c.8 BCE) was a political adviser to the Emperor Octavian, patron of Horace and Virgil, and generally renowned as a generous patron of the arts.

68. State lotteries were financed and administered by the government, but responsibility for ticket sales and promotion was contracted out to private firms: Richardson, Goodluck & Co. were one of only a few licensed offices before the abolition of state lotteries in 1826.

69. Adam Smith, *An Inquiry into the Nature and Causes of the Wealth of Nations*, 3 vols (Dublin: Whitestone, Chamberlaine, W. Watson et al., 1776), I, 158. Smith proves that lotteries are intrinsically unfair, since tickets are not worth the price paid by subscribers, gaining a fictitious value based on the vain hope of winning one of the big prizes.

70. This is the anecdote that Mrs. Howard recommends to Charles's attention before he starts school: see note 49 above.

71. This phrase is attributed to William Pitt (the Elder), 1st Earl of Chatham (1708–78).

72. This passage about the Marquis's letter (beginning with 'When Mrs. Howard returned home' and ending with 'sealed and sent') is present in the seventh edition (1816), but was omitted from later editions

of the tale. It reinforces Edgeworth's critique of party spirit and bias and her tale's emphasis on the values of independence and individual integrity, so is retained here.

73. *Break squares*: to violate an agreement with someone or to contravene the customary order.

74. Joseph Warton's 'Ode to Fancy' (1746) was anthologized in William Enfield's *The Speaker*, and thus known to generations of children.

75. Bryan Edwards, *History, Civil and Commercial, of the West Indies*, II, 67.

76. Edgeworth disagrees with Rousseau's assertion that all children are naturally gluttons in *Practical Education*, (2003), 80. See Rousseau, *Emile*, trans. by Barbara Foxley (London & Toronto: J. M. Dent, 1911), 117.

77. Edgeworth here alludes to a phrase used by her father that deeply impressed her when he visited her at school in England in the late 1770s: 'Tell me my dear little daughter if there is anything you wish for or want—and remember what I now say—*You will always through life find your father your best and most indulgent friend.*' (Butler, *Maria Edgeworth*, 57.)

78. Antinous was the lover of the Emperor Hadrian; he died suddenly in 130 CE, very young, in mysterious circumstances, possibly by his own hand. The Antinous Mondragone, a Roman bust of this beautiful youth now housed in the Louvre, depicts him with head slightly bowed, a sombre expression on his downcast face.

79. *Choused*: cheated (slang).

80. St John de Crèvecoeur's *Letters from an American Farmer*, mentioned earlier in this tale, has a chapter ('Letter IX') on Charleston, South Carolina, a major trading-port whose wealth was based on slave-trading and slave labour.

81. *Davy Jones's locker*: the bottom of the sea (proverbial).

82. Jefferies echoes Bryan Edwards's arguments here: William Preston accuses Bryan Edwards of 'dwell[ing] on their supposed inferior nature and blameable propensities, their slowness of apprehension, their...disposition to thieving and lying, as a justification of the severities exercised on them, and a pretence for retaining them in slavery': *A Letter to Bryan Edwards* (London: J. Johnson, 1795), 25.

83. August von Kotzebue published his anti-slavery play, *Die Negersklaven*, set in Jamaica, in 1796; it was immediately translated into English as *The Negro Slaves, a Dramatic-Historical Piece*. Bryan Edwards's *The History, Civil and Commercial, of the British Colonies in the West Indies*, was published in 1793, with a second edition in 1794 (the edition cited by Edgeworth in 'The Grateful Negro'), and an abridged edition in 1798. All further references in these footnotes are to the second edition (London: John Stockdale, 1794). Edwards defends planters against widespread allegations of cruelty, claiming that the general treatment of West Indian slaves is 'mild, temperate, and indulgent; that instances of cruelty are not only rare, but always universally reprobated when discovered; and, when susceptible of legal proof,

severely punished' (II, 143). The anonymous editor of the abridged version of Edwards's *History* (London: B. Crosby; Mundell & Son; J. Mundell, 1798) assembles 'some facts' that counter Edwards's 'evasive confession of West Indian cruelty', detailed directly after Edwards's claim about planters' humanity (195–7). See Introduction for a discussion of the influence of Edwards and Kotzebue in 'The Grateful Negro'.

84. Edgeworth's Mr Edwards echoes Bryan Edwards here: 'That I am no friend to slavery, in any shape, or under any modification, I feel a conscious assurance in my own bosom. [...] Of this I am certain, that an immediate emancipation of the slaves in the West Indies, would involve both master and slave in one common destruction [...] Hasty measures [...] will probably never end but in the extermination of either the Whites or the Blacks' (*History*, II, 150–1).

85. Bryan Edwards argues that slaves' workload should be made 'certain and determinate', that once they have finished the set task their time should be their own, and that they should be paid 'wages for extra labour'. He suggests that this is 'calculated to produce a spirit of emulation and industry, which the dread of punishment can never produce' (*History*, II, 151).

86. The different effects of hope and fear upon the mind are among the subjects Edgeworth discusses in *Practical Education* (1798), especially prominent in chapter IX, 'On Rewards and Punishments': 'Hope excites the mind to exertion; fear represses all activity. [...] would you rouse the energies of virtue, you must inspire and invigorate the soul with hope. Courage, generosity, industry, perseverance, all the magic of talents, all the powers of genius, all the virtues that appear spontaneous in great minds, spring from hope' (2003, 149).

87. As George Boulukos suggests, it is probable that Abraham Bayley is named after a real Jamaican planter, Zachary Bayly (Bryan Edwards's uncle), and his overseer, Abraham Fletcher: Edwards recounts their part in the suppression of a slave rebellion, Tacky's Revolt, in 1760, and claims that they were known for their 'singular tenderness and humanity' towards Bayly's slaves. See *History*, II, 64–6. Boulukos argues that 'The Grateful Negro' is largely based on Edwards's account of this uprising in 'Maria Edgeworth's "Grateful Negro" and the Sentimental Argument for Slavery', *Eighteenth Century Life* 23 (February 1999), 18.

88. Much of this paragraph about slaves' provision-grounds and slaves being sold to discharge their owners' debts is taken directly from Edwards's *History*, II, 153–4.

89. This naming may be a nod to Aphra Behn's *Oroonoko* (1688), the story and characters of which were known to a wide eighteenth-century audience through Thomas Southerne's stage adaptation (1696). Behn's hero is renamed Caesar when he is enslaved: 'he wanted no part of the personal courage of that Caesar, and acted things as memorable'. Caesar eventually kills Imoinda, his beloved, to save her and their unborn child from rape and other brutalities at the hands of whites,

knowing that he is likely to be executed for his part in a slave uprising. At one point he promises the narrator of *Oroonoko* that he will
'act nothing upon the white people', but he later organizes a rebellion
and urges his fellow-slaves to kill those who have punished them by
flogging them until the blood ran down their bodies, 'blood whose
every drop ought to be revenged with a life of some of those tyrants',
Oroonoko, ed. by Janet Todd (Harmondsworth: Penguin, 2004), 49, 62.
Caesar is eventually mutilated and executed by the governor of the
colony. Suvendrini Perera observes that slaves were often named for
fallen kings (*Reaches of Empire* (New York: Columbia University Press,
1991), 24); see also Peter Fryer, *Staying Power* (London: Pluto Press,
1984), 24.

90. Bryan Edwards makes a similar claim: *History*, II, 108.

91. Boulukos links this suggestion to Adam Smith's argument about the
advantages of waged labour over slavery ('Maria Edgeworth's "Grateful
Negro"', 16): see Smith, *Wealth of Nations*, I, 118–19.

92. Here Jefferies seems to echo Bryan Edwards again: 'the legislative
authority in many of the sugar islands has been, and still is, most
humanely and laudably exerted in exalting the condition of the slave
in all respects, and circumscribing the power of the master' (*History*,
II, 141).

93. In the Mansfield judgement of 1772 on the case of James Somerset,
Somerset v Stewart, Lord Chief Justice Mansfield ruled that Somerset's
master could not deport him from Britain and return him to slavery in Jamaica. The ruling was widely taken to guarantee the emancipation of all slaves once on British ground. The phrase, 'As soon
as a man sets foot on English ground he becomes free' is therefore
popularly associated with Mansfield, but was actually part of a ruling made by Lord Chancellor Northington, Robert Henley (1708–72),
in the case of Shanley v Harvey (1762). Harvey had been brought to
England as a child slave. Sir William Blackstone echoed Henley's
words in his *Commentaries on the Laws of England*, 4 vols (1st edition,
Oxford: Clarendon Press, 1765–9), I, 412 (1765): 'a slave or negro, the
instant he lands in England, becomes a freeman'.

94. Bryan Edwards quotes a 'valuable Friend' whose opinion it is that a
negro 'may be said to imbibe with his mother's milk, that whatever
he can cheat his owner of, in any direction, is clear gain to himself'
(*History*, II, 155).

95. Koromantyn was a fort and trading-post established in the seventeenth century on the west coast of Africa, a few miles east of the
modern Cape Coast in Ghana. The name 'Koromantyn' was loosely
employed to indicate most of the coast of modern Ghana, and the
Africans taken from that region, who were highly prized, many
of them from Fanti and Ashanti tribes. Bryan Edwards describes
'Koromantyn negroes' as having a 'firmness both of body and mind;
a ferociousness of disposition; but withal, activity, courage, and

stubbornness, or what an ancient Roman would have deemed an elevation, of soul'. By contrast, Edwards describes 'Eboes' (Igbo people) as characterized by a 'constitutional timidity, and despondency of mind' (*History*, II, 63, 75).

96. Mr Edwards here justifies Bryan Edwards's claim that masters never interfere with the property accrued by slaves' labour (*History*, II, 137).

97. Bryan Edwards comments: 'we find that the Negroes in general are strongly attached to their countrymen, but above all, to such of their companions as came in the same ship with them from Africa. This is a striking circumstance: the term shipmate is understood among them as signifying a relationship of the most endearing nature; perhaps as recalling the time when the sufferers were cut off together from their common country and kindred, and awakening reciprocal sympathy, from the remembrance of mutual affliction' (*History*, II, 79).

98. Edgeworth quotes from Edwards's *History*, II, 95–9 for this long footnote on Obeah. The 'Popaw or Popo' country borders on the area next to what Europeans called Koromantyn (*History*, II, 73). Edgeworth makes use of the material on Obeah in her novel *Belinda* (1801), when she depicts Juba, a black manservant and ex-slave, being terrified by what he believes to be the spectre of an old obeah-woman; Belinda exposes the spectre as a trick perpetrated by the anti-heroine, Harriet Freke. Alison Harvey's essay, 'West Indian Obeah and English "Obee"', in *New Essays on Maria Edgeworth*, ed. by Julie Nash (Aldershot & Burlington, VT: Ashgate, 2006), 1–29, offers an interesting reading of this incident.

99. The description of Mrs. Jefferies echoes Anna Barbauld's description of 'voluptuous' and 'languid' planters' wives in her anti-slavery poem, 'Epistle to William Wilberforce' (1791), and tallies with contemporary accounts of the cruelties of women 'of respectability and rank' towards slaves in Jamaica: see *A Short Sketch of the Evidence, for the Abolition of the Slave Trade* (Glasgow, 1792), 14.

100. *Indian*: West Indian.

101. Edgeworth's description exactly resembles a picture of a 'Negro Festival' in Bryan Edwards's *History*.

102. Edwards mentions the use made by Obeah men and women of a 'narcotic potion, made with the juice of an herb (said to be the branched *Calalue* or species of *Solanum*) which occasions a trance or profound sleep of a certain duration'. They thus 'endeavour to convince the deluded spectators of their power to reanimate dead bodies' (*History*, II, 91). Branched calalue is probably Solanum nigrum, the Black Nightshade: this contains high concentrations of hallucinogenic tropane alkaloids, including atropine.

103. Bryan Edwards writes of the 'Koromantyn yell of war' being uttered by the rebel slaves in Tacky's Revolt: *History*, II, 65.

104. This is a detail from Bryan Edwards's account of Zachary Bayly's response to Tacky's Revolt: *History*, II, 65.

Printed in China